RECIPIENT

H.L. VOSS

Published by:

5 Prince Publishing and Books, LLC

DBA 5 Prince Publishing

PO Box 865

Arvada, Colorado 80001

Digital ISBN: 978-1-63112-436-5

Print ISBN: 978-1-63112-438-9

Cover design by Marianne Nowicki

Interior design by 5 Prince Publishing

First Edition

F04032026

For more information about this title, visit: www.5princebooks.com

To Rosie, my North Star,
and Skyler, my Twin Flame.
Thank you for lighting my way.

ACKNOWLEDGMENTS

Thank you to everyone at 5 Prince Publishing for the opportunity to share my work with the world. Thank you to Bernadette for taking a chance on me; I feel so honored to join the strong catalog of authors she has built here at 5 Prince Publishing. Thank you to Cate for holding space for the core of my work and helping my prose shine.

Thank you to Callie for helping bring this book from rough draft to something that I could query. Thank you to everyone at the League of Utah Writers, without whom it would have taken me much, much longer to feel ready to share my stories. I want to particularly note Rachael, Alex, and Christina, who have believed in me from the start and been with me on this journey. Thank you to the members of my writing group that helped me find the courage to see beyond my fears and into possibility, particularly Skyler, Jez, and Joann. Thank you to Linda, my middle school English teacher, for instilling a love of writing in me that persists to this day. Thank you to my family: to my parents for holding space for my creativity and to my brother for showing me that a creative life is possible.

And last but not least, thank you to Rosie, for seeing the potential of this book in its infancy and helping me dare to dream.

RECIPIENT

1

"Stop fidgeting, mijo. You're making your son nervous."

Javier winces and settles back onto his heels. He's been rocking back and forth on them where they stand outside the Denver Zoo for the last five minutes at least. His ankles hurt, and his abuela is right; the last thing he needs is to get Alejandro riled up before Javi's fiancé gets here. "Sorry."

Alejandro looks up from his wheelchair and grins at Javi, all teeth in that way that nine-year-olds are. "It's okay to be nervous, Dad. We haven't met Mr. Carmichael yet, and I always get nervous when I meet new people."

Javi offers his boy a smile. "That's fair," he murmurs, "but your bisabuela is right, too. Mr. Carmichael is being very kind to us, and there's really nothing to worry about."

Ále hums and looks away, scanning the crowd for their companions. He's unlikely to find them by sight alone; Javi didn't share pictures of his Provider-to-be with his son, preferring to let Ále meet him for the first time in person.

Part of Javi regrets that right now. He's already uprooted his son from the only life he's known to chase this life. Maybe he should have given Ále more context. But they were both buckling under the weight of Javi's parents' expectations, and they need a fresh start.

And that fresh start's name is Gavin Carmichael.

"You know you have nothing to worry about," his abuela says from where she stands at Javi's elbow.

"I have everything to worry about," he hisses back. "I'm supposed to be the cautious one, and now here I am listening to Bianca and moving halfway across the country to marry a man I've only ever met on a video call. What was I thinking?"

His abuela places a hand on his forearm, stopping him from reaching up to tear his hair out. "You were thinking of your boy, and the life you could give him with a Provider that can truly provide for the two of you, especially for Alejito. He deserves two parents taking care of him. You were thinking that you trust your sister to find you a matchmaking agency that would do right by you. Even if you're doing this for Alejito, you deserve to be happy, too. And you were thinking that maybe, just maybe, it's time you got out from under the thumb of my son and his Recipient."

Javi startles. "Abuela, you can't mean that."

"I can and I do. They've always held you to a higher standard than your sisters, and it shows. They've always been more critical of the way you raise Alejito than they are of how Teresa raises your little sobrinos. They have never approved of what you do to take care of your son and they always try to fix the two of you. You don't need to be fixed. You and Alejito deserve to have your own lives, just like your sisters and sobrinos do, and you deserve to give your son the life you want to."

Javi doesn't quite know what to do with that declaration. His whole life he's been told he should be the Provider in his marriage, the one to work outside the house and take care of the family in that way. Today, Javi is yielding to the reality of his life: that having a Provider rather than being one means he'll have more time to spend with his son the way he wants and the way his son deserves. After all, that's what marriage is about. Their kids. Or, in this case, Javi's kid.

Before he can reply, Javi catches sight of Gavin.

The man stands almost a full head over the crowd at the zoo entrance, and Javi recognizes those curls from their one video call through the matchmaking company that introduced them, *CPR Agency—Connecting Providers and Recipients*. Javi pulls his shoulders back and stands up a little taller, lifting a hand in a wave.

It takes Gavin only a few seconds to catch sight of them. When he does, his eyes widen, and then his whole expression brightens. He turns away for a moment, seemingly talking to someone at his side. His chaperone, no doubt. His sister.

Then he steps out of the crowd, and after registering the preschool-aged child on Gavin's hip, Javi reassesses everything he'd thought about his Provider-to-be. While Javi knows that Gavin is a firefighter, he hasn't thought about what that really means. He knows Gavin is pale, knows he has bright blue eyes, knows he has fair, curly hair. What he hadn't known or realized is that Gavin is broad and clearly built, and though Javi is plenty strong himself, there's something about Gavin's bulk that should be intimidating.

It isn't, but it probably should be.

As Gavin and his chaperone approach them, Javi shifts his weight, trying to look less nervous than he really is. Gavin's smile is clearly an attempt to put him at ease, but there's too much at stake here for any expression on Gavin's face to calm him. All of this—the move, the engagement, the change—could mean nothing if today doesn't go well.

Javi glances at his abuela, his eyes wide and a little worried all at once.

She smiles softly and takes Javi's hand in hers. "It's going to be fine."

Javi nods wordlessly, and then, before either of them can say anything more, Gavin is in front of them, his sister at his side.

"Hi," Gavin says. He sounds a little breathless from the walk, but there's a steady warmth in his eyes that settles Javi.

"Hi," Javi holds out a hand, then starts to retract it when he remembers that Gavin is holding a kid.

Gavin smoothly switches the pre-schooler to his other hip and takes Javi's hand in his. "Gavin Carmichael," he says swiftly. "Which you knew already, of course." He chuckles, and something about the sound puts Javi at ease.

"Javier Pérez. But," he adds, feeling oddly cheeky, "You knew that, too."

Gavin's ears go red, but his smile widens. He squeezes Javi's hand, then pulls away, turning to the woman at his side, who is pushing a double stroller with a single toddler in it. "And this is my sister, Evelyn. She'll be chaperoning us."

With a glance at Gavin, Javi notes the lack of a last name in the introduction. He looks back at Evelyn, his eyes catching on the Recipient ring on her finger. Married, then, but Gavin is making his unhappiness with the match clear. Javi smiles and takes her hand, shaking it, too. "A pleasure." Then he reaches out for the toddler in the stroller, taking the tiny hand in his. She can't be more than two, with chubby cheeks and a nervous look on her face. "And who is this?"

Evelyn smiles. "This is my youngest, Sierra. And that's Elaine," she adds, nodding at the pre-schooler on Gavin's hip. "Their big sister Genesis will be coming with their dad later tonight." Then she turns to Ále. "And this must be your son?"

Javi places a hand on the back of Ále's wheelchair. "Yes. This is Alejandro. And this is my grandmother, Citlali. She'll also be chaperoning us."

Gavin's expression softens at the edges. He reaches out to take Citlali's hand, but rather than shake it, he leans down and presses a kiss to the back of it. "It's a pleasure to meet you."

Javi's abuela gives Gavin a once-over before fanning herself lightly. "Well. If I was sixty years younger..."

"Abuela," Javi says, scandalized.

She just smirks at him. He can't help but wonder if she caught him looking Gavin over on his approach.

"It's fine, Javier," Gavin murmurs. "I get worse on the job."

Javi opens his mouth to ask, then shifts gears smoothly. "Well, shall we see the animals?"

Ále grins up at the adults. "I looked at the map online before we came. This place is way bigger than the zoo back home. I can't wait to get through it all."

Javi winces at the mention of Vegas as home. When he glances at Gavin, though, the man looks more concerned than upset. Then the expression clears, and he grins down at Ále. "Well, you've clearly done your research. Why don't you lead the way?"

Ále lights up at the offer, but as he turns away Elaine pipes up from her uncle's arms. "Uncle Gavin?" She points at Ále. "Why chair?"

Gavin pauses, looking taken aback at the question. Javi is used to it, though, and turns to Ále to see if he's up for explaining today.

Ále's grin makes it clear that he is. "I have something called cerebral palsy," he says. "There are lots of different kinds, but mine makes it hurt for me to walk sometimes. So when we go somewhere like this, where there's a lot of walking, I get to use my wheelchair to move around instead."

Elaine frowns like she doesn't quite understand. "Hurts?" she asks.

"Sometimes," Ále agrees. "But not right now."

Elaine smiles at that. "Okay." She looks back at Gavin. "Elephant?"

Gavin shakes himself from where he's staring at Ále, eyes wide, and puts on a smile. "Sure. Why don't you ask our tour guide Alejandro where they are?" he adds, gesturing at Ále.

Elaine starts bouncing in Gavin's arms. "Elephant?" she asks again, this time directing the question at Ále.

"Sure." Ále glances at Javi, and then, based on whatever he sees in Javi's face, looks back at Elaine and adds, "Do you want to ride with me in my wheelchair?"

Javi, long used to Ále's kindness, can't stop the smile on his face. Still, he checks. "Are you sure, kiddo? We need to make sure that Elaine is safe."

Ále rolls his eyes at him. "I'm sure, Dad. I can hold onto her in my lap." Then he pauses. "Oh. But you'll be talking to Mr. Carmichael, won't you? Privately? So you won't be able to push me."

"No, kiddo," Javi agrees. "Sorry."

"We don't have to talk in private," Gavin cuts in. "It's okay with me if you help him with his chair."

Javi pauses, weighing his options. He knows he'll need to be a bit more reserved around Ále than he would be if it was him and Gavin alone, but he'll also feel better if he can stay close to his son. "Alright, then. If it's okay with her mom, it's okay with me."

Evelyn frowns a little. She glances at Javi and asks, softly, "He can hold on tight enough to keep her in the chair?"

"If he says he can, he can. He's a good judge of his strength."

Evelyn nods. "Then that's fine with me."

Elaine cheers as Gavin moves to settle her into Ále's lap. Javi takes a moment to test and adjust Ále's grip on Elaine, and, deeming it safe, they start off toward the exhibits.

Ále leads the way with Evelyn walking beside him so she can keep an eye on her daughter. It takes Javi a moment to notice that his abuela is trailing behind him and Gavin, who are walking side-by-side as he pushes Ále's chair. He glances back at her, but she smiles at him knowingly. She's leaving enough space for them to talk privately while still technically being close enough to chaperone them.

All at once, when Ále starts talking to Evelyn and her

daughters, Javi is virtually alone with the man he's going to marry tomorrow. He has no idea what to say. One glance at Gavin is enough to remind Javi that despite Gavin's choice to work in the public sector, financially and socially they grew up in different worlds. Gavin holds himself tall and proud, his step sure and his eyes clear as they look straight ahead. Not for the first time, Javi wonders why Gavin chose him out of all the potential Recipients he could marry. After all, it's not like Javi brings much to the table. What if today is all it takes for Gavin to realize he's made a mistake? What if Javi uprooted his son for a potential relationship that will never come through?

The thoughts still his tongue. If they're going to have a conversation, Gavin is going to need to be the one to start it.

2

It's taking all of Gavin's self-control not to stare at Javier. The man is even more beautiful than he'd appeared in either his interview video or the singular video call they'd had before today. He's shorter than Gavin would have thought, though only a couple inches shorter than Gavin himself. His brown eyes hold hints of gold in the sunlight that hadn't shown on camera, and his bronze skin is smooth in ways that have Gavin's fingertips tingling. His dark hair looks soft to the touch, and there's this one piece that keeps falling over his forehead from where he's slicked the rest back. It's damn cute is what it is.

Javier is also quieter than he'd been on camera, now that the kids are right there with them. His eyes are on Alejandro, and the thought of how important Alejandro is to Javier is enough to turn Gavin's knees to jelly. He may not be a traditional man in most ways, but, to him, marriage has always been about the kids. Literally, historically, it's been about the kids. It's been about raising young people in loving homes that give them the lives they deserve. Wanting a marriage that is all about his kids is one of the few traditional things about Gavin Carmichael, and he needs to make sure that Javier understands that, if only because he really needs this marriage to work.

The trust fund his grandparents set up for him ensured that there were plenty of Recipients for him to choose from. Listening to Javier talk about Alejandro had sealed the deal for him. Even though Gavin doesn't want to leverage his family's background to find a life partner, he needs to get Evelyn out of Boston and out here where he can protect her from her piece-of-shit Provider. The trust fund, locked behind a clause requiring him to get married before accessing it, is the only way to do that. Things are out of his hands now. Well, mostly.

"So," he says softly, sensing that Javier doesn't want to talk too much where Alejandro can hear, "Tell me a little more about yourself."

Javier glances at him, then turns his gaze back to his son. "What do you want to know?"

"Well, we can start simple if you want. What's your favorite breakfast food?"

That gets Javier's eyes on him, a hint of incredulity in them. "Seriously?"

Gavin laughs. "Seriously. I've got to make sure we have it in the house for tomorrow morning."

The apples of Javier's cheeks go pink and he ducks his head away from Gavin. "I'm not that picky."

"Okay, but if you had your choice."

Javier hesitates, taking until they pull up in front of the hyena exhibit. He helps Alejandro get steady, then they back a few feet away from the kids and their chaperones, gaining the illusion of privacy. When Javier finally speaks, it takes Gavin by surprise. "Molletes."

Gavin blinks. "What's that?"

"It's something my mom used to make for me. It's simple enough, just beans and pico on toast, but she used to make the bread herself. There's something about homemade bread that just can't be beat."

There's a hint of melancholy in Javier's voice that settles against Gavin's sternum, a steady weight. He wants to ask about the story there, but he doesn't know how. Not when Javier is staring into the middle distance instead of at his son.

Then Javier turns to him. "What's yours?"

"Mine?"

Javier's nose wrinkles, and it might be the cutest thing Gavin has seen so far today. "Your favorite breakfast food."

Oh. Right. "Well, I feel like anything I say now isn't going to be as good as yours."

That startles a laugh out of Javier. "It's not a competition, Gavin. If I'm going to be your Recipient, I want to know how to take care of you."

Gavin can't shake the discomfort those words give. When he'd thought of his marriage, he'd always seen himself in a Partnered marriage of equals, instead of a traditional Provider-Recipient marriage. But life doesn't always end up the way one expects, and this is just one more example of that.

Gavin glances at Evelyn before he can stop himself. "My mom never really made anything special like that, but Evelyn…" He pauses, swallowing past the lump in his throat. "Mom never liked to keep cereal in the house, but every year on my birthday Evelyn would go out and find the sugariest cereal on the shelves and bring it home for me. It's not even that I like it all that much anymore, so much as it just…"

"It's home."

Taking a moment to settle himself before he turns back to Javier, Gavin blinks hard. The understanding in his fiancé's eyes sends a shiver down his spine. It's exactly what he'd expected and nothing like it at the same time. "Yeah. It is."

Javier's smile is soft when Gavin can see past his teary eyes. "Okay, then. My turn."

"Your turn?"

"What's one thing you never leave home without?"

"Pocketknife," Gavin answers immediately. "I can't tell you how many I've had confiscated at airports over the years. I learned early on to never bring my good ones along with me. I almost lost the one Evelyn gave me for my high school graduation because I forgot it was in my pocket. That was a hell of a chase through the airport. I almost missed my flight. I refused to give it up, so I had to go back through security, drop it off in a mailbox to the house, and then go back through security." Gavin can laugh at the memory now, but at the time it had felt like a big deal. "What about you?"

Javier rubs the back of his neck. "Honestly? Wet wipes."

That startles Gavin a little. "Why's that?"

"It started when Ále was little. Before we knew about his CP there was a certain expectation about his progression. He spilled a lot when he was smaller, and so having them on hand was a necessity. Now it's mostly just habit."

"Huh," Gavin murmurs. "Makes sense."

Alejandro and the rest of their group seem to have grown tired of the hyenas, so Alejandro turns to them and waves so they can set off for the next stage in their journey. The girls are chattering with Alejandro and it warms Gavin's heart.

Gavin and Javier are left to linger at the back of the group each time they stop at another exhibit, with Citlali glancing back at them every once in a while. They exchange questions through the next two hours, playing at getting to know one another with a muddled game of twenty questions. Through it all, though, Gavin feels like Javier is holding something back. That there's something he wants to ask but isn't ready to yet.

That's alright. They're getting married tomorrow. There will be plenty of time to tease it out of him.

They catch up to their chaperones at the bongo exhibit just past the elephants, where they'd spent quite a bit of time. The girls are starting to lag, and when Javier checks on Alejandro, he admits to his fatigue.

"It is getting hot out here," Gavin acknowledges. "Is anybody hungry enough to need to eat something here before we go?"

Alejandro perks up at the mention of food. "Can we, Dad?"

Javier hesitates. "I'm sure we can just get something on the way to the house. There's no need to pay zoo prices for something to eat."

Alejandro wilts a little, but doesn't say anything.

Gavin's chest squeezes at the easy way Javier points to cost as a contributing factor and the just as easy way that Alejandro agrees. Gavin glances at Elaine and Sierra, both of whom look like they could fall asleep where they're now seated in the double stroller. Maybe going straight home is the right call.

But Gavin isn't ready to let go of this yet. He isn't ready to walk away from the warmth and ease that came from this time together, familiar and welcome despite its newness. Javier's posture loosened question by question as they talked and he's relaxed into their time together. Now, Javier's shoulders are back up around his ears, and Gavin just wants to soothe everything away for his fiancé. So he does what his parents always did.

He lets the money do the talking.

"Don't worry about that," Gavin says. "I can cover it. Besides," he adds, tossing Evelyn an apologetic look, "It's not a visit to the zoo without ice cream, is it?"

The girls immediately perk up. "Ice cream?" Elaine asks.

Evelyn rolls her eyes and shakes her head at Gavin. "Only you, Gav."

"We're here," Gavin says with a shrug. "Might as well enjoy it while we are."

Gavin turns to Javier, expecting a similar sort of laughing exasperation. Instead he's met with pinched lips and a furrowed brow. Javier's shoulders are even higher than before. Gavin pauses. Swallows. Tries to figure out his misstep.

Alejandro shakes his head. "It's okay," he says, "We can just go home. I don't mind."

"Oh." Gavin isn't usually a soft-spoken guy, but in this he can't help but be. "Are you sure you don't want to eat here?"

Alejandro glances instinctively at Javier. Gavin can see the words forming in Alejandro's mind, but Javier's face goes blank and he looks down at his son.

"It's okay," Javier says softly without looking at Gavin. "Whatever Gavin wants is fine."

"Yeah?" Alejandro asks.

Javier nods silently.

Alejandro lights up. "Awesome. I know just where I want us to go."

With Alejandro directing, their group troops through the zoo, presumably toward somewhere with food.

As Javier quickens his pace so he and Alejandro are next to his grandmother, Gavin drifts toward Evelyn.

"I upset him."

Evelyn hums. "You're the one that saw his interview and talked to him before today. What do you know about him that might explain it?"

Gavin looks ahead to where Citlali is speaking to Javier in low tones. "He's a single father. He's been living with his parents, taking care of Alejandro on his own. Oh." Insight comes like a lightning bolt. "He's used to being the one making the decisions for Alejandro. I took that away from him."

"That could be it," Evelyn agrees. "It could be a lot of things. But all you can do is take it in stride and either ask him what you need to do differently or figure it out yourself. You're going to be his Provider, Gavin. To a lot of people, that means you're going to be the one making the decisions."

"I'm not other people," Gavin argues.

"But Javier doesn't know that yet, does he?"

It's a fair point. Gavin worked hard to shed the version of

himself that his parents wanted—self-important, egotistical, with no regard for the people that helped him get to where he is—but there are some things that are hard to get rid of. Even with years at the fire station under his belt and spending time with people outside the tax bracket he was born into, he still has a lot to learn.

"Fine," Gavin says. "I'll talk to him."

"Just be careful with how much you say. We both know that sometimes you don't know where to stop. You don't want to scare him off by oversharing."

She's not wrong. But Gavin is invested enough in the potential in this relationship with Javier that he'll do his best not to be too much. After all, if he's going to get what he needs out of this marriage and get Evelyn and his nieces to safety, he needs to keep up appearances. The last thing he needs is anyone sniffing around why he's now moving so fast to get the inheritance he's spent years denouncing.

3

Lunch isn't as awkward as Javi expected. Evelyn and his abuela entertain the kids while Javi goes to help Gavin order and carry the food back to the table. Gavin offers an apology for insisting about the food, and Javi tries to be as blasé about it as he can. After all, this is his future. Javi may have offered himself up as a Recipient to Gavin because he'd seemed the most down-to-earth of all the potential Providers that the matchmaking agency found for him, but Gavin still grew up rich. That can make people look at the world differently, and it's something that Javi is going to have to learn to live with. Not to mention, Gavin is the Provider here. He has all the power.

After lunch, and at Elaine's insistence, Gavin does a speed run past the ice cream place over by the flamingos and comes back juggling three cones, one for each of the kids. Ále is almost reverent as he takes the cone from Gavin, smiling up at him and offering his thanks. Gavin accepts the gratitude awkwardly, and something about that reminds Javi of the man he'd seen in the interview video. When weighed against the quiet insistence that he felt when Gavin got them lunch, this just feels like someone that wants to be there for Javi's kid, and that, more than anything, might be the way to his heart. After all, that's what marriage is supposed to be about. Isn't it?

Once the kids are focused on their treats, Gavin steps into Javi's space again. "You have the address for the house?" he asks.

"Yes," Javi says with a nod.

"Okay. I can take Evelyn and the girls and meet you there. The girls will need to go down for a nap soon. I have to meet my grandparents at the wedding venue later, but I'm happy to show you and Alejandro around the place before I leave."

"Oh," Javi starts, "you don't have to do that."

"I want to. It's your home too, Javier. I want it to feel like your home."

Javi swallows down the last of the lingering weight in his throat. "Okay. I'd like that."

When Gavin smiles back, Javi thinks its brilliance could power the whole city.

Once the kids finish their ice cream, and Javi and Evelyn have cleaned them all up, armed as they are with wet wipes, they all head for the exit. Javi's truck is near the front, courtesy of the blue and white placard on his rearview mirror, so they say their brief goodbyes there before separating.

There's a moment when Javi thinks that Gavin is going to kiss him, but it passes quickly enough, and then Gavin double-checks that Javi has the address before guiding Evelyn and the girls to his own car.

Javi watches them go before helping Àle into the car and getting in himself. His abuela is up front with him and Àle is in back, so he can't exactly assess his son's experience.

At least, he doesn't think he can. As usual, his son proves him wrong.

"That was really fun," Àle says.

"Oh yeah?" Javi asks.

"Yeah! Miss Evelyn was really nice, and the girls were really cute. They had a bunch of questions about the animals and stuff, and they took turns riding in the wheelchair with me."

"Yeah? You were able to keep them safe okay?"

"Yeah. Bisabuela and Miss Evelyn always helped me get us buckled into the wheelchair so they wouldn't fall out."

Even though he already knew that, the tension that Javi had been holding about it dissipates. "That's good. And you enjoyed the zoo?"

"I did. I wish we could have gone to see all the primates, but when Miss Evelyn and I looked at the map she thought the girls would get tired before we got all the way through if we did that. Besides," Ále says lightly, "She said we could come back another time."

"She did, did she?"

"Yeah."

There's room in the budget for that, Javi supposes, but he also doesn't want to lean on those funds too hard this soon into his relationship with Gavin. "Well, we'll see, kiddo." His abuela smacks his arm lightly, and he adjusts. "If you're excited about it, we'll find a way to make it work."

"Thanks, Dad."

Javi bites his lip on an apology. He hasn't been able to give Ále the life he wants to, but this marriage to Gavin could be a step in the right direction.

"Your prometido is quite handsome," Abuela says, interrupting Javi's thoughts.

"Yes, well. He is that," Javi agrees. His cheeks are heating up, but he doesn't think he can really be blamed for that. Gavin really is quite attractive.

"You're still worried, though," his abuela says softly.

"I know the service that matched us is reputable," Javi says with a shrug, glad that he needs to keep his eyes on the road and can't actually look at his abuela. "There was nothing coercive about it, and most of the Providers seemed fine enough. Bianca did a bunch of research about the agency before she told me to do it, and we both know she can research with the best of them."

"But you knew what you were looking for."

Javi glances at his son in the rearview mirror. "I did."

"And you went for it."

She isn't wrong. Still, Javi clenches his hands around the steering wheel.

"Be patient, cariño. You've always had good instincts. If he is the one that you chose, it was for a good reason."

Javi swallows. His abuela has never steered him wrong before, and he hopes that she isn't about to start now.

As Javi turns the truck down the street their new house is on, he distantly registers the fact that all of the houses are rambling single-story places. His heartbeat quickens in his chest as that fully registers. He hadn't thought to hope, but maybe he can.

When he pulls into the driveway in front of the house indicated by his GPS navigation next to Gavin's car, he pauses in wonder. Ále's always struggled with stairs, but he hadn't told Gavin that. For Gavin to choose a place like this feels nothing short of remarkable.

Then Javi catches sight of the clearly recently redone walk up to the front porch. It's slow and slanting and there are no stairs to be seen, and for a moment Javi's knees go weak.

"I told you that you picked a good one," his abuela says. Javi can hear the smirk in her voice.

Javi ignores her, turning to Ále instead. "Come on, buddy, time to get out."

Ále dutifully and carefully undoes his seat belt. It's one of the fine motor skills they've been working on, and Javi is quietly proud of the initiative Ále is taking even when they're in a new place. As soon as he's unbuckled, Javi undoes his own seatbelt and gets out, rounding the car to help Ále wrangle his crutches and get down from the truck. Once Ále is settled, Javi goes for the back of the truck to grab the suitcase that has most of Ále's clothes. He pulls it and another bag with more of Ále's things in it out of the back before traipsing up the front walk after his son and his abuela.

Gavin opens the door with a wide smile. "Hey guys, come on in."

Ále moves slow and steady as he makes it up to the porch, and smiles up at Gavin once he's there. "Hi, Mr. Carmichael."

Gavin glances at Javi, and Javi realizes that, other than when they met, Ále hadn't called Gavin by name at the zoo. He winces, wondering if this is a misstep. Before he can intervene, though, Gavin grins down at Ále.

"Hey, Alejandro. You know what, though? You can call me Gavin. If you want."

Ále looks over his shoulder at Javi, his eyes wide and worried. Javi tries to think of an adult in Ále's life that he calls by their first name that isn't family and comes up blank.

Then again, Gavin is going to be family now, isn't he?

The thought isn't as settling as Javi thought it would be, and some of that must show on his face, because Ále turns back to Gavin. "That's okay, Mr. Carmichael. Are the girls here too?" he asks before Gavin can say anything more.

"They are. Do you want me to show you where they are?"

"Yes, please."

Ále carefully clears the small lip at the base of the doorway, and Javi watches a shadow cross over Gavin's face. It passes in a moment, though, and then he's walking Ále down the hall, presumably toward Evelyn and her daughters.

"I think this Gavin is going to be good for you, mijo," his abuela whispers, following Javi into the house.

"Yeah," Javi says, his heart in his throat and his eyes a little misty. "I hope you're right." He shakes off the swell of emotion in his chest and follows Gavin. "Come on. We've been in the sun all day. We should let you rest."

Once inside, Javi leaves the two bags by the door and follows the sound of voices into the house. The hall that extends from the wide open foyer is wider than the ones at his parents' house or, frankly, any of the houses he's been in lately. There's also the sharp smell of fresh paint in the space. That, coupled with a quick glance at the floor and the hints of drywall dust that reside here and there, makes it clear that Gavin did more renovations here than just the front walk.

That same swell of emotion fills Javi's chest, and it's all he can do to keep walking down the hall. He makes it to the open door to see Evelyn tucking the girls into the full-size bed that takes up most of the space in the room. Ále is perched on the side of the bed, grinning down at the girls.

"And you'll be here when we wake up, Ále?" Elaine asks sleepily.

"Yeah, I will."

"Hmm, okay." In moments, the pair of them are out, and it's all Javi can do not to melt at the sight of his son smiling down at his new cousins.

Well. Cousins-to-be.

"Cute, huh?"

Javi whips around to see Gavin standing in the hall beside him, hands in his pockets as he rocks back and forth on his heels. His lips are quirked up in a smaller smile than Javi expected, and his eyes keep darting from Javi to Ále and back again.

He's nervous, Javi realizes, and that settles the nerves in his own stomach.

"Yeah. It is."

Gavin exhales and drops onto his heels. "I can show you and Ále the rest of the house now, if you want?"

"Yeah." Javi smiles. "I'd like that."

"Okay. Okay, good."

"Although, maybe let's start with where my abuela will be staying tonight? Let her get off her feet for a bit?"

"Oh," Gavin says, "of course. My apologies, Citlali."

Abuela waves off the apologies. "I can find my way to the kitchen for now. You boys go see what your new home looks like." Gavin opens his mouth to argue, but one stern look from Abuela is enough to have his jaw snapping shut. "Go on," she says, looking back at Javi. "Let your man show you around."

4

Gavin insists on showing Citlali to the kitchen before starting the grand tour of the house. She smiles at him indulgently, patting his arm as he sits her down at the kitchen island.

"There isn't much in the fridge," Gavin apologizes. "I'm going to pick up some essentials after I finish at the venue, but I wanted to wait to get some input from Javier and Alejandro."

Gavin wants to ask how to help them feel at home here while he's in the kitchen with Citlali, but after the way Javier was so jumpy at the zoo, Gavin wonders how much he's allowed to.

"I'll make you up a list," Citlali says. There's a twinkle in her eye that settles Gavin rather than unnerves him. "I know these boys like the back of my hand."

"That would be lovely." Gavin lets himself settle into the easy assertion and smiles at her. He hesitates for a moment, then turns to Javier and Alejandro. "The dining room is this way," he says, jerking his head toward the opposite side of the kitchen from the one they'd entered through.

Once he's pretty sure the two of them will follow, he walks into the dining room, then steps off to one side. This was one of the trickier rooms to set up for Alejandro, but as he watches

Alejandro enter, he's pretty sure that he's done enough. Though he'd carefully chosen the place for its large kitchen and dining room, he'd been intentional when he picked out the dining room table so there would be enough room for Alejandro to easily walk around the table with the chairs pushed in, and probably with them pulled out as well. At least, it looks that way as Alejandro circles the room, his gaze on the walls.

"It's purple," Alejandro says, turning back to Gavin with a grin.

"It is. Do you like it?"

"I do."

"I'm glad." Gavin glances at Javier to take in his expression. His eyes are a little distant as he stares at Alejandro. Gavin wants to ask what he's thinking, but he doesn't dare. Not when things feel so tenuous with his fiancé. He turns his attention back to Alejandro. "Do you want to see your room?"

"Yeah." Alejandro winces, glancing at Javier, but whatever he sees on his dad's face settles him. "Yeah, I'd like that."

Gavin steps around the dining room table and out an open doorway to the hall they'd been in to start. The door to the first guest room is closed, meaning Evelyn is probably resting with the girls. Gavin hopes she isn't buried in the stress she brought with her when he isn't there to counterbalance her. Then he turns away and down the hall to the last room. He opens the door and gestures Alejandro in.

Alejandro steps into the doorway, then pauses, his jaw slowly dropping. After a moment, he turns to look at Gavin. "This is mine?" he whispers.

The nerves bubble up in Gavin's chest at the incredulity in Alejandro's voice. "Yeah. Is it okay?"

Alejandro nods, his head moving slowly as he turns back to the room, taking it all in.

Gavin would be lying if he said he wasn't proud of the work he did on Alejandro's room. One of the first—and only—things

Javier had mentioned about his son in their video call was how much he loves space. There's a solar system mobile in one corner and he'd found a Milky Way decal to put on the wall above the headboard of the full-size bed that takes up a good chunk of the room. There's a nebula on the comforter on the bed, and as Gavin's focus lands there, Alejandro steps into the room and reaches out, his fingers tracing over the arcs and spirals of the nebula.

Gavin smiles at Alejandro, then braces himself to look over at the boy's father.

Javier is staring at the room with wide eyes and parted lips, his gaze traveling over everything once, twice, and then settling on Gavin. "You did all this?"

Gavin shrugs, suddenly self-conscious. "I guess."

Javier turns back to the room, letting Gavin exhale his worries. "It's incredible."

That isn't the first time Javier said something to imply that he truly appreciates what Gavin is trying to do, but it feels more intentional than before. And for it to be something to do with Alejandro means even more. Gavin relaxes. Maybe he's on the right track.

Gavin waits until Alejandro checks the closet, the dresser, and the door that leads to an ensuite bathroom that Gavin had modified for Alejandro's needs. Javier drifts around the bed and over to the bathroom after his son. When he turns back to Gavin at the door, he's got one eyebrow raised.

"It was originally a guest suite," Gavin says. "I figured he would do better in here than in one of the rooms without a bathroom."

Javier hums and turns back to look around the bathroom.

As he does, Gavin lets himself admire him. Javier has a strong jaw that only softens when his son is smiling at him. His hands are work-worn but large and steady, and though there's been a sort of uncertainty in his eyes all day, he inhabits his body in a way that Gavin admires.

Javier turns to him, as though sensing his gaze. Gavin watches his Adam's apple bob as they stare at one another and distantly registers the desire to kiss the thin skin above it.

Not that it matters. This marriage is a business arrangement for both of them, and even if they one day end up sharing a bed, it won't be as lovers. That was the deal, after all. No matter how beautiful he finds Javier's form, no matter how much he wants to hold him in his arms, they're here for the family that each of them are bringing with them, not the family they could make together.

Gavin forces a smile. "Do you want to see the rest of the house?"

Javier backs out of the bathroom. "Come on, mijo. There's more to see."

Alejandro steps out after his father, a wide smile on his face. "Thank you, Mr. Carmichael."

The unprompted gratitude takes Gavin by surprise, but he tries not to let it show. "It's no big deal."

"It is," Alejandro insists. "This is so cool."

"Then, you're welcome. I'm glad you like it."

Alejandro grins, making his way quickly to Gavin's side. "What's next?"

The highlight of the family room for Alejandro is, predictably, the television, but Javier takes in the furniture with a knowing, critical gaze. He looks over at Gavin again with a question in his eyes.

Gavin shrugs, unsurprised that Javier picked out the extra supportive nature of the furniture for Alejandro's sake. "I like to research." Javier's eyes drift to the sliding glass door at the back of the room, and although Gavin hopes he won't notice the size of the lot just yet, he has no such luck.

Javier's eyes start to shift past the door only to cut back over to it. He walks to the back door in four long strides, stopping short when he sees the full length of the backyard.

Gavin didn't mean to buy a place that was three quarters of an acre all told, but it was the one that had most of the things Gavin knew Alejandro needed and would be most easily and quickly modified to ensure that the rest were present as well. It's more house than Gavin might have anticipated for himself or his family, but he can't say he's upset.

Javier turns to him with wide eyes and a slack jaw, his whole body turned away from Alejandro and pointed at Gavin. It's the first time Gavin has been the focus of his attention like this, and the realization settles warm and sure over Gavin's shoulders, an anchor point amidst all the newness. Alejandro is still preoccupied by the television and the couches, leaving Gavin to make his way over to Javier.

"You okay?"

Javier shakes his head, looking numb and dumbfounded. "Gavin, this is too much."

Before Gavin can say anything, Alejandro crosses the room to stand beside his father. "Whoa," he says, "that's a big yard." Then he scrunches his nose and looks up at Gavin. "Why are there so many weeds?" he asks.

"It's not a brand new house," Javier says when Gavin comes up blank. "The last family that lived here must not have spent much time back here."

"Huh," Alejandro says. Then he shrugs and turns back to the yard. "Okay."

"I know it's going to need a lot of work," Gavin can't look at Javier when he speaks, "but the realtor said it had potential, and my captain said the same thing when he came to look at it with me. And we don't have to do anything with it if you don't want to, but I figured..."

When Gavin can't finish the thought, Javier turns to him. He doesn't say anything, staring at Gavin with clear, curious eyes.

Gavin inhales slowly, then exhales just as slowly. "I figured since it already needs so much work we could make a space that's good for Alejandro. Not just safe for him," he's quick to say over Javier's burgeoning protests, "But a space that works with his physical therapy to make it helpful for him. Good for him. A space that helps him get stronger, in whatever way he wants to be stronger. And if he doesn't want any of that, we can do whatever he wants with the space. It's his, Javier. His and yours." Gavin glances at Alejandro and says, "How does that sound to you, Alejandro?"

Before Javier can say something, Alejandro looks up at Gavin with something sharp in his eyes. "You mean we get to make it whatever I want?"

"Well, whatever your dad is okay with," Gavin amends, glancing once at Javier. He doesn't want to overstep. Javier still looks stunned by the whole thing, moreso than he's been about anything else, so Gavin turns back to Alejandro to clarify. "We want to make sure that it's what you want, but we also want to make sure you're safe. Does that make sense?"

Alejandro stares at Gavin for a long moment before turning back to the backyard. "Yeah, I guess so." Then he smiles. "I think I'd like that."

"Oh." All the air leaves Gavin's chest as he stares at Alejandro. His throat is tight, and he swallows past it to speak. "Good. I'm glad."

Uncaring of Gavin's distress, or perhaps unaware, Alejandro looks at Javier. "Can we put in a slide?"

Javier hums and turns to the yard again. "We'll see, kiddo," he says. "We can reassess once I get it cleaned up back there, okay?"

Alejandro pouts, but nods. "Okay."

"Javier," Gavin says, "If it's a matter of cost, you know that's no barrier."

"It's not," Javier snaps.

Gavin startles, his eyes going wide.

"It's a matter of accessibility. I need to make sure that he can stay safe."

"Right," Gavin says, chastised. "Of course."

Alejandro shifts closer to Javier, his eyes flicking between Javier and Gavin, trying to read the moment.

"Well," Gavin shakes off his reaction to Javier's words, "as long as you have what you need to make the space what Alejandro wants. That's all that matters."

Javier stares at him for a moment, then looks away. "Gavin," Javier pauses, his eyes on the backyard. "Thank you."

Gavin waves his words away, unconcerned. As long as he didn't go too far, everything is fine. "It's nothing. Really. Like I said, all of this is for you and Alejandro. Whatever you two need, I'll do whatever I can to take care of it."

Javier takes a moment before he looks away. "Still. Thank you."

And Gavin has nothing to say to that, but "You're welcome."

The rest of the tour of the house goes quickly after that. Gavin feels skittish about it all now that Javier has seen his hand. Showing them to the second guest room, where Javier's grandmother will be staying tonight, the playroom for Alejandro, and the study Gavin put together for Javier all feels a little bit ostentatious now.

And then there's the primary bedroom, the one that Gavin fully intends to give to Javier once everything is all said and done. There's no easy way to insist on it when protocol dictates that it's Gavin's room first, but once there's no one else in the house with them, it'll be easier to kick protocol to the curb.

He hesitates outside the door to the primary bedroom, feeling Alejandro's curious eyes on his back.

Javier saves him, though. "Ále, will you go check on your bisabuela?"

Alejandro looks like he's about to argue, but the look Javier gives his son is enough to quell the protests before they come.

"Fine," he says. He casts one last look at the closed door before turning and heading back down the hall to the kitchen.

Javier watches him go, and Gavin watches Javier watching. He's distracted enough, though, that he's too slow to school his expression when Javier looks back at him.

"It's your house, too," Gavin blurts out before he can stop himself.

Javier blinks before his expression softens into a tentative smile. "We both know that's not true."

Gavin shakes his head, but before he can say anything, the alarm on his phone goes off, reminding him that he needs to head to the venue if he wants to make it in time to meet his grandparents there and assuage their concerns about Javier and the wedding. Still, he hesitates. He's scared that he's messed up beyond repair, and that Javier might bolt if given enough reason to.

Javier must see the fear in his eyes, because he closes the distance between them and grips Gavin's wrist. "We'll be right here waiting when you get home."

The words don't silence all the worries in Gavin's mind, but they make things a little quieter. "Alright," he says, refusing to let the unknown that Javier represents get in the way of the joy that is coming. "Alright. I'll see you in an hour or two, then." He hesitates, the instinct to kiss his fiancé swelling in his chest. He refrains, though, shifting his hand in Javier's grip so that he can lace their fingers together and squeeze tightly.

Javier's expression softens.

Gavin lets himself trust that Javier is as in this as he is. Maybe with different histories, and different goals, but they're in this together in ways that Gavin could only have hoped for when he connected with the matchmaking agency weeks ago.

Javier squeezes Gavin's hand in return and nods at him. "We'll be waiting." Then he lets go.

Gavin forces himself not to sway into Javier's space, and

instead turns on his heel and heads for the door. He has a meeting to get to, and the sooner he gets there, the sooner he can come home.

Gavin's running late to meet his grandparents by the time he makes it to the venue. He valet-parks his car because of it, even knowing he'll consider it extravagant later. Rather than dwell on it, he hustles inside and sees his grandparents waiting for him just inside the front doors to the venue. Neither of them look particularly impressed with his tardiness.

Granddad Carmichael was always a bit severe and today is no exception. "Gavin," he says, holding out a hand. No hugs among the men on this side of the family.

Gavin takes his hand and shakes it firmly. "Granddad," he says. Then he leans down to let his grandmother press a kiss to his cheek. "Grandma."

"Gavin," his grandmother says. "What took you so long?"

"I was getting Javier and his son settled at the house."

"Your father set you up with a good house?" his granddad asks.

"Yessir." Gavin assures him. He doesn't mention the few accommodations he'd added after the fact. It won't be well-looked upon. "Shall we tour the venue?"

His grandma slips her hand into his granddad's elbow and they turn away from the front door, expecting him to lead, which he does. "I still don't see why you're in such a rush with this all of a sudden, Gavin," she says, prying. "You've never been in a hurry before. And it's not like you need someone to look after one of *your* children; you don't have any. Unless an old girlfriend has come forward?"

Gavin can't tell them the truth. That, a month ago, Evelyn called him in the middle of a shift at work, crying. That he slipped away from team lunch to listen to her confide the truth in him. The truth he'd always feared. That her Provider Shane had finally laid hands on one of the girls. That they were trying for a fourth before that. That she'd been terrified that she was already pregnant and that she didn't know how to keep the girls safe anymore. That he'd researched every minute of downtime for the rest of that shift until he found *CPR Agency* and signed up for their service so he could meet the stipulations to get his inheritance and be able to afford to get Evelyn out of Shane's clutches in Boston and out here to safety.

He found Javier and Alejandro, and immediately wanted to save them too, even if he's still not quite sure why Javier chose now to ask to be saved. Surely he'd be snatched up by anyone else the second they saw him. Gavin isn't totally sure how he got so lucky as to get to marry someone that's as dedicated to their kid as Javier obviously is, but he's going to do his best to be worthy of the trust that Javier has placed in him.

He's going to bring Evelyn here and earn his right to be Javier's husband. That's all he wants out of this.

Gavin keeps his tone cool and even and doesn't say any of that to his grandparents, though. "It's like you and Granddad have been saying for years. It's time I settled down and made a family of my own."

Grandma Carmichael hums like she doesn't quite believe him. She doesn't ask anything more, though, instead letting him lead them through the venue.

He points out all the things he knows his grandparents will want to see, like the slightly outlandish Recipient suite, the high ceilings, and the space for the reception. He doesn't point out any of the things he'd actually sent his captain's Partner Diana out looking for, which were a single-floor venue with level entrances and wide hallways in case Alejandro needs his wheelchair. He doesn't say anything about his afternoon at the zoo with Alejandro and his nieces, instead focusing on making sure that he keeps his grandparents happy.

His grandmother purses her lips at the size of the hall where the ceremony is going to be held. “I still don’t see why you couldn’t have held it at church, darling,” she says, “there was no need for all this rigmarole.”

“I didn’t think I could get that organized in time,” he hedges. “I thought this would just be quicker and easier on everyone.”

“Again,” she says, “there was no need to be this quick.”

Gavin keeps his face carefully neutral. “What can I say?” he says, shrugging. “I can’t wait to be married.”

5

After convincing his abuela to rest in the unoccupied guest room, Javi spends the bulk of the time between Gavin's departure and his return helping Ále get his things unpacked. He lets Ále set the pace and listens intently each time his son pauses to talk about their trip to the zoo, or ask a question about the planets in the mobile or the stars on his headboard. Javi does his best to answer any questions, but mostly just revels in the time he gets to spend with Ále. They get his clothes put away first, then arrange and rearrange his toys three times.

Once the room is mostly organized, Javi leads them to the kitchen so he can check on the food situation and see if he can start making dinner before Gavin gets home. Unfortunately, Gavin's assessment was dead right. There is next to nothing in the refrigerator and there is even less in the pantry. Javi scrubs a hand over his face. He opens his mouth to offer to turn the television on against his better judgment when Evelyn steps out of the guest room with a sleepy Sierra on her hip and a wide-eyed Elaine following her.

"Oh, hello, Javier."

"Hi there." Javi waves at Sierra, who tucks her face into her mother's neck with a grumpy noise. Javi chuckles. "Well, hello to you too, Sierra. And how did you sleep, Elaine?"

"Good!" she says, bouncing a little on her toes. "Snack now."

"I see." Javi nods at the assertion with all the seriousness afforded to such a statement. He glances up at Evelyn. "I think Gavin got some food for the girls and left it in the fridge."

"Thank you," she says. She gives him a wide berth as she joins him in the kitchen.

Javi notes this, then turns to Ále. "Do you want to sit with your cousins or put on the TV?"

Ále thinks for a moment. "I want to sit with my cousins."

"Okay." Javi doesn't let his surprise show. "Do you want me to stay with you, or is it okay with you if I head out to the backyard for a little bit?"

Ále perks up. "You can go look at the backyard. That means we can put the slide in sooner, right?"

"Sure thing, kiddo." Javi says. "I'll see what I can do."

Ále grins up at him, then resettles his weight on his crutches and makes his way to the kitchen table to sit with Elaine.

Javi waits until he hears Evelyn greet Ále before turning to the backyard. He slips out the back door and steps into the early summer heat. He's not a good judge of space, but he can tell that there's a lot of land here. Plenty to set up a play space that's safe for Ále and maybe have some room left over for a garden. He's never had a garden before, but that's one of those things that Recipients are supposed to want to do, right? Take care of a garden?

Javi shakes off the immediate reaction to the thought. There have always been male Recipients in larger family groups, and there have been female Providers for just as long, but his parents raised him to think he was supposed to be a Provider. It was one of the things he knew from a young age: that his parents expected him to provide for his family and be the kind of man that didn't let his spouse take over. After all, if the family unit exists to take care of the children, it's his responsibility to take care of his own.

With one hand on the high wood fence and his eyes on the yard, Javi walks the perimeter, idly checking for spots that might need patching. He pauses periodically to take pictures of the different, larger plants that skirt the edges of the yard so he can get some advice on which ones to keep and which ones to get rid of. He'll have to look up gardening stores nearby.

Javi tried not to let his son fall into the same thought patterns as the ones his parents instilled in him. He'd already figured out how much they messed with his head before Ále was four, and he's done his best to keep him from the worst of it. That doesn't mean that he himself was spared.

He'd tried, is the thing. He'd tried so hard to be the kind of Provider that Ále's mother Casey needed. But as much as she loves Ále, she had one foot out the door years before she actually left. Video calls and holiday visits only go so far. Javi has been alone in this for years, and he'd started to think he always would be. Then Ále's tenth birthday started creeping up. It left Javi remembering his own tenth birthday and the way the world seemed to change on a dime. The way expectations changed in his parents' house and he was asked to take on so much more. Asked to be the man of the house when his father was away.

He'd seen the beginnings of that in the way his parents shifted in their treatment of Ále and known he needed to get his son out before things got any worse. So now?

Now he has a chance to screw it all up. He doesn't know what Gavin expects of him, doesn't know what he's supposed to do here. He'd known that they would be coming to the house after the zoo today, but he hadn't thought far enough ahead to think about whether he's supposed to make dinner tonight. That is, he's definitely supposed to, but how is he supposed to do that if Gavin's the one getting the groceries?

Javi's on the far side of the yard when he hears the garage

door open. He pauses, trying to decide if he should hustle back into the house. But he's almost done with the circuit of the yard, so he might as well just finish up.

Once he's done, he steps carefully up onto the slab of concrete serving as a back porch, pulls off his shoes, and heads inside. He pauses just outside the kitchen to check on Ále. Seeing nothing concerning, Javi goes to drop his shoes off at the front door. Then he heads back to the kitchen, catching his abuela coming out of the guest room.

"Mijo," she says with a smile.

Javi hums, leaning down to press a kiss to her upturned cheek. "Did you get some rest?"

"I did, preocupado. Where's your man?"

"In the kitchen with the kids, I think," Javi says as his cheeks heat up. He extends an arm for her to lean against, though she doesn't need much support. She smiles at him and he leads her into the kitchen.

"Citlali." Gavin's voice is bright as he calls out to them. He maneuvers around the kitchen expressly so that he can pull out a chair for her.

She smiles at him, patting his cheek. "You can call me abuela, you know."

Gavin's eyes widen. He glances at Javi, who can't read the expression on his face. Javi offers his Provider-to-be a small smile, but he must be too slow on the draw, because Gavin's answering smile is wobbly.

Gavin looks back at Abuela. "Maybe someday," he says softly. "But not today, I don't think."

Javi can't see the expression his abuela makes, but Gavin looks away. "If you say so, mijo."

Gavin chokes on a laugh. He stands up. "So, dinner, anyone?"

"Yes," Javi says, ready to slip into this role, at least. "I'm not sure what all you got at the store, but I can make us something to eat."

"It's okay," Gavin says, waving him off. "I've got this."

Every muscle in Javi's body freezes. "What?"

"Dinner. I got everything I need to make lasagna. It'll be a minute, but I can do that while you all spend time with the kids."

Javi's lips go a little bit numb. "Oh. Got it."

Is he not expected to do this? To help? Does Gavin really think him this incapable?

Gavin turns to look at him, but Javi manages to plaster on a smile before they make eye contact. It feels as uncertain as so much else with Gavin has. He can tell that Gavin doesn't know how to read his expression any more than he knew how to read Gavin's, and, at the moment, that's a blessing in disguise.

Ále pipes up before Javi can say anything. "Dad, can we go get my Switch so I can show the girls? We can sit in the family room."

"Sure thing," Javi says, eyes still locked on Gavin. "I'll meet you there in a minute."

Ále hesitates, then gets to his feet, grabbing his crutches to head to his room.

Evelyn pulls Sierra a little closer to herself, as though sensing the tension in the room. Javi tries not to take it personally. Gavin looks over at his sister and nods, as though giving her permission to slip away, which she does immediately. Then it's the two of them and one of their chaperones. Javi considers sending his abuela away, too, but he's pretty sure he's going to want a witness to this.

Gavin stares at him, his brow drawn together in a frown and his eyes darting between Javi's face and the door through which Evelyn had just slipped out.

Javi needs to try, at least one more time.

"Are you sure you don't want me to make dinner?" he asks.

Gavin's shoulders lift to his ears. "I told you, I've got it."

"Okay," Javi allows, "but you don't have to have it." It's my job, he doesn't say. It's my job to take care of you like this. Not the other way around.

But Gavin just shakes his head. "I want to do this for you. Let me."

The instruction, which sounds almost like an order, rankles, but Javi keeps his face carefully neutral. "Okay. Do you need help?"

"It's fine." Gavin smiles tightly. "Go be with your son. I'll let you know when dinner is ready."

Throat thick with unfamiliar weight, Javi nods. "Okay. I'll be there when you're ready." Then he turns away and heads for the doorway, feeling his abuela follow.

Gavin's voice comes from behind him. "Javier."

Javi glances over his shoulder. "Yes?"

Gavin hesitates, as though holding something back. Then he sighs and nods. "Nothing. Don't worry about it. I'll let you know when dinner is ready."

Javi's jaw tightens, but he doesn't drop the smile. "Okay." Then he turns on his heel and heads for the family room.

Evelyn already set the kids up on the couch, with Elaine and Sierra on either side of Ále. The three of them really do paint a lovely picture. The girls are already enamored with Ále, and he seems just as taken with them. Javi gives himself a moment to just observe, letting their comfort with one another settle against his sternum. There's something about the ease of children that he can settle into in a way that he can't when he's with adults.

So the shrewd look that Evelyn is giving him is a warning he wants to obey.

But if this is going to be his marriage, then she's going to be his sister-in-law, and there's going to be no avoiding her in the long run. He might as well start to make nice with her now.

Evelyn is propped up in one of the recliners, and though Javi could avoid her by sitting at the other end of the room, he knows he needs to give her what she's challenging him to keep hidden. Whatever story she wants, he's going to have to at least hear her out before he decides if it needs to stay hidden or not.

He crosses the room and stands at her side, his hands in his pockets as he stares at their kids. He can still feel her eyes on him, but he's on her brother's home turf. If one of them is going to make the opening volley, it's her.

"So," she says, breaking the silence after a moment. "Javier."

He hums, but doesn't give her anything more than that.

"Tell me your side of this story."

That makes Javi turn to look at her. It's far more leeway than he might have expected, but it's in his nature to clarify where he can. "Story?"

A small smile quirks her lips, though it disappears quickly. "How did you two connect?"

He almost pushes back on that, too, but he relents at the last moment. "We met through a matchmaking agency."

"Yes. A rather obscure one, if what Gavin tells me is true."

Ah. So that's her angle. She wants to know if he sought Gavin out deliberately. After all, he and Gavin have already discussed the fact that they both chose the *CPR Agency* as their agency of choice precisely because of its obscurity. Gavin must not have told Evelyn that. Still, that's Gavin's story to tell, not his. "My sister Bianca likes researching things. It's why she's the one of us that's headed for graduate school. She found the company for me. Said they have some of the highest success rates for long-term matches."

"And you just went with it?"

Javi raises an eyebrow at her. "She's my sister. I trust her."

Evelyn's only reaction to that is a slight tightening of her brow. "This agency. How much do they charge a Recipient?"

And there's the money angle. "That's the beauty of the *CPR Agency*. They don't charge Recipients a dime. It's rather progressive," he adds when she opens her mouth to speak, "and I wanted a Provider that could see the value in that."

For a moment, he thinks he's stymied her. Then she nods and

leans into what he's given her. "And why Gavin? Why my brother?"

That question is at once the easiest and hardest one to answer. "Your brother." He pauses, trying to find the right words. Words have never been his strong suit, and some days he thinks that's why Ále's mother left them, but for this—for his son—he'll try. "Your brother is a good man," he says softly. "I knew that from the second he told me he decided to be a firefighter rather than spend his time in the gilded tower of your family's company walls. I know he still does work for them but that clearly isn't where his heart is. He could have had the world handed to him on a silver platter, and instead he chooses to be in the world in a more authentic way. He knows what it is to be one of the people, and it's clear that he prefers it. Not to mention that as a firefighter he works closely with paramedics and EMTs." This is where Javi almost slips up, almost shows too much of his hand and alludes to the fact that, of all the Provider profiles the *CPR Agency* had given him, Gavin had seemed the safest. The kindest. He holds back, uncertain how Evelyn will interpret such an assertion. "I can imagine he'll be better able to help me with Ále than most other potential Providers."

It's only part of the truth, but from the way Evelyn's expression softens, he knows it was the right part to share. "Alright," she says softly. "I can't say that I trust you completely, but it's clear you're both in this for the same reason. For family. I can accept that for now. But if you hurt him, I can assure you, there will be hell to pay."

Javi nods grimly. He knows what's in his marriage contract with Gavin. He'd gone over it with a fine-toothed comb, and then asked Bianca to do the same. She'd done as he asked, and she was the one to find the clause that Gavin put in about the college fund for Ále. That, provided Javi married Gavin on the predetermined date, Gavin would put an obscene amount of money into a fund for Ále's studies post-high school. No strings attached.

That was one of the things that would make Javi completely willing to jump in with both feet, and Gavin obviously saw that from the start. So if Javi has to stay with Gavin until Ále graduates to give his son the life he deserves between now and when the fund matures, he will. He'd do anything for his son. That doesn't mean that he likes it. He doesn't like being strung along like this and then treated like the bad guy in this situation. After all, Gavin's the one that's after the inheritance money he'll get when they get married, and quickly, too. There's been no clear reason for it, but that doesn't mean that Javi has to like it, or that he gets to ask.

Evelyn's eyes finally slide off of his face and back over to the kids. She settles back in the recliner and places a hand on her abdomen. "Thank you."

"For what?" Javi asks.

She shrugs. "For telling me the truth."

Javi bites his lip to hold back a comparable deluge of questions. After all, he knows his place as a Recipient. He keeps house and takes care of the kids and is occasionally arm candy for his Provider. Not that he thinks there will be much of that last one, what with Gavin's attitude toward the family business. That's fine, though. Javi can do his best with what he's been given, and will do whatever Gavin lets him do around the house.

It doesn't seem cooking will be part of that, but that's okay. He can find other ways to be useful.

6

Javi and Evelyn don't talk much after that. They watch their kids and share one another's company but otherwise keep to themselves. Ále glances up at them a few times, but seems content enough to just sit with the girls and entertain them. He's patient with them in a way that Javi saw with his other cousins back in Vegas, but dialed up to a level that is unfamiliar.

Eventually, just as Sierra is starting to get squirmy and distracted, Gavin calls out to them. "Dinner's up."

Evelyn carefully levers herself to her feet and heads for the couch, where she scoops Sierra up and takes Elaine by the hand. "Come on, girls. Uncle Gavin has dinner ready."

Elaine cheers and would no doubt be scurrying off ahead of her mother if not for her hand in Evelyn's.

For his part, Javi waits as Ále leans forward to set his Switch down on the coffee table before grabbing his crutches. Then, as Ále makes his way into the dining room, Javi goes to get his abuela from the kitchen.

When Javi and his abuela get to the dining room, Evelyn is already seated at the foot of the table with the girls on either side of her. That pulls Javi up short. He hadn't considered seating arrangements, and from the way Gavin is looking at him, he hadn't either. Evelyn clearly needs to be between the girls, but Javi also desperately wants to be next to his son so that he can help him with anything he might need. The table is set for seven, though, and Gavin is standing behind the only remaining pair of adjacent chairs, which means...

Gavin must realize this at the same moment that Javi does, because his face breaks out into a shaky smile and he says, "Citlali, why don't you sit at the head of the table?"

Abuela squeezes Javi's shoulder. "Of course, Gavin, dear." She slips out of Javi's reach and smiles up at Gavin as he pulls her chair out for her.

"And then, Alejandro, why don't you sit over here with your dad?" Gavin pulls Ále's chair out, too, before scuttling around the table to take the chair in front of Javi.

It takes a moment of maneuvering for them to get around each other, each shifting the same direction at the same time as they try to pass the other. In the end, Gavin goes still, and Javi places an instinctive hand on his elbow, using that to shift past him. The muscles in Gavin's arm tense at the touch, so Javi pulls away immediately and makes quick work of the space between him and Ále.

He doesn't let himself think too hard about the way Gavin tensed, instead settling in and following Gavin's lead as Gavin serves up the lasagna he'd made. There's salad and warm garlic bread and a bottle of red wine at their end of the table. For a moment Javi wants to sink into the care that Gavin is showing them. Wants to let Gavin have all the control. But that feels too much like what Javi had with his parents, and he can't risk someone leveraging their control over him again to make Ále feel inadequate. He doesn't think he'd survive it.

So he sits up a little taller and keeps one eye on Ále as he eats, ready to help in whatever way he needs to. But Ále's fine motor control has gotten better the older he's gotten, and he doesn't need as much help as Javi half-wishes he did. Not that he wants his son to feel like he needs to constantly ask for help. He wants Ále to always know he can ask for help, but he doesn't want his son to feel like he needs to.

No, this is all about Javi himself.

Evelyn and Gavin keep the conversation light between them, pulling Abuela into the conversation periodically. Javi only chimes in when asked. It isn't until about halfway through the meal that Javi notices that the wine is only half gone between the four adults. He and Gavin had half a glass each, and Abuela has had at least one, but, as Javi glances at Evelyn, he sees that she keeps eyeing the wine without taking any for herself.

The thought that Evelyn might be pregnant is an idle one at first, but the more he watches Evelyn with her daughters and thinks about the way Gavin hadn't named her Provider or asked after them all night, the clearer the picture becomes. If she's here without her Provider and she hasn't said anything overt about a pregnancy, he can't help but wonder if Gavin is doing the same thing for her that he's doing for Javi himself.

Because if there's one thing that Javi understands now about Gavin, it's that, although he is willing to spend money on the people he loves, he doesn't feel the need to flaunt it like some other Providers. Part of what drew Javi to Gavin's information packet was the speed with which he wanted to get married. It aligned with Javi's own need to get the hell out of his parents' house, and though Javi hadn't thought much of it at the time, now it feels like there might be more to it than just a money grab.

No discussion of Evelyn's Provider. Her abstaining from alcohol. And a brother on an apparent money grab that seems out of character for the little Javi knows of him. It paints an ugly picture of Evelyn's home life, and one that leaves Javi also avoiding the wine for the rest of the night.

If he's about to be in the middle of a rescue mission for a

pregnant woman, then he needs to be at his best for as long as this takes.

Still, he doesn't ask, and when the time comes to clean up after dinner, he's the first to start collecting plates. Ále offers to help. Javi accepts before anyone can say otherwise.

"Why don't you grab everyone's silverware while I get the plates?" Javi offers.

"Then, I'll bring in the serving dishes," Gavin is quick to insist.

Javi doesn't fight him on that, simply smiling and gathering everyone's plates. The three of them make their way into the kitchen, and Javi waits until Ále puts the silverware in the sink before he reaches around his son to open the dishwasher. He starts rinsing off plates and passing them off to Ále, watching his son out of the corner of his eye to see if he needs help arranging the dishwasher. He doesn't seem to need any help, so Javi settles into the familiar, albeit slightly altered, routine of cleaning up the kitchen.

Gavin hovers near the edge of the room, as though uncertain if he should be in here or not. Javi gives him a moment to decide before glancing at him. "Why don't you go sit with your sister? Ále and I have got this."

"Are you sure?"

"I'm sure." Javi says, bristling. He tries not to let it show. "Thank you, though."

Still Gavin hesitates. After a moment, he nods and turns away, stepping back into the dining room.

Javi and Ále work in easy silence until Ále breaks it. "Hey, Dad?"

"Yeah?"

"Do you think Mr. Carmichael would let us go to the zoo again sometime?"

Javi's heart squeezes in his chest. It's not that he's embarrassed about how hard he needed to work to keep the bills paid back in Vegas, but he does sometimes wish he'd had more time to spend with his son. It's one of the biggest reasons he'd caved to Bianca's scheming and connected with *CPR Agency*. He's always wanted to be able to do more for Ále, and this, marrying Gavin, is just one step in that direction.

"I think he'd like that," Javi says.

"Yeah?"

"Yeah. He seemed like he was having almost as much fun as you. You wouldn't believe the number of facts he just has in his brain about all those animals."

Ále's eyes widen. "Seriously?"

"Yep. Any time he wasn't asking about me, he was telling me about the animals we were walking past."

"Wow," Ále murmurs, "that's so cool."

With a smile, Javi hands Ále the last dish from the table. He dries his hands quickly, then reaches out to ruffle Ále's hair. "Why don't you go see if the girls want to watch you play on your Switch a little more?"

"Okay." Ále gives him one more smile and then he's off to the dining room.

Javi listens with half an ear as one of the girls, probably Elaine, cheers loudly at Ále's offer of more time with the Switch. There's more quiet conversation in the dining room that sounds like Gavin and Evelyn, but Javi can't tell if his abuela is still there with them. Even if she is, he doesn't need to know what they're talking about. Not just yet.

He moves on to the larger serving dishes, packing away the leftovers and making quick work of cleaning everything from the table, and it isn't until he's looking for any other dishes from the assembly of the dinner that he realizes that there aren't any, other than a pair of cookie sheets that must have housed the garlic bread, the last thing to come out. Javi washes those off quickly, rummages around until he finds the dishwasher fluid, and starts the dishwasher.

For a moment, Javi stands still, at a loss as to his next steps.

Then he straightens his shoulders and turns to the entryway to the dining room. He might as well spend some time with his abuela and Evelyn while they're here.

By the time Javi gets there, Evelyn is in what was Sierra's seat next to Gavin, and Abuela is across from Evelyn. There's another glass of wine in front of his abuela. Javi looks up at her sharply, one eyebrow raised in question. Her answering smile is just as sharp, and that's all it takes for Javi to conclude that she knows about Evelyn, too. It's almost enough to have Javi asking Gavin about it then and there. Except if Gavin hasn't brought it up yet, he must have a reason, and Javi is really in no position to be making demands. Whatever that reason is, Javi can respect it. After all, he has sisters, too, and there isn't much he wouldn't do for them if push came to shove. Including a rushed marriage to safely get them out of a bad situation.

Still, as he slides into the seat across from Gavin, he figures the least he can do now that he knows, is help, in whatever form that takes. After all, after tomorrow, Evelyn is going to be family, too.

"So, Javier," Evelyn says shortly after he's joined them. "What do you think about the ceremony tomorrow?"

"Evelyn," Gavin says sharply. "You don't have to ask him that."

"No, it's fine," Javi says, finding that he believes it. "I've let your brother make most of the arrangements, though. He said in our video call two weeks ago that he wanted to surprise me."

"Did he now?" There's amusement in Evelyn's tone, and Javi can't hold back a grin at the blush that spreads over Gavin's pale cheeks. "Now, that certainly does sound like my brother."

Javi blinks, but before he can press, Evelyn tosses him a wink. "Is that so?" he asks, planting his elbows on the table and his chin in his hands. "Tell me more."

The tension in the corners of Evelyn's eyes softens. "Gavin has always been big on surprises," she says. "Likes to keep everybody guessing, I think. If you ask his buddy Tyler from the station, though, you'll get a very different definition of the word surprise than you'd get from Gavin, here."

"Oh," Javi says, turning to Gavin with a helpless smile, "so you're a prankster?"

Gavin looks seconds away from blurting out apologies and promises to never do that here before he seems to catch Javi's tone. He rolls his eyes. "Ha ha," he says, turning his attention back to Evelyn, "very funny, sis. I don't need you embarrassing me in front of my fiancé."

Evelyn laughs brightly. "Oh, trust me, Gav, you'll be embarrassing yourself in front of him in no time." She grins over at Javi. "You don't need my help."

Javi leans back with a smile, watching the siblings banter. He knows his abuela will get in on this soon enough, but that doesn't mean that he's going to light the way for her. She'll just have to do that herself.

It isn't until Sierra wanders in rubbing her eyes with a tired, cranky expression that any of the adults realize how long they've been talking. Evelyn is quick to grab the girls and take them to the guest room, and Javi only needs to glance at his abuela for Gavin to offer to take her to her room.

"Thank you, Gavin, that's so kind of you," Abuela says before Javi can even think to argue. "But if I'm here to chaperone, I think I need to know where my Javi is going to sleep tonight."

Gavin glances at Javi, looking wildly out of his depth for the first time all day.

"Teasing, dear," Abuela says lightly. "Teasing. I know you two will be safe tonight," she adds with a cheeky wink in Javi's direction.

Javi just rolls his eyes as his abuela lets Gavin help her from her chair and threads her arm through his.

Once he's certain that she's in good hands, he heads to the family room to get Ále to bed. "Okay, kiddo, bedtime."

Ále is already sitting forward on the couch, his arms in his crutches and his Switch on the table.

"What," Javi asks with a worried smile, "you don't want to bargain for more screen time?"

Ále shakes his head, but doesn't say anything.

Immediately concerned, Javi moves to sit next to his son on the couch. "What is it?" he asks, "what's wrong?"

"Where's Mr. Carmichael?"

"He's taking Bisabuela to her room, why?"

Ále hesitates a moment longer. Then, "Dad?" he asks. "Do you like Mr. Carmichael?"

Javi pauses for a beat, then settles back into the couch cushions. "Why do you ask?"

"Well, I know you said that we were gonna be living with him. That you're getting married. And I think I like him okay. But I want to know if you like him."

Javi almost gives a knee-jerk approval of his Provider-to-be just so his son doesn't have to worry. But that's not the kind of relationship they have and it's not the kind of relationship he wants them to have. So he pauses and thinks before giving a slow, careful answer. "I think that Mr. Carmichael and I have a lot of the same goals. I think he's a nice man. I think we could be a good match. But I also don't know him very well, yet. So, I guess the answer is, I don't know if I like him yet, but I think I will."

"Soon?"

"I hope so," Javi says softly. He can't hold back a smile at the hope in his son's voice.

"Okay," Ále says after a moment, "I'm glad." He nudges Javi with his shoulder. "I also think Mr. Carmichael is a nice person, and I hope you like him soon, too."

Something tense in Javi's chest loosens. "Okay. You're sure you're okay with this? Me, getting married?"

Ále shrugs. "You said it would let us spend more time

together." He bumps his shoulder against Javi's again. "I want that."

Javi's heart swells in his chest. "Okay. That's good."

Ále is quiet for a moment, before he murmurs, "I love you, Dad."

Javi's heart can't take much more of this. He leans over and presses a kiss to Ále's temple. "I love you too, kiddo."

He gets Ále to his room and ready for bed in silence, and Javi only slips away to go check on any expectations Gavin has for tonight. He knows they won't be spending the night together—it would be improper, and their conversations have made it clear that Gavin's grandparents are all about appearances—but he wants to make sure there isn't anything left for the two of them to do tonight.

"Oh," Javi adds, turning back to Ále before he slips into the hall. "And if you want to call Mr. Carmichael by his first name, that's okay with me."

Ále lights up. "Really?"

"Really."

"Thanks, Dad."

"You're welcome, kiddo," Javi murmurs. He smiles and taps the doorframe twice before slipping out into the hall.

He finds Gavin in the kitchen, staring blankly at the sink.

"You did all the dishes," Gavin says when Javi leans back against the counter beside him.

"Isn't that kind of my job?"

Gavin's head snaps up to meet his eyes. "What? No."

"Look, Gavin," Javi starts. He purses his lips, then forges ahead. "I get the sense that you're trying to be chivalrous, but you don't need to. I know what I signed up for, here, okay? I know what's expected of me."

Gavin looks away again. "Oh yeah? And what's that?"

"I'm the Recipient. I take care of the home and the kid and the life you've built. And you go out into the world and make the difference that you're here to make. I get it," he adds, shaking his head when Gavin opens his mouth to argue, "but this is how it goes. Okay? You don't have to, I don't know, pretend that we aren't what we are."

"Right." Gavin closes his eyes. "Okay."

The kitchen is quiet for a moment, before Javi gently asks, "I assume I'm sleeping in Ále's room tonight?"

Gavin's hands clench and unclench on the edge of the counter. "Sure," he says hollowly. "That's what I was thinking."

Suddenly worried that he's misstepped somehow, Javi steps into his Provider-to-be's space. "Gavin…"

Gavin jerks away. "No, it's fine. I guess I misunderstood."

That takes Javi aback. "Misunderstood?"

"I'd hoped…" Gavin shakes his head and smiles bittersweetly. "Never mind. I thought we were building something together here. Guess I was wrong." The weight of Gavin's words crashes over Javi's head. Javi needs to say something, wants to say something, but Gavin turns away and steps out of the kitchen before he can find his words.

If Gavin thinks they're going to be something more than just companions, that could be a problem.

7

Gavin wakes feeling ragged and exhausted, but some of the hope from before last night is back in his chest. He can only imagine how defensive Javier must be feeling right now. Javier is the one that picked up and moved, Javier is the one that doesn't necessarily have the money to get out of this if need be, and Javier is the one without any control.

And if Gavin had needed to text his sister last night from the too-large primary bedroom to deescalate himself, well, that's his own business and no one else's.

He doesn't eat breakfast, too nervous to keep anything down at this point, but he does pour Evelyn a bowl of apology cereal for not being up for making her anything either. Evelyn just smiles and shakes her head when she makes it out of the guest room with the girls in tow. She gives him a hug, downs her own food while Gavin helps the girls with theirs, and then gets the three of them ready for the day, before hustling Gavin back to the primary bedroom to grab his tux for the wedding.

He'd gone more ostentatious than he might have under his own power, but his best friend Tyler had seen his eyes lingering over the white tuxedo jacket with red lapels while they were on shift and joked that Gavin should go for it. Then he'd looked at Gavin a little more closely and realized how much he wanted to do it. That was more than enough for Tyler to grab the phone out of Gavin's hands and order the damn thing for him, only pausing to ask his measurements while their friend and coworker Kelsea ran interference and kept Gavin away from Tyler.

It's the one and only thing Tyler has done in support of the whole wedding, and it meant more to Gavin than he could say.

With his clothes in hand, he slips out into the kitchen to check on Evelyn and the girls. "Are you three ready to go?"

"Just about." Evelyn finishes doing Elaine's hair and then the four of them are off to the venue.

By the time they're two hours out from the ceremony, Gavin is bursting at the seams with energy, and it's only Evelyn's hand in his elbow that's holding him back from becoming a full-blown groomzilla. He's bouncing on the balls of his feet, watching his family of origin interact with his firefighting team, the family he's chosen, as they all make sure everything is going the way it needs to. The way *he* needs it to.

It's odd watching his captain's Partner Diana talk to his mother as they arrange chairs for the ceremony, and even odder to see his grandparents being held back by an excitable Tyler. He may not have told his team that he needed them to run interference with his family, but that doesn't mean they hadn't noticed the awkwardness every time he discussed his grandparents. They'd figured him out, and even though he has to have his grandparents here for the ceremony, that doesn't mean he can't also have his chosen family here, too.

The venue looks amazing. There are balloons in white and silver all around the space, simple centerpieces on the reception tables that Diana's daughter Meg insisted on making, and the chairs are already out and arranged for the ceremony. The day may not be perfect, but he's starting to believe that it's going to go well.

Evelyn squeezes his elbow. The girls are running around, carefully kept in check by Kelsea's son and Diana's two kids. Which means that all of Evelyn's attention is on him. "Gavin," she says, "you know Javier is a sure thing. What's got you so worried?"

"I don't know that. You know how our conversation went last night. He's got all these preconceived notions about me and isn't giving me a chance to fix things. I know you think he's all-in, but I'm worried." Gavin huffs out a breath and reaches up to run his hand through his curls.

Evelyn swats his hand away from the gel she'd used to tame the usual chaos of his hair. "What are you worried about?"

Gavin looks away from her, taking in the scene around him. The location was chosen largely for the availability on short notice, but the view of the mountains doesn't hurt either. Plus, he'd made sure the space was accessible for Alejandro, to make sure that he can get in and around safely. He just can't be certain that it's enough.

"I'm just worried that I'm not good enough for him."

"Gavin," she scolds, "you're his Provider. Of course you're good enough for him."

"That's the thing, though." Gavin pulls away from Evelyn's grip and starts pacing again. "I'm just a necessity to him. A means to an end. And that's okay. We both knew that coming in. But Evelyn, I think this could really be the kind of companionship I've been looking for." The last words come at a whisper, and Evelyn's face softens.

"I don't think you have anything to be afraid of. The kind of relationship you're talking about, the kind that lasts? They take work. This guy was willing to pick up and drive seven hundred miles—"

"Seven hundred and fifty, give or take."

Evelyn chuckles, shakes her head, and approaches him. "This guy picked up his life and drove seven hundred and fifty miles to get to you. I think he's willing to put in the work. Are you?"

"You know I am."

Evelyn gestures someone over to them. "Then you'll be fine. Now, I think you said that you wanted to check on the table decorations for the reception, correct?"

Gavin narrows his eyes at Evelyn. He knows a diversionary tactic when he sees one, but that doesn't mean he's immune to it. Instead, he leans into the distraction and lets himself be pulled into the hubbub that Diana and his captain Charlie initially insisted on managing.

Within five minutes, he's landed himself in Charlie's orbit near the reception tables. He'd seen Meg's work from afar, but he's let himself be drawn in to enjoy it up close. The simplicity of the white taper candles above the bouquets of red and white flowers are a perfect offset to the bright red tablecloths he'd jokingly mentioned to Charlie last shift.

His captain keeps looking at him in that way that means he has something to say, his dark skin pinched around his darker eyes. Gavin isn't sure if it's wisdom or more of the gentle admonishment Gavin's been subjected to over the last few days.

"Penny for your thoughts?" Charlie leans his hip against one of the chairs across from Gavin at the reception table.

Gavin jumps from where he'd stopped short to adjust a bouquet on one of the reception tables. "What?"

Charlie's smile softens, and he rounds the table to stand at Gavin's side. "You look like you have a lot on your mind."

"I'm getting married, Charlie." Gavin huffs. "Of course I have a lot on my mind."

Charlie hums and rocks back and forth on his heels, as though preparing his words.

"What?" Gavin finally asks.

"Look, Gavin. I know you know what the team and I think of this whole wedding thing."

Gavin purses his lips. He does. He's been hearing about their concerns since he started on the *CPR Agency*. Everyone but Kelsea was less than supportive, and he can tell that she's skeptical too. It's only gotten worse since he and Javier matched and the possibility of his getting married swiftly became an inevitability.

He knows most people don't get married this quickly unless there's a baby involved. Even then, there's a lot more talk of roles and responsibilities than he and Javier have had. They'd chosen their roles, then they'd chosen each other, and that's all there is to it. It's like Evelyn said; relationships take work, and jumping into one feet first is something the Gavin of yesteryear would have done, back when he was desperate for any scrap of affection. Now, he knows he has a family that loves and supports him in his team at the station. He wouldn't even have looked for a Recipient if it wasn't for Evelyn.

Gavin casts his gaze over to find his sister. Their eyes meet, and he lifts a hand in greeting before he turns back to Charlie with a raised eyebrow.

Charlie winces at the expression, but keeps going. "That doesn't mean we aren't going to support you. It's your life, and even though we want to protect you, we can't make your choices for you. If you think this man is for you—"

"Javier. His name is Javier."

Charlie swallows and nods. "If you think Javier is the right companion for you, then I will support you. You deserve all the happiness in the world, Gavin. It's about time you took some of your own."

Gavin's throat is tight. He bows his head. "You know it's not really like that."

"Still." Charlie waits until Gavin looks up at him again. "I've seen you smile more over the last few weeks than with any of your previous partners. Whatever this relationship is, you seem like a happier man."

Gavin stares at Charlie, trying to find the words to thank

him. He'd been a young firefighter when he'd been assigned to Charlie's station, young and reckless. Charlie did more than any captain should be expected to do to keep Gavin safe. Eventually, Gavin realized that he needed to be more than just the reckless guy without a plan, and Charlie helped him become that man.

To hear that Charlie still has his back means more than Gavin can really say.

So instead he just bows his head and nods. "Thanks."

Charlie claps him on the shoulder. "I'm going to go check on the caterer." Charlie's voice is choked up but clear. The sound pulls a laugh from Gavin's throat.

"Sure thing."

"Oh," Charlie says before he's gotten too far away, "one more thing. When is Javier going to get here? Are you meeting him out front?"

"Of course not." Gavin frowns.

"What?" Charlie asks.

Gavin shifts his weight so he can lean back against the table beside him. He crosses his arms. "You know I'm not supposed to see him before the ceremony."

Charlie stares at him for a moment before bursting out in laughter. "You're really sticking to an old superstition like that?"

"Yes." Gavin blushes but holds his head high. "There's plenty of documentation that this is a sacred part of the Provider-Recipient marriage."

"But not in Partnered marriages?"

"There isn't enough conclusive evidence," Gavin says, waving Charlie off. "And anyway, this isn't a Partnered marriage."

Charlie stares at him for a moment before his features relax. "You just want everything to go right."

Gavin shrugs. Charlie isn't wrong, but that isn't the point.

"Okay. Well, I'll put Kelsea and Tyler on the front door to keep an eye out for him, shall I?

"If you don't mind," Gavin says with a nod. "I'll see you in the Provider's dressing room in thirty, yeah?"

"You've got it, kid."

Gavin looks up at Charlie just long enough to smile at him, and then turns back to the centerpieces.

He stares at the bright red tulips, interspersed with lilies of the valley, arranged across the tables. One of the first things Javier let slip about his son was his interest in the solar system, and that he's been specifically interested in Mars lately. Gavin took that and ran with it. The table decorations are all red and white—red for the planet itself, white for the ice caps—with some silver interspersed to add a bit of shine and give the illusion of spaceships through the reception area.

It doesn't hurt that the red reminds him of his team at the station.

Through all of their texting, Javier asked for exactly one thing at the ceremony. Two seats at the front: one for his sister and one for his grandmother. Aside from that, he hadn't asked for anything.

Gavin asked as many times as he thought he could from the perspective of the companion on the other side of a sight-unseen marriage, but it hadn't been enough. Javier's request was easy enough to accommodate.

That meant that Gavin had been almost on his own preparing for a rush ceremony. With Evelyn busy and distracted, his parents out of town, and his grandparents' exacting standards with no intention of getting involved, he'd thought he'd be doing it all alone. Kelsea was the first to throw her hat in the ring to help him, and brought her Recipient along to choose flowers and help him taste test cakes. Charlie got wind of that last bit and immediately insisted on being the one to vet the caterers. Diana, as one of two people that knew that Javier's son has a disability, assigned herself the responsibility of picking out a venue. Tyler took longer to bring around, but yesterday he'd agreed to go pick everything up from the various vendors—the flowers and the cake and the damn balloon arch—as a last-minute apology and show of support.

Not that Gavin needed the apology. He knows all of them just want him to be safe and happy, and they're scared that this won't do that. But he loves Evelyn so damn much, and that matters more than anything else. He needs to keep her safe and well, and if this helps with that, then he'll do it without fear.

It doesn't hurt that Javier's attractive, or that his son seems like one of the sweetest kids in the world. Gavin's always wanted companionship. Even if this is an organized Recipient and his son, Gavin had started to think that he wouldn't even get that much. That he'd be doomed to a life of bachelorhood.

Instead, it's a Saturday afternoon, he's staring down the rest of his life, and he's pretty sure he's never been happier.

Now all he needs is his Recipient to arrive.

8

Javi wakes on the morning of the wedding stiff in ways he hasn't been in ages. He's not surprised; a full day at the zoo after two days of driving will do that. The stiffness is all the more intense because the room is quiet aside from Ále's soft breaths and the buzz of Javi's thoughts. Javi turns to look at Ále, just barely visible in the light from between the heavy curtains. One look at his son is enough to remind him of why he's jumping feet first into this marriage.

Part of him thinks he should be more concerned than he is. He's always been the methodical one out of the three Pérez siblings, always done things only after long and careful consideration. He's so careful that he's never broken a bone; he's so careful he's only ever worked jobs that guaranteed a certain level of security in the contract. And while one of the few times he'd acted without all that care and precision had led to the best part of his life, it had also led to the part that takes the most time, energy, effort, and care.

Alejandro.

Javi's phone alarm goes off next to him. He turns it off, which leaves the image of his son on his lock screen smiling up at him.

He hesitates. He signed the marriage contract back in Vegas six days ago, but he hasn't said his vows yet. There's still theoretically time to bail.

He'd be lying if he said he wasn't scared. He is. He just trusts Bianca to have done the research into the matchmaking agency, and that their lawyers would have looked over the contract before sending it to him. He needs to trust that he has more than enough legal leeway to leave if cause arises.

So Javi takes a deep breath, puts on a smile, and wakes Ále.

"Morning, buddy."

Ále mumbles a little and looks around, disoriented. As he comes awake, though, understanding dawns on his face, and he looks back at Javi. "Wedding day?"

"That it is."

Ále yawns. Then he offers Javi a wide smile. "Stretches first?"

"Stretches first."

Javi grabs their yoga mats and sets them out on the floor of Ále's room. Ále gets himself out of bed under Javi's watchful eye; morning mobility was one of the things that Ále personally chose to master first in his physical therapy. His CP made it more challenging, but Ále persisted in ways that have always reminded Javi of Casey. Now he's able to get to the yoga mat with a minimum of struggle, although Javi can tell by his expression that he's in more pain than usual.

That's not a huge surprise. Ále pushed himself a little at the zoo the day before, and with the girls, and before that it was two days on the road. While Javi could have made the drive to Denver in one long day, they'd stayed in Glenwood Springs night before last to give Ále some much-needed rest and time to stretch. Today, it's time for yet another drive, and though Javi wishes his Provider-to-be had chosen a wedding venue closer to Denver proper, he hasn't been in a position to disagree throughout this process. After all, he's the Recipient in this marriage; that means that any monetary decisions would always be the purview of his Provider.

That also means that he isn't too upset that only two people from his family are coming. His parents are still too angry at him, and with the short notice, his sister Teresa wasn't able to get away for the ceremony. Bianca, though, begged, bartered, and pleaded with her Partner to come with her for the ceremony. Her Partner Dominic gently insisted on holding down the fort at home with their fur babies, but he was more than happy to have Bianca go to Denver for the ceremony on her own. He'd encouraged it, in fact. With her work, though, she wasn't able to get out to Denver for more than the weekend, so Javi was on his own for packing and transit.

Not that he'd minded. There wasn't much to pack, and most of it was Ále's. Javi didn't have much he wanted to bring with him, just a suitcase of clothes and a photo album of Ále's younger years to hold onto, from back when Casey was more of a presence in their lives. Oh, and the suits for him and Ále that he'd burned through his last paycheck to buy for the wedding.

"So, big guy," Javi says, gently distracting his boy while they stretch. "What are you thinking about today now that you've had a chance to sleep on it after we met Gavin?"

Ále makes a noise that might be easy agreement or might be distaste, so Javi waits until he's done with that count of ten before he asks again. "I'm excited, I guess," he says, tilting his head to the side. "Like I told you last night, I like Gavin plenty. And I think this could be a cool place to live. I'm excited about today, you know? Only, I don't want to be the ring bearer."

Javi pulls up short at that. "Did Gavin ask you about that?" And then, more importantly, "Why not?"

Ále shrugs, but Javi can tell Ále is bothered by the need to state that preference.

For his part, Javi hadn't thought about that, hadn't thought that would be something Ále would want to do. But from the furrow in the brow of his son's usually smiling face, Javi knows he needs to double check. "Alejandro. ¿Por qué no?"

Ále waits long enough that Javier is considering using his full name again, but Ále looks up before he can. "Because I don't want everyone to watch me mess it up."

Javi gets up on his knees to look Ále in the face immediately. "Hey. Buddy. If this is something you want to do, we can do it together. We can practice walking down the aisle together this morning, and at the venue, too. And then, if you want to, at the ceremony, you can walk down the aisle with me. That way, if something goes wrong, we can handle it together."

Ále worries his bottom lip between his teeth, then looks up at Javi. "You really think it would be okay?"

"I know it would. If that's what you want, I'll text Gavin to tell him right now."

Ále turns away for a moment before he looks Javi in the eye. There's just a hint of hope in his eyes, a hint of desperation that Javi can't quite place. "And you don't think he'll be mad?" Ále whispers.

"Not at all." Javi takes Ále's hands in his. Ále doesn't look away from his face, and that's how Javi knows this is the right call. "He wants us to be a family. If that means you being the ring bearer at the ceremony, he'll do it in a heartbeat."

Ále's face splits in a grin. "I want to do it."

"Okay. I'll let Gavin know right now. But you still need to finish your stretches, mister."

Ále just grins at him. "Aye aye."

Javi grabs his phone and shoots off a quick text to his Provider-to-be and gets an affirmative almost instantly. They text back and forth a few more times, just to ensure that the rings get to Ále without the two of them running into each other—something about old traditions? Javi doesn't worry too much about it—and then he locks his phone and finishes his own morning exercises.

Ále sits up from the last of his stretches, and Javi does an extra ten sit-ups, groaning through them the whole time purely for dramatic effect. Ále giggles at his father's antics, then tackles him as he finishes the last sit-up. Javi cries out dramatically.

"Argh, you got me!" Javi says, much to Ále's delight.

They roll around on the floor for a few minutes before Javi's next phone alarm goes off, this one signaling that it's time for them to really get up if they're going to have time to head down to the car and drive to the venue. Javi does his best not to tense, but from the way Ále goes quiet, he's pretty sure he doesn't manage it.

"Okay, bud, time to get ready." Javi kisses Ále's cheek and disentangles them from one another. "Shower and clothes and teeth and then we're going to head out."

Ále contemplates him for a moment before nodding. He gets carefully to his feet and heads over to the ensuite bathroom where Javi left his clothes the night before.

Javi doesn't let himself linger. He makes a quick detour to his abuela's room to rouse her, then makes his way over to the hall bathroom and starts the shower running so he can get ready for the day ahead of them.

The drive out to Castle Rock for the ceremony is easy enough, but as they get closer, Javi realizes that Ále is getting progressively quieter through the whole drive. He and Abuela are carrying the conversation more and more. With about five minutes until they make it to the venue, he glances into the rearview mirror. "Ále?"

"Yeah, Daddy?" Ále's eyes are wide and Javi is instantly on high alert. It's the 'Daddy' that does it.

"What's going on, mijo?"

Ále looks down to his lap where his fingers are no doubt

tangled together. Javi wants to pull them apart and take Ále's hands in his, but he knows better than that.

He waits until Ále looks out the other window without saying anything before he finally asks, "Are you okay?"

One of Ále's shoulders twitches up in what might be a shrug or might be a spasm. They'd spent more time than usual on his stretches in anticipation of the long day of sitting, so he might have overworked his muscles. Or he could just be tense and scared out of his mind by the unknown.

Javi runs a hand over his face and turns his attention wholly to the road again, wishing he'd asked Abuela to drive instead so he could be in the back with his son. But right now, the GPS is shouting directions at him, and he needs to follow them if he doesn't want to get lost. If that also gives his son a chance to recover, that's just a bonus. It's the same drill as when Ále starts the new school year. It's a big event, a big change, and Javi knows by now that validating those nerves is the only way to move forward.

Except Ále still hasn't said anything to him by the time they pull up in front of the venue.

Javi takes a moment to gather his thoughts before he speaks. "You know, this is a big change. It would make sense if you're not completely certain about it. Or if you're worried about something. And if you want to go back to Vegas, we can."

"I don't."

"Ále..." Javi closes his eyes at the sharpness in Ále's voice.

"You said I'd get to see you more. You said it would be better. *You* said this would be good, so why would we go back?"

Javi swallows. It's a valid question. Maybe he's just as scared as Ále about this change in their lives. He opens his eyes and looks back at his son. "I don't know."

"You've been happier since you started talking to Gavin." Ále's voice is soft but firm. "Even if you're scared, you did it. So, it was the right thing to do. Right?"

How can Javi tell his son that it was the right idea almost exclusively because it means Javi can take care of him better? He can't. Instead he glances once at his abuela before he turns around, reaches back, and ruffles Alejandro's hair. "Well, I'm glad you think that, because I think so too."

Ále untangles his fingers, reaches for the buckle of his seatbelt, and carefully presses down on the button. Javi waits. When Ále is done, he smiles up at his dad. "Come on. Let's go. We have a walk to practice."

9

Javi takes stock of the venue. The sprawling ranch house looks to only be one level with easily a dozen cars in the lot around him. He'd known to expect Gavin's grandparents, as they're the ones footing the bill for the bulk of this; and his parents, as they're the ones that bought the house for them; but other than that, Javi can only imagine that it's Gavin's coworkers filling out the rest of the parking spots.

After a single deep breath, Javi opens his door and steps out. He moves slowly to open the back door and grab Åle's crutches and their suits. He scans the venue, checking for stairs and uneven areas while Åle gets out of the car. The place looks fine, and he's just about to start heading for the door when two people emerge from the house: a tall Southeast Asian woman with a shaved head and a white man that only just comes up to her shoulder. Neither of them resemble Gavin, making it unlikely that they're family. They're dressed nicely and they must be friends with the way they're eyeing him with something not quite like suspicion. Caution, maybe.

Javi straightens to meet them. He holds his and Åle's suits in front of himself like a shield, feeling suddenly underdressed in his t-shirt and jeans, and meets their eyes with his chin held high.

The woman moves forward, holding a hand out to Javi. "I'm Kelsea," she says, shaking his hand with only a fraction of the frigidity he'd expected. "Is this your son?"

"Yes." Javi places a protective hand on Ále's shoulder. "This is Alejandro."

Kelsea nods her head in the direction of Ále, a wordless request for permission. Javi nods back.

Kelsea crouches down in front of Alejandro with a smile on her face. "Hi," she says.

Ále glances at Javi, then back at Kelsea.

"I'm Kelsea," she says. She starts to hold her hand out, only to glance at Javi again.

Javi raises a challenging eyebrow.

Her jaw sets and she extends her hand the rest of the way. Ále shifts his weight so he can shake her hand. Smiling as though she's just passed a test which, to Javi's cautious relief, she has, she shakes his hand before pulling away. "My son Dakota is getting dressed in the house, would you like to come meet him?"

Ále looks up at Javi. Javi's chest twists, not from the fact that Alejandro is turning to him for decision making, but from the cautiously hopeful look on his face. He forces himself to smile back. He looks up at Kelsea. "If he'd like to come meet us, I'd be okay with that."

"Oh," Kelsea looks surprised, though Javi wonders if it's faked. She's probably testing him too. "Well, I figured, since it's just your people and Gavin's people here, you wouldn't mind."

Javi files that away; it's good to have confirmation that these people are in Gavin's corner. Javi puts his hand back on Ále's shoulder, fighting to keep his grip relaxed. "I'm afraid that I do mind." Then he catches on to the other part of that sentence. "My people?"

Kelsea nods. "Your sister, I think?"

As she says it, Bianca comes out of the house, her high heels doing nothing to slow her step.

"B?" Javi asks, shock and relief mixing on his tongue. "What are you doing here? Why are you here already?"

"I'm here for your wedding," she says. "Duh." There's an edge to her smile that makes Javi nervous. She closes the distance, kisses his cheek, and embraces him. "I was starting to wonder if you'd gotten lost."

"Gavin said one-thirty." Javi returns the embrace instinctively. "Did I misunderstand?"

"No, no, I just worry about you, hermano, you know that."

Javi relaxes. "No es nada, Bianca."

"It's something," she mutters. Then she pulls away and pulls Abuela into a hug. "¡Abuela! ¿Cómo estás?"

"Bien, bien, mija. But I think I'll go in and have a seat now, hmm? No, don't worry about showing me in," she says when both Bianca and Javi move to do so. "I can find my seat on my own."

Then she's off, heading into the building, and Javi is still standing out here with two people he's never met and only Bianca for backup.

Before he can say anything, Kelsea cuts in again. "Javier, what would you think about Bianca here coming with me and your son so he can meet Dakota? That way he's with someone you know. It'll give him a chance to get the rings for the ceremony," she adds when Javi hesitates.

Javi holds his ground as best he can, but he knows he's going to give in when he sees the hope in Ále's eyes again. Still. Still, Javi isn't there yet. "Why don't I have B go with you to pick up the rings, and then bring them to us?"

Kelsea looks thoughtful, then purses her lips with a nod. "I'll show you where they are." she says to Bianca.

The two of them walk away, chattering in that way that implies that they're sizing each other up.

Javi watches them go until the man clears his throat, and

when Javi meets his eyes, he's scrutinizing Javi with more intention than Javi expected. He gestures for Javi to follow him into the building.

With Ále next to him, Javi follows, one hand hovering at Ále's elbow in case he loses his balance as Javi checks for any potential mobility hazards. It's not that Ále can't look out for himself but Javi's a father first and he isn't going to let his son be embarrassed today. He casts his gaze around the front entrance and the short hall they're led through. There are streamers and curtains in red and white and silver, and, as he's ushered past the room where he presumes the ceremony will be held, he sees that the space behind the altar is draped in white cloth with red trim. To his surprise, the place looks to be completely accessible. It's definitely a single level, with mostly level floors and wide doorways. His heart climbs into his throat, suspicion crawling up after it. Did Gavin choose this place because of its accessibility? Or was that a happy accident?

"You're in here."

The words startle Javi. He turns to see their guide gesturing at a doorway. With the knowledge that Bianca is here settling him, Javi is able to actually take the man in. He's dressed in a fine charcoal suit with a boutonnière featuring a red carnation affixed to it. He carries himself with authority, perhaps acting as Gavin's best man. For a moment, Javi considers confronting the casual dislike the man is displaying, but before he can, the man relents.

"I'm Tyler," he says. He doesn't hold out a hand to Javi the way Kelsea had, and he keeps going before Javier can try to offer his. "I'm Gavin's best man. He asked me to show you in."

Javi squints at an open door to what looks like the larger suite, usually reserved for Recipients. Even so, it's far more space than he and Ále need, and Gavin should know that. "Shouldn't Gavin be in here? He's the one with a crew of people."

"Yeah, I noticed you only brought a couple people." The man

nods into the room, not answering Javi's question but clearly implying that he needs to go inside.

Javi complies, contemplating how to respond to the jab. He doesn't mention the huge, blowout fight he had with his parents the night before he'd left, or how he'd taken Ále and left first thing the morning they'd left rather than listen to them snark at him about his parenting choices over breakfast again. He didn't want them at the wedding in the first place, so after they'd fought him, he didn't tell them anything about it, other than that it was happening.

He does have people on his side, though, he knows that. "Abuela came into town to chaperone, so she was here already, and Bianca is the reason I'm getting married in the first place. She wouldn't miss it."

Tyler hums but doesn't say anything more to him. "I'll let you get dressed, then."

Taking it as a dismissal, Javi turns to Ále. "Why don't you go to the bathroom before we get you dressed, mijo."

Ále slips into the enclosed bathroom, leaving Javi alone with a still-present Tyler.

Tyler starts to leave when Javi looks back at him, then seems to change his mind. He turns around and comes back over to Javi. "Look," he says in a low tone. "Gavin told us not to do this, and normally I'd respect his wishes. But here's the thing. Gavin's important to me, and I can't let you come in here and hurt him. He's one of the best, kindest people in the world, and he deserves a companion that loves him. One that will take care of him. One that will do right by him.

"I don't know you. I think he's rushing into this headlong without looking where he's going, but that's how he's always been. So I'm telling you now, if you're only in this for the money, or for your kid... If you *hurt him...*" He shakes his head. "You're not going to like what happens."

Javi stares at Tyler for a long moment. It's not the same as his refusal to let Ále go off with Kelsea alone earlier, but it's not dissimilar either. Tyler obviously cares about Gavin, and that's another vote in Gavin's favor. Javi doesn't owe this man anything, but he owes Gavin a lot. He can give this man the truth. "I am here for the money, and for my kid, and I'm not going to lie about that. But I know that he's putting a lot on the line for me, too." Providing the kind of safety net Gavin offered him is more than Javi could ever have expected. He knows how lucky he is to have found Gavin, and he's not going to mess this up. Not if he can help it. Not when he knows how much family means to Gavin.

"Gavin seems like the kind of guy that puts himself on the line like that a lot." Javi meets Tyler's eyes, thinking of the situation he thinks Evelyn is in.

Tyler's face twists in bitter understanding. "He is."

Javi nods again. "I'm not going to betray that trust intentionally. I will do whatever I can to deserve him, I guarantee you that."

Tyler contemplates him with a curious expression for a long moment. Then Ále slips back into the room and Tyler sighs and shakes his head. He mutters something under his breath before leaving Javi to get changed.

Javi takes that as a signal to start getting dressed. He starts with Ále's suit, pulling it out of the protective bag. It's a navy blue and cut to Ále's size while still allowing him plenty of freedom of movement. Javi doesn't know how much extra help Ále is going to need getting dressed today, but he is going to offer whatever his son needs.

Once Ále is out of his t-shirt and jeans, Javi sits down on one of the many chairs around the room and starts handing Ále pieces of his suit. Javi helps Ále into his pants first, then his belt, which Ále slips through the first loop before turning around so that Javi can put it through the rest. Javi feeds the end through the buckle and Ále tightens it.

This version of getting dressed—the one that involves fancy clothes that Ále isn't used to—is not a practiced routine, but is similar enough to their usual routine that they don't need to talk. Ále gets his shirt on, tucks it in, and starts on the top buttons; Javi does the bottom buttons and they meet in the middle. Ále puts his jacket on, and then it's time for socks and shoes. The socks are the hardest part, and Ále doesn't try to argue about putting them on himself today. Same with his shoes. Nerves twist in Javi's gut, and though he wants to check in with Ále again, he also doesn't want to pressure him to say something he isn't ready to. Whether Ále doesn't want to talk or is just picking up on Javi's nerves, Javi isn't sure.

"All good?" Javi asks.

Ále nods.

"Okay. Do you want to go walk the aisle with me?"

"Right now?" Ále asks. "But you're not dressed."

"Well, there are these superstitions, things people believe about weddings, where they think that if the Provider and the Recipient see each other the day of the wedding before they meet at the altar, then it's bad luck."

Ále gasps. "Bad luck?"

"Yes," Javi allows, "but I think Gavin is too busy to notice me if we go into the place where the ceremony will be right now. What do you say? Super secret spy mission?"

Ále giggles and nods, before taking his crutches and letting himself be led back out to the main area. They walk the aisle twice, and neither of them says anything about how Ále might be expected to carry the rings, because neither of them wants to break the careful ease between them. Everything about being here in Denver, here at Javi's wedding, feels tenuous enough right now, and there's nothing either of them can do until Bianca gets back with the rings.

Then they head back to the Recipient suite to find Bianca

there with two ring boxes and a seam ripper for Ále's pockets to put the ring boxes in.

Javi relaxes. Gavin had thought about this beforehand. Something even he had missed in considering Ále's request to be ring bearer. His chest tightens, hope twining around his ribs, but he puts it aside. There will be time enough for gratitude later.

He lets Bianca help Ále put the rings in his pockets, not listening as she murmurs instructions to him. Instead, he pulls his own suit out of its protective bag. It's black, because although Gavin didn't lay out any expectations, Javi had figured him for a traditional man. Gavin later implied that he's less traditional than Javi feared, but it was too late to do anything about the suit order. Besides, more than Gavin's inclinations, *Javi* is a traditional man at heart, and getting married in black was always the plan. If he's getting a chance at marriage, even if it's to someone he barely knows, he wants to do it right. Even if only in his attire.

The suit fits like a glove. He smooths his hands over the fabric of his sleeves, shivering a little at the way it presses his dress shirt against his skin. It makes him feel new. Powerful. *Free.* He stands up a little taller and tries not to feel lonely with the knowledge that there is no one living in Denver proper that knows him. No one to truly turn to. But Javi's spent this much time believing in Gavin and he sees no reason to stop now.

It's up to Javi to make sure it stays that way.

10

Gavin has spent the bulk of the last hour greeting people and directing them to their seats. Once the influx slows to a trickle, he heads back to the Provider suite. He freshens up, then waits for his mother and Tyler to let him know that everything is ready. Stepping out into the venue again, ready to pledge himself to Javier, feels more settling than he'd expected.

Tyler leads the way out, stopping by the Recipient suite to pick up Javier's sister, Bianca. Gavin turns away in time to miss any chance at seeing Javier, and his mother only looks at him in exasperation.

"Give us a couple minutes, Javi," Bianca says as she closes the door behind her. "You'll hear the music."

Gavin can't make out Javier's reply.

The four of them make their way to where the guests are all gathered in front of the altar. The chairs on the aisle are bedecked in red and white flowers and the arch at the front is similarly adorned. The whole thing feels a little too ostentatious for Gavin, but if it means that he gets to help Evelyn and have Javier and Alejandro too, he won't complain.

It isn't until they make it to the beginning of the aisle that his eyes catch on his third niece, Genesis. That means her father Shane made it here with her.

Fuck. In the joy and revel of meeting Javier and Alejandro and finalizing his marriage, he'd almost forgotten the reason behind it.

For as glad as he is to see Genesis in her flower girl dress, he can't help but scan the crowd for Shane. Predictably, he's seated next to Evelyn near the front, one arm spread proprietarily over the back of her chair.

Bastard.

Gavin keeps his body as relaxed as he can and lets his eyes scan over the rest of the crowd in the hope that his mother won't notice the slip. She doesn't seem to, and then the music is starting and holy shit, this is all going to be real.

He's about to get married.

He clings to his mother, and she shifts a little, looking up at him.

"Oh, Gavin," she sighs. Her tone isn't upset, but there is a hint of the familiar disappointment.

"I'm alright." Gavin looks down at her, forcing a smile. "Let's go."

Tyler crouches down and pats Genesis on the shoulder, and he and Bianca follow her down the aisle. The procession is shorter than his grandparents might have wanted, just the four of them, but there really was no one else to ask. Well, no one other than Alejandro, that is, and that was not an option.

Then his mother taps his arm and he lets her lead him down the aisle with her arm in his. Genesis is already sitting with her parents when he makes it to the altar, and Tyler is showing Bianca to her seat. Gavin kisses his mother's cheek and does the same, before stepping up to the altar with Tyler at his side.

Then the music changes.

Gavin fought his grandparents on very few things when it came to the ceremony. He pushed Javier on even fewer. It worked out for the most part, until four days ago when his grandparents asked him who would be walking Javier down the aisle. He hadn't known the answer. By that point he'd known that only two members of Javier's family would be joining him and his son at the ceremony, and he'd been uncertain how to ask. Tradition would dictate that Javier's Provider parent walk him to the altar, but that wasn't happening.

So he'd asked Javier if he wanted someone to walk him down the aisle. He'd felt guilty texting the question instead of asking him face-to-face, but Javier was busy packing at that point, getting ready to get on the road to Denver, and Gavin wasn't going to ask anything more than he was already being forced to.

To his surprise, Javier answered immediately. *Ále will.*

Your son?

He's the most important person in my life. He's the one that I want to agree to see me married. Isn't that the whole point?

Gavin wasn't able to argue with that.

Now, as he stands at the altar watching his fiancé and his son walk down the aisle toward him, his heart clenches. Not because it's bad, but because it's so damn perfect that he can't imagine anything else.

Alejandro has his forearm crutches on, a bright red that somehow perfectly complements the navy of his suit. His suit jacket moves heavily with the weight of the ring boxes in his pockets. Javier doesn't take his eyes off of his son, though not in the sense that he wants to intervene so much as that he wants to make sure that he doesn't have to.

Gavin has a weak spot for kids, and the way Javier moves slowly and carefully beside Alejandro, letting the boy lead, endears him to the pair of them even more than before. They're a duo that Gavin doesn't want to hurt, and though he doesn't know how he'll ever be worthy of them, he'll spend the rest of his life trying.

And then there's the perfect cut of Javier's suit, the way it molds to his body, showing him off without being too much. The black sets off the bronze of his skin, and, for a moment, Gavin can't take his eyes from Javier's face. There's an expression there that Gavin almost recognizes but can't name, not at first. It's not a look he's seen on Javier's face yet, but it's one that he always wants there.

Because Javier looks content. Settled. At peace.

It's more than Gavin thought he'd get, and he'll hold onto it no matter what.

Then Javier is standing before him. He has Alejandro at his side, and Alejandro has one hand hooked into Javier's jacket. Alejandro smiles up at Gavin toothily, and it slows the rapid beating of Gavin's heart. Gavin makes himself look away from Alejandro and up to Javier, and is grateful that he did. He gets another moment's look at Javier's love for his son before Javier meets Gavin's eyes and nods.

They're ready.

The ceremony itself is brief, with a few words from the officiant and some basic vows from himself and Javier. They'd worked together to create closely matching vows beforehand just to prevent any potential surprises.

At least, that's Gavin's intention.

As planned, Javier goes first. "I, Javier Pérez, take you, Gavin Carmichael, to be my Provider. I pledge to stand beside you as your Recipient, in the foreknowledge of joy and pain, strength and weariness, direction and doubt. To respect you in everything as the leader of our family and the provider of all that is. I pledge to be true to you in good times and bad, to forever be yours, that we may grow together for all our days."

Gavin swallows at the words. Even having known Javier's vows were coming, hearing them is nothing like he expected.

Javier's eyes widen, and Gavin wants to take back his reaction. He didn't outright say that he wants a romantic bond, but he's pretty sure Javier knows Gavin is settling for this. But this was their deal. That's how this goes. Gavin doesn't get to change the rules no matter how much he might wish he could.

He opens his mouth and speaks.

"I, Gavin Carmichael, take you, Javier Pérez, to be my Recipient. I pledge to stand beside you as your Provider, in the foreknowledge of joy and pain, strength and weariness, direction and doubt. To respect you in everything as the authority of our home and the protector of all that is."

Gavin glances down at Alejandro where he stands at Javier's side, one hand still tangled in Javier's jacket. He looks back at Javier. With the image of Javier's son behind his eyes, he can do this. With the courage born of years as a firefighter and a beautiful day with Javier and his son, Gavin goes off script.

"I pledge to serve you and Alejandro to the best of my abilities. To provide for you both in all your needs. In everything that you are."

Javier gapes at him. Gavin hadn't planned this, which means Javier didn't know it was coming. But surely Javier knows how much Gavin will do for the two of them? Surely.

Seeing Javier's distress, Gavin quickly returns to the agreed-upon vows. "I pledge to be true to you in good times and bad, to forever be yours, that we may grow together for all our days."

Gavin looks down at Alejandro with a smile and a nod. Alejandro steps forward, slipping the ring boxes from his pockets. With a careful glance at the two boxes, he holds his right hand out to Gavin. Gavin takes the box, popping open the top. He pulls the ring out and closes the box again, eyes on Javier the whole time. Then Alejandro holds his other hand out to Javier. Javier mirrors Gavin's movements, taking the box, opening it to take out the ring, and closing it again. They both hand the boxes back to Alejandro, who slips them back into his pockets.

For a moment, neither of them move. Then Gavin reaches out and takes Javier's left hand in his. Javier takes a step closer to him. It's small enough to still be appropriate, but enough to make

Gavin's heart beat faster in his chest. Slowly, and only breaking eye contact for a split second, Gavin slides the ring onto Javier's finger. White gold, with three recessed gems and space for more. A symbol of their family as it is and as Gavin hopes it might be.

Javier stares at it for long enough that Gavin starts to wonder if he'd been too presumptuous. He lets go of Javier's hand.

Javier looks up at him, eyes wide and wondering. A slow smile crosses his lips, and he turns his hand over to hold it out for Gavin's. Gavin meets him partway, holding his left hand out, an invitation and a promise. Javier hardly breaks eye contact either as he slides Gavin's ring over his finger. It's the same style, but in a non-silver metal to mark him as the Provider of the two of them. The gold is cool against his skin, and it takes all his willpower not to cling to Javier immediately.

Distantly, Gavin is aware of the officiant saying something. He feels the pause before the kiss more than he hears it, and it's enough for him to step in close and kiss a chaste yet sure kiss to Javier's lips.

For a moment, Javier stays still. Then he pushes up a little into the kiss, one hand coming up to cup Gavin's jaw. Gavin sinks into the touch, almost losing himself in it.

That lasts right up until Alejandro gives a happy shout, startling Gavin into pulling away. Then Gavin laughs brightly, crouching down to sweep Alejandro up into his arms. For the first time since he joined the fire station, Gavin feels like he has another place he belongs.

11

There's a split second, standing at the altar beside Javier and Alejandro when Gavin forgets himself. Forgets that this is the middle of their wedding ceremony, that his friends and family are watching. Nothing matters more, in that second, than reveling in Alejandro's joy with him.

A split second later, Gavin remembers that they still have a lot of building to do to make this the family he wants them to be.

With Alejandro in his arms, Gavin looks to Javier for confirmation. It was instinct to reach for him, to lift him in the air, but he doesn't know how Alejandro or Javier will feel about it.

But Javier just smiles at both of them and nods at Gavin, washing the fear away. Gavin smiles in relief and looks at Alejandro instead, who looks just as pleased. "You ready to go eat some really good food?"

Alejandro grins back. "Yeah."

Gavin sets Alejandro down intentionally but without making it too obvious. He links his fingers through Javier's, and tugs gently, inviting him to stand closer.

Javier allows it, and Gavin's heart flutters. He's been so

focused on the ceremony and making sure that everything is in order for Javier and Alejandro that he didn't stop to think much about this part. The after.

He swallows down the guilt and worry and waits until Javier's other hand rests on Alejandro's shoulder. "Shall we?" When Alejandro nods at him, he adds, "We're headed down the hall and to the right. You want to lead the way?

Alejandro grins at him, and Gavin glances at Javier, ready to catch his eye and smile.

Javier isn't looking at him, though. He's watching his son lead them down the aisle. The expression in his eyes is soft, warm, devoted in a way that takes Gavin's breath away. He swallows thickly and forces himself to look away so that he doesn't trip over his own feet.

As they walk down the aisle, Gavin lets himself see it all through Javier's eyes. He has a brief moment to worry that he's gone too far, been too extravagant. He'd tried to keep things reasonable, but his grandparents insisted on a larger venue and a larger head count than he would have. He'd be happy to just have the closest members of his team and their partners, his family, and whoever Javier wanted. But his grandparents gave him the look that allowed for no argument, and he'd caved. The bigger venue led to inviting more guests and ordering fancier decorations and requesting a larger spread for the reception, and before he knew it he'd been talked into the kind of wedding that Evelyn wanted the first time around but their grandparents had only partially financed. They'd wanted her to be Provider in her marriage and help carry on the Carmichael legacy, but Shane hadn't wanted to be the Recipient. When Evelyn tried to suggest a Partnered marriage as a compromise, both sides had refused. In the end, Evelyn had sided with Shane instead of their grandparents. She had gone through a small chunk of the inheritance she did receive for getting married on her wedding so it would come close to what she wanted, but he knows she'd never felt that it was everything she'd dreamed of.

He just hopes he hasn't upset her.

Alejandro leads them through the rest of the guests and toward the reception hall. Javier's eyes never leave Alejandro, and Gavin's never leave Javier. He sees it the moment Javier clocks the level of decoration in the reception hall. Javier's eyes go wide and his lips part as he takes in the gentle lighting that softens the red table runners and reflects off the silver ones. It's the first time that Gavin fully understands how little Javier had cared about the presentation of the wedding. He'd no doubt expected something simple given how fast it came together, and probably isn't sure how to handle this.

Before Gavin can apologize, though, Javier turns to him with a wondrous expression. Gavin can't tell if it's gratitude or relief or something else, but whatever it is fills Gavin's stomach with bubbles. He wants to lean in and kiss Javier again. He glances down at Javier's lips, and when they twist a little in uncertainty, Gavin holds back. He won't do anything that Javier doesn't want, but that doesn't mean that he can't want. He squeezes their linked fingers instead and leads the way to the table at the front.

Javier stops short when they round the table. "Three chairs?" he whispers to Gavin.

"One for Alejandro. Is that okay?"

"It's good," Javier says softly. He tugs on their joined hands until Gavin wheels around to look at him. "It's perfect."

Gavin relaxes. Javier is in this with him, and that's what matters.

Alejandro, who Gavin expected to want to sit next to Javier, insists on sitting between them. Javier's eyes widen before cutting over to Gavin and then back to Alejandro. Gavin can see the way Javier wants to say something, but holds himself back, as though afraid of offending Gavin.

"That's fine with me," Gavin squeezes Javier's hand again and holds out his free hand for Alejandro to fist bump. "He's the one that brought us together, after all. He gets to choose where he wants to sit."

Javier stares at Gavin for a moment, his eyes still wide and his mouth still half-parted on words he hasn't spoken. Then he closes his mouth and nods. He pauses just long enough for Gavin to get the hint that he's supposed to sit down first. He moves around the table, letting Alejandro slip directly into his seat and Javier follow him. Javier gives him that scrutinizing look again, but doesn't say or do anything more than that.

As they sit, someone taps their glass, calling on them to kiss. Gavin frowns. It's probably Tyler, shit-stirrer that he is. Before he can say anything, though, Javier reaches around the back of Alejandro's chair to settle a hand on his bicep.

"I don't mind."

Gavin searches Javier's expression for any hint of deceit or uncertainty. When Javier's eyes flicker out to the crowd, who have now taken up the tapping as well, Gavin shakes his head. "I think you do. You don't have to do things just because you think it's expected of you, Javier. No one will think any less of you."

Javier opens his mouth to argue, but Gavin catches Javier's hand in his own, tangling their fingers together again.

"You don't have to do anything you don't want to do."

"Do you want to kiss me?"

The question startles Gavin. He knows there's only one right answer to this, and he has to hope that he has the right one. "I only want to do what will make you happy."

Javier's eyes widen a fraction before he schools his expression again. "Then, if you want to, I think you should kiss me."

Gavin still can't quite make heads or tails of what Javier wants, but the steady expression on his face is enough to convince him that he isn't lying. Instead of a proper kiss, though, he takes Javier's hand from his bicep and kisses his knuckles. Even if Javier looks willing, Gavin can feel the tension in his hand. Gavin won't take more than Javier is offering.

He rubs his thumb over the ring on Javier's finger, and Javier startles. Gavin smiles and kisses his fingertips before he pulls away, registering the whoops and hollers from his assembled friends and family. His eyes, however, flit to the table where Charlie, Diana, Evelyn, Shane, his three nieces, Citlali, and a woman he doesn't know yet are seated.

Javier's sister.

At the moment, it's only Javier's sister that is looking at them. Her eyes are on Javier, but as soon as Gavin looks at her, she shifts her gaze to him. She purses her lips and lifts her chin, and Gavin knows she's probably about as happy with this arrangement as his friends are. He inclines his head toward Javier, in deference, and she nods once in understanding.

He knows she's going to come up and talk to him soon enough, but he's pretty sure she'll wait until he's alone to do it. That's okay. He knows Javier is going to be subjected to plenty of grilling from both of Gavin's families, blood and chosen. The least he can do is subject himself to Bianca interrogating him in turn.

A quick glance at Javier reveals the same thing Gavin saw on his way up the aisle. Javier's eyes keep darting around the room, as though taking everything in, from the centerpieces to the favors for the guests to the seating chart. He's nervous, but holding steadfast in his decision. Seeing him in person is different than seeing him through a phone screen. And yet, for all his beauty, where he was almost vibrant when they'd spoken before, he now seems subdued, almost resigned. Gavin isn't sure how to assure him that he has a say in this relationship, but he needs to, sooner rather than later.

As the food is brought out, Gavin takes his cues from Javier regarding Alejandro. More than once, he's tempted to intervene when it looks like Alejandro is struggling with his adapted utensils, but Gavin holds back, waiting to see what Javier does. Each and every time, Javier waits until Alejandro asks for help to reach out and cut his food for him, or shift his water glass closer.

It takes a few such instances for Gavin to look at Javier instead of Alejandro, to really understand what's going through his head. When he does, it's clear that Javier wants to intervene just as much as Gavin does, but learned to hold himself back for Alejandro's sake.

Gavin did his research. Even before he'd closed on the house his realtor found for them, he'd found a physical therapist that specializes in childhood CP. When he'd gone in to meet her in person, she'd covered what Alejandro would need, and he'd set up Alejandro's bedroom with a set of free weights and a full range of resistance bands. He considered getting an electric stimulation machine, but he didn't know what Javier already had for Alejandro. The other thing he hadn't gotten despite wanting to was an exercise ball. He could guess how tall Alejandro was, but he didn't want to get the wrong size. He's done what he can to set Alejandro's room up for him to be successful, but he still isn't sure he's done enough.

He tries more than once to strike up a conversation with Javier, and though Javier smiles and tries to respond, there's an awkwardness between them that wasn't there before. Gavin wants to poke at it, to prod and understand why, but he gets his answer before he can ask.

"So, what's the plan for tonight?" Javier asks.

Fork halfway to his mouth, Gavin pauses. "What?"

Javier flushes, but tilts his chin up the same way his sister had. "What's the plan for tonight?"

"You really want to ask me that in front of your kid?"

Javier raises an eyebrow, a challenge in his expression.

Gavin smiles and shakes his head. "I figure we'll head back to the house. Get Alejandro settled in. And then," He shrugs, letting his expression soften. "Whatever you want," he murmurs. "Tonight can be whatever you want."

Javier's eyes widen. "What do you mean?"

"The guest room is all set up, and I'll stay the night there if you want. Just because it's our first night together, that doesn't mean we have to spend it *together*."

Javier wets his lips and glances down at Gavin's mouth. "I..."

Gavin would be lying if he said he didn't wish that tonight would end with Javier in his arms, but he won't press. Not with someone that's going to be as important to him as Javier. Still, that doesn't mean he won't meet an offer from Javier with an offer of his own.

Gavin leans in slowly, offering Javier a chance to pull away. Javier doesn't. He leans in, behind Alejandro's head, and lets Gavin brush their lips together. Then Javier reaches up and presses his palm to the base of Gavin's neck, pulling him closer and parting his lips on a sigh. Gavin's heart thunders in his chest, hope twisting through his veins. It's more than he'd expected, more than he'd dared want, but that doesn't make it any less powerful a kiss.

Any less than exactly what he wants.

He slips his tongue past Javier's lips, tasting the glaze on the salmon from dinner. Then he gets ahold of himself and pulls back, blinking past the stars in his eyes.

Javier seems just as dazed, and Gavin takes a small thrill from that. Maybe Javier isn't as uncertain as he'd seemed.

Dessert is brought out next, and some of the guests come up to congratulate them. No one else tapped their glasses to call for a kiss, and Gavin is grateful that his guests know better than to pressure Javier. Everyone shakes Gavin's hand, then Javier's, then, occasionally, Alejandro's. They only rib Gavin a little bit and only tease Javier in the context of Gavin. There's no pressure, and Gavin can see Javier relax the more people come up to greet them.

It's Tyler that seems to really get under Javier's skin. Though Gavin can guess why, he doesn't want to get angry with his best friend in the middle of his wedding reception, so he lets it slide with no more than a raised eyebrow in Tyler's direction. Tyler winces, but doesn't say or do more than that, understanding that he's in trouble, but that they're going to be okay.

The food is cleared away, Alejandro finishes his dessert with his father's help, and that means it's time for the last part of the ceremony.

The dancing.

12

Javi knows what's coming when Gavin leads him and Ále back to the room where the ceremony was held. The chairs have been cleared to create a dance floor, and there's a DJ set up in the far corner and a cash bar in the other. Javi doesn't let himself cling to Ále like a lifeline, but it's a very near thing.

"Do we have to?" he asks Gavin softly.

Gavin looks surprised. He opens his mouth, thinks, then shrugs. "I'd like to," he says honestly, "but we don't have to."

Javi doesn't know much about dancing outside of what he learned from his cousins, and that kind of dancing is definitely not what he should be doing on the dance floor at his wedding. And though he tries to use that as an excuse, Gavin just smiles at him and chuckles.

"Then let me lead. If you're okay with that. I just want to hold you. If that's okay with you."

And, really, what can Javi say to that? So he passes Ále off to Bianca and lets himself be led to the center of the room to the meager applause of Gavin's friends and family. One of Gavin's hands is in his and the other is at the small of his back. Then Gavin steps past him and turns to face him, bringing them both to a stop. That hand is still gently holding Javi, warm and damning all at once. Gavin nods at someone off to the side, and music starts playing. Music that Javi doesn't quite recognize, but knows all the same. It takes more than a few beats, but eventually he recognizes the familiar melody from amidst the violins. The sound is softer and sweeter than the more bass heavy, alt-rock version he's used to.

For a moment, he's transported back to middle school and the first dance he'd been asked to. For a moment, he's a kid, uncertain and unsure of the girl in front of him, even as he tries to step in and take charge.

Then he looks up into Gavin's face and is met with a shit-eating grin.

"Seriously?" Javi asks. "Did you literally go back to your sixth-grade playlist to pick something out for our first dance?"

"Come on now," Gavin says with a laugh, and a tension that Javi hadn't noticed rolls off his Provider's shoulders. Gavin pulls him in closer by that damn hand, until their chests are pressed flush. The dim lights of the hall set off the blue of Gavin's eyes.

Javi feels pulled into those eyes, feels himself melting against a man he's only just met. But between the work that Gavin's done to put the ceremony together so fast, every kind, gentle word he's offered Ále, and the caution with which he's touched Javi himself, Javi can't help but feel drawn to him. He tightens his grip on Gavin's hand.

Gavin's expression softens. "It wasn't sixth grade. It was eighth grade."

And Javi can't help it. He laughs at that, his heart swelling in his chest, warm and bright and somehow *more* than it was just minutes before.

It isn't until a good minute into their glorified swaying that their closeness really registers for Javi. "Aren't we supposed to leave room for a little light to show between us?" His voice comes out just a bit breathier than he intends.

Gavin smirks at him in a way that makes him look boyish and young. It's endearing, if a bit disorienting. Gavin spins him away, then pulls him back in even closer, and Javi's breath stills in his chest. "Is that what you want?" he murmurs.

"What I want?" Javi stares up at Gavin, still trying to figure him out. "Gavin," he says softly, "I'm your Recipient. This isn't about what I want. This is about what you want."

"I don't want things to be like that between us." Gavin twirls Javi around, showing him off a little.

"Like what?"

Gavin winces, and Javi understands immediately. He'd thought that they both knew this was all for show, that this was a money grab for both of them, but if Gavin doesn't want the traditional Provider-Recipient roles, that means he wants something else from Javi. Probably romance. Maybe more. That means this isn't exactly what Javi thought it was.

Where does that leave him? When Javi looks back at Gavin, his expression is drawn and worried. "Javier, I didn't mean anything by it."

"Didn't you? It's what's expected nowadays, right? Romance? Love? Sex?"

"That doesn't mean I'll do something about it. We have a contract."

They're whispering low enough and the music is still playing, making it unlikely that any of Gavin's friends or family can hear them, but Javi's heart is pounding in his chest regardless.

It's not like he doesn't know this is his place. He's the Recipient, and that usually comes with certain expectations. Sexual expectations. No matter what's in the contract, Gavin must have hoped for something more. Must have thought they could come to some sort of agreement.

The thing is, Javi knows Gavin's objectively attractive. He knows this. He knows anyone would count themselves lucky to call Gavin theirs, even before the kind heart that Javi has seen from the start.

That kindness doesn't mean Gavin is impervious to societal expectations.

If Javi's supposed to fake interest to cover their bases, he'll need to figure out what, exactly, he's willing to ask for tonight.

Gavin's hand flexes against the small of his back, but he doesn't pull Javi in closer. "I'm not going to do anything you don't want."

Javi smiles sharply as the sound of whispers hits his ears. "They're talking."

Forcing his feet to move, Javi takes a half-step closer to Gavin, unintentionally forcing his Provider to stumble back. He recovers beautifully, though, and then they're moving across the dance floor again. Javi can see Gavin trying to find the right thing to say the whole time, but nothing comes out of his mouth. Then the song ends and the flower girl springs up between them, demanding a dance with her Uncle Gavin, giving Javi the perfect escape to a seat at the edge of the dance floor where Bianca had set Ále up.

His reason for this marriage. His only good reason for anything he does.

Before he can get too far away, Gavin catches his wrist. Javi closes his eyes and lets himself be reeled back in.

"I'm not going to do anything you don't want," Gavin mutters against Javi's ear. "I'll sleep in the guest bedroom for our whole marriage if that's what it takes to make you believe that. I'm not going to do anything you don't want."

Then he lets Javi go. He takes a split second to look into Javi's eyes, to insist without words how serious he is, before he looks down at his niece with a grin.

Javi doesn't quite stumble away, but it's a near thing. He collects himself quickly, but before he can head to his son, Bianca intercepts him.

"Everything good?"

Taken aback, Javi falls into step with her out of instinct alone. "Yeah, B, everything's fine."

"Really? Because you looked ready to cut and run from your Provider a second ago. What gives?"

Javi shakes his head. "I'm not actually sure."

Bianca doesn't say anything, just sways in front of Javi and turns them in a slow circle. She knows how to wait for his brain to sort itself out. His eyes catch on his abuela as they turn, and he nods at her expectant look. He'll need to connect with her soon. Not tonight, though. There's too much going on tonight.

"I don't have anything to compare this to," he finally says to Bianca.

"Compare what to?"

"The whole intimacy thing. It's different," he's quick to say as Bianca makes a face, "because you're Partnered, and Teresa is the Provider in her marriage and I'm not talking to her Recipient about this, and Mom..." He shakes his head. "Who am I supposed to talk to about this?"

"The sexual relations clause?" Bianca asks. "I thought you said you were happy with it," she says when Javi nods.

"I am. I mean, I was. I just think his expectations are different."

"Then talk to him. No, seriously, Javi," she adds when he shakes his head, "with that clause you have all the power. Talk to him, tell him what you're willing to have and do and make sure he understands. He seems like someone that will."

"B. You can't possibly know that."

"You're right," she agrees, "I can't. But I've got a good feeling about him. Besides, I know you and Casey made Ále together, but goodness knows you two can't communicate for shit."

Javi throws his head back on a laugh. He pulls her in, then throws her out in a spin. "B, come on," he says as she spins back in toward him. "You don't have to call me out like that right now."

Bianca isn't laughing. "Javi. You always think you know what's going on in other people's heads. You don't."

"What does that mean?"

"It means you need to tell him how you feel, and then listen to what he's saying, not what you think he's saying."

The music ends, and, with it, Javi's excuse to talk to Bianca.

She takes pity on him, though, and pulls him into a hug. "Listen to what he's saying, and then say your piece too. Okay? If this is going to work for you, you need to give him a chance to be who he really is, not who you think he is." She squeezes him tight. "Abuela and I have an early flight tomorrow and a long drive to our hotel, so I'm gonna see if Abuela's ready to go and head out. I love you."

"Yeah." Javi squeezes her back. "Love you too, B."

He ignores the fact that he's standing in the middle of the dance floor as he watches Bianca intercept Gavin briefly and give him a hug as well before heading out.

Before Gavin can look at him and try to catch his eye again, Javi heads back to where Ále is waiting.

"Daddy?"

Javi grins at Ále even though it feels shaky. "Hey, buddy."

Ále stares at him. He opens his mouth to say something, then looks out at the dance floor, which is now populated by plenty of other guests. It doesn't take long for Javi to guess what's going on in his son's head.

"How are you feeling?"

Ále contemplates this, then gives him a so-so motion with his hand, meaning he's not completely comfortable but he isn't straining himself.

"Do you want to go dance? Are you up for it?"

Ále perks up immediately, then slumps a little. "Is that okay?"

"Why wouldn't it be okay?"

Ále takes a moment to respond. "Abuela always says that I

should be more careful. There's so many people. I don't want to hit somebody with my crutches."

Sending up a silent curse on his mother's name, Javi keeps his expression carefully schooled. "Well, do you wanna know a secret?"

Ále looks briefly skeptical, but nods and leans in.

Javi leans in close and whispers, "Your Abuela isn't here. I think that means we should do whatever we want."

Ále stays very still. Then he looks at Javi with a tiny giggle, almost like he doesn't believe what Javi's saying.

Javi gives Ále his brightest grin. "Now, are you going to get out there and dance and make some new friends or not?"

Ále stares up at him for a long, slow minute, before a matching grin breaks out on his face. Javi takes his crutches from where Bianca stored them against the back of Ále's chair. Ále gets sorted and hops off his chair. He leans in dutifully so Javi can press a kiss to his temple and then makes a beeline for a group of kids on the dance floor. The five other kids make space for him right away, and when the flower girl grabs him by the sleeve and, presumably, asks him to dance, his eyes light up.

Javi's chest aches, and though he's alone on the outskirts now, he doesn't feel as isolated as he might have expected to. He watches as Evelyn hovers just at the edge of where the kids are dancing and catches her eyes flitting from the flower girl that asked Ále to dance to Ále and back again.

It takes some doing to keep his hands loose and relaxed in his lap, and even more doing to keep himself in his seat. Evelyn looks like she's going to intervene with Ále somehow, and he doesn't know her well enough to know whether or not it will be helpful. When she starts to move toward the kids, Javi gets halfway to standing to make his own intervention before Gavin intercepts Evelyn. They have a brief conversation that includes Gavin glancing at the kids. At Ále. Javier stands up completely, but

Gavin shakes his head and motions at an empty table nearby. Evelyn glances over, then relaxes with a nod.

Then, instead of heading for the kids, she grabs a chair from the table. She doesn't take it all the way to the kids, but she moves it closer to the edge of the dance floor and angles it so that it will be easy for Ále to drop right into it. Javi relaxes. She was probably worried about him and trying to help. Javi may know that his son is usually pretty good with his limits, but she wouldn't. It's a kindness that Javi hadn't expected in this setting.

Then Gavin drags his sister into a dance and Javi can breathe easy for a moment.

"So," a voice says from over his shoulder, "how'd you bag a Carmichael?"

Javi freezes, then turns to see a white man standing beside him and leaning into his space almost threateningly.

He's tall, almost as tall as Gavin, dressed down in just a button down and slacks, with an extremely unattractive smirk on his face.

"Excuse me?" Javi asks.

The man gestures to Gavin and Evelyn. "That's my Recipient. I hear you all had a grand old time yesterday. My girls can't shut up about your kid."

"Is that a problem?" Javi bristles.

"Nah. Just thought I'd come see what you have that's got Gavin so interested. The guy's never wanted anything to do with his family's money, but then you show up and he's getting married?" The man scoffs. "I don't think so. Though," he adds with a leer, "if you put out the way your ass is offering, I can see why a horndog like Gavin would be interested."

All at once, Javi feels small. Gavin implied that they weren't going to be sexual together, but this is apparently Evelyn's Provider, so he must know better than him.

Except didn't Javi figure out that, for Gavin, this whole money grab is probably about Evelyn? There's no way this guy knows

Gavin better than Evelyn does, and she trusts Gavin over her Provider, that much is obvious.

Javi looks away and breathes deeply three times, counting each breath as he does. Then he stands up. "Excuse me," he mutters. Then he's across the room in a second, posting up by the cash bar. He's not interested in drinking right now, but if he needs to deal with Evelyn's Provider again, that might change.

Five minutes later, though, Javi catches sight of Evelyn's Provider approaching Evelyn and Gavin with purpose, two glasses of champagne in his hands. With what he knows, Javi might have to intervene. The last thing either of them need is Evelyn's Provider handing her alcohol when she's pregnant.

He turns to the bartender. "Do you have any sparkling apple cider for the kids?"

13

"Gavin!"

Gavin's spine goes taut at the sound of his brother-in-law's voice. Evelyn's hand tenses in his, and he sees the mask she plasters on as the man approaches.

God, Gavin hates the guy.

Still, he has to play nice, for now at least. Can't have him catching on too soon. He turns to Shane with a smile. "Shane. Glad you could make it."

"Of course, of course." Shane gives him a one-armed hug before insinuating himself between Gavin and Evelyn. "I'm only sorry Genesis and I couldn't be here yesterday."

"Yes, well, we both know how work can be, and I didn't want you to have to take Genesis out of kindergarten any more than necessary." That last part is a lie. If he could have gotten Genesis here with her sisters and kept the three of them and Evelyn safe, he'd have done it. But he can't, not yet, so all he can do is stay as close to her as possible. Protect her the only way he knows how.

"Still, I want to toast to your new Recipient. Where is he anyway?"

"Right here."

Gavin startles a little when he feels Javier's arm slip around his back. "Javier?"

"Hi, dear." There's something sickly-sweet about the way Javier says it that rankles him. Then he's kissing Gavin's cheek and Gavin has less than no idea what is going on.

"Ah, yes, the newest Carmichael."

"And who is this, dear?" Javier says in that same tone. "I don't think we've been introduced."

"This is, uh." Gavin swallows, taken aback and not clear at all on what's happening right now. "This is Evelyn's Provider, Shane."

Javier hums. He passes off a glass of champagne to Gavin before reaching out with his free hand to shake one of Shane's.

Shane pauses, looking down at the two glasses in his hands.

"Oh, my bad," Javier says. He deftly slips one of the glasses from Shane's grip and hands it off to Gavin. He shakes Shane's hand. "Pleasure to meet you."

"Oh, no, the pleasure is all mine."

Gavin's neck heats up at the almost sultry tone in Shane's voice. It's not enough for him to make a scene over it, just enough to make him angry.

Javier titters, almost as though he's flattered. Then he reaches for the glass in Gavin's hand. "Now, I think I heard something about a toast?"

Gavin tosses Javier a wide-eyed look. Evelyn can't drink alcohol. He holds firm on the glass in his hand. He doesn't know what game Javier is playing, but he doesn't like it.

Javier leans in as though to press a kiss to Gavin's temple. "Trust me."

And somehow, against all odds, Gavin does. He nods.

"Okay. Distract him."

Gavin nods again, turning to Shane as he lets Javier take the glass from him. "You really don't have to do that," he says, drawing Shane's gaze.

Out of the corner of his eye, he sees Javier pass Evelyn the drink from his other hand and nod at her. She blinks, then lifts the glass to her nose. Her eyes widen and she looks at Javier like he's just saved her and all at once Gavin knows that he has.

When they'd set up the cash bar, Gavin insisted on sparkling apple cider, both for the kids and for his sober captain. But for Javier to think of that to distract Shane is more than he ever could have asked for.

All at once, Gavin finds himself falling a little bit in love.

"Nonsense."

Shane's voice startles Gavin out of his reverie. He turns back to Shane.

"I want to do this."

"Alright," Gavin acquiesces, "but nothing big. Just the four of us is fine."

Shane pouts, but relents. He pulls Evelyn in against his side and lifts his glass.

Gavin mirrors the motion, pulling Javier to him as though that might protect him from whatever Shane is about to say.

"To Gavin and Javier. May your love be strong, your family large, and your sex life extraordinary."

Javier stiffens at Gavin's side.

"Shane," Gavin starts, but Javier pinches his side.

"Thank you, Shane," Javier says deferentially. "We appreciate it." Then he lifts his glass and the four of them clink their glasses together before downing the champagne.

Well. Champagne and, in Evelyn's case, the sparkling apple cider.

Once they're all done, Javier offers to put the glasses back, and though Shane tries to coax him into staying, he steps away with nothing more than a kiss to Gavin's cheek.

"I tell you what, Carmichael," Shane says with a leer. "You found yourself a good one."

As Gavin watches Javier pass the glasses off to a waitress, he sees Javier nod in their direction and say something to her. The waitress nods and slips away. Gavin can only hope that Javier did what he should have done hours ago and told the staff that Evelyn isn't to be served alcohol.

"Don't you think, sweetheart?" Shane asks.

"Yes." Evelyn's voice trembles as she speaks. "Yes, I think he did."

For the first time—and probably the only time—Shane is exactly right. Gavin really did find a good one.

Gavin beats Javier and Alejandro back to the house after the reception. It isn't intentional, but he figures he's just more used to Denver traffic than Javier is.

Gavin is out of his suit and dressed in something more comfortable when Javier pulls up in front of the house instead of the garage. Gavin opens the front door to ask what's going on only to see Javier juggling a half-asleep Alejandro and his crutches while trying to shut the door.

"Here," Gavin hustles down the walk. "Let me get the door."

Javier's shoulders tense briefly before relaxing again. "Thanks."

"No problem." Gavin closes the door as quietly as he can. "Do you want me to take him?"

Javier pulls Alejandro a little closer against his body. "That's okay," he says sharply. "I've got him."

"Sure. Is there something else I can do to help?"

"No." Javier hesitates before Gavin can turn away. "Actually, if you want to put the truck in the garage, that would be nice."

"Sure thing. You have your keys?"

Javier deftly maneuvers his son and the crutches to grab the keys from his suit pocket. He passes them off to Gavin. "Thanks."

"No problem."

Gavin pulls the car into the garage. It's a tighter fit than he'd expected, but it'll work for them, at least for now.

He shuts the car off, closes the garage door, and heads inside to where he finds Javier just finishing helping a still-sleepy Alejandro out of his suit.

"Come on, buddy," he says. "Teeth, face, toilet, and then bed."

Alejandro grumbles a little but lets himself be led to the ensuite. Gavin hovers at the door to Alejandro's bedroom, uncertain of his welcome. Javier and Alejandro come back out a few minutes later and Javier helps Alejandro into bed.

Through it all, Javier is intentional without being overbearing, present without hovering. It's clearly an art that he perfected over the years, and Gavin wonders how long it will take him to do the same.

Javier runs his hands over Alejandro's curls. "You want a story tonight, buddy?"

Alejandro shakes his head. "Tired."

"Okay." Javier leans forward and kisses his forehead before helping him under the covers. He kisses Alejandro's forehead one more time before tucking him away and moving to turn off the light. "I love you, mijo."

"Love you too, Daddy," Alejandro mumbles back.

"I'll see you in the morning."

Alejandro's answer is unintelligible. Javi chuckles, and it warms Gavin's heart.

Then he's stepping into Gavin's space, easing him out of Alejandro's room, and closing the door behind them as quietly as he can.

Javier looks up at Gavin, then, his eyes glittering in the hall light. All at once, Gavin wants him more than he'd ever thought possible. He takes a half-step toward Javier, then hesitates. One of his hands is half-raised, reaching for his Recipient, but he pulls back at the last moment.

"Fuck, Javier." Gavin's whispered words have Javier pressing his back and palms against the wall. "The way you are with him… you're an incredible father. And then the way you covered for Evelyn at the reception…" He shakes his head. "You're going to be an incredible husband. You know that, right?"

Javier considers him briefly before asking, "And if I can't give you what you want?"

Gavin pulls back, searching Javier's face. "What do you think I want?"

Javier's laugh is brittle and sharp, yet soft in deference to his son. "Come on, Gavin. What every Provider wants."

The words sting, but something about the way Javier says it gets under his skin. It's almost like he's practiced the words, like he's expecting something specific to come of them. No one at the ceremony would have given him the impression that this is anything like that, except maybe Shane.

"What did Shane say?" Gavin says, his voice low and dangerous.

"What?" Javier asks. There's something guilty in the tone. "Nothing."

"Javier."

Javier exhales. "He may have implied that you were just looking for a bedwarmer."

"And you believed him?"

"I mean, why else would you want me?" Javier snaps back.

Gavin reels away as though struck.

Javier looks just as startled by the outburst, but he doesn't stand down. If anything, he stands up straighter.

"Is that really what you think of me?" Gavin asks. "After today? After yesterday?"

Javier runs a hand over his face. "It's not like that." He sighs. "I don't know what you want from me."

"What's that supposed to mean?"

"It means," Javier says sharply, "that you didn't let me cook yesterday. You offered to take Alejandro in. You don't seem to want me to take care of the house or my son or anything. If you don't want me to *do* anything, then what else am I here for except to look handsome and meet your needs."

The bottom drops out of Gavin's stomach. "I hadn't thought of it that way."

Javier tips his head back against the wall. "I'm starting to figure that out. But, Gavin, I need some expectations, here. I'm in a new city where I know no one other than you and your people, and I need to know what I'm supposed to do. What you want me to do."

"Okay. Okay, I can kind of see that." He huffs. "I should have known I'd choose someone that doesn't want to sit idle."

"Not even a little bit."

"Okay," Gavin laughs. "Well, for now what I want is for you to put on something more comfortable than that, and then for us to maybe get some sleep. We can talk more about this in the morning.

"And you'll let me make breakfast this time?" Javier asks.

"If you wake up before me, sure."

Javier muffles his laugh quickly as they're still standing outside of Alejandro's door. "Oh, you're on."

Gavin grins widely for a moment before settling into a softer expression. "There's one more thing," he says. He waits until Javier is looking at him directly. "I want you to take the primary bedroom."

Javier is shaking his head before Gavin can even finish the thought. "Gavin…"

"I want you to know that this is your home, too. Alright?" Gavin huffs, running his hand over his hair. "I'm not the singular boss here. At least, I don't want to be. I want us to be a team. I want us to do this together."

Javier stares at him for a long moment. Then the apples of his cheeks go pink and he ducks his head. "Alright. I think I can work with that for now. There's just one thing."

"What's that?"

"I'm not sure I'm up for changing the sheets tonight."

Gavin blinks, the thought not computing until he realizes that he'd slept in the primary bedroom last night, which means that if Javier sleeps in there tonight, Gavin's cologne will still be all over the sheets.

Oh.

Oh.

Javier gives another muffled laugh at the look on Gavin's face. "I think I'll take the room my abuela slept in last night, and we can worry about changing bedsheets and stuff tomorrow. If that's okay with you?"

After a moment, Gavin nods. "Yes, yeah, yes, of course, that's fine. Tomorrow."

"Okay." Javier pushes off the wall and leans into Gavin's space. He reaches up and cups his jaw. "Tomorrow."

With the unspoken promise, Javier slips down the hall toward the guest room Citlali slept in the night before, leaving behind a very flustered Gavin.

14

The room is dark when Javi wakes. He luxuriates in it for a moment before his internal clock starts to register its discontent. He reaches for his phone, which he'd of course forgotten to plug in last night, and sees that it's already well past 9:00 a.m.

He sits up in a rush, his worry for his son and his morning needs outstripping any other thoughts. He turns on the bedside lamp, ready to clamber out of here in yesterday's underwear only to stop short.

His suitcase is in the room with him, the one thing of his own he'd brought to Denver. All the other space in his truck was saved for Ále's things. If his suitcase is in here, that must at least mean that Gavin is up already, so Ále isn't alone.

Javi slips out of bed, fighting down the flutter in his chest at the fact that Gavin came in to drop off his suitcase but didn't wake Javi. He's not sure how that makes him feel, but it leaves his throat dry and his skin overheated. Once he's shaken the feeling off, he pulls out underwear, a pair of jeans, and a loose-fitting Henley and gets dressed. Then, gearing up for the day ahead, he opens the door.

He winces away from the light around him. Blackout

curtains, then. Gavin definitely installed blackout curtains in the bedrooms. It's an unnecessary touch of kindness that Javi doesn't know how to process. An extra layer of comfort that he never would have expected. Then again, they're just curtains, not an offer of marriage. Besides, they're married already anyway.

Instead, he walks through the house in search of Ále. He wouldn't be surprised if Gavin has work today and Javi's the only one here to look out for his son. He moves through the house, silent in his bare feet, until he reaches Ále's room.

"Dad!" Ále clambers off his bed and makes his way carefully across the room to hug Javi. Javi wraps his arms around Ále's shoulders and drops a kiss into his curls.

"You slept in so late!" Ále says, grinning up at him.

"That was the deal, Alejandro."

Javi looks up to meet Gavin's shining eyes. His focus isn't on Javi, though. It's on Ále.

"I know," Ále says with a huff.

Gavin laughs and turns back to where he's putting a pile of Ále's Legos away. "I'm happy to see him too."

Javi's heart flutters in his chest. Gavin made himself perfectly at home in Ále's room, and for all that Javi thought he wanted a partner to help take care of Ále, this level of forwardness strikes him as odd. "Gavin?"

Gavin tosses him a grin. "There's omelet bites keeping warm in the oven if you're hungry, and plenty of coffee in the pot."

"Oh." Javi frowns at the redirect. "I'm just fine." Except his stomach chooses that moment to growl loudly.

Ále laughs. "Come on," he says, taking Javi's hand, "they're really good."

Javi tosses Gavin a nervous smile. He hesitates, uncertain whether he should wait for Gavin to finish putting Ále's Legos away, or if he's supposed to leave with his son and let Gavin finish his task. If they're a family now, are they supposed to do things as a family? Gavin said something about them being a team last night.

"Go get some food in your belly," Gavin says, waving them off. "I'll be over in a sec."

Javi still hesitates until Ále tugs on his hand. He's helpless in the face of his son's insistence and lets Ále lead him to the kitchen. Even so, he glances over his shoulder at Ále's bedroom door and thinks about the man beyond.

Everything Gavin has done so far this morning, from slipping his suitcase in quietly enough that Javi didn't wake, to making breakfast, to getting Ále unpacked, is something that Javi expected to do himself as the Recipient. The kids, the food, the moving around silently so the other can sleep; those are all classic Recipient moves. Whatever it is that Gavin expects of Javi, it truly doesn't seem like he has any expectations of sticking to their traditional roles.

Javi wants to be relieved, wants to be grateful that Gavin is doing so much, but it leaves him unsettled, too. Just as Javi learned how to be a Provider from his father and the men he surrounded himself with, Javi learned how to be a Recipient from his mother and the other women in the neighborhood. If he doesn't have to be what he thought he had to be, what does that leave for him? Idle hands have never been his strong suit, and he thinks he might go stir crazy the second Ále goes back to school if he's left to his own devices. He knows the marriage contract calls for a divvying up of chores that leans more heavily on him, but surely there's more that Gavin expects than what he's been doing. Surely.

Ále moves carefully but with a kind of confidence that Javi's only ever seen a few times. It warms something in him, the part that hoped that this marriage would be more than just a safety net for Ále. That, maybe, Ále could be happy here, too.

Ále clambers into a seat at the small table at one end of the spacious kitchen. Javi finds his way to the oven and pulls out the tray of omelet bites. They do look good. He spots the salt and pepper off to the side and grabs them both to bring to the table with the plate of omelet bites he puts together for himself. Then he takes the time to pour himself a mug of coffee as he watches his son.

A yawn threatens, but Javi swallows it down. The fatigue has been there since they left Vegas, but it feels more acute now. He wonders if his exhaustion was obvious to Gavin. If it was, it makes sense that Gavin would have gotten up with Ále long enough ago to entertain him. Ále has always been an early riser, and even though it makes it easier to get him to school, it's a task to keep him from moving so fast he gets himself in trouble. Though Ále's energy is infectious, it sometimes makes him want to rush through his morning stretching and strengthening. Javi allowed that exactly once, the first week Ále was in kindergarten, only to have Ále come home crying quiet tears of pain that tore at Javi's heart.

After that, their mornings became more disciplined, even if Javi tried to ensure that they never became less fun.

Now, he wonders how their mornings are going to have to change. Will Gavin expect to be a part of their mornings? Or will he leave that to Javi? This marriage is a business arrangement; they'd both agreed on that from the start. He'd figured that he'd need to talk to Gavin about Ále's needs and how to support him effectively. He'd figured they'd wake Ále together. So why is Gavin trying to support Ále on his own like this?

Javi shakes off the thought. He can't do anything about it now. "You ate already?" he asks as he moves to the table to sit next to Ále.

"Yup." He's gets his Switch out and pokes at it idly.

"Hey," he says, gently tapping the table between them. "Not during meals."

Ále doesn't argue, turning it face down and placing it off to the side.

"And you did your stretches this morning?"

"We did them together," Gavin says as he rounds the corner.

"What?" Javi pauses with a bite halfway to his mouth.

Ále pipes up. "We did my stretches together this morning."

Javi puts his fork down and looks at his son. "You showed him?" he asks, wonder in his tone.

The grin falls off Gavin's face. "Is that okay?"

"Of course," Javi says, waving off the concern, "He's just never been super open about that. My father…" He cuts himself off, startled at how close he'd come to revealing more information about his family than he'd planned.

His parents may have professed to love Ále, but his dad never understood why Javi was doing yoga and stretching with his son instead of "toughening him up." On the rare occasions when Javi left his father with Ále and the even rarer ones where his father actually tried to do the stretches with him, Javi would come home to Ále moving with less precision than he was used to. Ále finally admitted that his abuelo only wanted to do the strengthening parts of the exercises, not the stretching.

Javi put a stop to that too, refusing to let his father help with Ále's stretches anymore.

Gavin's face darkens, as though filling in the unspoken words. "I see."

"It's nothing bad," Javi rushes to assure him. "He just thinks Alejandro is less capable than he actually is."

Gavin's lips pull into a grimace, and his shoulders hunch up to his ears. "That's worse."

Javi laughs self-deprecatingly, turning away from Gavin. "Well, he raised one mess-up of a son," he says, covering the phrase that wants to spill from his lips instead. "It shouldn't have been too hard for him to think his mess-up of a son would mess up his son."

"What did you say?" Gavin leans in close in Javi's space. When Javi doesn't immediately look up at him, he tips his chin back with two fingers until their eyes meet. "You are not a fuck-up," he hisses, speaking low enough that Ále might not have heard.

The ferocity in Gavin's voice leaves Javi blinking at him, words failing him.

Gavin takes this as permission to continue. "You have raised a brilliant, funny, strong kid with a better head on his shoulders than most adults I've met on the job. You were brave enough to ask for help when you needed it and brave enough to accept that help from a complete stranger. You are not a fuck-up. You're incredible."

A lump forms in Javi's throat, and even though he wants to raise a son that knows how to handle his feelings, Javi himself is still learning how to do that. "Well," he says, changing the subject "you're pretty incredible, too."

Gavin hums, as though trying to decide whether or not to let this slide. In the end, he pulls away. "I'm glad you think so."

There's no threat or malice in the tone, no matter how hard Javi looks for it. Javi swallows down his surprise with his third bite of omelet. Back home his mother rarely had the time to cook in the mornings. With three kids under ten and his father off providing for the family, she'd often been rushed and too busy to put together a breakfast that took more time than popping something in the toaster or the microwave, and then she'd just never broken the habit.

Abuela, though. Abuela taught him everything he is now grateful that he knows.

"Better than you expected?" Gavin sees the surprise in Javi's eyes if the way he laughs is any indication.

"Delicious." Javi chooses his words carefully. "I'm impressed."

"What, you thought I'd turn you into my little house husband?" Gavin laughs, though the sound cuts off when Javi flinches.

Gavin's at his side again in an instant, hand wrapped around

Javi's wrist. "Hey. I don't want that unless you do, okay? I'm happy with this, just being here for you and Åle."

Javi takes a quick sip of his coffee with his free hand, hoping to hide the tremble in his lip. His parents never picked up on it when they said something too sharp or too harsh, but Gavin sees right through him. It leaves Javi feeling cracked open and raw. Even as a Recipient—especially as a Recipient—his needs are secondary to the Provider. Tertiary, with Åle involved. If Gavin can see right through him, Javi is going to have to be even more careful with how he reacts. He can't let Gavin think that he's unhappy or ungrateful, lest he drive a wedge between him and Gavin. He can't afford that.

Literally.

"Okay." Javi shakes off the melancholy before mustering a smile. He doesn't believe Gavin, but it's certainly the thought that counts.

Gavin still seems to see through him, but he doesn't pry. He lets go of Javi's wrist, leaving a rash of goosebumps in his wake, and pulls away. The smile on his lips is tentative, cautious, and it leaves Javi even more wrong-footed.

Javi opens his mouth to say something more, but words, as they so often do, fail him. He closes his mouth.

Gavin turns instead to Åle as he settles into a seat. "You sure you don't want any more, big guy?"

Åle grins at him. "I'm good," And then, at the stern look from Javi, "thanks."

"You don't have to thank me." Gavin ruffles Åle's hair. "Besides, you helped me make them."

That gets Javi's attention. His mother never let Åle help in the kitchen, which means Gavin was patient and careful enough not only to let Åle help, but to *teach* him. It leaves Javi's throat tight. "Did he?" His voice cracks on the words.

Gavin gives him another one of those searching looks but doesn't say anything. When he speaks, it's with a lightness that at once soothes Javi's nerves and has him wondering what his Provider is up to. "Yeah," Gavin says. "He's a great helper."

The words send a flutter through Javi's chest. He knows that Ále can do most things with help, even those things that some people might consider outside his skillset, but to have someone that's known his son barely two days feel the same way? It's a hell of a thing.

He meets Gavin's gaze, nodding in gratitude. Gavin's face softens and he reaches out to squeeze Javi's shoulder. "I told you," he says softly, "I'm in this for the both of you."

Javi hesitates, then offers a small smile, hope welling in his chest. "I'm glad. Thank you."

Maybe this isn't going to be as bad as he'd feared.

15

Gavin and Ále carry the conversation, while Javi finishes eating, the three of them still seated around the kitchen table. As soon as Gavin mentions something about a book he's reading about black holes, Ále is off to the races, sharing facts he's learned and hanging on every last word Gavin shares from his book. They trade information freely and there's an easy joy in those words that is unmatched by any conversation Javi has ever seen Ále have before.

Javi can't stop smiling at the easy way Gavin interacts with Ále, or the way he keeps himself carefully attentive and just serious enough to let Ále know he isn't making fun of him. The light grows in Ále's eyes the longer he and Gavin talk, and Javi can already tell that, no matter what happens, this was the right call for Ále.

Javi shifts in his seat. He wants to add to the conversation, but doesn't quite know how. It's been just him and Ále and his parents for so long that he can't find a way to get a word in edgewise in their conversation. He wants to do what's best for his son, and for a long time that's meant protecting him from the people around him. Javi knows he's good at that.

But this, Ále having Gavin as a role model, can only be good news for Javi's son, no matter how uncomfortable it makes Javi himself. Javi will do whatever it takes to keep this going for him, because he'll stop at nothing to give Ále the life and the childhood he deserves.

And if Gavin looks at Javi himself the way he is now, with a warmth and kindness that Javi doesn't deserve, then that's just icing on the cake.

When there's a lull in the conversation, Javi turns to Ále and asks, "Where did you two do your stretches? I didn't see your mat in your room."

"The playroom," Ále says with a grin. "There's more space in there, so Gavin said we could do my stretches in there."

"Oh yeah? And then you went back to your room for the toys?"

Ále laughs. "We didn't have time to bring them all to the playroom before you woke up. Do you want to help us move them now?"

Javi doesn't lick his plate, but he's pretty sure Gavin can tell he's thinking about it. He stands up before he can change his mind. "Sure. Just let me put this in the sink and then we can get started."

Gavin's eyes are hot on his back as he heads to the sink. He's not quite sure why, but he pays attention to the feeling of Gavin's eyes as they follow Ále to his room.

"Where do you want to start?"

Ále ends up directing Javi and Gavin through most of the arranging of all his things. They look sparse in the extra space that Gavin's home affords him, but Javi has an inkling that Gavin is going to do something about that, too. Eventually, at any rate. For now, it's the two of them following Ále's orders and getting everything situated.

Gavin takes orders from a nine-year-old surprisingly well. He teases and jokes and the whole thing is just so reminiscent of the kind of family Javi always wanted for his son, the kind of family he saw his friends have over the years, that he can hardly contain himself.

That's why, when there's a moment where they cross paths in the doorway to Ále's playroom, he stills rather than just shoulder past his Provider. He looks up just in time to see Gavin looking back down at him, his pupils blown wide as he stares.

Javi forces Gavin's name past his lips, an unspoken plea. His eyes drift down to Gavin's lips, lips that spoke of such easy devotion at the altar the day before. Lips that have defended and uplifted Alejandro at every turn.

All at once, Javi knows that he wants those lips to kiss him again.

Gavin doesn't seem to care what the sound of his name on Javi's lips is supposed to mean. That, or he knows what Javi needs better than Javi himself. He leans in and kisses Javi deeply. He only reaches out with one hand, the other busy with a box of Legos, but even with only a single hand on Javi's jaw, he kisses like he wants to take on all of Javi's pain. Like if he just kisses hard enough, deep enough, he can remake Javi in the image of love. Javi shudders under his touch and reaches up to grasp him by the biceps. Gavin deepens the kiss, tilting Javi's head back and maneuvering him against the wall of Ále's playroom.

It's the thought of where they are that has Javi pulling back from the kiss. The second he starts to lean away, Gavin pulls away completely, his free hand falling to his side. His eyes are wide and wild and keep flitting down to Javi's lips. "Sorry," he whispers. "Sorry, I should've asked and I didn't. Sorry."

Javi stares at him for a moment. He's just as caught up in the closeness of another person, another adult, as Gavin is, and he's almost willing to yield to it and just melt against Gavin.

Then the words register. "That's what you're worried about?" Javi shakes his head. "You don't have to ask permission to kiss me, Gavin. I'm yours."

"That doesn't mean you'll always want to kiss me," Gavin argues. "I shouldn't have done that."

Javi hesitates for a breath before he steps back into Gavin's space. "And if I do want you to kiss me?"

Gavin's breath hitches. "If you ... oh." He reaches up with his free hand and cups Javi's jaw again. "Is that what you want?"

"Yeah." Javi grins, letting the light of Gavin's affection fill his chest. "Yeah, that's exactly what I want."

Gavin hums. "You want me to kiss you here?" He brushes his lips over Javi's cheekbone. This time it's Javi's turn for his breath to hitch at the delicate touch. "Or here?" The next kiss is against the hinge of his jaw. "Here?" The arch of his eyebrow. "Here?" The hollow of his throat.

"You know what I want." Javi's breathless with it, his knees weak from wanting. "Really kiss me."

"I am."

Javi fists his hand in Gavin's hair before he can think better of it. When he yanks Gavin's head away, his pupils are wide. "Kiss my mouth, Carmichael. Kiss me like you mean it."

Gavin surges forward, his teeth catching on Javi's lip as he moves in close. Javi's fingers spasm in Gavin's hair, and his other hand comes up to grasp at Gavin's hip. His fingers find skin as he rucks up Gavin's shirt and he shudders. Gavin's got their chests pressed together and Javi is only just holding back from arching up against him like he's a teenager all over again.

"Dad?"

Any remaining interest in kissing Gavin again dissipates at the sound of his son's voice. Gavin releases Javi as soon as he starts to shift away. Though Javi's more used to covering things up for his son than Gavin is, he still feels unsettled and out of sorts. He's supposed to be doing all of this for Ále, not for any sort of relationship with Gavin.

Fighting down his guilt and embarrassment, Javi smiles down at Ále.

"Yeah, buddy?"

Alejandro looks between the two of them for a moment before his nose wrinkles. "Were you two kissing?"

Javi opens his mouth to deny it, but then Gavin makes a sound somewhere between a huff and a laugh and Javi can't hold back his own chuckle. "Yeah, buddy. We were."

"Oh."

Javi frowns at how small his son's voice sounds and leans in to catch his eye when he looks away. "Hey, Ále. What is it?"

Ále bites his lip and shakes his head, as though afraid of speaking his mind.

"Mijo." Javi tamps down on the flush of anger at his parents that rushes through his body. "You know you can tell me anything, right?"

This time Ále's eyes slide up to Gavin and then skitter away.

Javi stands, but he doesn't even need to look at Gavin before his Provider is moving away. "I'll be in the kitchen when you're done talking, okay, Alejandro?"

Ále nods, but still waits to say anything until Gavin's well out of range. Even then, he tugs Javi all the way into the playroom and shuts the door behind them.

Ále stands there for a minute before he turns to Javi, tears in his eyes and shoulders hunched, avoiding Javi's eyes. "I thought you liked Gavin."

The words diffuse his worry that Ále is upset with him for kissing someone other than Casey, his ex, but leave him stumped as to the reason Ále's upset. "I do."

Ále frowns. "Were you fighting?"

"Were we … Ále, what are you talking about?" Javi doesn't follow the logical jump. He knows Ále saw him and Casey fight, but he can't think of anything that he or Gavin have done to suggest that they're fighting.

"You and Mom always kissed after you were done fighting. I know other people kiss because they like each other, but you don't." Ále swallows and looks away. When he speaks again his voice is soft. "I thought you liked Gavin."

There's so much to unpack there that Javi really isn't ready to acknowledge, but he knows he has to. He crouches down in front of Ále so that he's looking up at him instead of down at him. "I just want to make sure I understand. You think that, because Gavin and I were kissing, we were fighting?"

Ále nods.

It takes Javi a minute to find the words to explain. "We weren't fighting," he says as gently as he can. "I used to kiss your mom because I liked her too. Gavin and I were kissing because I like him."

"You said that yesterday," Ále says, his shoulders hunching, "and you say that now, but what if… what if that changes, like it did with Mom?"

"Mom and I kissed after we fought," Javi allows, "as a way to make up with each other."

Ále wrinkles his nose.

Javi doesn't have the words to explain to Alejandro that kissing—and sex, for that matter—was all part of the ritual of argument that he and Casey used to fall into before she moved out for grad school. Kissing to make whatever argument they'd just had go away, sex to get back to normal. Then again, maybe he should have known the end was coming when the sex became less and less frequent.

Javi reaches out to take Alejandro's clenched hands in both of his. "You know I still love your mom because she's your mom, though, right? We still care about each other and we love you. I thought I was supposed to take care of her, and you, but our idea of taking care of each other was different. She wanted something I couldn't give her back then. I don't know if I could ever have given it to her. We weren't a good match."

"Then, you and Gavin, you're a good match?" Ále asks, his

hands unclenching and his face relaxing. There's hope in his eyes, and Javi relaxes. He hasn't fucked this up completely.

"I think so." It's more complicated than that, but Javi doesn't know how to distill that for Ále. He and Gavin have an arrangement, to be sure, and Javi can't deny that he's attracted to his Provider. But everything is still new, and there's so much more to building a life together than expectations and attraction.

Even if they can build a functional life together, that doesn't mean that he's going to be able to fall in love with Gavin. That Gavin can fall in love with him. He just doesn't know.

In the end, it's easy to assuage Ále's fears. "We're a good match right now, at least."

Ále straightens up, his shoulders relaxing. Then he looks up at Javi. "Okay."

Javi and Casey stopped loving each other a while ago, but they'd stopped liking each other as anything more than co-parents even longer ago. However Ále interpreted that, Javi will need to keep an eye on it. He nods seriously at his son. "Okay."

Ále nods as though he's satisfied.

Javi just isn't sure he himself is satisfied.

16

Gavin doesn't run from the room when Alejandro interrupts them, though it is a near thing. He heads for the kitchen, his heart hammering away in his chest and his hands trembling as he presses them against the back of a chair. He's suddenly ridiculously grateful that Charlie insisted he take some time off after the wedding to get settled in. He'd be absolutely useless if he needed to go into work like this.

What was he thinking, kissing Javier like that? He knows Javier is skittish about physical affection; he made that clear last night. Sex comes easily for Gavin, but the idea of having a partner to stand beside him means more to him than getting off. If he's going to make this work, he needs to remember that. The thought that he might have taken more than Javier meant to offer sits like a stone in his belly. Still, he can't ask in front of Alejandro, so if he's going to ask, it will have to wait until they're alone.

He'll explain where he was coming from, and let Javier do the same.

When his thoughts stray to what Javier and Alejandro are discussing, he can't pull his mind away. Once he's worried himself into a tizzy about how long they might talk, his focus shifts to the content of their discussion. Are they talking about Gavin kissing Javier? About why they were kissing in a space that belongs to Alejandro? Or maybe Javier gave Alejandro some expectations about what their relationship would be like, and Gavin tore those to shreds. What if neither of them trust him anymore?

Javier's coffee mug stares at him from the kitchen table. Gavin reaches for it, then hesitates. Javier had drunk maybe half of it before Alejandro dragged them both out of the kitchen. Gavin wavers for a moment, wanting to provide, but not wanting to overstep. A quick touch to the mug reveals that it's gone cold. Though he doesn't know Javier well yet, he knows how to read a cup of coffee.

He tops the mug off and adds a touch of cream, matching the initial shade as closely as he can. He holds it in his hands for a moment before setting it down on the counter beside him. Then he braces his palms against the granite. He'll give Javier a way out, give him a way to take care of Alejandro and let them both live their best lives. If they don't need Gavin beyond that, then they'll take the money from their marriage and make their way out of his life. It'll suck when it happens, but at least maybe Gavin will get to play house with them for a while.

Shaking off the encroaching melancholy, Gavin grabs his phone. He shoots off a text to his sister, checking in on her and his nieces.

We're all okay, Gavin. Gavin can hear the fond exasperation in her words. *Shane got us to the airport in one piece and our flight leaves in about an hour. We're all okay.*

I wanted to make sure, Gavin answers.

And I appreciate it. But shouldn't you be with your Recipient and kid?

Gavin swallows. *They're talking. I'm giving them some space.*

Oh, Gavin.

Gavin closes his eyes and sets his phone aside. Taking care of Alejandro is easier than he'd expected, honestly. The second he'd seen Alejandro at the zoo two days ago, he'd known beyond a shadow of a doubt that he'll do anything to protect this kid. He'd already loved him from Javier's stories, but seeing him and shaking his hand and letting him settle into Gavin's new life solidified that love, and this morning only intensified that affection. Alejandro insisted on doing his stretches before they started unpacking his remaining boxes of toys, and Gavin followed along as best he could with the help of Alejandro's instructions and a YouTube video they'd found. Making breakfast was a different kind of fun, this time with Gavin in charge instead of Alejandro. But watching Alejandro's delight in learning to whisk the eggs made up for any nerves he had around having Alejandro in the kitchen with him.

Although he knows he loves Alejandro, he'd expected Javier to want to stay in charge of his son's life. What he hadn't expected until this morning was to want to fill in wherever Javier would let him.

Okay, maybe he expected that part a little. He'd known how he felt about wanting to protect Alejandro even before they met. His feelings about kids aren't a secret to anyone. Haven't been since his first month at the firehouse. Still, it's different when the kid is one you'll have more than passing contact with. He'd known on some level that wanting to protect Alejandro like that would translate to wanting to help make decisions with and for him too. And, most of all, he'd known how badly he wants a family. He doesn't want to just play house with Javier, he wants to be his companion in all things, including parenting. But even though Javier does his best to let Alejandro learn and grow on his own, he's also protective of Alejandro, almost to a fault. Gavin isn't sure if or how he's supposed to grapple with that.

Gavin pushes away from the counter and moves to the sink. Their breakfast dishes are still stacked there; three plates, one mug, and a small plastic cup that Alejandro insisted on using instead of a full sized glass. It was a quiet insistence, one that Gavin didn't completely understand. Still, he honored Alejandro as best he could. He swallows thickly and reaches for his own mug first.

Gavin's never been a father, and yet Alejandro treats him like more of a parent than any of the other kids in his life. Gavin only gets to see his nieces a few days out of the year, and already there's a marked difference in the way they treat him as opposed to Alejandro. Evelyn will let him dress his nieces up and take them out to the park, but at the end of the day, they always go home to their mother.

Alejandro, on the other hand, sat right down in his playroom and insisted that Gavin do his exercises with him. Insisted that Gavin be part of his daily routine. And, at the end of the day, Alejandro is coming home with Gavin. There's a certainty and a comfort there that settles in Gavin's chest, a bloom of hope that he doesn't dare hold onto too tightly. Alejandro treats him more like a second father than an uncle. It's the kind of family he's wanted for years, and he can only hope that Alejandro's reactions persist.

"Gavin!"

Gavin jumps at the sound of Alejandro's voice behind him. He forces his expression to relax as he turns to Alejandro and Javier. He smiles at Alejandro, but still tosses Javier an uncertain expression. Is Alejandro upset? Is *Javier* upset? Gavin doesn't know how far he's overstepped, but he has to believe that Javier will tell him.

Javier just smiles and nods back at Gavin, sending relief spinning through Gavin's stomach. He looks back at Alejandro, his smile coming back in full force. "What's up, buddy?"

"I wanna play more Legos with you now."

Gavin chuckles. He picks up Javier's warmed mug of coffee and makes his way over to them.

Javier gives him a grateful, slightly exasperated smile. Then he takes a sip and his eyes light up. He glances at Gavin, but demurs before meeting his eyes directly. "Thank you."

Gavin's chest warms, and he smiles back at Javier. "You're welcome."

They follow Alejandro down the hall, and Gavin stays close to Javier, close enough to touch, though he tries to keep from crowding him. Although he wants to kiss Javier again, wants to insist that they're building a family together, this isn't the time. They both need to unpack where their relationship is going, and that's not something they can do in front of Javier's son.

The two of them pause at the doorway to the playroom as Alejandro steps in, his eyes searching the Lego boxes to find the one he wants. As they watch, Javier looks up at Gavin with more warmth than Gavin thinks he deserves. Gavin wonders how he got so damn lucky. Javier looks relieved, overjoyed, *hopeful* in a way that makes Gavin's stomach twist. Before he can say anything, though, Javier brushes his fingertips against Gavin's jaw and leans up to kiss the corner of his mouth. "Thank you."

Gavin's eyes flutter shut, but he can't lean into Javier's touch no matter how much he wants to. He wants to seal the deal and fully commit to being in this relationship, this *family* with Javier and Alejandro, but he can't do that if he's alone in the commitment. He can't quite make himself open his eyes again when Javier pulls back.

His heart has always been easily won. He knows that. He just thought he'd shielded it better than the last time someone important walked into his life. Evidently there is more work to do to keep from falling all-in when Javier isn't there with him.

Javier clears his throat and Gavin's eyes fly open in time to see Javier smile back at him. Then Javier turns to Alejandro. "So," he says, "what do you think, Ále? You want to do your homework in here with me once school starts back up again? Or do you want to use Gavin's study down the hall?"

"My study?" Gavin tilts his head, and quirks his lips in a smile. "Why would I need that space?" he asks gently. When Javier doesn't respond, he continues, "For now, at least, you're the one at home. I figured you could use it however you like. I did set it up as a study so that you could help Alejandro with his homework in there, but if you want something else, we can set it up differently."

"I..." Javier's voice is a croak. Gavin's brow furrows with worry, but he waits for Javier to say his piece. "Thank you."

Gavin grins back. "Of course." He keeps his voice as soft and warm as he can. "I want to give you everything you need. This is just the beginning."

Javier blinks hard a few times before turning back to Alejandro. "So, what do you think? Playroom or study for homework?"

"The study is definitely for homework," he says, giving them a toothy smile. Then he seems to remember something and goes quiet as his face falls.

Javier's on his knees instantly, his attention on his son. Gavin's heart shivers in his chest at the immediate shift in Javier's focus and attention. He swallows down the words he wants to say to them both and lets Javier speak instead. "What is it?"

"All my friends are still in Vegas," Alejandro says, his voice small. "I don't want to make new friends."

Javier glances at Gavin, his eyes wide and aching, before turning back to Alejandro. "I know, buddy. But we'll find you a really good school with really good kids, and I bet you'll make tons of friends in no time."

"You promise?"

"We promise." Gavin says, speaking up before Javier can. He may not be able to bring Alejandro's friends to Denver, but he can certainly set him up for success with where they send him to school. There are plenty of good options around town; he's already asked Kelsea for ideas. Even if none of those pan out, he knows he and Javier are going to do everything they can to make Alejandro's transition easier. "We'll do whatever it takes to make sure that you have a good experience there."

Gavin may not know what it's like to have the kind of family Javier and Alejandro have between the two of them, but he hopes they'll be able to build a family together, the three of them. There's still a distance between him and Javier, but maybe, someday, they'll be able to bridge it. He doesn't want to be on the outside looking in at the love that Javier and Alejandro share, and yet if that's all they need from him, he'll find a way to be okay with it. This family, whatever form it takes, it's still his, still theirs, and that's going to be enough to bring him through.

They're going to be fine.

17

Gavin spends most of the first week after Javier and Alejandro move in, unpacking alongside them. The days of early morning stretches, afternoon laundry and tidying, and late night video games on the couch don't feel as monotonous as they would without Alejandro's infectious smile and Javier's steadfast presence at his side. More than once, Gavin has to hold himself back from asking for more. He can't ask for more from them after they've already moved across the country for him, so he offers more of himself up instead. Every other day, though, they take the morning to get out of the house and explore some of what Denver has to offer.

On their fifth day together, Gavin finds himself standing with his hands in his pockets in the entryway to the Museum of Nature and Science, staring up at the fin whale that takes up the majority of the ceiling above him. He rocks back on his heels, trying not to let his hopes get too high. He enjoys this museum, and he desperately wants to impart that same love to Alejandro.

If that's largely because he wants to have an excuse to come more often, that's no one's business but his own.

To his delight, Alejandro is positively transfixed by all of it, lingering longer than Gavin would have expected on some of the displays. Alejandro stands so close to some of the permanent gemstone displays that Gavin's surprised he doesn't leave behind smudge marks from his nose, and he makes a friend in the space section, both of them giggling as they pilot a mock space shuttle together.

Gavin enjoys getting up close and personal with the displays with Alejandro, but he also keeps an eye on Javier, who, as usual, lingers behind them. Javier keeps his attention on Alejandro, gauging his enjoyment and engagement with the displays with a small, soft smile on his face. Periodically, he'll claim a need to sit down, encouraging Alejandro to join him on the bench he's found. Alejandro never fails to join him, though he also stands up periodically, leaning on his crutches and craning his neck to see more. Gavin admires the care and concern with which Javier treats his son, and it leaves warmth bubbling up in Gavin's chest. He repeatedly forces it down, reminding himself that that's not what this arrangement is about. He's here to do right by these two and give them everything that their previous life denied them. That's all.

When they stop for lunch, Alejandro leans a little against Gavin's side, lagging from the effort of all that they've done.

Javier smiles at the pair of them as they finish eating, his expression slightly strained as he focuses on Alejandro.

Gavin gleaned from Javier's profile and their few text conversations before the wedding that Alejandro was important to him, but knowing that and internalizing it are two different things. He's not sure he even fully understands it, yet, but he's closer than he was. That said, Gavin is sure he *doesn't* fully understand why Javier is attached to controlling as many aspects of Alejandro's life as possible, but he can certainly guess.

For as much research as Gavin did about raising a child with a disability—most of it done at work—he doesn't *understand* what it's like the way Javier does. Doesn't know if he'll ever understand it the way Javier does.

Not that he needs to, but, well, maybe he wants to.

"What do you say we head home for the day, hmm, Ále?" Javier asks.

Immediately Alejandro sits back up and shakes his head. "We haven't done anything on the third floor yet."

"Those exhibits will still be there later on." Javier's voice is placating, and Gavin isn't sure why Javier is making such a big deal out of this. Alejandro is having fun, and he seems ready to do more. "We can come back another day."

Alejandro pouts. "Please, Dad? Can't we stay a little longer?"

Gavin intervenes before Javier can say anything. "It's fine with me to stick around a little longer," he says. "What can it hurt?"

"Yeah, Dad. I'm fine. Let's keep going."

Javier stares at Gavin, looking like he's going to argue. His brow is wrinkled, and there's heat in his gaze that Gavin doesn't recognize. After a moment, Javier swallows thickly and nods. "Alright. If you're both sure."

Two hours later, after seeing the temporary exhibit about a set of well-preserved fossils found in a town near Colorado Springs, Gavin helps Javier maneuver an exhausted Alejandro into the back of the truck. "There," he says softly to Javier, "that wasn't so bad, was it?"

"He certainly enjoyed himself," Javier allows, but he doesn't say anything more. The wrinkle in his brow is back, and he's brushing the curls off of Alejandro's forehead with a far-off look before he heads for the driver's seat.

The drive back to the house is silent, presumably in deference to Alejandro's dozing. Gavin doesn't try to start the conversation, no matter how much he wants to understand why Javier wanted to leave early. He's still not sure if he misstepped, or why Javier hesitated so long, and he desperately wants to understand so he doesn't make the same mistake again. But Javier's driving, and Gavin doesn't want to distract him. His confusion can wait.

Javier takes custody of Alejandro to get him into the house, and Gavin keeps his distance, sensing that his presence would not be welcome right now. As Javier and Alejandro disappear into Alejandro's room, Gavin retreats to the guest room he's been staying in since they changed the sheets after that second night, leaving the main bedroom to Javier. Gavin unpacks some of his own things that he's been avoiding unpacking, taking the time to set the guest room up the way he'd intended to set up the main bedroom. Each item that finds its place is another opportunity to worry about how he overstepped this afternoon with Javier. He's always been too big for whatever room he's in, taking up more space and time than he really needs to. It's not the first time he's upset a partner by stepping in where he wasn't wanted. But it was instinct to defend Alejandro, to lift up his voice the way his own was always quieted in his parents' house. He's not sure he knows how to avoid advocating for Alejandro's needs and desires. Then again, Javier seems to be an attentive father, so maybe there was a reason he'd been insisting that they leave. More of a reason than Gavin can think of, at least. There's something Gavin is missing, but if he can just explain his own line of thinking, maybe Javier will be able to forgive him.

When it starts to get late and Gavin is tired of thinking himself in circles, he walks down the hall and raps on the doorframe to Alejandro's bedroom.

"Dinner?" he asks. Javier turns to look at him from amidst the organized chaos of clothes around him. Most are folded, though there's a section by the window that has been left for last. Alejandro's eyes are drooping, and as Gavin watches, he slowly folds a t-shirt and adds it to a pile to his left.

"Sure," Javier says. "Whatever's easy."

Gavin worries his bottom lip between his teeth at the easy dismissal as he turns away. After Gavin cools off, he definitely needs to talk to Javier about this afternoon. Maybe after dinner, or after Alejandro goes to bed for the night.

An hour later, when the pasta bake comes out of the oven and the rolls and salad are ready, Javier rouses Alejandro from the corner of the room he's dozing in. He helps Alejandro to his feet and out to the dining room, one hand hovering behind his back the whole way. Alejandro slouches in his chair and glares at his plate throughout dinner, moving his food around without really eating anything until Javier gently encourages him to actually eat.

"I already told you I'm not hungry," Alejandro says, his hands moving jerkily as he gesticulates. Gavin's eyes widen; up until now, Alejandro has been soft-spoken and deferential. He glances at Javier, ready to take his cues from him this time.

"Ále…"

"No," Alejandro snaps, his movements growing wilder and unsteadier. "I said *no*." With a twitch of his hand, Alejandro knocks over his glass, spilling apple juice all over the table.

Gavin stares at the spilled drink, his pulse hammering in his neck. He needs to do something, grab a towel, tell Alejandro that it's okay, but he's frozen in his spot. After this afternoon, he needs Javier to do something first. He needs Javier to give him permission to move. Then Alejandro shrieks and rears back from the table as tears start to fall on his cheeks.

Javier is out of his seat immediately, crouching down beside Alejandro. He doesn't shush Alejandro, instead running soothing hands along Alejandro's arms. "It's okay, buddy," Javier says softly. "It's okay. It was an accident and we can clean it up. I'm right here, mijo."

Despite the adrenaline still flooding Gavin's system, he marvels at the easy way Javier aligns himself with his son and makes the problem theirs instead of just Alejandro's. There was no hesitation in his movements, no moment of thinking to chastise Alejandro instead of help. His stomach twists with some bizarre amalgamation of gratitude that Alejandro has someone like Javier and pity that he himself never did.

Alejandro pitches forward into his dad's arms. "I didn't—I don't—Dad, I—"

"I know, buddy." Javier runs his hand through Alejandro's hair. "I know, you're tired. It's okay. We'll just clean this up and then you can eat a little bit more and then we can go to bed, okay?"

"Daddy, I—I didn't *mean to,* I—I'm *sorry.*"

"Ále..."

"Don't worry about it," Gavin interjects, desperate to do something to help.

Alejandro looks up at him with wet eyes.

"I can clean it up in no time."

"No." Javier's voice is strict and sharp and Gavin doesn't know how to respond. "We've got this."

Gavin startles, taken aback by the ferocity in Javier's voice. He's misstepped again, and this time he has even less of an idea of what he did wrong. He was only trying to mirror what Javier did. Is he not supposed to back his Recipient up?

With a swallow, Gavin tries again. "Javier?"

"I said we've *got* this."

"Right." Gavin straightens. "Okay. I'll just... let you handle this."

Javier's eyes dart from Gavin to Alejandro and back again. For a moment, he softens, and Gavin thinks he might be about to be let in. Then the expression fades and Javier is back to being the sharp, angry man he'd been moments ago. He nods jerkily and turns back to Alejandro.

Gavin hesitates for a moment longer before grabbing his plate and retreating to the kitchen. He listens with half an ear as Javier speaks to Alejandro in low tones, nursing his hurt. He knows Javier is Alejandro's father, and that he'll get the final say every time. That's his right. But Gavin didn't think it would be too far outside his boundaries to offer assistance. He was just trying to make sure Alejandro knew Gavin was on his side, like Javier. Is that not his place? But *surely* they're supposed to be a team just as much as they're a family. Unless they're not a family in Javier's eyes.

The thought sinks heavy in his gut and he blinks back the rising desire to cry. He's the one that isn't playing by Javier's rules; he doesn't get to cry. Not until they've talked and Gavin fully understands what he did wrong, and why Alejandro acted like that.

He hasn't seen Alejandro act that way before. It's unsettling, watching the usually mild-mannered boy shift into a tantrum that felt unbecoming of his age. This must be what Javier meant when he said sometimes things with Alejandro were hard. Maybe the reason living with Javier's parents was so hard for him was because his parents didn't know how to respond when these things happened either. Maybe they froze the way he did, or, worse, maybe they got angry at Alejandro. Gavin shivers at the thought. Alejandro doesn't deserve that, and he deserves better than whatever happened with Gavin tonight. Gavin needs to do better, and that starts with talking to Javier about what he did wrong as soon as Javier will talk to him. If he's the reason Alejandro had this reaction, he needs to do better.

That's when Gavin finally understands why Javier tried to insist that they leave the museum early. Why he'd repeatedly insisted that Alejandro sit beside him. Gavin drops his fork onto his plate and plants his elbows on the table so he can bury his head in his hands. Gavin knows Alejandro needs his crutches and his other supports, but he hasn't fully connected to the why of it all until just now. Alejandro has needs that are different from an able-bodied kid—Javier made that clear from the start—and that means needing more support and more rest than an able-bodied kid. And Gavin pushed him beyond his limits. Limits that Javier knows. No wonder Javier was so upset with him.

Alejandro walks into the kitchen to grab a towel and doesn't so much as look at Gavin before he's walking back out.

With a tight throat, Gavin nibbles at his dinner. The knowledge that he got too close in his attempts to help stings more than Gavin wants to admit. It stings, but he knows it wasn't his place to step in, either. They're playing by Javier's rules when it comes to Alejandro, and Gavin knows he needs to accept that if this is going to work. If he wants to keep this family, even just for a while, he needs to follow Javier's lead in all things, but most especially with Alejandro.

A minute later, Javier walks in and drops the wet towel in the sink. Gavin doesn't grab him, doesn't get in his way, but he does call out to him before he can leave the kitchen. "I'm sorry," he says. "I didn't mean to..." But, no, that's not right. "I know I'm still learning how to help you and Alejandro. I should have followed your lead today. I'll do better next time."

Javier's head jerks in what might be a nod or might be an aborted turn toward Gavin.

Gavin holds his breath and waits for the verdict.

"Thank you," Javier says softly. "I appreciate that."

Gavin winces. It's not the forgiveness he wants, but it's the forgiveness he deserves. It's a reminder that Javier is in charge here, in every way that matters. "I know you're the one that knows him best," Gavin adds. "And if there are things that I'm doing wrong, I want to know that. I want you to correct me in front of Alejandro if you need to. You're not—" *alone,* he doesn't say.

And here is the moment of truth, the moment that could make or break this apology. He changes course. "I am in your corner because I want to be in your corner, but you get to decide what that means, always. Okay?"

It takes a moment, but eventually Javier's shoulders lower from where they were raised around his ears. He looks over his shoulder at Gavin and says, "Okay."

Although Gavin may still be learning to help with the specifics of Alejandro's disability, he can certainly fund Javier doing so instead, and he can follow Javier's lead into the depths if need be. They're in this together, no matter what.

Javier hesitates, then says, "You want to finish eating dinner with us?"

Gavin melts at the offer, one he hadn't expected. "Is that okay?"

Javier hesitates, clearly weighing his options. Then he nods. "Yeah, Ále would... *We* would like that."

Gavin nods and grabs his plate to head back into the dining room. He settles slowly down into his seat, tossing a glance at Alejandro, who's staring down into his plate. Gavin switches his gaze to Javier and waits for him to make the first move.

"So, Ále," Javier asks, eyes on Alejandro as he spears a bite of salad. "What was your favorite part of the museum today?"

Alejandro glances at Gavin, who, with a matching glance at Javier, smiles back at him. "I'd like to hear too."

Alejandro immediately brightens and regales them with the story of his friend from the space exhibit, which was expected. His admission that the gemstone exhibit was a close second surprises Gavin, and he makes a mental note to ask Javier if he can get Alejandro some books about gemstones. He'll need to ask what the right level would be for him, but it would be nice to be able to do something concrete for Alejandro, even if it's just to get him a book or two.

After that, Javier takes Alejandro to put him down for bed while Gavin cleans up from dinner.

When Javier finds him there doing the last of the dishes, he huffs. "You know I can do that," he says.

"I wanted to help."

"You already made dinner. And you help in more ways than you know."

"Yeah?" Gavin tosses Javier a hopeful glance.

Javier huffs and smiles up at Gavin. "Yeah. You really do. And things like today will get easier. They did for me."

"So you're telling me to be patient?"

"I'm telling you to be patient."

Gavin sighs dramatically. "Well, if you say so."

Javier's smile widens. "I do."

18

Javi stares out the passenger side window at the school. It's the last of the three they're visiting today after three yesterday, and has the best ratings of all the places Javi has researched. It's past the typical enrollment period, but Gavin pulled some strings to at least get them an interview. It's a hell of a counterpoint to the way his parents would have handled the situation. They would have leapt at the chance to tell Javi where to go and how to help Ále best, but they wouldn't have taken either Ále or Javi's opinions into account. Gavin, on the other hand, is letting Javi make all the decisions, and it leaves Javi feeling wrong-footed and disorganized. But he can't squander this chance for Alejandro just because he isn't used to being allowed to make these decisions. This place may have the best ratings and the best reviews, but the price tag alone isn't enough to ensure that it will be a good fit for Ále.

Despite the last two interviews going fine and the facilities looking fine, this one feels like it has the most riding on it. If his research is accurate, it could be the best fit of all of them. Just because Javi's a little uncomfortable being offered control over the decision doesn't mean he can fumble at this point in their path. Not when his son's happiness is at stake.

His son, who's in the backseat playing on Javi's phone, perfectly content and more than a little excited about the prospect of helping to choose his school. The first school they'd gone to yesterday recommended bringing Åle along, and it went so well that they'd brought him along to the other interviews as well. Åle leapt at the opportunity to do something as a family other than go to museums and the like. Not that he hasn't enjoyed them all, but he was ready for something else.

"Penny for your thoughts?" Gavin asks.

Javi turns to Gavin, who's dressed just as nicely as Javi himself, both in suits that Gavin insisted on getting and having tailored for them for these meetings. He looks even hotter than usual, or at least, a different kind of hot than Javi is used to around the house where it's all fitted t-shirts and basketball shorts or jeans. He looks nice like this, and it's almost enough to distract Javi from his train of thought.

Almost.

"I'm just not sure this is the best move for Åle." Javi tugs at the lapel of his suit. "Just because this place has the price tag it does, that doesn't mean that it will be the right place for him."

Gavin's brow furrows. "I thought you said it has the best ratings for accessibility and IEP support."

Javi blinks, surprised that Gavin remembers that much. "It does. But if I have to dress up like this," he tugs at his lapel again, "to get him in, then maybe it isn't the right kind of place."

"Because?"

"Because this isn't who I am. And it isn't who Åle is either. And it doesn't mean that they have the skills and tools to give him what he needs."

Gavin turns in his seat so that his body is facing Javi. "You did the research. You filtered out places that would be no good and found the ones that you thought would be best. Now it's a matter of deciding if any of these places is what Alejandro needs."

Javi huffs and looks away.

"Or you could homeschool him."

That startles Javi into looking back at Gavin. "What?"

"You could homeschool him if you prefer." Gavin says with a shrug. "I imagine there are programs to support parents with that, and you do know his needs better than anyone."

It's the out that Javi hadn't realized he was looking for. Permission to hold Ále close to home and protect him from anything and everything that might come his way. Permission to keep him safe the only way Javi knows how: by not letting anything bad happen to him.

"I hadn't thought of that," Javi murmurs.

Gavin tilts his head, considering. "Okay." His voice is soft and understanding. "What do you want to do?"

It's a tempting thought. To turn around and just go back to the house. But Javi knows Ále needs friends his age more than Javi needs to keep him safe. So he turns to the backseat and holds a hand out to Ále. "Okay, mijo, we're here. Phone time is over."

Ále barely grumbles as he hands Javi his phone back. He's been more excited than Gavin and Javi combined about finding a school for him, and it's made him even more agreeable than usual.

Gavin is smiling at him when Javier turns back, pocketing his phone.

"What?" Javi asks.

"I'm just so grateful that you're letting me join you in this decision."

"Why wouldn't I?"

Gavin shrugs. "Let's go rock this place and get your son into the best school this side of town."

The principal's secretary greets them in the main office, and they only wait a few minutes before Principal Collins steps out of her office to take them on the tour. She moves to shake Gavin's hand first, but he steps back, avoiding her touch.

"Javier is Alejandro's father. I'm just here for moral support."

Javi tries to maintain his cool as he shakes the principal's hand. "It's nice to meet you."

"And you," she replies. "And this must be Alejandro."

Ále grins up at her, balances carefully on his crutches, and holds his hand out, too.

She shakes it with a smile before turning to look back at Javi. "Your son is welcome to join us on the tour, but he may have more fun joining our summer STEM group that's meeting right now. It might be a good way for him to get to know a few students before the year starts.

"You have summer programs?" Javi asks. "How extensive are they?"

"We have morning, afternoon, and all-day options throughout most of the summer. The only exception is the week before school starts, because our teachers are here getting ready for the new year."

Javier hums. Summer options aren't necessarily a requirement, but he knows how important it is to avoid summer learning loss. He'd never been able to offer Ále much in the summer. Just the library's reading program and whatever his school in Vegas was offering, but those programs weren't very robust. "I'd love to hear more about your summer options after the tour."

Collins nods. "And Alejandro?"

"I'd prefer he stay with us for now."

Collins nods again. "Of course." Then she sets off on the tour, Javi, Ále, and Gavin in tow.

The tour is thorough. When they walk past the STEM summer group, Ále lights up, and Javi relents, letting him join the group instead of following him and Gavin on the tour. He hovers for a minute before letting himself walk away, but he knows at some point he needs to let go and let Ále fly. He doesn't have to let go completely today, but maybe he can loosen his grip a little.

From what Principal Collins is telling them, Javi can tell that this really will be a good fit for Alejandro. They have a speech-language pathologist that comes by once a week and their teachers are all well trained in what the principal calls SEL—social-emotional learning, she explains at Gavin's confused expression—and how to encourage healthy boundaries and displays of emotion in their students.

Javi aches at each assertion, at the promises that his sweet little boy doesn't have to be molded into some arbitrary image of manliness. That he's found a world safe enough and warm enough to let Alejandro grow up to be the best version of himself, with less of the dark, tamped down places that Javi carries with him.

It's perfect.

He turns to Gavin, ready to say as much, when the principal drops the bomb.

"Of course, we'll want to meet with Alejandro's mother to complete the family interview process."

Cold grips Javi's stomach. "I'm sorry?"

"His mother. I assume she's your Recipient, Mr. Pérez? We want to make sure that the whole family is on board with this transition."

"Oh, his, uh." Javi swallows, trying to get his heart out of his throat. "His mother isn't really in the picture when it comes to decisions like these. We're separated."

Principal Collins purses her lips. Her eyes dart over to Gavin, and Javi can see her connecting dots that aren't there. His shoulders hunch, but he doesn't let himself say anything until he has his wits about him.

Before he can, though, Gavin's arm wraps around his shoulder. "He has full custody. Alejandro's mother won't be an issue."

"Mmhmm," Principal Collins says, her eyes skeptical as she looks Gavin up and down. "Tell me again who you are?"

"Oh, didn't I introduce myself?" Gavin is smiling a shark's smile as he reaches out to offer her a hand. "Gavin Carmichael. I'm Javier's Provider."

Gavin's proclamation doesn't seem to clear up the concern in Principal Collins' face. "I see. Well, we tend to prefer students that come from households where both biological parents are involved, rather than those with separated parents. Stability is important in a child's home life. I'm sure you can see where I'm coming from."

"Of course." Gavin's smile goes even sharper. "That being said, if you think our family isn't a good fit, we'd be happy to take Alejandro elsewhere. Though, I must say, I'd hate to see word get around that you're discriminating against a blended family, just because the Recipient father chose not to marry his son's mother."

Principal Collins' eyes go wide. It's an underhanded tactic and it makes Javi feel a little dirty. Before he can say anything to Gavin, though, she's apologizing profusely, to Gavin instead of Javi, Javi notices dimly, and clearly trying to backtrack that they're a family-oriented school and they just wanted to make sure that all of Alejandro's parents were on board, but of course they'd be happy to have him here if Gavin is there to provide a stable home life.

The swift change in her attitude leaves a bad taste in his mouth, but she isn't talking to him anymore, she's talking to Gavin. He should have expected it. Even though it's one of the few times anyone really treated him like a Recipient since he married Gavin, Javi knows how this goes. He's sure it doesn't hurt that Gavin's white and Javier isn't, but even without that, in his experience, Recipients have always gotten a bad rap.

Shame curls around his stomach, leaving him acutely aware of how little power he has now. He knows there's nothing really wrong with that, knows he and Casey separated for a reason, even though sometimes he wonders if it would have been easier if they'd just stuck it out together. He knows there's plenty of power in being a Recipient, even if some people don't remember that. It just sucks to see that prejudice played out so overtly in front of him.

Except then Gavin's hand tightens on his shoulder. "I'm not the one you should be apologizing to, Principal Collins. Alejandro's father is the one that matters here." Gavin's hand slides from Javi's shoulder to his low back, and he presses against it gently. Javi straightens automatically. He shouldn't be surprised that Gavin is letting him take control again. He's gotten enough insight into how Gavin feels about Åle and who gets to make decisions for him. And yet, it still startles him a little.

Javi settles into his power again. The power that Gavin gave him, deferring to him as Åle's father. "Thank you for your time, Principal Collins. I am impressed with your facilities. I would, however, like to meet with the teacher that would be over Åle's homeroom class if we enroll him. I want to make sure that they don't have a problem with him having separated parents."

Principal Collins grimaces. "I do apologize, Mr. Carmichael," she says.

"Pérez," Gavin says, cutting across the conversation. "He didn't take my name."

That startles Javi out of his sense of deference to the principal. He starts to turn toward Gavin, but Gavin squeezes his hip in warning. "No," he says, trying not to sound breathless. And then, in a bolt of inspiration, "I wanted to keep the same last name as my son."

Gavin's fingers flex against his hip but he doesn't say anything.

"I see," Principal Collins says. She looks more and more intrigued by them by the moment, and Javi feels some of the shame roll off his shoulders. Even if he hates that they only got an in with the principal because he's a Recipient with his Provider instead of a single father with a friend, if this place really is as wonderful as it seems, as wonderful as Principal Collins made it seem, then maybe he can put up with a bad first impression of the principal. "I can certainly understand that."

"His teacher?" Gavin prompts after a too-long silence.

Principal Collins takes them to meet his teacher, a sweet, kind woman that has been in education for twelve years, all of them in elementary and most with the third and fourth grades. Her understanding of curriculum brings a smile to Gavin's face, and her kindness settles the fear in Javi's stomach. He can handle Ále only learning so much in school, but he can't handle anything bad happening to his son.

At the end of the conversation, Javi holds a hand out to the teacher to shake. Gavin doesn't, his eyes still keen on the principal, but Javi's happy to smooth things over if it will be what's best for Ále. He shakes the principal's hand as well and promises to be in touch with the enrollment paperwork in order to start the official application process. After confirming that she'll need a few other forms as well and collecting them from the main office, the tension in his body leaks, leaving him calmer and more relaxed than he's been since the conversation around Ále's schooling began.

Gavin, on the other hand, is a study in hard lines and sharp angles as they pick up Ále from the STEM camp before he ushers Javi and Ále to the door. He keeps one hand on Javi the whole time, either on his shoulder or at the small of his back or, at one point, just threading their fingers together. It's the most upset Javi has ever seen him, but he can't put his finger on why. He doesn't want Ále present if they're going to have a blowout fight over the school, but he also isn't certain that that's what he's upset about. He's been perfectly content to defer to Javi on these decisions, and Javi doesn't think that's changed. The school really is as good as it looked online, which he hadn't expected. And yet, his joy is overshadowed by whatever is going on in Gavin's head. He just hopes whatever it is doesn't break them.

19

Gavin is grateful that Javier waits until they make it all the way home before he asks. It isn't until Alejandro is asleep and Gavin is settled at the kitchen table with his phone that he brings it up.

"You were upset today, at that last interview," Javier says softly. "What's wrong?"

"Nothing," Gavin says, his eyes still on his phone.

"Gavin. Come on."

Gavin clenches his fist around his phone. He hesitates, then sets it aside. "It's that principal. She was so disrespectful to you. The things she said…" He cuts himself off, huffing sharply. "No one should talk to my Recipient that way."

Javier pauses for a moment before he sits down across from Gavin and takes his hand. "She didn't know. You didn't really introduce yourself at first; you told her you were just there for moral support. When she found out that you're my Provider, she obviously would defer to you."

"But I *was* just there for moral support," Gavin says before Javier even finishes. He's your son, you get to make the decisions."

"I know that," Javier says. "But you're the *Provider*. To the rest of the world, you're the decision maker."

Gavin purses his lips. "Well, the rest of the world is wrong," he mutters. "The whole thing is bullshit."

Javier's hand twitches in Gavin's hand. "The Provider-Recipient marriage structure?"

"Yes." Gavin knows plenty of Partnered couples that work out just fine, and just as many Provider-Recipient couples that defy societal norms. He hates that Javier seems to buy into it so deeply that he doesn't mind being treated like a second-class citizen by anyone over the age of fifty.

"Oh." Javier withdraws his hand.

Gavin glances at him, needing only a moment to understand his misstep. He reaches out and tangles his fingers with Javier's again. "I'm grateful it led me to you," he says, tripping over the words. "You and Alejandro. You've made my life so much better since we got married. I wouldn't trade it for anything. I just wish people could see you the way that I do. I wish they could see all that you do and all that you bring to the table instead of what they think you lack."

Javier stares at Gavin and whispers, "You mean that?"

Gavin pulls Javier's hand to his lips. He kisses his knuckles gently. "More than anything."

Javier smiles, something fond and amused in his expression. "Okay. But I'm still seriously considering that school."

"I know you are." Gavin sighs. "I won't have to make nice with the principal or anything, will I?"

Javier laughs. "Don't worry, I'll handle all the PTA meetings and parent-teacher conferences."

Gavin's fingers tighten around Javier's, and for a second he can't breathe. That isn't at all what he'd meant; he wants to be involved, he just doesn't know how yet. But if Javier needs to keep him separate, then he'll stay separate. He'll be the Provider

Javier wants instead of the one he wants to be for Javier. "Good," he says softly. "That's what I want to hear."

A small wrinkle appears in Javier's brow, and he searches Gavin's face for something Gavin hopes he won't find. Then he opens his mouth to say something, only to startle as though just remembering something. "Oh, but that reminds me. The principal was kind of right. I need to call Casey soon."

"Who?" Gavin blinks at the non-sequitur.

"Ále's mother. I..." He pauses, then gives Gavin a sheepish grin. "With getting settled here and everything, I haven't reached out to her yet."

Gavin pulls his lips between his teeth, not sure if he's holding off a laugh or a shout. Once he's sure neither will escape his lips, he says, "Why not call her tonight?"

Javier glances at his phone. "I texted her to check in and she hasn't gotten back to me, which means she's on site and will be out of touch until she gets back. That's in her hands, now."

"On site?" Gavin asks.

"Yeah. She's working on her environmental engineering degree and will go on-site for some of her research."

"Huh." Gavin sits back, the question of why Javier isn't with her on the tip of his tongue.

Javier must see right through him, because he rolls his eyes. "We weren't a good match. She's always had bigger dreams than me. This—Ále, a home, a family—that's all I've ever wanted. She... needed something more. Something that I couldn't give her."

Gavin watches Javier hunch further and further in on himself the longer he speaks. There's shame there, and maybe even some guilt, but that doesn't mean that Gavin is going to let him wallow in it.

Instead, he reaches out and takes Javier's hand in his. "Well, her loss is my gain. I get you *and* Alejandro, and I can't say I would ever want for anything more."

Javier's breath catches, and a moment later he's standing up and leaning across the table to kiss Gavin. "Thank you," he whispers against Gavin's lips. "I…" He settles back into his chair and stares at Gavin with starry eyes. "Thank you."

"For accepting you?" Gavin asks with a frown. "You never have to thank me for that."

But Javier shakes his head. "You can call it what it is, Gavin. It may not be love yet, but you care about me, just the same as I care about you."

It's Gavin's turn to gasp, Javier's words landing harder than he probably intended them to. "Javier…" Gavin swallows, then looks away. "You, Alejandro, and this… this family, you are everything I want. I will do whatever it takes to keep the two of you safe and healthy and happy, okay?"

Javier stares at him, as though trying to parse a hidden meaning from the words. Then he gets to his feet and walks around the table. He bends down and rests his forehead against Gavin's.

Somehow, it's more intimate than any of the few times they've kissed.

"I know you will," Javier whispers. He leans forward and kisses Gavin's lips gently. "I know you will." Javier reaches out and tangles his fingers in Gavin's lifting them to his mouth. "And someday I'm going to be able to take care of you the way you are working to take care of us."

Gavin's heart stills in his chest. "You mean that?"

Javier bites his lip and nods slowly. "I don't know when, but I will. Someday."

Gavin leans up and kisses Javier with all the affection in his chest. "Take all the time you need."

After three days of his Recipient's deliberation, Gavin ends up at the kitchen table across from Javier, discussing Alejandro's school. He bites his tongue when Javier officially decides to enroll Alejandro in the final school they'd visited, The Marion School. He understands that Alejandro had fun with the STEM group he'd gotten to join, and, though he doesn't know much about accessible facilities yet, what few accommodations he saw seemed up to snuff. He just can't get over the way the principal treated Javier.

"All the research I've done points to it being the best of the six," Javier says from across the kitchen table. "They've got the best rating for students with disabilities, and his teacher seems like the best of the lot."

Javier pauses, his eyes on Gavin. His expression is concerned, though Gavin can't pinpoint why it would be.

So he asks.

"It sounds like you've made a decision, then?"

Javier blinks hard a few times. "Is that… I mean, I know you weren't too keen on the principal. Is that okay with you?"

"It's your decision," Gavin says, looking down at the mug of coffee Javier plied him with for this conversation. The admission aches in his throat. He wants to be involved in this decision, but knows he doesn't get to have any say in Alejandro's life. He's not Alejandro's father. He knows this, but the stark reminder hurts. "He's your son."

Javier makes a sound, but when Gavin looks up at him, his expression settles into something neutral. "But you don't want to send him there."

"I—" Gavin cuts himself off. He wants everyone in Alejandro's life to know how hard Javier worked to give him a good life. How much Javier gave up and did to keep Alejandro safe and healthy and happy. He doesn't want Alejandro to be at the mercy of someone that looks down on his father.

Javier raises an eyebrow, cutting Gavin's white lie off at the pass.

Gavin blows out a sharp breath. Abandoning his coffee, Gavin pushes away from the table, away from this conversation, though he knows he can't escape it. Desperate for something to do with his hands, he opens the dishwasher and starts unloading it.

It takes a moment before Gavin finds his words again. "Look, you're absolutely right that I am not a fan of that principal. She was sharp with you and she doesn't know how our—" Gavin bites off the word *family* when it wants to slip past his lips, knowing he can only get away with that for so long. "How our arrangement works. Alejandro is your son, and that isn't going to change. You get to make these decisions, Javier, not me."

"It's your money," Javier takes a moment before responding. Then he gets up and places one hand over Gavin's right, stilling his motions. "That matters."

Gavin is shaking his head before Javier finishes speaking. "This was the deal. I needed to get married to access my inheritance, and you helped me get that. Now that money is yours, too. It isn't just mine anymore."

"You really mean that."

It's hard not to take offense at the fact that Javier didn't believe Gavin the first time. Javier was reluctant to accept the unconventionality Gavin wants in their relationship from day one. "I really mean that."

Silence reigns for a moment. Then Javier nods. "Okay. I can live with that."

The phrasing gets under Gavin's skin, as though Javier is dismissing the role he played in getting Gavin access to his inheritance. "What's that supposed to mean?" he asks.

Javier gives him one of his rare smiles, and Gavin has to tighten his grip on the mug in his hands to hold back the desire to lean in and kiss him. It's a familiar impulse, but one he's mostly kept in check so far. "It means that I think I can start actually spending your money."

Gavin frowns. "What have you been doing so far on your grocery runs and stuff?"

"Using the card attached to the account you set up for me specifically. I get it now," Javier says when Gavin opens his mouth to protest, "I just didn't at first. The other one you gave me a card for is for shared funds, things we both are responsible for. I'm just finally starting to accept that Ále is included in that category."

Unable to find the words to tell Javier that their little family of three is what he's wanted for years, Gavin smiles and nods. "Yeah," he says softly. "Alejandro is definitely included in what I want to help you take care of."

Those words get Gavin another one of those gentle smiles. Javier reaches along the counter and places a hand on Gavin's wrist. "Thank you."

Frustration at Javier's decision wars with gratitude in Gavin's stomach. "You're welcome." Then, thinking he might as well try, he adds, "But does that mean I can talk you out of sending Alejandro to school with that devil woman?"

Javier tilts his head. "Would it really bother you that much?"

There's something different in Javier's tone that Gavin can't figure out, but he forges ahead regardless. "I mean, does it matter?"

"It does," Javier insists softly. "If Alejandro is a shared responsibility, then this is part of that. You get to start helping me make the decisions."

"Oh." Gavin exhales softly. He pauses for a moment before asking, "You really think it's the best place?"

"It's definitely the most accessible," Javier says with a nod. "And I like the information they gave us about the social learning that they do, too." He squeezes Gavin's wrist. "I really think it could be good for him."

Gavin stares at him for a long moment, then exhales in a huff. "Alright. If you're sure."

Javier turns away to grab a stack of papers off the kitchen

table and hold them out to Gavin. "They just need your signature."

"My signature?"

Javier's expression turns indulgent. "You're the Provider, remember?"

Gavin bites his tongue on the words Javier won't want to hear. Words that won't matter in this situation. He just takes the papers and turns away to grab a pen.

Javier grabs his elbow before he can go too far and presses a kiss to Gavin's cheek. "Thank you."

"You don't have to thank me."

"Hmm," Javier murmurs, "and yet I am anyway."

So saying, Javier slips out of the kitchen and down the hall toward the main bedroom, leaving a stunned, hopeful Gavin in his wake.

20

Gavin's first day at work after Javier chooses a school for Alejandro goes relatively smoothly, other than the two minor medical calls and a fender bender late on shift that doesn't even require them to get into their turnouts. There's plenty of downtime that leaves Gavin the time to sort out inventory both in the station and in the trucks after the day from hell that C shift had the day before. It also leaves time to mess around and bond with his team, both at the pool table in the rec room, and in the gym. Although Gavin would usually love that time, today it gives him too much space to think about all sides of his life and the ways he could, and should, be better. Despite the excess of downtime, two interesting things of note happen before dinner.

One is Kelsea checking in with him about the school Javier chose. He whines to her just enough to make it clear that, while he has opinions, he hadn't complained about his issues to Javier. She'd been appropriately supportive.

The second is a call from his grandparents' lawyer about the funds from his trust fund being released.

That leads to one long and furtive phone call with Evelyn that includes offering to buy a plane ticket for her and the girls immediately, before the two of them decide to wait until he's gotten a place set up for them here, and one equally long but less furtive phone call to his realtor to start looking for said place to get set up.

It's a relief to know that things are moving on that front, even if that relief is tempered by some disappointment about the way his relationship with Javier keeps changing. Not that he wants to push Javier, not at all. He just wants to feel more like they're a family than they do right now.

Things with Javier are still settling into a new normal. It's not like Gavin knows Javier completely after just three weeks of living together, but those first ten days when he was off work taught him a lot. Being away from Javier and Alejandro is hard on him, even though it's only about once every three days. Gavin always enjoyed the one-on, two-off schedule, even enjoyed picking up extra shifts before he got married, because it keeps him busy. But missing out on Alejandro's bedtime a third of the time is starting to wear on him.

Maybe he can talk to Javier before the next time he has to go into work and ask if he can video call at bedtime when he's at work, just so he can see them both. It might be too much, but he won't know if he doesn't ask.

He runs his hands through his hair for what feels like the hundredth time since he came in today. He's hiding out in the bunk room even though it's only just past dinner time and nowhere near the time he usually goes to sleep. He doesn't know how to be among his friends right now, especially when Charlie keeps giving him this knowing look any time he starts to get too down.

Gavin isn't ready for a deep talk about this burgeoning relationship, and Charlie will try to draw the truth out of him. It'll be caring and supportive and come from a place of concern, but it'll just needle against Gavin's ribs to have Charlie looking at him with something a little too close to pity.

So Gavin hides, and he ruminates, and he tries to stay as alert as possible even as his mind spirals out of control.

It's not even like his anxiety got worse after Javier moved in. On the contrary, it got better. Javier's a constant, an anchor, a *home* that Gavin started to believe would never come to him. Sure, he's only thirty, and he knows he has a whole life ahead of him, but part of him finally feels like he's stepping into his own. Getting married and getting Evelyn away from Shane both felt like the cherries on top of the life he's built.

But marriage is different from dating, and for all that he'd known that, too, it's another one of those things that he thought he understood but didn't actually understand. The last thing he wants is for Charlie to come in here and tell him all about what marriage is for him and Diana, what marriage could be for Gavin if he tried.

Gavin flops back on the bed, careful to fall at a diagonal so he doesn't fall all the way off. He covers his face with his hands and breathes as steadily as he can, grounding himself. He's trying. He's trying so damn hard. He wants to get to that magical place that Charlie has with Diana, and that Kelsea has with Janie. He'd never admit it aloud, but he's always been a bit of a romantic. Having his every move and offer of support rejected is not his idea of a good time. Not in the least. He'd love to be allowed to fall in love with Javier the way he thought he could on their wedding night, but he's not entirely sure that they're ever going to get there. Which is okay, of course. This is a business arrangement first. He knows that.

Then there's Alejandro. He's been more open to accepting Gavin's help than his father, but that isn't as much of a comfort as Gavin wishes it was. He wants to be able to support Alejandro, be a father like Javier is. He wants to matter to Alejandro the way Javier does, even if he'll never mean as much. But he doesn't have that, and he doesn't think Javier will ever let him have that.

The thing is, he gets it. He'd be protective of his kid in this situation, too. Hell, he's already protective of Alejandro, and he's known him barely a month. But that doesn't mean he likes it.

Tyler finds him still in the bunk room a solid hour after dinner, still flopped on his back with one arm thrown over his face and his mind spiraling out of control. Tyler sits beside him. He doesn't say anything at first, clearly waiting for Gavin to break the silence. When he doesn't, Tyler sighs, lies down next to him, and cuffs his shoulder gently.

"You're gonna figure it out."

Gavin hums, but doesn't reply. It's not the first time Gavin has talked to Tyler about Javier, but usually it's idle complaints over text, or whispered hopes in the bunk room in the middle of the night. He's been patient with Gavin's fears and uncertainties, even though Gavin knows Tyler still isn't sold on Javier.

Tyler shakes him. "You are. You may be an idiot, but you're a lovable idiot, and if Javier doesn't know that yet, he'll figure it out soon. I can't think of a single person that's known you for more than a month that you haven't won over."

"What about Diana?"

"She was worried you'd give her husband a heart attack with all the stunts you used to pull," Tyler says with a shrug. He props himself up and taps Gavin's elbow until Gavin moves his arm and looks at him directly. "Once you got your head out of your ass and learned how to be part of a team, she was ready to love you just like the rest of us."

"That's all I'm trying to do, though," Gavin mutters, putting his arm back over his eyes. "I'm trying to be on his team."

Tyler goes quiet. Gavin avoids his gaze for as long as he can, but the silence is damning, and Gavin is nothing if not curious. Not to mention, Tyler is persistent. When Gavin finally gives in and moves his arm again, Tyler's expression is more serious than Gavin has ever seen it.

"What?" Gavin asks.

"Maybe he's not ready to have you on his team," Tyler says, his eyes sharp and his voice hard.

"What's that supposed to mean?"

"I talked to Evelyn at the wedding."

The non-sequitur makes Gavin sit up.

"She told me how invested you were in Javier and his kid at the zoo. How important it is to you that this relationship works out. Have you thought about why?"

Gavin twists his hand in the sheets beneath him. It's a question he's only asked himself once, and refused to look at any closer. "Because he's my Recipient. Obviously I just want him to feel safe and cared for, but I'd like that to happen with me instead of on his own."

"Well, maybe what he needs is a little time on his own."

"He's been on his own since Alejandro was born."

Tyler raises an eyebrow. "Has he? He had his parents, right? He wasn't completely alone. Not like—"

And suddenly Gavin understands. He tears his gaze away from Tyler before he can finish the sentence. Tyler falls silent, and Gavin is pretty sure he knows where he screwed up. "Not like me."

The thing is, Tyler isn't completely wrong. His parents weren't bad, they were just distant. His dad got married to appease his parents and his mom was the perfect Recipient in front of the in-laws, but neither of them really wanted kids. The only reason they had him is because Grandfather Carmichael told Dad he wanted a male heir in addition to Evelyn. Gavin knows his parents were distant.

That's different from the way Javier's parents treated Alejandro.

"I didn't mean it like that," Tyler says, waving a hand between them.

"Then how did you mean it?" Gavin asks. When Tyler can't seem to come up with an answer, Gavin nods. "That's what I thought. I'm not abandoning him," he says sharply before Tyler can say anything more. "Alejandro's mother already abandoned both of them. I'm not going to be another person that walks away."

Tyler stares at him. Then he looks away and shakes his head. Gavin can't tell what he's thinking, but he can tell he's frustrated with Gavin himself.

Gavin doesn't care. He stands up and leaves Tyler behind, his heart in his throat and his stomach in his shoes. Maybe there's more to the tension between him and Javier, but he won't go getting ahead of himself.

Right now, he's going to keep following Javier's lead, because Alejandro's the one in all of this that matters, and Javier's the one that gets to decide where Alejandro ends up.

21

Javi meant to email Casey a while ago. He hasn't sent her photos of Ále in over six weeks, what with the time with the matchmaking agency, the lead-up to the wedding, and everything that's come after. Even though he knows she's up to her eyes in her summer research, he also knows how much she loves getting those emails. Besides, she deserves to know what's going on in her son's life, especially now that he's closer to her.

Which. Yeah. He might have forgotten to mention that to her *or* Gavin. CU Boulder is just a lot closer to Denver than it is to Vegas.

It's been a week since he finalized his decision to send Ále to Marion. He's in Ále's room helping him try on and organize the new school clothes they bought today with Gavin. They were going to go yesterday while Gavin was on-shift, but Ále insisted that Gavin come along too. Ále is leaning into the fact that Gavin is here to help them even harder than Javi is. Not that Javi doesn't rely on Gavin. The days he's gone are a throwback to the days when Javi was alone in taking care of Ále, and he doesn't like that. But it also makes the time he does have Gavin as a tentative co-parent so much better.

Which brings him back to Casey. The woman that he'd thought would be his co-parent once upon a time. When he thought about it, he never wanted to raise his children alone, and doing so with Ále is one of the hardest, if arguably the most gratifying, things he's ever done. He's always wanted to raise his son in a family, even if now, after all these years, he's accepted that that family can't be with Casey.

At this point, it makes more sense to call Casey and hope she isn't on site instead of sending an email or another text and waiting for the fallout when she calls him. He waits until Ále is helping Gavin with lunch to slip into his bedroom and call her.

"Javi?" Casey's voice is sharp and a little panicked when she picks up, and there's a lot of sound around her. "What is it, is something wrong? Is Ále okay?"

Javi winces. He hadn't thought what a phone call after his prolonged silence might look like to her. "Ále's fine," he assures her. "We're both fine."

"Oh." She sounds relieved, and Javi's heart slows in his chest from the moment of frantic beating. "Good, I'm glad." She says something he can't make out, as though she's covered the mic to talk to someone, and when she speaks again, the space around her is quiet. "So then, why'd you call?"

"I, uh. I have some news."

"Okay? Is it bad news? Because if so, I should probably go find somewhere a little more private."

"No, no, it's not bad news. At least, I don't think it is? I don't think it is."

"Well, that's not ominous at all," Casey says with a laugh. Javi's heart lurches toward the familiar sound. It's one of the first things he fell in love with about her. "Go on, then, hit me with it."

Javi genuinely means to lead with something else. Maybe that he and Ále are in Denver now. Or that he wants to double check his decision about Ále's school. Something safe. Something easy.

Something that focuses on the commonality of their son instead of what he actually says, which is, "I got married."

Silence resonates down the phone line. Javi winces, realizing his mistake too late. When Casey speaks, it's with that low, dangerous tone that he's come to associate with her at her angriest. "You what?"

"I got married. To a... He's my Provider."

Casey's breath hitches. "Hang on. I'm switching to a video call."

Javi's heart speeds up again. Casey made it clear when Ále was born that she didn't want to get married, at least, not then. And not to Javi. That doesn't mean he should have gone out on a limb like this without conferring with her. Not with Ále involved.

The telltale sound of Casey switching things up on him almost makes Javi balk, but the thought of what she'll say if he doesn't take the call is worse. He taps the accept icon and tries not to wince when she comes on the screen clearly sweaty and in the middle of her research. "Casey..."

"You got *married*, Javi? What the f—" She stops short. "Is Ále there?"

"No, he's in the kitchen with Ga—with my Provider."

Casey gives him a sharp look. "We're talking more about that in a minute. But first, what the fuck, Javi?"

"Case..."

"No. No, you don't get to just act like this isn't a big deal. This isn't *like you*." She steamrolls over him before he can ask what she means. "You don't just make decisions willy nilly like this. What happened?" And then, after a moment of Javi trying and failing to find the words, she asks, "Did B put you up to this?"

"It was her idea," Javi allows, "but I'm the one that pulled the trigger."

"I just... Javi, you've always wanted a family. Why this? Why now?"

Javi bites back the sharp words he wants to spit at her, that he wanted a family with *her*, and that when it became clear that that was no longer an option, that he couldn't help but want to look elsewhere. It's not true—or, at least, there's more to that truth than those words—but it still feels true some days. He's spent ten years waiting for them to be a family; so sue him if he got tired of it and decided to get married on his own. He bites that all back and just says, "It's complicated."

Casey sees right through him. "Your parents," she says, narrowing her eyes. "What did they say?"

"What they always do," Javi spits out. "That they think they can take care of him better than we can. That we should stop trying to raise him on our own. That they could give him such a good life. It was exhausting."

"Then why didn't you just move out?"

"You know the answer to that." He runs a hand through his hair and starts pacing. He walks across the sliver of daylight shining through the blackout shades as he paces from the bed to the door and back again. The only thing keeping him level is the sound of Ále laughing with Gavin in the kitchen. It's the only reminder that he did this for his son, above all else. "If I did, I'd just be paying rent somewhere, and they'd still be looking after him while I was at work. I couldn't afford that."

"Javi, if you needed more help with money, you know I would have."

"I didn't. I mean, I did," he allows at her skeptical expression, "but Case, I wasn't going to pull you back to Vegas just because I couldn't handle my finances."

"Our finances. This was always supposed to be a team effort, Javi. This was always supposed to be about us as a team, a united front. What the hell are you doing making unilateral decisions for our family?"

"Because," he says harshly, "it's like you said. We're not family. Not the way I wanted us to be."

"You're not being fair."

"And you are?" Javi's breath hitches. "Case." He closes his eyes and shakes his head. "Please, don't make this any harder than it needs to be."

Casey is silent for long enough that Javi forces himself to open his eyes and look at her. There's a grimace on her face, and though Javi can't pinpoint what part of the conversation made her look like that, he's at least grateful that it doesn't seem to be directed at him. "I just don't want you to put yourself in a position you can't get out of, just because we decided on me going out to grad school and leaving you alone there with them."

Javi laughs weakly. "It's not like that. My parents were always going to be overbearing, but Gavin is a good man. He's gonna do right by Ále."

"And what about you?"

Javi shrugs. "I'll figure that part out."

Casey makes a sound in the back of her throat, like a scream being held back. She stares at him. "Why would you do this?"

"I couldn't ask you to leave," he says honestly. "But I couldn't stay there any longer. I'd rather he be close to you than close to them."

"Close to me? Javi, where are you?"

"We're in Denver. That's part of why I called. There's this school we found for Ále, and you came up in the entrance interview. Do you mind if I put him in private school? I mean, is that okay?"

"Of course it's okay," Casey says, waving a hand. "You know I trust you with that. I just wish you'd told me before you got married." And then, softer, "I would have come."

Javi's heart leaps. There's sincerity in Casey's eyes, the kind that he forgot she was capable of. "Oh."

"Yeah, you big dummy. Oh."

"Casey."

"It's fine, Javi," she says before he can apologize. "I know how you are. If you made this decision it wasn't totally impulsive. You wouldn't do that with Ále's heart and safety at stake."

Javi's heart lurches. "You know I wouldn't."

"I know. And this guy. He's good with Ále?"

Javi contemplates the question for a moment, making sure he gives her an honest answer. He steps toward the door and cracks it open, letting the sound of Gavin's warm voice wash over him along with Ále's giggles. "He is. He's only known Ále a couple weeks and he's already as infatuated as you or me. He'll do whatever it takes to keep our kid safe and happy, I know it. He just doesn't always know what it takes."

"Did we know at the beginning?"

Javi inclines his head in acknowledgement.

"Okay," she says. "Good. I'm glad you called. It's good to see your face."

"You too. Did you want to see Ále?"

Casey glances over her shoulder. "I should probably get back to work but, yeah, I'd like to see him real quick."

"You've got it." Javi heads for the kitchen. "And Casey?"

She makes a humming noise down the line, and he can tell he's already losing her to her work.

"Thanks."

"Hey," she says warmly, "Anything for you and Ále. You know that."

"Yeah," Javi murmurs. "I do."

Ále is delighted to get to talk to Casey, even if it's just for five minutes. His grin is wide and his eyes are sparkling and Javi realizes that he's going to need to make time for calls like these more often, if only for Ále's sake. He may not want to talk to Casey more than once a month, but his son deserves to have a chance to talk to his mother.

Eventually, she's apologizing and heading back to work, and Javi is retaking his phone from Ále's hands. Javi notices Gavin scrutinizing the pair of them, but his expression clears as soon as he catches Javi looking.

"Who wants pad thai?" Gavin asks, and Javi lets himself be led astray by his bright smile, forgetting the scrutiny as though it never happened.

22

Javi's curled up on the couch and partway through a mystery novel the afternoon after his phone call with Casey, while Ále's finishing up his first day at school and Gavin's on shift. It occurs to him near chapter thirty-two that his abuela hasn't called since the wedding, nor has he texted to reach out. He knows why he hasn't reached out: he's been too caught up in figuring out what his role in this new life with Gavin is supposed to look like. He knows he's been in his head about what they're supposed to be to each other, but he thinks they're finally starting to understand one another.

He thinks maybe, some day, they could become a family.

That doesn't change the fact that his abuela hasn't reached out either. It's been about two months at this point; what on earth is she waiting for? He calls her to ask, but she switches to a video call and sends him to the kitchen to pull out the chocolate to make himself a mug of her cocoa before he can get a word in edgewise. He does as he's told, then sets his phone up on the kitchen table so he can see her and talk to her while he sips on his cocoa that it's really too hot outside for.

"I was waiting for you to need space from that man of yours

and call me," she says with a sparkle in her eye when Javi brings it up.

Javi flushes. "Come on, Abuela, you know I didn't do this for a relationship. I didn't get married to fall in love."

His abuela's expression sobers. "No. You did it because my son and his Recipient made you think you needed to behave in a certain way to be a worthwhile father. I told you, you could have just moved in with me if you wanted to leave so badly."

Javi smiles and takes his mug in his hands, holding it loosely. "You know we would still be too close to them if I did that. Besides, I couldn't take advantage of you like that."

"Oh, like your man is taking advantage of you?"

"Abuela."

"Don't lie to me, young man," she says, narrowing her eyes at him. Javi shrinks a little in the face of her frustration. "I know you've always needed more than sex to make a relationship worthwhile to you. Is he giving you what you need?"

"We're not even having sex."

His abuela pulls back. "You're not?"

"No. He won't let me."

"Won't let you what?"

"Have sex with him." Javi says plainly.

Abuela turns away and lifts her own mug to her lips, muttering in Spanish under her breath. Javi knows better than to push when she's like this, but it's hard to hold back. Eventually she turns back to him, her brow pinched and her nose wrinkled. "Do you want to have sex with him?

Javi opens his mouth to give an automatic answer.

Before he can, Abuela leans forward, close enough that the view in the phone is more of her eye than of her face. "Tell me the truth."

Javi's mouth snaps closed. He knows she won't accept a half-baked answer from him. She never has. So instead he looks out the kitchen window, trying to gather his thoughts.

It's not that he and Gavin are perfect together, not by a long shot. But they do care about each other, and Javi's pretty sure that matters. More importantly, though, Gavin genuinely cares for Ále. Just the other day he spent a solid two hours working with Ále on the summer homework he'd gotten, while Javi looked on. Who knew fourth grade science was so confusing?

But Gavin had nothing but patience with Ále, and Ále mirrored that patience, which left Javi admiring his Provider. More than two months, and he's already learned what took Javi far longer to learn. Patience, and support. Love unconditional. Javi still can't shake the lingering fear that this relationship is transactional, no matter how much Gavin reminds him that it isn't. He's trying to truly trust in Gavin and their relationship, the one that saved him and Ále from the life Javi was giving them in Vegas. He's trying to trust and, for as difficult as it is, it seems to be getting easier every day.

"Ah."

Javi looks at his abuela, whose expression is soft and relieved. "What?"

"He's good for you."

"He's good *to* me, Abuela," he counters. "I don't know what else he might be, but he's good *to* me, and to Alejandro."

"And he provides for you? He takes care of you?"

"Honestly?" Javi chuckles and shakes his head "Almost too well. I didn't even have to drop anything I was doing to call you today."

"That means he knows how to show you your value."

"Sure." Javi looks down into his mug. "But you know I don't like being idle. He even gave me a project, you remember. Something to work on around the house to make it really feel like it belongs to me and Ále as well as him. I just wish there was more I could do for him."

"He's the Provider," Abuela says with a hint of sternness. "It's not your job to do anything more for him than I know you already are."

"Meaning?"

"Cleaning, chores around the house, taking care of Alejito," she waves her hand, implying everything else Javier does for their burgeoning family. "That's plenty."

"But he helps me with all of that," Javi protests. "He cooks half the time, and he insists on helping with the dishes no matter who made dinner. He even folds half the laundry if I make the mistake of doing it on his day off. Sometimes I feel like I should be doing more than I am. He's already giving us so much."

"You dealt with a lot of change to be with him, Javi."

"It's not the same."

"No," Abuela agrees, "it's not. But you both have dealt with a lot of change to make this relationship work, and now it's time to decide what it looks like from here on in."

"I still wish I could give him more."

"Why?" Abuela asks. "You're not the Provider."

Javi doesn't have a good answer to that. He isn't, that's true, he's just been raised to think he was supposed to be for his whole life. He changes tactics. "Gavin says he's happy, and I want that to be enough, it just—isn't."

"It wouldn't be, yet, for you. Relationships have always been more than just the physical for you, Javi," she says again. "They always have."

Javi raises an incredulous eyebrow at her, but her expression goes hard.

"If he's pressuring you—"

"He's not, Abuela," Javi says, cutting her off. "Just the opposite. He hasn't really even kissed me, not since early on. I just—" He huffs and doesn't finish that sentence. He knows how she'd react to hearing that Javi thinks the only thing he can offer in his relationship is sex.

"You just what?"

"Nothing."

"Javier *Cesar* Pérez," his abuela says sharply, "you tell me right now."

"I just feel like I need to give him more."

"More what?" Abuela asks.

"More of a family."

"Ah." Abuela sits back from where she'd leaned toward her phone. "But you're not ready to let go of Alejito yet."

Javi doesn't deny it.

Abuela sighs, understanding his protectiveness. "Well, he did give you a project when you moved in. How is that going?"

"He didn't give me any parameters." Javi says with a shrug. "I don't know how to do it the way he wants."

"The way he wants?"

With a sharp exhale, Javi stands up and turns partly away from his phone, resting his hip on the kitchen counter.

"From what it sounds like, he doesn't want you to do it the way he wants. He wants you to do it the way Alejito wants."

Javi sips at his cocoa.

"Isn't that what you want?"

"Of course it is," he says vehemently. "He said it was the only part of the house that he couldn't get looked at in time, and that I would probably want to put it together for Ále anyway. But he didn't give me contacts or a budget or limitations or anything. I only have an inkling of how to do that if he doesn't tell me what he wants. I can start ripping out what needs ripping out, but there's so much more to it than that. There's structures to choose from, and we need to decide what kind of ground material we're going to use, and there's just so *much*."

"Did it occur to you, mijo," Abuela says with that amused glint back in her eyes, "that maybe he wanted you to make those decisions together instead of him making them unilaterally?"

"What? No, that's not… that's…" Javi shakes his head, reeling from the possibility. "There have to be rules. Don't there?"

Abuela's smile widens. "Maybe you should be asking that man of yours that question instead of me."

"Maybe," Javi agrees. He huffs and settles back in his seat. He doesn't want to, but maybe Abuela has a point. Communication is the most crucial part of his time with Gavin. It's what got them through school interviews, and it's what's getting them through understanding how to raise Ále together. Maybe, if he can't ask about the backyard yet, he can ask about something else.

Javi considers bringing his concerns up with Gavin, but there's an ease between them that he doesn't want to break. Not yet.

It happens too soon anyway.

Javi gets home from dropping Ále off at school the next morning and settles down at the kitchen table to start working through September's bills. This is one of the few comforting things that he gets to hold onto these days: paying bills. Ále's doctor's appointments are one part of the move that stayed consistent from their time before, but the bills feel less intimidating with Gavin's money behind him. He makes quick work of the bills in front of him and goes to file them away in the study.

He pauses, looking down the hall toward Ále's room. Ále is settling in well, taking to Gavin far more easily than Javi anticipated. Not that Gavin made that hard. He's engaged with Ále in every way he can, and made sure to invest time in Ále's interests so that he can match his energy. Javi's noticed a suspiciously large pile of books about space and the solar system in the guest bedroom when he goes in there to clean.

He teased Gavin about it at first, and though Gavin had been bashful, he was also insistent that this was part of being supportive of Ále. "Hell," he said from where he was seated next to Javi on the couch with a movie playing on low volume, "if I had half an idea of what would bring you joy, if I knew anything about it, I'd be researching that too."

Javi scarcely held back the insistence that all the time Gavin spent learning about CP had more than done the trick. Instead he'd muttered something about playing baseball in school and offered to go over stats with him if he ever wanted to.

Gavin lit up, and soon a few memoirs about the baseball greats were added to the pile of books in Gavin's room.

Although both he and Ále have grown to enjoy Gavin, Javi still isn't sure where he himself falls in Gavin's estimation. The way Gavin danced with the kids at their wedding reception made it clear that he has a soft spot for kids, Ále included. But frequently when they talk, Gavin will start to say something or do something only to cut himself off mid-word or action. Javi hasn't had the courage to ask yet, and he wonders if a reckoning is coming. If, whatever it is that Gavin's holding back, is going to overflow one day soon and leave Javi shattered in its wake.

The door opening and closing pulls Javi out of his reverie. It's a little late for Gavin to be getting home—almost 9:30—which means there was probably a big callout right near the end of his shift. Instead of making a beeline for the shower like Javier expects, Gavin steps into the kitchen. He pauses, looking surprised, then moves into the hall where he meets Javi's eyes.

"Everything okay?" Javi asks.

"We need to talk."

Javi's chest constricts at the seriousness of Gavin's words. When he moves toward Gavin, Gavin's head jerks so that he's looking past Javi instead of at him, which Javi realizes with a start, he's never done. Dread settles in Javi's stomach. "What's wrong?"

Gavin hesitates, then takes two long strides toward Javi. "It's not wrong, exactly. But I think we need to clear the air."

"Okay." Javi hesitates for a moment before matching Gavin's stride, taking two of his own steps toward his Provider. He keeps his hands loose at his sides as he moves. Slow. Steady. Deliberate. Not giving anything away. "Go ahead."

"I was talking to Tyler on shift last night. He said some things."

"Okay," Javi says. "What things?"

"I need to know what you need from me. What you expected when you agreed to marry me. I know we have a contract," Gavin says, waving his hand dismissively and leaving a pit in Javi's stomach, "but that was hardly specialized for your situation."

Javi blinks hard and consciously keeps his hands relaxed. "What does that mean?" Is he talking about the fact that Javi had been so resistant to spending his money? Or could this be him wanting to take back the generosity of their sexual relations clause? But no, he wouldn't. Would he?

"It means that I know how much Alejandro means to you. How much you mean to each other. I just need to know where I fit in all that."

For a long moment, Javi's lungs feel too small. Filled to capacity, but unable to sustain him even so. Doesn't Gavin already know that Ále cares about him? Loves him? That Ále may even see him as a dad already? That Javi's terrified of asking his son any of those things lest they turn out to be true?

Eventually Javi swallows and nods. "I think what you've been doing has been good." It's more than he wants to give Gavin, and less than Gavin deserves, but it's all he has.

Gavin tilts his head to the side. He starts to reach out toward Javi.

Javi jerks away before he can stop himself.

After staring at him for a moment, a wounded look on his face, Gavin pulls back. "Right."

"Ále," Javi says, grasping for the part of this conversation he understands. "Ále knows how to ask for what he needs. If he needs more from you, he'll let you know."

Gavin opens his mouth. Pauses. Closes it. Pauses. Opens it again. "Right."

"So you don't have to worry about him." The words taste like ash on Javi's tongue. He doesn't want to raise Ále alone. He always wanted to raise him in a family. But that doesn't mean that he knows how to ask that of Gavin, who has already given them so much. "He's going to be okay."

Gavin's shoulders hunch. "Right."

Silence reigns for a long moment before Gavin moves around Javi, his work boots heavy on the floor. "I'm gonna go grab a shower."

"Right." Javi swallows thickly, fighting down an apology. He's not even sure what he'd be apologizing for. "Okay."

"Yeah." Gavin huffs softly. "Right."

The door to the bathroom opens and closes, leaving Javi to wonder how he went so wrong.

This was a conversation about Ále. But, no, that's not entirely right either. This was a conversation about family, and where Gavin fits in the family that Javi and Ále have built for themselves already. Javi knows what his gut reaction to that is: nowhere.

He winces at the thought. It's not accurate, not anymore. It's just what he thought he was supposed to think when he got into this whole… it's not a mess, anymore, not really. But there are elements of it that are still messy. Like Gavin insisting that they stay longer at the museum that day over the summer.

But, then again, he hasn't tried to override Javi's decisions since then. He even helped soften the blow of them once or twice when Ále was fighting him.

Gavin is more than generous with his funds, shelling out for Marion and offering to get Ále private help with his academics on more than one occasion. Gavin is the support that Javi needed to be the father he wants to be, but none of that points to Gavin's role in this family.

Except, perhaps, as a proper co-parent.

The thought is too much to sit with right now, especially when Javi still can't be completely certain that Gavin wants that. It seems like he wants to be a co-parent, and his actions point to wanting to help take care of Ále, but Gavin never actually asked to be Ále's father. Hell, maybe Javi is being presumptuous and Gavin was hoping Javi would tell him not to be involved anymore. Not likely, but Ále's mother herself explicitly asked not to be involved.

Javi shakes off the worst of his melancholy. No, Gavin won't ask for nothing, but he may ask for less than Javi hopes he will. If he doesn't want to be kept in the dark, he'll have to find a time to broach this topic with Gavin again, no matter the potential outcome.

23

Three days of silence and awkwardness later, Javi drives himself to parent-teacher conferences alone. He'd expected Gavin to want to come with after the way he'd asked after Ále and their family. Expected to make the trip with all three of them. Instead, Gavin insisted on staying home with Ále to help him with a Lego solar system project they'd been working on since the weekend.

"You go," Gavin said, half-distracted by the project already when Javi went to ask about it after he'd finished the dinner dishes. "I can hold down the fort for a few hours."

So Javi goes to the school, woefully uncertain about the conversations he's about to have with Ále's teachers. He knows Ále is still struggling to adjust after the move, knows he probably should be more involved at the school to help him be successful, but the truth is that *he's* been struggling with the move too. Second guessing everything Gavin says and does, trying to figure out what is expected of him, waiting for the other shoe to drop. This is all too good to be true, and if he lets himself get too comfortable then it's going to be so much worse when it all comes crashing down around his head.

If it hasn't already.

But his world isn't ending today, and his son needs him to go in and face the music, listen to the experts tell him what he's doing wrong, and then adjust to support his son better. After all, this whole thing—the move, the marriage, the school, everything —was all for Ále, wasn't it? What good is Javi if he can't give his son everything he promised him?

With a tightness in his throat, Javi gets out of the car and makes his way into the school. He feels bare, unprotected, like anyone that looks at him knows exactly what he is. A Recipient, abandoned by his Provider and sent here alone. Never mind that that's what Javi has told Gavin he wanted all along. It's different when it's in public like this. Still, he needs to do this. It's for Ále. He can do anything for Ále.

He stands tall and approaches the table at the front. There are two women, presumably PTA parents, seated at the table, both eyeing him up with interest. He adjusts his hold on Ále's report card to flash the white gold of his ring at them. One of them turns her gaze away deferentially, but the other's gaze lights up as it settles on his ring. She leans forward and bats her eyes at him.

Javi's throat goes dry. He's never understood people that aren't faithful to their partners. That's the whole point of having someone. To hold onto them and give them everything they've ever wanted. That was the goal with Casey and it's just as much so with Gavin. Maybe more so. Part of him wants to turn and run, wants to escape the awkwardness that he knows will come.

The rest of him knows that he owes Ále at least this much and forces his feet to move.

He aims for the woman that demurred at his ring, but another parent steps up to her before he can. He steels himself and turns to the other woman. She's smiling at him warmly with a light in her eyes that makes his stomach twist. But that's not why he's here. Her expression is sultry, and though she no doubt has a terrible pickup line ready, he opens his mouth before she can say anything.

"I'm here to pick up my son's schedule." He bites back the instinct to say more. He doesn't need to be seen chatting up someone's mother.

"Of course." Her smile doesn't waver as she turns to the box of schedules in front of her. "Last name?"

"Pérez. Alejandro Pérez."

She hums and flips through the schedules twice. Javi would insist that it shouldn't be that hard to find Ále's schedule, but he knows better than to give her an opening to start chatting him up. When she's figured out that he isn't going to talk to her, she heaves a sigh and hands over Alejandro's schedule. "Here you are."

"Thank you."

"There's a map on the back if you need it."

Javi nods as he turns away, already focused on where to go from here. He definitely needs to meet with Ále's IEP file holder and see what more he needs to do to help his son. Then art and music, and he'll probably save homeroom for last. Oh, and he'll need to check in with the PE teacher to see how Ále's accommodations are working out. A check of his watch shows that he only has an hour to do all that. With a soft swear he clocks the fastest way through the school to each of Alejandro's teachers. It means finishing with art, which he isn't particularly excited about, but he'll make it work.

He's pleasantly surprised when every one of Alejandro's teachers emphasize their confidence in his abilities.

"He's been through a big change," his file holder Mr. Slater says. "He'll get caught up in no time."

"He's enthusiastic and engaged," the PE teacher Mrs. Harrison says. "And the kids are all really supportive of his needs. They make sure he never feels pressured, and he keeps up with them anyway."

"You've done a great job with him," the art teacher Ms. Dominguez says. "You should be really proud."

She's the first and only one that Javi isn't completely at ease with. He can feel her interest in him, and on some level, he can see the picture they would make. Her warm brown skin and long hair, the perfect picture of a Recipient. Latina, which his mother would approve of. Deferential and refined, the kind of Recipient his father would have chosen for him. And he can admit that she is beautiful. The kind of woman that he could make the perfect family with. The kind that he used to think he wanted. The kind of woman that his parents would approve of. Being with her would give him a life that would be easy, simple. Quiet and calm and straightforward. Expected. Perfect.

Empty.

That's the part that catches on his heart and scrapes against his ribs. They would be the perfect picture, but there would be no substance underneath it. She would love Ále. She's said as much, though not in so many words. She can probably cook and probably doesn't mind cleaning, and he would go out to work every day, be the breadwinner his father thought he should be. He'd go out and do the work of a Provider and come home to his Recipient and that would be that. Easy. Straightforward. Hollow.

Nothing like the ease he feels with Gavin's support.

Even though they're on unstable ground right now, uncertain in each other's space and uncomfortable with where they go from here, Javi still wants that. He wants that support, that comfort, that knowledge that there's nothing Gavin wouldn't do for their son. For their family. That they've *chosen* each other for life, or at least for now.

He doesn't want anyone else. He wants Gavin, and if that means taking a leap of faith and trusting him the way he's never trusted anyone before, so be it. There isn't a lot he wouldn't do for Ále, but he's starting to wonder if Gavin is something he did for himself too.

He smiles at Ms. Dominguez, gets to his feet, and extends a

hand. She takes it in more of a handhold than a handshake. "Thank you," Javi says. "I'm glad he's fitting in well."

She holds his hand a moment longer than is appropriate and Javi almost lets himself give in to what she's offering. Almost lets himself start walking the path to be the person that his parents wanted him to be. But he has a son and a Provider to get home to, and the last thing he wants to do right now is jeopardize that. He pulls his hand from hers and gives an awkward nod. Then he's leaving, walking past the front table with the aggressive mom that tries to catch his attention again, and into his truck.

There, in the half-dark of the evening, he grips the steering wheel until his knuckles pale. He presses his forehead against the wheel and closes his eyes. Twice. Twice someone thought they could pull him away from Gavin. Could offer him something better than what he has now. He doesn't want that. Not when he has Gavin. Gavin, who is kind and warm and intentional in every interaction with *both* Javi and Ále. He's shown nothing but compassion and care in their relationship, and Javi met his request for truth with fear. Maybe it's time for him to lean into the evidence instead of his fears. Maybe it's time to trust Gavin. Maybe it's time to entrust himself to his Provider the way he used to think he needed to.

Maybe it's different when it's his choice.

With his heart still in his throat and his fingers trembling with potential, he puts the car in gear and goes home.

24

When Javi gets home, Gavin is already holed up in the guest room for the night. Javi takes a moment to poke his head into Ále's room and make sure that he's sleeping. For a moment, he lingers in the comfort of knowing that his son is safe and well and resting, before he makes his way to the main bedroom. The one he should be sharing with his Provider. He undresses and gets ready for bed.

The knowledge that he's here, alone, unsupervised, is simultaneously a thrill and an admonishment. He almost goes to bed to get off alone, but in the end chooses the shower instead. Easier to clean up and easier to hide the evidence. Not that he needs to hide what he's doing from Gavin, but there's something to be said for discretion.

As the water pounds on his shoulders and spills down his back, he takes himself in hand and thinks about his Provider. He thinks about Gavin's eyes, his strong arms, his easy demeanor, and the reverent way he always touches Javi. He thinks about what it would be like to be held close to him, what it would be like to feel his breath on his skin. What his careful promises might feel like as they lie in bed beside each other, warm and sated and present in one another's lives in a way that he's never had before.

Casey is the only person he's ever had sex with. After her there was Alejandro to think of. Coupled with the fact that he isn't one for casual sex, that had left him sadly lacking in this area. He wants to believe that there's no shame in that, wants to believe Gavin wouldn't want him to think poorly of himself for it.

He tightens his grip on his cock and runs his thumb along the underside. It draws a soft cry from his lips that leaves him aching. He wants this to be enough. *He* wants to be enough. And although he wants to believe Gavin might want him—has to believe it, at least, because he doesn't know where it leaves them if Gavin *doesn't* want him—he's also starting to understand that Gavin needs him to commit. Needs him to show that he wants to be with him, that he wants to be Gavin's. To belong to him. Even if that isn't the way Gavin thinks of things, it's how Javi feels, and it's time to remind his Provider of just who his Recipient is.

He slaps one hand to the wall, holding himself up as he strokes his cock with more intention. It's the thought of Gavin that drives him forward. He can imagine the feel of Gavin's calluses on his own fingers as he jerks himself off, can imagine that it's Gavin's heavy breaths mingling with his own instead of the pounding of the water. There's so much he can imagine is Gavin, so much that he knows of his Provider that he can replicate in this setting.

It aches something fierce to be alone and imagining Gavin rather than be in Gavin's arms. In this in-between space while he waits for Gavin to be ready to hear from him again, though, he'll take what he can get. It may take a while, but that doesn't mean that Javi won't wait. He will. As long as he has to. He's not going to abandon Gavin, and when he has his chance he'll tell him the truth.

Javi will tell Gavin that he's committed to him, and that means he trusts Gavin with his life, his safety, and his son, the heart of his that walks around outside his body. And maybe, someday, once he's had enough time, he'll finally be ready to trust Gavin with the heart of his that still lives in the sanctity of his ribcage.

The thought of that—of the consummate perfection that could be his heart held in the safety of Gavin's hands—is what finishes him off. He tries not to think too hard about what that means for him.

Once he's out of the shower, Javi towels dry and curls up in bed. There's no one waiting for him here right now, not really, but he feels the commitment to Gavin all the same as he slips between the sheets and settles his head on the pillow. This may not feel so much like their room right now with Gavin sleeping down the hall, but that doesn't mean Javi can't hold true to his principles with his Gavin. His Provider.

His home.

The high from his orgasm carries him softly to sleep, and he sleeps through the night, right up until it's time to take Ále to school. From there, it's an easy thing to smile and nod and squeeze Gavin's hand when Javi makes it to the kitchen for breakfast. He gets a nod and a tentative smile back, but there's nothing more than that between them.

Ále, of course, picks up on it, finally voicing the uncertainty that Javi's seen in his eyes for days. "Are you and Gavin fighting?"

"Nope," Javi says, his smile widening as he watches Gavin's ears go pink on his way out the door to run some errands. "Just figuring things out."

Ále hums, his tone sounding skeptical, but he doesn't press the issue. Javi ignores the increasingly weirded out looks his son is giving him as they get him ready for school and into the car. He ruffles Ále's hair once they make it to Marion and gets a wrinkled nose for his trouble.

Once he's watched Ále make his way safely into the building, he pulls away and heads to the hardware store. He needs some heavy duty tools if he's going to start working on the yard. It takes him an hour and two conversations with three different salespeople to find what he needs, but once he has it all, he makes quick work of the drive back home.

Gavin should be home by now. Javi sits up straighter in the car at the thought, hope in his chest.

Except by the time he gets home, Gavin's car still isn't in the garage. The errands must be taking longer than usual. That's fine; he can get some work done in the yard while he waits for Gavin to make it home.

Javi dresses down in an old long-sleeved shirt and the rattiest pair of jeans he has—not that he has much in the way of gardening-appropriate clothes; he left most of that in the garbage back in Vegas—and steps out into the backyard.

He can't rush into this, so he starts by walking the perimeter, then slowly moving toward the center. The easiest thing would be to start with the weeds, as he's mostly just working with his hands right now, at least until he can have Gavin order a garden waste dumpster to sit out front while he deals with the worst of the yard. He'll need some heavy duty power tools to get through some of the fallen branches, and he doesn't want to do that until he has somewhere to put the resulting debris. He'll get that sorted once the dumpster is here.

Which leaves the bushes. He'd done his research on how to handle them and asked the people at the garden center at the hardware store. It's time for him to get his hands dirty, quite literally in this case, but if he doesn't want to be scraped up and bruised, he needs to wear all the protective gear he got. There's a moment where he worries the gloves he got are too small, but as soon as he starts reaching down to find the bushes' root system, he realizes they're exactly the right size. A good grip will be crucial, and that means smaller gloves than he might otherwise have chosen.

As he walks, trying to choose a spot to start, the back of his mind drifts to Gavin. Last night was an eye-opener, in that he hadn't expected to have such a strong response to being flirted with. He's always been a loyal man, but the intensity of his reaction was surprising. Overwhelming, even. But it felt true in a way that everything with Gavin does. A way that he's been avoiding.

The south end of the yard has most of the smaller bushes, so he starts there. The yard is on the north side of the house which means it gets less sun, so the bushes closest to the house are the ones that are going to be easiest to tackle. He works his hands down through the stems and leaves of one of the smallest bushes until he gets to the roots, tugging futilely at them for a few minutes. When the direct approach doesn't bear fruit, Javi grabs the trowel he'd picked up and starts loosening the dirt around the bush's roots. They give much more easily than they had for his hands, and after a few minutes of work and two more rounds of fruitless tugging, he eventually manages to get the first bush loose.

He stays there, crouched on the ground, staring at the bush when something rattles loose in his head. He cares about Gavin. That doesn't come as a surprise, but it's the intensity with which it comes that is. He'd thought he cared about him in that distant way he's come to realize he cares about Casey. As someone involved in his kid's life, but nothing more than that.

But Gavin wants more than to be just *involved* in Ále's life. He wants to be *in it* with Javi. Ever since that first meltdown, Gavin has watched with careful eyes as Javi supported Ále through another one. Javi thought he was, perhaps, being judged, but now he thinks that it was evaluation rather than judgment. A desire to understand instead of a desire to demean. It's the same with Ále's homework on the rare nights Ále lets Gavin help. Gavin's been careful and patient and gentle while still coaxing Ále to acknowledge what he knows. And all the studying he did and continues to do into CP. It's more than Casey ever did.

Gavin isn't Javi's person, but Javi can suddenly see a world where he could be. A world where they calm Ále down together instead of Javi alone. A world where he even starts to truly lean on Gavin for some of the decision making instead of refusing to let him in.

It's not an easy thought, but it is, at least, a welcome one.

Conclusion reached, he realizes he isn't sure what to do with the bush in his hand now that he's gotten it out. He glances around the backyard, his eyes settling on a relatively clear patch near the gate. He tromps his way over there and drops his first trophy to the dirt. One down, who knows how many to go.

Javi never would have considered himself a gardener, nor even interested in it. But there's something satisfying about working with the earth, with his hands, in a way that he never has before. At least, nothing beyond mowing the lawn growing up, and that hardly feels like it counts compared to this. He works for two solid hours before the back door slides open and he hears Gavin call his name.

He turns to Gavin, eyes wide as he stares up at him from the yard. At the sight of his Provider, he grabs at the hem of his shirt and tugs it up to wipe the sweat from his face. When he drops it, Gavin is staring right back, his eyes wide and lips parted. And suddenly, it's the easiest thing in the world to speak those three words into existence.

For a moment, Javi lingers, letting them settle on his tongue, sweet and warm and kind. He holds them there for as long as he can, lets them swell and grow behind his teeth, until there's nothing he can do but speak them into existence. Until there's nothing he can do but gift them to Gavin the way Gavin gifted him with so much already.

"I trust you," Javi says.

Just like that. Simple. Easy.

Terrifying.

Gavin goes completely still.

"I trust you." Javi's voice is softer that time, but from the way Gavin's eyes light up, he knows his Provider is listening.

Except then Gavin shakes his head sharply, turns around, and marches back into the house.

Javi stares after him. Is he supposed to follow? Or is this Gavin's way of telling him that he doesn't want to talk about this right now? Or ever? He takes one step toward the open door, but hesitates even longer. There's no way he's supposed to just follow Gavin, is there?

Before he can make up his mind, Gavin returns, a glass of water in each hand. He sits down sharply on the back step. "C'mere." His voice is rougher than usual, but the words are clear. "You look parched."

Javi moves closer slowly, trembling a little with the way that he wants to reach out to Gavin and hold on for dear life. He doesn't, though. He sits down, takes the glass of water, and waits instead.

He watches Gavin out of the corner of his eye as he sips his water.

There's a far-off look in Gavin's eyes, now, and he doesn't move his glass to drink. It makes Javi want to ask what's wrong, what he *did* wrong, but he's learned by now that Gavin doesn't take kindly to Javi's assumptions of his own guilt. So he waits.

When Gavin speaks, his words are as rough as before, but laced with more emotion. "We'll go slow."

Javi wants to argue, but the set of Gavin's jaw deters him.When Javi doesn't say anything, Gavin turns to him, then reaches out to trace his fingertips over the arch of Javi's cheekbone. "I want to trust that you mean what you say, but the whole time you've lived here, you've held me at arm's reach. I don't think I could stand it if we start this and then you changed your mind. It would hurt too much." Gavin pauses, then forges ahead. "I won't take advantage while you're still figuring out how you feel about this. Us. Or at least," he says before Javi can argue, "while what you are feeling is still so new."

Javi looks away. He can't deny any of it. He certainly did try to keep Gavin at bay for the longest time. He doesn't know now if that was to protect Ále or to protect himself, but he can't deny that he has been the one driving a wedge between him and Gavin the whole time.

"We can try being together like this. You know I want that. I just want to make sure that you're completely certain you want it too. So let's take this slow, until we're both sure that this is what you want."

It takes a moment for Javi to process Gavin's words. "That makes sense."

Gavin leans in and kisses Javi softly, leaving Javi to melt against him. The kiss is warm and steady, a promise of things to come, even as Gavin holds back. Then Gavin pulls away. "We don't have to wait forever. I don't want to wait forever. But I'm going to need more than just your word."

"You don't even want to know what changed?"

Gavin snorts. "I can hazard a guess."

That makes Javi look at him straight on. "What?"

"That school. The PTA and all the other parents, they're mostly exhausted rich parents that think sending their kid to a nice school will make that kid a good person. More importantly, they think it makes *them* good parents. But it doesn't. Not when they—"

Javi knows Gavin can fill in the blank, but from the tortured tone in Gavin's voice, Javi won't make him. "Not when they hit on other people's Recipients?"

Gavin winces. "No. No, not then."

“Okay. I can accept that we need to take our time.” He reaches out and touches Gavin’s shoulder gently. “As soon as you’re ready for more, I’ll be here. I promise.”

Gavin nods, then leans in to kiss Javi again, a reminder that Gavin’s caution is only temporary. “Thank you.”

25

Right around the time that he and Javier have their conversation, there's a run of ten days where Gavin doesn't hear from his sister. He tries not to let it worry him, but it doesn't work super well. She'd insisted that he let her reach out to him, not the other way around, and he's been doing his best to comply, but ten days is really pushing it.

Then, just when he's considering texting her, she texts him. *out,* the text says. *15 hours?*

Dread pools in his gut. His hands are shaking. If it's bad enough that she can't even call, that's already alarming. If it's bad enough that she wants out in *under twenty-four hours,* that's even worse.

Fuck, how bad is it?

Hands shaking, Gavin likes the message and composes one of his own. *Text or email?*

text. screenshots. please.

Gavin navigates to the web browser on his phone. He finds a flight out of Boston that leaves in exactly fourteen hours and ten minutes. He buys four tickets and texts her the screenshots. *Uber too?* he texts.

please.

You got it. And Sis? I'll be there when you land.

She likes the message.

Five hours later, she calls him choking down sobs.

"I can't, Gavin. I can't, he'll kill me, he'll kill the girls."

"I won't let him," Gavin insists. "I'm going to keep you safe."

"How do I even get out? He'll notice if I pack, and there's no way I can get everything we need out of here in enough time to make the flight."

"Do you want me to get you another flight?"

Evelyn hesitates. "No," she whispers. "If I don't come now, I don't think I ever will."

Gavin inhales sharply. "Okay. Then here's what we're going to do. You're going to pack enough luggage to get you and the girls here but not enough that he notices that you're leaving for good. You're going to tell him that I just had a fight with Javier and I need you to come out here and help me, I don't know, wrangle him."

"Wrangle him?" Evelyn asks, choking on teary laughter.

"I said what I said," Gavin teases. Then he sobers. "I'm going to get in touch with Diana and make sure we can get you somewhere that he won't be able to find you. And then I'm going to keep you safe, okay, Ev? I promise."

Evelyn laughs wetly again. "Okay. As long as you promise."

"I do. God, Ev, I swear, I will do everything in my power to keep you and the girls safe."

Evelyn is quiet, but he can still hear her breathing down the phone line. "You know we won't be able to stay with you."

Gavin closes his eyes. "I know."

"But you'll keep us safe?"

"I'll do everything I can."

Evelyn exhales. "Then that's going to have to be enough." She pauses. "I love you."

"Love you, too, Ev."

He waits for her to hang up first.

Javier finds him still sitting at the kitchen table with his head in his hands an hour later. "Gavin?" he asks. "What's wrong?"

"It's Ev." Gavin can hear the scratch in his voice from holding back his tears. "She's coming out."

Javier inhales sharply. He sits across from Gavin and reaches out to take his hand. "What do you need?"

Gavin closes his eyes and bows his head. "I need to call Diana. I need her to be safe, Javier. I need her to be *safe*."

"Okay. Why don't you call Diana and put her on speakerphone? We can talk to her together."

"What if she can't help?" Gavin says, a little desperate. "What if there's nothing she can do?"

"Hey."

The sharpness in Javier's tone startles Gavin.

"You're focusing on the worst possible outcome before anything has even been decided. Let's look at what we *can* do first." He taps Gavin's phone. "Call Diana."

With his throat tight and tears in his eyes, Gavin allows himself a brief moment to be grateful for his husband before he does as he's told.

Gavin pulls into short-term parking just so he can be inside to pick Evelyn and the girls up. The last thing he wants right now is to force his sister to stand in the parking garage at DIA just to make *his* life easier.

The girls see him first, and Genesis tackles his legs just as he catches sight of Evelyn. His sister looks tired, and Gavin wastes no time lifting Genesis into his arms and letting her chatter a mile a minute into his ear.

He steps close to Evelyn, who has both hands on the double stroller in front of her now that he has Genesis. "How are you?" he murmurs.

She gives him a tight smile, then winces. "Been better."

Gavin almost reaches out, almost brushes her bangs from her forehead, but he holds back at the last moment, weeks of restraining himself around with Javier getting in the way of instinct. "I bet." Then he closes his eyes, exhales, and smiles at his nieces. "Do you girls want to go meet a friend of mine?"

"Who?" Elaine asks from the stroller.

"Her name is Officer Bevan. She's my captain's Partner, and she's going to show you where you'll be staying for a while."

"Like vacation?" Genesis is frowning at Gavin when he turns to look at her.

"Yeah, kinda," Gavin says with a glance at his sister. Her expression is tight, but she doesn't seem upset by the comparison. He turns back to his niece. "Is that good with you?"

"Yeah!"

Gavin winces a little at Genesis's volume, then turns to his sister. "Do you want me to get the stroller, too?"

"I've got them. Although, maybe you can help with this?" she adds and then nods at the luggage beside her.

Gavin catches on immediately. "You got it." He lowers his eldest niece to the ground and holds a hand out for her. "Come on," he says, grabbing the handle of the big roller bag in his other hand, "let's go find my car."

Genesis takes his free hand easily. She also grabs her own littler luggage that had come clunking along behind her as she'd raced toward him. "Did you lose it, Uncle Gavin?"

"I hope not." Gavin grins at her. "But just in case, I thought I would ask you to help me look."

After letting Genesis spot the bright red sedan he'd bought after graduating from the fire academy, he helps them all pile in. Evelyn juggles the two car seats for the littles, the ones she could easily strap into the double stroller, while Gavin sets up the one he'd bought for Genesis when they'd concocted this plan and concluded that there was no way Evelyn would be able to juggle all three car seats.

Besides, now that Evelyn lives in town, Gavin *wants* to be able to chauffeur his nieces around.

They get the luggage settled in the trunk, the girls all settled in the backseat, and Evelyn settled in the front seat. Gavin takes off on Peña Boulevard toward downtown. It's unfortunately close to rush hour, meaning more traffic than he would like, but he hands his phone off to Evelyn so she can keep Diana updated on their ETA. Genesis keeps staring out the window, her eyes wide and wondering, and it leaves Gavin comfortable enough to ask Evelyn what happened.

She sighs. "He hit Sierra when she just wanted his attention, and then when I told him off, he..." She shudders. "Let's just say there's a reason I didn't text you for ten days."

Gavin clenches his hands on the steering wheel tight enough that he can hear it creak. "Bastard," he mutters.

"Hey." Evelyn smacks his shoulder lightly. "Not around the girls."

"They're gonna know what I think of him anyway."

"Doesn't mean I want you swearing around them."

"Fine," Gavin sighs. "I'll behave."

"Good. You'd better."

The rest of the drive is quiet. When they make it there, Diana is there with Charlie and two vehicles, one of which Gavin recognizes as Charlie's. Charlie starts moving the girls to the other car while Diana talks to Gavin and Evelyn.

"I want Evelyn to give you her phone."

"What?" Gavin snaps. "No, absolutely not."

"We have no reason to believe that her Provider didn't put a tracking app on it. If you want to keep her safe, you'll let her hand it over."

Gavin looks between the two women desperately. "But how will I know she's okay?"

Diana holds her hand out. “Give me yours so I can program her new number in.”

“Oh.” That makes a lot of sense. He’s already handed his phone off when he realizes a flaw in this plan. “Wait, if he does have a tracking app on there, won’t he notice if she keeps going to the firehouse?”

“That’s why I want you to give it to that Recipient of yours and let him be in charge of it for a couple days. When everything is ready, I’ll come pick it up and have it entered into evidence in her case.”

Gavin nods. “That makes sense.” He turns to look at Evelyn. “Is this okay with you?”

She smiles affectionately and nods. “I’m just grateful that I have you to run to.” She shivers. “I don’t want to think of what I’d do if I had to do this on my own.”

Gavin grips her upper arm. “You’re never alone in this. I’ll be here every step of the way.”

But Evelyn shakes her head. “You already have a family. You need to be with them.”

“Javier understands,” he says with a smile. “He wanted to be here, but we wouldn’t all fit in my car or his. I had to talk him out of renting a van just so he and Alejandro could come along.”

“That’s sweet. But I’m glad you talked him out of it. I think the girls are already overwhelmed enough.”

Diana hands Gavin his phone back. “I’m taking you to the apartment we’re putting you up in temporarily, just until we can get you situated. I assume you’ll be in charge of that, Gavin?”

He nods. “We’ll need to figure out how to keep it out of public record that I bought it, or else buy it under someone else’s name to keep her safe, but I can handle the real estate portion of it all.”

“Good,” Diana says. “Then I’ll see you in a couple days, Gavin.”

Gavin reaches out to give his sister a hug, which she returns tightly. “Stay safe, sis.”

“You too, Gav.”

He gives her one more tight squeeze, then pockets both her phone and his and gets back in his car. He almost waits for Diana and Charlie to drive away first, but Diana just raises an eyebrow at him. He gives her a sheepish look, and then pulls out, heading to the house.

Javier is still awake when he gets home, though Alejandro is asleep, it being a school night and all. When Gavin explains the ruse with the cell phones, Javier agrees readily.

"She's your sister," he says earnestly. "I'm happy to help."

Gavin can't help it. He's exhausted from the day and all he wants is to be held. He leans in and presses a kiss to the corner of Javier's mouth. "Can I come to bed with you? Not to *do* anything," he says when Javier stiffens, "I just don't want to be alone right now."

Javier turns his head so he can kiss Gavin full on the mouth. "Of course, honey," he says as he pulls away. "Why don't you just go get ready for bed? We can read for a bit or something before we go to sleep."

"Yeah," Gavin melts a little at the easy words. "I'd like that a lot."

Javier's answering smile is brilliant.

26

A week later, Javi's elbow-deep in dishwater when his phone goes off in the living room. He groans.

"Javier?" Gavin calls out. "Your phone."

"I hear it. Who is it?"

There's a moment of quiet while Gavin grabs the phone. "It's, uh. It's someone named Melissa?"

Javi swears. "That's Haley's mom." Melissa is one of the few parents Javi has really connected with, and her daughter is an incredible friend to Ále.

"Alejandro's friend Haley?"

"Yeah."

"Do you want me to bring it to you?"

"No, you can answer it," Javi says after only a moment of hesitation.

"What?"

"I'll be out in a minute anyway, just see when she wants to schedule a playdate and then check Ále's calendar."

"But, Javier," Gavin starts.

"It's okay, Gavin," Javi insists, "I trust you, remember?"

The phone goes off one more time.

"Gav—"

"Hello?"

The familiar sound of Gavin's phone call voice relaxes Javi. He turns his attention back to the dishes and listens intently.

"No, this is Gavin. I'm Javier's Provider. But I can get him." Gavin pauses, as Melissa says something. "Right. What day did you have in mind?" And then, "Let me check his calendar."

Javi slows down, making sure he can hear what Gavin says next. He trusts him, yes, but that doesn't mean that Gavin knows how to read Ále's calendar easily yet.

"Thursday?"

Ále has physical therapy on Thursday. Javi's throat tightens, but Gavin speaks before Javi can call out.

"Alejandro has physical therapy on Thursday. No, he usually needs to rest after those appointments. Yes, I'm sure he'd want to see her too, but we need to make sure that he's taking care of himself too. What about—" Gavin pauses, and Javi can almost see him scrolling through the calendar to find a better date. "What about next Wednesday?"

Javi frowns. Tuesday would have worked too.

"I know, but I'm on shift on Tuesday, and I'd like to come with him to meet you. Not because I don't trust his judgment," Gavin is quick to add, "I just would like to meet the parents of Alejandro's best friend."

Javi closes his eyes. It's every kindness he could have hoped for and just reinforces his trust in Gavin. Gavin has always trusted Javi with Ále the way Javi's parents never did. That's been clear from the start. But for Gavin to trust *himself* with Ále is a new thing.

"So?" Gavin places a hand at the small of Javi's back, startling him. "Do I pass?"

"What?" Javi asks.

"Your little test, or whatever that was. Do I pass?"

"I don't know," Javi says with a frown. "Do you?"

The return question pulls Gavin up short. “Isn't that your call?”

With a hum, Javi relaxes. “I already told you that I trust you. This was about seeing if you trust yourself.”

“With what?”

“With Ále.”

It's Gavin's turn to frown. “I wasn't, though. I was just trusting myself in reading his calendar.”

“And you knew not to let him have a playdate on the same day as his physical therapy. You drew that boundary with her even when she asked. And then,” he adds when Gavin starts to argue, “you insisted on a day when you could come with me.”

“You know that wasn't because—”

“You don't trust me?” Javi smiles. “I know. You've made it clear since day one that you trust me with him. Coming with us means that you want to be involved. That you want to know his friends and their families too. That means something to me, Gavin. More than I can say.”

“Oh.”

“Yeah.” Javi sets aside the last dish and dries his hands off. “Oh.”

Then he approaches Gavin and steps into her personal space.

Gavin inhales. “Javier, I…”

When he doesn't say anything more, Javi smiles. “I'd like you to kiss me, now.”

Gavin's answering “Really?” is soft and reverent.

Javi's heart thuds in his chest, his trust in Gavin and his usually absent trust in himself merging into a warmth that he can't contain. He steps an inch closer. “Really.”

Gavin is tender and careful as he leans into Javi. He cups his jaw in one hand and traces the pad of his thumb over the arch of Javi's cheekbone.

Javi's eyes flutter shut and his lips part as his heart redoubles its pace.

The first touch of Gavin's lips is soft and tender. It's a ghost of a touch on his bottom lip that scarcely seems real. Then he presses against Javi's lips more firmly. It's still chaste, but it makes the breath catch in Javi's chest. Their first kiss had been heat and vigor, tinged with the newness of their vows. Their kisses since then have mostly been brief and casual. But this.

This.

This is coming home to the smell of lasagna cooking. This is watching his Provider run around the playroom with his son. This is comfort and space and all that Gavin gives him.

And then Gavin pulls away.

Javi doesn't mean to make a small sound of loss when Gavin moves away, but it ends up being a good thing, as that sound is all it takes for Gavin to press back in and kiss Javi with intent.

He slides his hand down to the back of Javi's neck and nips at Javi's lower lip and dips his tongue past Javi's still-parted lips.

Javi reaches up to cling to Gavin's upper arms, his knees going weak at the intensity of being the sole subject of Gavin's focus.

Gavin pulls away again, and Javi chases him this time. Gavin chuckles. "Yeah?" he whispers.

"Hmm?"

"You're sure you trust me?"

"I'm sure," Javi says with a smile.

"With—"

"With everything. With our finances. With our home. With my son. With… me."

Gavin inhales sharply. "Yeah?"

"Yeah."

"Okay." Gavin starts to pull away, but Javi clings to him a little longer.

About to reach out, Javi stops, his nerves failing him when he opens his eyes and is reminded again of what Gavin does to him.

"What is it?" Gavin asks.

Javi swallows and looks away, but before he can turn his head, Gavin's fingers are back on his jaw, turning Javi back to face him.

"What is it?" Gavin presses.

Blinking hard, Javi tries to find the words.

"If you trust me," Gavin says, "trust me enough to be honest with me."

That's all it takes. "Will you spend the night with me?"

Gavin stares at him. "Are you sure?" he whispers.

"Just to sleep."

"Of course," Gavin agrees.

Javi nods, his bravery failing him as he stares up into Gavin's clear blue eyes.

The smile Gavin gives him turns Javi's stomach to liquid. It's all the assent Javi needs, but Gavin gives him more as an extra kindness. "Yes," he whispers. He brushes a kiss over the apple of Javi's cheek. "Yes."

"Okay." A laugh bubbles up from deep in Javi's chest. "Okay." And then, with a bravery that he hadn't known he possessed, "Move in?"

"What?"

"I want you to move into our bedroom. Listen," he says when Gavin seems to be gearing up to protest, "I really am grateful for the time and space you've given me. It means a lot to me. But I know you better now than I did in June. I've seen the way you are with Ále. With me. I won't go so far as to say that I know you, but I definitely know you better than I did this summer, and that matters to me." Javi pauses, his voice failing him briefly. Then he swallows and meets Gavin's gaze directly. "I want to get to know you better."

Gavin doesn't take his eyes off of Javi. He's still staring at his Recipient when he croaks, "That doesn't mean I have to move into the bedroom."

Javi's heart leaps. It's not a refusal, it's a test. He can handle that. "If you don't want to, that's okay. But I'd really like it if you did."

Gavin's eyes light up, but he pauses before he answers. "You're sure?" he asks.

"I am."

Gavin steals another quick kiss. "Tonight?"

"Yes. If you want to. I'd like that."

"Okay. Then… I mean, I don't have to grab everything, I guess, but I just want you to know I—"

Javi laughs and shoves Gavin gently toward the guest room. "Go on. Just grab whatever you'll need for tonight and tomorrow. We can figure out the rest while Ále's at school."

"Yeah?"

Javi nods with a smile that could split his face in half. "Yeah."

27

Ten days later, Gavin's day at work starts with two routine medical calls and a car accident with no major injuries. He makes it to the end of the sunlight hours ready for a nap only because Alejandro ran him hard the night before. They'd spent the evening chasing each other around the backyard to "test" the work Javier has done so far. There's a small section with the new rubber surfacing that Javier painstakingly chose, and he'd asked Alejandro to help him decide if it was any good. Javier watched Alejandro's every move when he'd been on it with a soft smile on his face that Gavin wrapped up tight in his memories.

It's that smile that Gavin thinks of when they all pile out of the bunk room and into the app bay at two in the morning for a fire callout. He's in his turnout pants and halfway into his jacket when he hears the report that it's one kid still stuck in the house, along with one of his mothers. Gavin's throat goes tight and he forces himself to keep putting on his turnouts. Major calls with kids are always the hardest. They get plenty of minor medical calls for kids, and he doesn't have a problem with those. That's routine stuff. Something like this, though, where a kid's life is in danger, isn't as common as people think it is.

Tyler slaps Gavin on the back, pulling him out of his thoughts. "We've got this," he says, as he pulls himself up into the truck.

The words are familiar, but they carry a different ring now that Gavin can't put his finger on.

He nods at Tyler regardless and focuses on getting his head in the game as he follows him into the truck. He hasn't lost a kid on a call yet, and he's definitely not going to let that change today.

He settles in across from Tyler and next to Fletcher, a newer addition to the house. Gavin likes the way they hold themself. They're small, barely taller than Tyler, but their strength is obvious. He'd always rather be paired with Tyler when they go into a well involved structure, but he'd be proud to work with Fletcher as a substitute if time is of the essence.

The house is well involved by the time they get there, and Gavin is chomping at the bit to get to the kid.

The truck pulls up behind the ambulance and the engine, making them the last ones on scene. Gavin jogs over to the semicircle of his fellow firefighters standing around their captain. Their bulky turnouts make it so no one is standing too close, but the heat rolling off the house fire more than makes up for any absent heat.

Charlie can undoubtedly tell Gavin wants to get into the house immediately. He silences Gavin with a look before sizing up the situation. "Two stories," Charlie calls out to the assembled team. "The smoke from the back is worse than the caller reported. One child reported trapped inside." He turns to his team. "Don, Tyler, Simon, get on the hoses. Kelsea, see if you can get around back to get to our caller and her daughter. And Gavin—"

Gavin stands up taller, eyes sharp on Charlie. He waits for the disappointment of being assigned to the outside of the house where he can't help the kid.

"You head in with Fletcher and see if you can find the kid and the mom."

"Okay." Gavin exhales. He doesn't thank Charlie for the chance to go inside. This isn't the time, and he can offer his thanks later.

He and Fletcher finish gearing up for entry, masks and SCBA tanks in place, then lead the charge. Tyler and the rest of the crew on the hose are close behind. Gavin and Fletcher forge ahead much faster than the team on the hoses, weaving through the fire as they go, calling out for survivors to respond. The smoke is intense enough that he's relying almost entirely on sound to find their survivors. There haven't been any flashovers yet, but he keeps his eyes on the walls as they go, peering through the smoke to keep an eye on the state of the fire. In any other well involved situation, they would wait until the hoses were on the fire for a while, but with survivors in the house, there's no time for that.

Kelsea's voice comes over the radio. "Gavin, Fletcher, it's Kelsea."

Gavin holds up a hand. Fletcher stops walking behind him

"I have our caller."

"Good," Gavin pants, eyes still scanning the hallway they're in. "Names?"

"Stacey and Caleb."

"Copy that."

With the kid's name, and his mom's, Gavin changes his calls. "Stacey," he calls out as they head for the second floor, "Caleb! Denver FD, we're here to get you out. Stacey," he calls again, "Caleb!"

He hears a cough, somewhere ahead of him to his left, just loud enough to be heard over the roar of the flames. He can't see much other than a vague outline of a doorway through the smoke, but he's already moving toward the sound when a voice calls out to him, too.

"Firefighter?"

Gavin makes a beeline toward the voice. As soon as he's close enough, he crouches down to smile at the kid. There's soot under his nose and around his mouth, along with a definite reddish tinge to his skin. They need to get him out of here immediately. "Hey there. Are you Caleb?"

"Yeah."

"Hi Caleb, I'm Gavin. My friend Fletcher and I are going to get you out of here, okay?"

Caleb coughs again, and Gavin's chest aches in sympathy. They need to get him out of here and into fresher air immediately. "Caleb? Is that okay?"

"Yeah." The boy, who can't be more than seven or eight, reaches his hands up to Gavin. "Out of here."

"Okay. I can't see very well because of the smoke, did you fall? Hurt yourself? Are you stuck?"

"Hurt my leg," Caleb says, "but I'm not stuck."

"Okay, good." Gavin feels around the boy's torso and down to his legs. As soon as he's confirmed that they're clear, he sweeps him up in his arms. It's hard to tell from this far inside the structure, but the fire doesn't seem to be getting any worse, at least. "Caleb," he asks, as his eyes seek out Fletcher, "do you know where your mom is?"

"Isn't she in her room?"

"I'll go look," Gavin says as he waves Fletcher over. "Where is her bedroom?"

Caleb points further down the hall. Gavin follows his arm. The fire is worse further down the hall, but not so bad that he won't be able to make it to the next two or three rooms. Past that, he'll have to call it.

"Thanks." Gavin deposits Caleb in Fletcher's arms. "You get Caleb out of here," he says. "I'm gonna go get Stacey."

"Gavin, you can't do that. SOP says we've gotta stay together."

"Look, you can come with me or you can get Caleb out of here. Your call."

Gavin doesn't wait for Fletcher's answer. He turns around and heads down the hall. When a glance over his shoulder doesn't show Fletcher hot on his heels, he exhales in relief. At least the kid is safe.

"Stacey," he calls out again. "Stacey, where are you?"

"Here," a voice calls out. "I'm in here."

Gavin hurries toward the voice, only to find a woman with a leg pinned under a partially collapsed bed frame. He starts testing the trapped leg and the frame on top of it, trying to determine how much pressure he has to deal with to get her out of here. As his hands work, he looks up to the ceiling instinctively, checking for flashover predictors. The smoke is thick above them and heading toward the door. That doesn't give him a lot of time.

"I was trying to get low, under the smoke, like they say you're supposed to," Stacey says, "but something happened."

"Looks like the bed caught before you could get out," Gavin tries to keep his voice calm. They're running short on time. "Okay, Stacey, I'm going to get you out of here."

Stacey's only answer is a hacking cough.

Gavin filters out the sounds of her labored breathing and starts looking for a way to get the bed off her leg. It isn't a huge section that's holding her in place, but the bed as a whole is bearing down on it; if he could just shift the weight and get some leverage, he could get her out in no time.

Just as he's about ready to give up and try to manhandle the bed frame off of her on his own, his radio crackles to life. "Attention all respondents to the structure fire at 6831 Elm, this is an order to evacuate. The structure is unstable. This is an evacuation order."

Stacey looks up at Gavin, and even through the smoke and the fog of his mask he can see her terror. "You're leaving me?"

"I'm not leaving you," Gavin rushes to say. "I'm getting this off of you and then getting you out of here."

Stacey exhales and closes her eyes, leaning her head against her arm.

Gavin gets his shoulder under the part of the bed frame that is closest to her leg. "This is gonna hurt, but as soon as you can, I need you to pull your leg."

Stacey nods. The smoke is thicker under her nose than he'd initially seen, which makes sense given how much he'd seen on the ceiling. They're running out of time.

"Okay." With a swallow and a push, Gavin heaves the bed frame high enough off Stacey's leg. "Go!"

Stacey doesn't scream. She doesn't cry out. Instead she whimpers as she yanks her leg out.

Dropping the bed and rushing to Stacey's side, Gavin skids onto his knees. "Stacey?"

She groans, but doesn't say anything more.

For a moment, Gavin hesitates, but he refuses to slow down again. It takes a moment, but he gets his shoulder under hers and hoists her over his back into a firefighter's carry. They have a straight shot to the door, and if he can make it to the hall, that's one less obstacle in his way.

His radio crackles as he steps out into the hall. "Gavin, I told you to get the hell out of there. Where are you?"

Gavin doesn't bother to answer. He just takes stock of what little debris he can actually see in the hall, and maneuvers around it as he heads toward the stairs back to the first floor.

He's halfway down the stairs when Stacey jerks hard against him. Gavin stumbles at the shift in weight and slams into the wall. He's barely gotten his feet back under him when she jerks again. Two stairs' worth of stumbling and then Gavin is tumbling the rest of the way down. He glances at her as she jerks and spasms against him.

Seizure. Not a common side effect of smoke inhalation, but not unheard of. But he can't treat her here. He needs to get her out to the ambulance. He needs to do something.

It takes an almighty effort to start moving again with everything he's focusing on at the same time. He's trying to keep hold of a seizing woman, track how long she's been seizing, and get the hell out of Dodge at the same time. The floor doesn't feel particularly sturdy underneath him, and he'd forgotten about the furniture between there and the door. He inhales from his SCBA tank one more time, and then charges for the open door.

Once more, his radio sounds. "Gavin."

But Gavin is already stumbling out the front door before Charlie can finish the call.

The clear air sends a shock through his system that almost leaves him staggering. The vision of his team standing arrayed in the yard and in the street settles him enough to tighten his grip on Stacey. Gavin opens his mouth to call out to the paramedics, but Kelsea is already there, helping support their patient. She and Gavin stagger a bit under the weight of Stacey and her seizing.

"How long?" Kelsea calls out.

Gavin rips off his mask, ignoring the way his helmet drops to the ground. He sucks in the unfiltered outside air, letting the shock of cold air on his face focus him. "About two minutes, forty-five seconds, give or take," he pants.

Kelsea swears under her breath and calls out to the paramedics. As soon as they grab Stacey, though, she gives an almighty shudder, arches hard and then goes still. Suddenly there are too many bodies around Gavin, forcing him out of the way. He can hear the paramedics counting off as they do CPR, as they call for equipment. Gavin can only stand there and watch, dumbfounded at what he knows is coming.

He's distantly aware of a section of the house coming down behind him. The hoses are still going, but it's all containment at this point. Nothing is going to be salvageable from there. Gavin's turnout coat is too tight all of a sudden. He marches over to the truck and starts yanking everything off. His SCBA tank, his gloves, his coat. He can see Caleb with two other people, the other mom and the other kid, no doubt. His eyes are too fuzzy from the sweat sliding into them to make much out, but they're sitting near the ambulance, which means Caleb's probably being treated.

There's a shout from where he'd just been standing, as the paramedics call Stacey's time of death. Gavin's whole body sags. He should have moved faster. He should have gotten to her sooner. If only he'd done something different, something more. Fuck, he should have *tried harder*.

But he didn't, and now those two kids are without one of their mothers, and their mother has to do this alone.

He slams his fist into the side of the truck, ignoring the pain that ricochets up his arm to his shoulder. He must have done something to his shoulder in there. What's he going to tell Alejandro when he wants to play later today and he can't because he's hurt?

And then, like a blooming flower in his chest, the question comes. Were these women in a Provider-Recipient marriage? If so, which one was Stacey? Has he just damned a Provider to exist without their Recipient? Or is it the reverse? Which one would be worse? Which one *could* be worse?

He hears the telltale wail of a spouse in grief from over by the ambulance. He turns to look, and he can just make out the family —now only a family of three—huddled in the back of the ambulance. Stacey's spouse is rocking side to side with Caleb and his sibling under her arms. They're safe, but the pain they're feeling must be immeasurable.

Gavin glances over his shoulder. The fire isn't fully contained, yet, but the worst of it seems to be over. The house won't be livable ever again, and Gavin hopes that they have insurance to cover the hotel costs, or supportive friends or family that will let them stay for a while. Something to make the hurt of this night a little less.

Closing his eyes, Gavin leans forward and rests his forehead against the firetruck, taking the small moment of quiet before Charlie comes and puts him on the hoses to put out the last of the blaze. It's a small blessing, he supposes, that it was the mother and not the child. He still hasn't lost a child, and he intends to keep that streak. Before it was a competitive thing but now, he realizes, it's about Alejandro.

Because now he has to ask, which one would hurt more, if it was a choice between losing Alejandro or Javier?

28

Javi has already dropped Alejandro off at school, and when Gavin walks in the door from his twenty-four-hour shift, he's wildly grateful for that fact for a split second. His Provider is soot-covered and his eyes are exhausted when he drops his gear bag. He stands there for a moment, staring at Javi, before he closes the distance and faceplants into Javi's shoulder.

Javi reaches up automatically to run his fingers through Gavin's sooty hair, fingers tangling in the normally golden-blond strands, now streaked with a deep gray. Gavin makes a pained noise into his shoulder, and Javi hums a gently encouraging sound rather than hush him. When that isn't enough to draw Gavin out, he murmurs, "Tough shift?"

"Yeah, you could say that." Gavin says, laughing humorlessly.

It's not the first time Gavin has come home disheveled from a job, but this is an intensity Javi has never seen. He's come home with soot under his fingernails before. Sometimes he comes home from fender benders with his hands and arms covered in motor oil. But he's never come home from what was clearly a serious fire.

For a brief moment, Javi wonders if anyone was hurt, and if

so, how badly. But that's not his business. Gavin is his business, and if Gavin needs his help right now, Javi wants to offer it.

Pressing a closed-mouth kiss to Gavin's temple, Javi hums again.

Gavin makes a broken little sound in the back of his throat and leans into the touch.

"Okay," Javi says. "What do you need?"

"Is Alejandro already at school?"

"Yes."

After a slow inhale, Gavin exhales with a kind of shuddery sound that sends a shiver down Javi's back. "Then I need you."

Javi shivers again. "Okay. How do you need me?"

Gavin shakes his head as though he can hear what Javi's thinking. "Just this. Like this. Next to me. Holding me. I just need to feel you. To know you're here. Safe. Alive."

Javi freezes for a split second. Something terrible must have happened for Gavin to respond like this. It occurs to Javi that Gavin's job sometimes—maybe even oftentimes, he can't know for sure—requires him to hold a life in the balance. What must that have felt like, the first time he saved someone? What must it have felt like, the first time he failed to? Javi relaxes and presses the flat of his thumb gently into the spot below Gavin's jaw. "We can do that. Do you want to take a shower first?"

"I probably should," Gavin says with a shrug. He makes no move to shift from his spot on Javi's shoulder.

"Do you..." Javi hesitates, but continues when Gavin makes an encouraging sound. "Do you want me to come in with you? Help you?" It's more of an offer than he's ever made for Gavin before, and yet it feels like the best way to support him. Gavin always leans into Javi's touch, always appreciates when Javi takes care of things around the house. This is no different.

Gavin gives a broken laugh. "You wouldn't mind?"

"Not at all. Whatever you need, Gavin, you have it."

"Promise?" Gavin leans more heavily on Javi.

Javi's heart skips a beat at the easy question. "Yeah," he says breathlessly. "I promise."

Javi bundles Gavin down the hall to their bedroom. It takes some time for him to ease Gavin out of his clothes, which turns out to be because he strained his shoulder and is still feeling it. He won't tell Javi how it happened, but it doesn't matter. Javi knows enough to know that means he had a hard save today. Maybe even didn't manage the save.

He presses a kiss to Gavin's shoulder and feels the muscles relax under his lips. It leaves an ache in his chest that he doesn't know how to fill. They linger there for a moment until steam starts to fill the room from the shower and Javi is out of reasons to linger.

Gavin hisses at the touch of the hot water, the scrapes and bruises that accompany the strained shoulder not particularly happy about the change in temperature. Javi steps behind him and reaches for the soap. He starts cleaning out the scrapes on Gavin's back and shoulders, careful of the rising bruises he can see there. Once those are handled, he reaches for the strawberry-scented shampoo that Gavin favors. He pours a generous amount and reaches up to massage it through Gavin's hair. Gavin hums contentedly, and Javi can't shake the little tendril of warmth that fills his chest.

He takes his time washing Gavin's hair. When he's done, he tugs gently on Gavin's uninjured shoulder until Gavin gets the point and turns around to tip his head back into the shower's spray. He reaches for the conditioner next, spending less time on that now that the soot and ash are out of Gavin's hair. Then it's rinse and repeat and Javi checking over Gavin's scrapes one more time. He bundles Gavin out of the shower and into a towel to dry off. He works another towel through Gavin's hair, getting it as dry as he can. Then he puts antiseptic on Gavin's scrapes over the man's protestations.

"I'm not taking any chances. I need you healthy and whole, and that means taking precautions."

Gavin sighs and doesn't argue anymore.

Although Javi opens his mouth to insist on putting Gavin into his sweats himself, one clear-eyed look from Gavin is enough to put a stop to that. Instead, he gets into his own loungewear and turns down the comforter.

Briefly, Javi watches as Gavin settles in. There's still a tension in his shoulders coupled with a furrow in his brow. Gavin is feeling better than he was, that's for sure, but he also isn't feeling completely himself.

Unwilling to let Gavin hide, Javi lets him slide into bed first and gets in beside him, filling the space he's left behind. After Javi is settled, Gavin moves in even closer, curling up against Javi's side and resting his head on Javi's chest. Javi shifts just enough so that his arm will be comfortable while still letting him run his fingers through Gavin's hair. Gavin exhales long and slow, his whole body going lax against Javi's side.

Javi waits him out. Despite wanting to know what happened, he also doesn't want to insist that Gavin share before he's ready. He knows that way leads to Gavin shutting down and retreating the way he sometimes does when tough topics come around. So he waits. He isn't disappointed.

"Lost a patient today," Gavin murmurs into Javi's clavicle. "House fire. Mom, two kids. Fuck, Javier, her son was only eight."

Just a little younger than their Ále, then. Javi inhales sharply. No wonder Gavin asked after Ále as soon as he'd gotten home. "I'm sorry."

Gavin huffs, his breath ghosting over Javi's skin. "Yeah. Yeah, that's really all there is, isn't there. Apologies and what-ifs."

Tears splash onto Javi's skin. He moves his hand down to Gavin's shoulders and pulls him in closer.

"I know it's part of the job. I know that's how it goes. But,

Javier, it's not *fair*," Gavin says, his voice breaking on the last word.

"I know," Javi whispers. "I know, honey. It isn't fair at all."

"Javier, that could have been you. And I wasn't fast enough to save her. I wasn't fast enough."

"I'm sure you did everything you could. You always do."

"I should have done more."

Javi tightens his hold on Gavin's shoulders. "You did everything you could. You put your body on the line to save her, did everything you could to take care of her. To get her out of there. Just because things didn't go your way today, that doesn't mean that you didn't do everything you could, because you did. I know you did."

Gavin's tears come faster, and Javi feels his own eyes gloss over in sympathy. "I hate this."

"I know, honey. You're allowed to."

Gavin shakes his head. "I'm supposed to shake it off. That's what I'm supposed to do."

"She had a kid, Gavin. Of course you're taking it harder than usual. After all, you have a kid of your own, now. Someone close to her kid's age. It should hit you harder."

"I'm supposed to be stronger than this."

"Stronger than grief?" Javi's hand slides up Gavin's back to cup the base of his skull. The additional point of contact settles them both—Gavin from his day, and Javi from seeing his Provider so distressed. "Strength isn't what gets us through grief quickly. Numbness is. If you numb yourself to the grief, it'll feel like it passes sooner, but really you're just waiting for all of it to come back again ten times worse. Feel it now, Gavin. Let it run its course. Everything else will still be here when you're ready."

Gavin goes quiet save for the sniffles between his still-streaming tears. Javi goes back to running his fingers through Gavin's hair, humming an old lullaby he learned to help Ále get to sleep when he was little.

Eventually Gavin's tears subside and he starts to breathe a little more evenly.

"Tell me something good?" His voice is wavering, on the edge of more tears, and Javi's heart breaks a little in his chest. "I need… I just…"

Javi kisses him quiet. "I know." He wracks his mind for something, and when he finds it, he can't help but smile. "I started researching some equipment to put in the backyard."

"Oh yeah?" Gavin tilts his head up, planting his chin on Javi's chest. "What did you find?"

"Well, I found a few structures that I think will fit in the yard. Nothing too fancy, mostly just slides or swings. I don't know if we'll be able to do both. I'll have a better idea about that once I get completely done with the yard and finish cleaning it out. I think it looks smaller than it is right now, which is making it hard for me to gauge how much space we have." Javi's chest warms with the thought of all the options he'll be able to give Ále. He still hasn't decided if he wants to go with the poured rubber or the rubber tiles, but he can figure that out once the space is fully cleared out. "So, first step is to pull out the last of the bushes and handle the weeds. Once that's done, we can get rid of the garden waste dumpster. Then I'll need to assess what the rest of the soil is like and what kind of base we want to put down." He glances at Gavin. The furrow in his brow relaxes, and Javi relaxes with it. If Gavin appreciates the distraction, Javi is happy to provide. "I'd like to do some native grasses, but something we can manage and won't get in Ále's way too much. Once that's all done, we'll finally be able to look at proper equipment."

Gavin hums, his eyes soft. "Alejandro's going to love it no matter what you do."

"Maybe. Or maybe he'll be one of those kids that ends up glued to his phone all the time. I don't know, I worry about him sometimes. He sounds like he's making more friends, but I never know for sure. What if he's lonely?"

"Hey." Gavin cups Javi's cheek in his palm and turns his head to face him. "He's a great kid, Javier, and he's going to be an even better man than either of us. We're just lucky enough to be on this ride with him."

Javi relaxes instantly at the words. "Yeah?"

"Mmhmm." Gavin adjusts so that he's resting his ear against Javi's chest again. "Now, come on. I wanna nap before we go get Alejandro."

"We?" Javi asks, a teasing lilt to his voice. "You're coming with?"

Gavin stiffens beside him. "Is that okay?"

"Hey, no, of course it's okay," Javi soothes, fingers finding their way to Gavin's hair again. He's known for a while that Gavin is holding back when it comes to Ále, but hearing it so blatantly is a harsh reminder of how hard he pushed Gavin out at the beginning. He needs to do something more to show Gavin that he's wanted in this family, and, just as important, he wants to do so. "Whatever you need. You're always welcome in the pickup line with me."

"Thank you," Gavin laughs wetly.

"You don't have anything to thank me for," Javi says, bewildered. "If anything, I should be thanking you. You've given me everything."

"And you've given me everything in turn, Javier. You helped me bring my sister and my nieces out here. You helped me keep some of the most important people in my life safe. But it's not just that," he says before Javi can interrupt. "You and Alejandro, you're everything to me, too. You always will be."

With that solemn promise, Gavin settles his cheek against Javi's sternum and lets his breathing even out into sleep as though he hasn't just dropped a bomb in the middle of Javi's view of the world.

29

Gavin is still asleep when Javi wakes. A quick check of his phone reveals that they still have another hour and a half before they need to leave to pick Ále up. He must have left the blackout curtains ajar, because there's light streaming into the room and falling across Gavin's mouth. His lips are softly parted and Javi doesn't think his heart could grow any bigger.

Javi hadn't known what to expect when Gavin came home straight from a fire, still covered in soot and the evidence of the danger of his work. He hadn't known what to do, but Gavin told him. And Javi did as he asked. And now there's nothing but their shared warmth beneath the comforter and the soft puffs of Gavin's breath on Javi's face.

The vulnerability Gavin showed when he came home is more than Javi expected. It's not that Gavin is particularly reserved so much as that he's tended to try to shield Javi from the worst of what's going on around them. It happened with Evelyn, and it nearly happened today. Javi doesn't want that. At the beginning, perhaps he wanted or needed it, but now? Now he's starting to understand that he wants to do this *with* Gavin, instead of just beside him.

"See something you like?"

Javi startles at the roughness in Gavin's voice. He takes a moment to process the words, and as he does, Gavin winces.

"Sorry. I shouldn't have asked it like that."

Gently, Javi takes those words in hand as well, weighing them against the warmth in his chest. Then, when he's certain of his answer, he leans in and kisses Gavin. "You can ask however you like," he whispers against Gavin's lips.

Gavin inhales sharply. "Javier..." And then, slower, "What are you saying?"

"I'm saying," Javi says, choosing his words carefully, "I'm ready for you to touch me. I'm not ready for everything, but I want to see what it's like to be with you in every way."

Gavin's eyes grow wider with each word. Hesitantly, he leans in and brushes his lips against Javi's. "Are you sure?"

Javi smiles and returns the gentle kiss. "I'm sure."

Gavin's shuddery exhale sends goosebumps over Javi's skin. "Tell me how you want me."

Javi's eyes fall closed. There's a reverence in Gavin's voice that sets his skin on fire. "Your hands," he says. "I want your hands."

Gavin hums his assent. Instead of going straight for his pants, though, Gavin traces the backs of his fingertips down the center of Javi's chest. Even through the fabric of his shirt, Javi can feel the tenderness in the touch.

When his hand gets to the hem of Javi's shirt, Gavin looks up at Javi for confirmation.

It's no challenge for Javi to give it.

Gavin smiles and gives Javi another featherlight kiss. Then he goes up on his knees and props himself up on one elbow.

As Gavin slides Javi's shirt off, Javi admires the strength of Gavin's chest in a way he hasn't let himself do before. He reaches up and catches a fingernail on the smattering of wiry hair across Gavin's chest.

Gavin's breath hitches, but he stays on course. "Arms up."

It's easy for Javi to obey and let Gavin strip his shirt off.

Then Gavin lowers himself back to the bed, half-sprawled across Javi's chest. He kisses Javi more firmly this time as he ghosts his palm along Javi's far side.

Javi shivers at each testing press of Gavin's tongue. He opens up to Gavin's touch and can feel the gratitude in the way Gavin searches his mouth.

Gavin's palm stills at Javi's waist, pressing into the skin there more firmly. "Is this what you wanted?"

"I want everything with you."

Gavin shivers. "But is this what you wanted right now?"

Javi brushes Gavin's bangs away again—the man really needs a haircut—and cups his jaw until their eyes lock. "I want you to touch me."

"Javier."

"And if this is about lube, I have some in my bedside table."

Gavin chokes on air, but then he's laughing, pressing his forehead to Javi's sternum.

Javi smiles and runs his fingers through Gavin's hair as the man's stress leaks out of his body and into the room. It settles into the baseboards and then, with a shared exhalation, into the earth.

"Thank you, Javier," Gavin whispers.

"You've been so patient for so long." Javi tips Gavin's head up to kiss him gently. "Let me give this to you. Please."

"You know I don't need this. I would be proud enough to be your Provider even if I never got to touch you this way again."

"I know. That's why I'm ready for this. I know what you are capable of, and I know what I can give you. I'll tell you if it's too much, but Gavin," Javi kisses him under the hinge of his jaw, "I don't think it will be."

A shudder wracks Gavin's frame. "Where's the lube?"

Javi disentangles himself from Gavin and rummages around in his bedside table until he comes up with the bottle he'd bought on a whim a few days ago, once he'd started thinking of being with Gavin like this. He hands the bottle off to Gavin, who eyes it.

Then Gavin grins. He grabs Javi by the back of his neck and gently pulls him in. "Gonna rock your world, Javier. I swear."

But Javi shakes his head. "Just be with me, Gavin. That's all I need."

For a moment, they both stay there, still as anything. Then Gavin gently eases Javi onto his back with a palm at his shoulder.

Javi goes easily, ready for whatever Gavin wants to give him.

Gavin starts by tugging Javi's pants down beneath his balls and wrapping a dry palm around Javi's half-hard cock. He strokes it gently, the friction just enough to get Javi's cock interested.

Javi's breath hitches as he watches Gavin work him over. He glances up at Gavin to see the tip of his tongue swipe across his bottom lip as he works. He has a split-second, vivid image of Gavin's mouth wrapped around his cock and he closes his eyes to hold that image close.

Gavin chuckles as Javi's cock jumps in his hand. "Eager little thing, aren't you?"

With a groan, Javi flops back against the bed.

Gavin's hand disappears for a moment, but when it comes back it's slick with lube.

Javi startles a little at the chill, but settles into it easily enough. Gavin's strokes are easy and measured, clearly there to rile Javi up instead of get him off. And, the thing is, it's working. Javi plants his feet and thrusts up into Gavin's hand.

"Yeah?" Gavin asks.

"Yeah."

Although Javi tries to match Gavin's pace, he's too impatient, too desperate. It's been years since he had anyone else's hands on him, and it feels incredible. Soon enough, though, that single point of contact isn't enough. Javi reaches up, unseeing, to pull Gavin to him.

The first kiss is messy and off-center, but it might be the best kiss Javi's had. It's raw and honest, with nothing hidden between them, no uncertainty or misalignment. It's everything.

Gavin must feel the same because he dives in and kisses Javi again and again, along his cheek, along his jaw, along his whole face.

Javi feels devoured, on fire from within, and he can't stop the way he moves against Gavin. "You too," Javi gasps, his body understanding his need to get his hands on Gavin before his mind does. "You too."

Despite the utter lack of clarity in those words, Gavin understands. He hands Javi the lube and then goes back to kissing up and down his neck, clearly only just holding back from leaving hickies behind. The thought sends a shiver down Javi's spine, but he doesn't say anything. Not yet. Not now.

Maybe next time.

Javi lingers in that thought for a breath, then drops back into the moment. He slicks his hand up and then reaches for Gavin's sweats with his clean hand, shoving them clumsily over his ass and down to his thighs. Through the chuckle he can hear from above him, Javi reaches for Gavin's cock with his lubed-up hand and wraps it around him.

Gavin inhales sharply. He pulls his head away from Javi's neck and punches his hips forward so he can shove his cock through the circle of Javi's hands. "Fuck," Gavin whispers. "Fuck, Javier."

"Yeah." Javi's voice is just as soft. He stares up at the utter bliss on Gavin's face—the slack jaw, the fluttering eyelids, the pulse thundering in his neck—and revels in it.

He did that. *He* did that. He made Gavin look like that.

Fuck.

Gavin's hand is opening and closing around Javi's cock, but Javi doesn't care. All that matters is the look on Gavin's face and the weight of Gavin's cock in his hand.

"Fuck, Javier, please."

"What do you need?" Javi chokes on the words, not because he doesn't want to speak them, but because they feel precious. Holy.

"I want you to touch me."

The words are a perfect echo of what Javi himself asked not so long ago. He understands, intrinsically, what Gavin means. He smiles. "Then come down here and kiss me."

Gavin doesn't hesitate to obey. He dives back in, kissing Javi deeply.

Javi responds in kind, stroking Gavin's cock first slowly, then faster as Gavin's hips move more with certainty against Javi's own. Soon enough, Gavin's hand tightens around Javi again, sending a gasp from Javi's lips.

"Beautiful," Gavin whispers.

With a shaky breath, Javi shudders and forces his eyes open. He stares up into Gavin's clear blue eyes, his soft, sandy-blond hair, and that mouth that always seems to have a smile and a compliment on the tip of its lips.

"Fuck, Javier, you have no idea how beautiful you are."

Javi doesn't have the words to convey the same to Gavin, so he whispers back. "You too. Gavin, you too."

Gavin buries his face in the crook of Javi's neck. His teeth brush over Javi's jugular there, and Javi can *feel* how badly Gavin wants to leave a mark there. Can feel how badly he wants to wear that mark.

"You can," Javi whispers. The shudder that wracks Gavin's frame isn't enough to deter him. "You can, if you want to."

"I want to." Gavin's voice is hoarse, tightly controlled in a way that Javi isn't used to. "But I—" He shakes his head. "Not now."

"Next time?"

The black of Gavin's pupils when he pulls back almost completely swallows the familiar blue of his irises. "Next time?"

The question gives Javi pause. "If you want—"

Gavin's mouth is on Javi's before he can finish the thought. "I want."

Javi reaches up with his clean hand and fists it in Gavin's hair. "Then, next time. I want you to..." The word trembles on his tongue, but he shoves it past his teeth relentlessly. "I want you to mark me up."

Gavin's eyelids flutter and his cock jumps in Javi's grip. With that thought close to his chest, Javi swipes his thumb over the head of Gavin's cock and smears the pre-cum there over Gavin's cock to mix with the lube. Gavin's hand starts to work Javi over in earnest. It's not a race, but there is something of a challenge in Gavin's eyes when he looks down at Javi. A question of who can get the other off harder.

Javi smirks and takes the challenge for what it is: an opportunity to give Gavin something that he hasn't yet been able to.

As Gavin strokes Javi with more fervor, Javi works his Provider over with more intent. Gavin's thighs shake above him and his grip keeps shifting from tight to loose and back again, and Javi knows that his Provider is as close to orgasm as he is.

In the end, Javi spills between them first, his head dropping back and his lips parting on a sigh. His hand goes slack around Gavin, but he can feel Gavin above him still fucking his fist, chasing his own orgasm.

"C'mon, Gav," Javi murmurs. "Come for me."

"Fuck, *Javier—*"

Whatever Gavin was going to say falls away as he comes in streaks across Javi's stomach and chest. They stay there for a long moment, Gavin's eyes wide as he stares down at Javi. It takes Javi a moment to understand what those eyes are for, and when he does, he just grins up at Gavin.

"That was perfect," Javi murmurs.

Gavin shivers. "Are you sure?"

Javi nods, then reaches up with a sweaty but lube-free hand to pull him down into a kiss. "I'm sure.

"Okay. Okay, that's good."

"Don't overthink it," Javi chuckles. "It's gonna be okay."

The panic in Gavin's eyes starts to fade, and after a moment, the familiar boyish grin is back. He clambers out of bed and holds a hand out to Javi. "Shower?"

"Yeah." Javi follows Gavin out of bed. "That sounds perfect."

30

Something changes between them after that. Javi isn't sure what it is, but it's something small, something important, because now he catches Gavin *looking* at him in ways he never has before.

The first few times, Javi barely takes note. Gavin's always kept more of an eye on him than Javi wishes he would, more than he really needs to, but Javi tries not to begrudge him that. He knows how much he and Ále both mean to Gavin, and he can't blame him for keeping an eye on them.

But this is different.

This is Gavin's eyes hovering on Javi when he's doing the dishes and Javi catching sight at the last minute. This is Gavin's eyes lingering on Javi as he dresses for work on days he goes out in the garden but Gavin has off and Javi refuses to let him help. This is Gavin's eyes tracing his form when he thinks Javi isn't looking, only for his face to flush when he sees that Javi's caught him out. Javi doesn't know how to read it, so he doesn't. He just goes about his days pretending nothing changed and goes about his nights letting Gavin pleasure him to no end. At some point this is going to come back and bite him in the ass, he's sure of it, but for right now, everything is fine. Everything is *fine*.

And if Javi finds himself looking back more now than before, he doesn't think anyone would blame him. Everything feels different, and new, and he wants to hang onto that feeling for as long as he can. But he has to stop himself from reading too much into Gavin's looks, lest he risk breaking his own heart. The closer Javi gets to Gavin, the more he wonders about his own relationship with Casey. Ever since Javi told Casey he'd picked up and moved to Denver, her calls to talk to Ále have come like clockwork. Every Sunday afternoon at 3:15 P.M. on the dot, Javi's phone rings with a video call from her number and she spends the better part of thirty minutes talking to their son. It's the perfect time for her to call, too: she can ask after his schoolwork and the upcoming week, and can learn all the hot schoolyard gossip from the week before. Ále revels in the time to talk to his mom, and Javi can't let his suspicions about the frequency and timing of the calls detract from that. He may be certain that she's keeping tabs on him as much as on Ále, but he won't let that take away from Ále's love for his mother.

And yet, when October rolls around with Halloween on the horizon, Javi doesn't actually feel all that bad about not stopping the train wreck he can see coming from a mile away.

"Mom?" They're nearing the end of the call, and there's something hopeful in Ále's voice.

Javi knows what's coming and hates himself a little for not cutting it off at the pass. He clenches his hand around the phone and waits for his son to speak it into being.

"Can you come to the Halloween party at school?"

"Oh." Casey both looks and sounds surprised to have even been asked. That twists some of the suspicion in Javi's chest to guilt. Then she keeps talking and the suspicion takes over again. "I, uh. I'm not sure I can, baby."

"Oh." The disappointment is apparent in Ále's tone, but he manages a smile anyway. "Okay. Maybe another time."

Casey smiles. "Absolutely," she assures him.

It sounds like a lie to Javi's ears, but he doesn't ask for more.

"In fact, why don't you let me and your dad talk for a minute and see if we can find a time for me to come down and see you."

The grin on Ále's face as he turns to look at Javi is enough to have Javi smiling back even through the dread rising in his stomach.

"Sure thing," Javi says. "Ále, why don't you go find Gavin so you two can go over your vocabulary for the week one more time."

"Sure." Ále maneuvers off the couch and makes his way carefully to the study. Javi waits until he's out of sight and out of earshot to look back at the phone.

"Casey."

"Javi, you know I can't come down without a little more warning."

"It's three weeks out," Javi argues "You can't get someone to cover?"

"I'm on-site at one of our projects that week. It was the only time we could get all of us out to Pueblo with our teaching loads this semester."

Javi huffs and runs a hand through his hair. "Which means that knowing wouldn't have changed anything either."

Casey bites her lip and looks away. "That's not the point."

"Then what is the point, Casey?" It's not the first time she's bowed out of Halloween, not the first time she's begged off of something important to Ále. It's not the first time she's asked him to cover for her with him. "Please, enlighten me."

"You know I want to be around for Alejandro when I can. But I need your help with that."

"I can't predict the damn future, Casey," Javi snaps.

"I'm not asking you to," she snaps right back. "I'm asking you to try."

Javi's breath stills in his chest. "Try what, exactly, Casey?"

Casey exhales, not understanding how close Javi is to

screaming. "I love that kid just as much as you do. I don't love him any less just because I wasn't ready to be a full-time parent."

"What, and I was?"

"You were more ready than I was."

Silence hangs in the air between them, dark and damning. When Javi finds his voice it's low and dangerous. "What the hell does that mean?"

"Javi."

"No, don't *Javi* me." He feels sick, his stomach twisting and churning as he tries to reconcile the words with his own memories of their relationship to this point. "You're telling me, what?" He shakes his head. "You thought I was more ready for Ále than you were?"

"You have younger sisters. You took care of them, you always said you did. You may have hated it, but it's more experience than I ever had. I just had older sisters. And I wanted..."

Understanding dawns, making him feel like the fool Casey played him as. "You wanted to go to college. You wanted to go to college and you knew I didn't. So you gave him to me." His lips are numb. "You never wanted a family."

"You knew that," Casey says desperately. "You knew I didn't want a family. I was always going to be happy to co-parent with you, but not..."

"You want to be the Disneyland parent. You want to be the fun one." He closes his eyes and huffs. "Fuck, I should have seen this a long time ago. But you didn't want me to, did you?"

"Javi..."

Javi's vision narrows. Even though he never wanted the life that Casey has, even though he loves Ále, even though he wouldn't change his life for the world, he still would have liked to know there was a choice. He still would have liked to know the decisions that were being made around him. For him. "I have to go. I can't do this with you right now."

"Javi."

"What?" Javi snaps.

"Can I still call next week?"

Javi barks a harsh laugh. "Of course you can. I'm not going to take that away from Ále just because..." He shakes his head again. "I'll text you if anything comes up, but you can plan on the usual time."

"I'm sorry."

Javi exhales sharply. "I'll text you later, Case. Don't call me."

"What about Halloween?" Casey asks.

"I will text you the information about Halloween so you can decide what you want to do." God, is that what they'd been talking about before he'd lost his cool? What the hell are they if they can't even put their shit aside for their son? "Don't worry about that."

"Okay. Thank you. And Javi, I'm—"

"Sorry. I know. You said." He lingers in the silence for a moment, not sure what he's waiting for but knowing that there's something there he still needs from her. He doesn't know what it is, so he just says, "I'll text you," again before hanging up.

He stands there in the living room breathing harshly as he tries to calm himself down. Every calm thought feels further and further away the longer he stands there. He needs to do something, to move, but he worries that if he goes for a walk he'll let himself get lost in his thoughts and in the neighborhood as a result and be late to put Ále to bed. If he starts working in the kitchen, he'll get distracted and tangled up in his thoughts and probably make things worse. So. That leaves the backyard.

He needs to work the soil to get it ready for the buffalo grass he'll put in in mid-March. He's confident he's gotten most of the weeds out at this point, but working the soil to be sure will be good both for his mind and for the lawn-to-be. So he dresses in his gardening gear and heads to the backyard, tools in hand.

The methodical nature of working through the soil to ensure that the weeds are well and truly gone without fully disrupting the mulching cycle he's working on soothes him more than he wants it to. He wants to stay mad at Casey, wants to stay mad that she took this choice from him without being honest about it. Intellectually, though, he gets it. They were eighteen, seniors in high school, with no time to really figure out their plans beyond making sure that they brought Alejandro safely into the world. Casey's parents were distant but financially supportive while his own offered up the space for Alejandro as an infant. It was hell, taking care of an infant and feeling like it was just the two of them while his parents were riding him about also going to school even as he worked part time. Sometimes he thinks it's a miracle that he managed to graduate at all. It would have been easier to drop out, but Casey insisted.

"He's going to need both of us to at least have our diplomas," she'd said. "If you're not going to college, you need this. You need to graduate."

She'd helped him study for all his finals, and sometimes he feels like that's the only reason he did manage to graduate. It's an uncharitable thought to both of them—he'd worked hard on his studies and she'd helped out with Alejandro as much as she could —but he can't shake it, really. She must have known even then that she was going to college and leaving him behind. That she was going to drop Ále into his lap and walk away.

He stabs at the earth with a trowel. That's not fair either. He loves Alejandro more than anyone in the whole world, and he'd do anything for his son. Anything at all. If that means letting Casey go to school and taking Alejandro on as a single parent, he'd do it again in a heartbeat. He'd do anything for his son, and he wouldn't let go of the last four months of taking care of him with no other responsibilities hanging over his head for anything. He loves all the time he gets to spend with Ále, all the ridiculous research Gavin does to help with Ále's projects, all the ways in which the three of them have become exactly the kind of family Javi always wanted. Exactly the kind of family that he wishes his was like when he was a kid.

Exactly the kind of family that Casey could never have given him.

The thought has him slowing down until he's just sitting with the trowel poked into the ground and his eyes cast into the fading sunlight. He'd never thought about it like that before. Casey was always career-driven, goal-oriented, and a hell of a perfectionist. They'd only had sex three times before she got pregnant, and she'd been meticulously, almost clinically careful about making sure they were using all the birth control options available to them. That wasn't enough, of course, but she'd still managed to be salutatorian of their class, only missing valedictorian because of the single A-minus she'd received in English at the end of their Junior year. She'd never be the kind of doting, engaged partner that Javi wanted even back then. She'd never be what Gavin is to him.

He drops the trowel and flops onto his back, letting the cool earth soothe his soul. It's better this way, he knows. Better that he has Gavin, and Casey has her work, and Alejandro has a Disneyland parent that will be able to dote on him and pay child support and help out in whatever way she can. It's better this way, no matter how hard Javi needed to work to get here. It's better this way.

Javi still spends another hour in the yard, staring up into the fading sunlight, until he hears Ále making his way outside.

"Dad?"

Javier tips his head back to look at his son. "Hey, mijo."

"Why are you lying on the ground?" Ále asks.

"The view's better from here."

Gavin snorts from somewhere behind him, and Javi smiles in spite of himself.

"Can I lie down, too?" Ále asks.

"Nope," Javi says, sweeping in and scooping Ále up into his

arms before he can hit the dirt. "Not if you've already taken a bath."

"Aw, c'mon Dad."

"Nope."

"But—"

"Saturday night," Javi says. "If you get all your homework done by Saturday night, we can watch the stars come out." It's an easy enough deal to make. Javi never could have afforded Marion on his own, but it's been the perfect fit for Ále. His teachers have worked with Javi to make sure that they're meeting all of Ále's IEP accommodations, and he's starting to settle into his classes and even excel in his science coursework. The gentle pressure to get his homework done early is mostly a way to keep Ále from trying to cram it all in on Sunday night.

Ále wrinkles his nose. "Can we even see the stars from here?"

Javi glances at Gavin, who shrugs.

"If we can't, we can always go up to the mountains and go camping," Gavin supplies.

"It's October," Javi says, gaping at him.

"Hey," Gavin says with a grin, "You're the one that's talking about stars in the middle of autumn."

Ále giggles, and Javi shakes him lightly. "You're menaces, both of you." There's no heat in his words, though, and soon enough he's helping Ále into his pajamas and into bed. Now that he's let Gavin really help take care of Ále, Gavin has more than stepped up. On the nights that he's home, Gavin asks Ále if he wants to help make dinner. Ále almost always agrees.

Tonight, Gavin must have seen that Javi needed more time in the yard, because there's a covered plate on the kitchen table when Javi walks in. They don't have a perfect family routine what with Gavin's shift schedule, but Javi and Ále enjoy their days to themselves just as much as they enjoy their time with Gavin. Ále is usually the one making plans for their shared weekend days off.

It's gotten easier for Javi to let Gavin help carry the load, and to help carry Gavin's load in turn. Gavin doesn't tell him everything about his days, but Javi gets to hear all the station gossip the moment Gavin gets home like he had this morning.

Once Ále is asleep and Javi eats the dinner Gavin and Ále left out for him, Javi takes a shower of his own. He stands under the spray, letting it work the tension out of his muscles and the ache out of his soul. He's allowed to mourn the youth that he spent on his son instead of on himself, but he isn't allowed to hold that against Ále. And he doesn't want to hold it against Casey either.

As soon as he's out of the shower and crawled into bed with a dozing Gavin, he texts her.

I wish you'd just told me.

I know that now. I'm sorry.

Javi stares at the apology. He may not be ready to fully accept it yet, but he can at least be grateful that she isn't pretending it away. *Thank you.*

You're welcome. I'll see what I can do about Halloween.

Javi locks his phone and drops it on the bedside table. He's certain she'll try, maybe even make time for a video call during the party, but he knows where her priorities are. He's known that for a long time. He's just finally ready to accept it.

31

Gavin generally lets Javier lead when it comes to his relationship with Alejandro's mother. But it's the Monday before Halloween when Alejandro asks him if he'll come to the holiday party at Marion instead of his mom, and Javier isn't there for Gavin to take his cues from.

"Tell you what," he says. "I'll ask your dad if they'll let me come too, and we can check and see if your mom is still able to come."

"She can't." Alejandro's voice is matter-of-fact. "She told Dad."

"Oh." Gavin mentally rolls through his schedule, then through the three guys on B-shift that owe him favors. "Let me make a couple calls."

Three days later, Gavin drives himself and Javier to Alejandro's school.

"And you're sure it's okay that I'm coming?" Gavin asks for what he knows is at least the fifth time.

Javier just chuckles. "I'm sure. His mom will want to call around her lunch to see him and his friends in their costumes, but in the meantime..." He pauses, bites his lip, and glances sideways at Gavin. "In the meantime, I'm glad you're here."

Gavin has been over the moon since he and Javier started spending the night together, and is even more so that Javier has chosen to be intimate with him too. He doesn't dare hope for more. He grins at Javier and steps out of the car, ready to face the day.

It's been years since he was at a school for Halloween and even longer since he was at an elementary school. His high school banned most of the fun costumes, so he and his friends didn't dress up after freshman year.

Walking into a private elementary school is a whole different ballgame.

The walls are decked out in black and orange with just enough green to make it clear that they're looking at pumpkins, not just orange blobs. The firefighter in him is immediately concerned about the amount of flammable material on the walls, but he quiets that part quickly. It's a holiday, and he's here if anything happens.

The kids are all laughing and shrieking and running through the halls. The teachers seem to have managed that careful balance of controlled chaos to keep the school standing, and Gavin is, frankly, in awe of them.

Javier leads the way to Alejandro's classroom. Gavin picks out Alejandro's friends Haley and Bryce right away, and they both wave at him. He grins back at them and waves in turn. Then he looks over at Javier, who, predictably, only has eyes for his son.

The costume was Alejandro's idea, but the implementation is all Javier. The bald cap and carefully placed rims on Alejandro's wheelchair make him immediately recognizable as Professor X. Gavin knew to expect that.

What he didn't expect was for Haley and Bryce to match Alejandro's costume. Haley is wearing a long red wig and Bryce has a pair of red sunglasses on, immediately identifying the pair of them as Jean Grey and Cyclops.

Warmth blooms in Gavin's chest at the sight and the knowledge that Alejandro has good friends on his side.

"Like it?" Javier asks softly.

Gavin glances at him.

"Their parents wanted to do a group costume, but they weren't sure how to include Ále, especially since he's been getting tired so easily lately. I didn't want him on his crutches all night, so this seemed like a good compromise."

"You planted that idea?" Gavin asks sharply.

Javier's expression is contrite. "Is that bad of me?"

Gavin looks back over at the kids, Alejandro too distracted to even notice that the two of them are talking. The smile on Alejandro's face and the sound of his laugh is enough to soothe the instinctive defensiveness Gavin has about parents controlling their kids. "No," he finally says. "You suggested that he take his wheelchair trick-or-treating this year, and you gave him a couple ideas that could match. You made it seem like it was his idea, but I think both of you know you're just looking out for him." When he looks back at Javier, Javier's eyes are aglow with relief. "You made the right call."

Javier exhales deeply before slipping his arm through Gavin's. "Come on, let's go see what the kids are up to."

Gavin makes sure to ask for Javier's blessing to invite Evelyn and her kids along trick-or-treating with Alejandro and his friends. He's been trying to get Evelyn out of the house more, especially now that Diana passed the phone along and things are starting, slowly, to move forward in her case.

Javier agrees readily. "I've been waiting for an excuse to get to know her better."

Haley and Bryce's parents keep an eye on the big kids while Evelyn, Gavin, and Javier hang back with the littles. They make easy small talk throughout the first part of the night, with Javier tossing Evelyn softball questions and Evelyn returning the throw each time. It isn't until well into the evening that Evelyn starts to tease at the edges of telling Javier about their childhood.

"Oh, he hasn't told you?" Evelyn asks with a smile.

"Evelyn." Gavin tries to cut her off, but she just smirks and forges ahead.

"After Gavin dropped out of community college he wandered the country bartending and working construction. Anything that could hold his attention for more than three months was something to be applauded. But as soon as he decided he was joining the Fire Academy, there was nothing that could stop him, not even Grandpa convincing him to get a bachelor's in fire science first."

Javier turns to Gavin, smirking at the pink Gavin can feel in the tips of his ears. "That so?"

"Shut up," Gavin says, shoving lightly at Javier's shoulder. "It wasn't that interesting."

"No, I think I'd like to meet bartender Gavin." Javier's laughing now, and it warms Gavin's chest. He's seen Javier laugh before, but this is the freest he's ever seen him. "Was he as smooth a talker as you are now?"

The flush spreads from Gavin's ears down his neck and spills across his cheeks. "Shut up."

Javier laughs again and lets the topic go. He turns to Evelyn. "And you? Gavin says you haven't gone back to work since you moved out here, but that you were a nurse back east. Is that something you'd like to do again?"

"Yes, but probably only part-time," Evelyn says. "With three kids, I need to be home a lot more often than when it was just Genesis, though even she was a handful."

Javier takes a moment before replying. "Well, maybe we can help each other out," he says. "If you ever need help with the kids, or just need an afternoon off, you just let me know."

"Thanks." Evelyn smiles softly at him. "And the same goes for you two. If you ever want me to take Alejandro so you two can have a date night, I'd be more than happy. It would be nice to get to know my nephew."

Gavin feels Javier freeze next to him, drawing Gavin's gaze from where it drifted to Alejandro and his friends.

"Oh," Javier murmurs. He glances over at Gavin, who does his best to keep his face neutral so as not to let the hope drift into his expression. After a moment, Javier smiles helplessly at Gavin. "Of course," he says, "I'm sure Alejandro would be more than happy to see his cousins again."

Gavin's eyes go a little damp at the knowledge that Javier really is trying to connect with his family. To make them a family of their own. He tucks his arm through Javier's and pulls him close.

"Great," Evelyn says. "Here." She holds out her hand. "Give me your phone. I'll put my new number in and we can set up a time. I know how hard it can be being stuck at home all the time, sometimes without another adult to keep your head on straight. I'd be happy to come over anytime you want."

Javier's head snaps around to look at Evelyn. Gavin can only just make out the wide-eyed expression on his face, but he can feel the line of tension he makes along his side.

Evelyn's eyes widen. She glances over at Gavin for a moment before looking back at Javier. "I'm sorry, I didn't mean to assume."

Javier shakes his head. "It's not that, it's just… you'd want that?"

"Of course I would," she says sharply. "You're my brother-in-law."

Javier opens his mouth to say something, but stops short. He stares at Evelyn for a long moment, his mind clearly sorting through a dozen different thoughts. Then he settles on his answer, a soft smile on his lips.

"Thank you. I would love to spend time with you, now that we know each other a little better."

Evelyn smiles warmly at him. "Thank you. I would love that too."

"Good." Javier glances once at Gavin before looking back at her. "Then it's a date."

32

Fall gives way to the chill nip of winter, and both Javi and Alejandro are feeling it. It's not that there isn't weather in Vegas so much as that the weather in Vegas is different from weather at elevation. Javi gets more and more comfortable with Henleys and sweatshirts around the house, and Alejandro gets better at prying himself out of unintentionally restrictive sweaters when he warms up enough to take them off.

The backyard is ready to head into the final stages, and just in time. Javi pulled out the last of the bushes and weeds before the first freeze, and is ready to have the rubber poured next week. After that he just needs to wait for the back-ordered structures and then he'll be able to finalize the space.

Javi spends more time with Evelyn in the next couple weeks than he has with any other adult besides Gavin since he left Vegas. Together they explore Denver with the younger girls in tow, and sometimes she'll sit on the back porch while Javi works the backyard. They become fast friends in a way that Javi hadn't expected.

"And what does Alejandro think of the yard?" she asks one Friday in late November. Ále's inside playing with Genesis, while

Elaine follows Javier around the yard and Sierra sits with her mother.

Javier settles back on his haunches and squints at her in the pale winter light. "He can't make up his mind about what kind of structure he wants. Can't seem to understand that if he doesn't decide now, it's gonna be months before I can even get the right one in. But," he continues, "I think he's excited."

"That's good. It means he's invested."

"Yeah." Javi chuckles. "Yeah, it does." He contemplates her. "How are you feeling about the hearing? Gavin said it got moved back?"

He regrets the question immediately with the way she curls in on herself. "Yes. Shane's lawyer requested more time to gather testimony, and the judge granted it."

"I'm sorry."

Evelyn smiles bittersweetly. "It happens."

"It does. Doesn't mean it should."

"Thanks, Javi."

Javi salutes her with his trowel and gets back to work, trying to put his worry for her out of his mind. Gavin kept Evelyn's story pretty close to his chest, but ever since they'd started hanging out together, she's given him plenty of detail. Knowing what he does now, he's even more grateful that he was able to help Gavin get her out of trouble. Her pregnancy is showing now, and although they'd worried that Shane's last hurrah would spell the end for her little one, they both seem to have come through.

The next morning, Gavin suggests a family outing. The weather is cold and ever so slightly overcast, but Javi is still more than ready to bust out of the house with the family. Sure, he's spent time with Evelyn and he's spent hours on the phone with his abuela, updating her on things in Denver. This family, though? The little one they're building together? Between Gavin's shifts and Javi's work in the yard and Ále's playdates and sleepovers, there hasn't been time to go out and spend time together as a family just the three of them. At least, not anywhere other than around the kitchen table and Ále's fourth grade homework.

All of which means that Javi is more than happy to bundle Ále up and into Gavin's car before he even thinks to ask about where they're going.

"The Museum of Nature and Science," Gavin says, practically vibrating in his seat.

Alejandro immediately perks up. "The one with the space movie?"

"That's the one," Gavin assures him. He turns to Javi with a grin on his lips and laughter in his voice. "You're gonna love it, Javier. I already got us tickets to the IMAX movie they have right now, it's all about the Solar System. I know I said I wouldn't indulge any more of Alejandro's requests, but this is a little one, and it's so special to have this here that I know he'll just have so much fun. I swear, I won't do anything more than this."

"Gavin," Javi says with a laugh, "this isn't what I meant when I said we needed to stop indulging him so much. I meant with bedtimes and desserts. This: time as a family? That's important."

"Oh."

"Yeah," Javi says, leaning across the center console as they stop at a light, pressing a lingering kiss to his Provider's lips. "Oh."

Gavin's breath hitches against him, and Javi smirks as he pulls away.

"Light's green," Javi says.

Gavin glares at him, but there's no heat behind it. He turns to face front again and refuses to cave to Javi and Ále's teasing despite the blush and grin that he can't hold back.

The day really is wonderful, and Javi appreciates the opportunity to be out in public with their little family. It leaves him wanting to make this happen more, no matter how much planning that will take. He makes a mental note to see if Gavin would be willing to go out to the zoo with them the weekend after next. It's one of the first weekends for Zoolights, and they already know that most of it is accessible if Ále needs his wheelchair. He's learning to lean into his trust for Gavin, and, no matter what happens, he wants to hold onto these memories.

This, the three of them. It feels precious in a way he doesn't completely understand. It feels so long ago now that it was just him and Alejandro that Javi can hardly imagine what life would be like without Gavin anymore. He's become so ingrained in their everyday movements through the world that Javi has to really think about what life was like before him. That's how his life is divided now: into Before Gavin and After Gavin. His kindness and softness and general existence mean so much more than Javi can put words to, and he can't help but lean into that warmth a little stronger every day.

His father would have some choice words to say about that, but Javi doesn't answer to him anymore. Not for as long as he's Gavin's.

So, Javi knows before they get there that watching Gavin and Alejandro geek out after the IMAX showing will quite possibly be the best day of his month. He follows the two of them at a distance, happy to watch them talk and bond, connecting in ways that he knows Gavin was holding back from in their early days together. Ways that Javi doesn't want him to hold back from anymore.

He strolls behind them, hands in his pockets, and watches how they move. They're just getting out of the IMAX movie, chattering animatedly about the film when Javi's phone rings.

It's his mother.

Javi stares at it for a long moment, wondering if he even wants to answer. It's been almost six months, and *now* she wants to reach out? His sisters have kept him up-to-date on the family's goings-on, but his parents haven't even tried to reach out, not once.

Until now.

Guilt has him accepting the call. "Hola, Mamá."

"Mijo." Her voice is stern in a way that makes him stand up straight against his better judgment. "You haven't sent us your travel dates for Christmas."

Javier blinks, feeling like he's missed several steps in this conversation. "Excuse me?"

"Christmas, mijo, Christmas. When are you and Alejito coming home?"

"When are…" Something too cold to be anger settles like ice in his veins. "We're not coming home for Christmas, Mamá."

"Bah," she says sharply, "of course you are. That richy-rich Provider of yours can surely spring for a pair of tickets for you, can't he? Or did you truly marry down?"

Javier was mad enough on his and Ále's behalf, but to hear her disparage his Provider tips him over the edge. "My *Provider* has much better things to do with his money and time than come out to Vegas. And before you ask, no, I'm not coming with just your grandson, nor am I sending him alone."

"Come now, Javi, mijo, of course you're coming home. We're family."

Javi closes his eyes. "Mamá, what's my Provider's name?"

"What?"

"What is my Provider's name?"

"What does that have to do with anything, Javi?"

"I'm sorry, Mamá, but this is the family that I will be spending Christmas with. You can call me again when you're ready to hear about my family and respect my choices."

He hangs up before she can say anything more. He lowers the phone and stares down at it, his heart beating double time in his chest. He's so focused on his now-dark phone that he startles when Gavin touches him, nearly clocking him in the nose for the trouble.

Gavin darts out of the way and lifts his hands placatingly. "Whoa, easy. You okay?"

Javi's still breathing a little too fast, and he can see the concern on Gavin's face. "Yeah," he whispers. "Yeah, I'm fine. Well, not fine," he says at Gavin's skeptical look. He looks down at his phone. "That was my mother."

"Oh? What did she have to say?"

"She wanted to know when we were coming back for Christmas."

"Oh?"

Javi threads his arm through Gavin's at the strangled tone in his voice. He goes up on tiptoe to press a kiss to Gavin's mouth. "We're not going back to Vegas. This is our home now. Here, with you."

"Oh." A slow smile spreads over Gavin's face. "Yeah?"

"Yeah. Now, come on," he says, tugging Gavin toward where Ále is settled on a bench a few yards away waiting for them, "I don't think we've gone in to see the minerals exhibit yet today." He grins up at a stunned Gavin. "Don't you know that's Ále's favorite?"

"Yeah," Gavin says softly. "I guess I do."

33

When they make it home from the museum, Javi gives Gavin a quick kiss before gently gathering Ále into his arms and taking him inside. Javi can't shake the warmth in his chest as he shuttles Ále to his room. Gavin has been more to them today than Javi ever could have seen coming of their situation. More than Javi would have let him be at the beginning. Ever since he opened up a little, Gavin has gently, carefully, patiently made a place for himself in the family when Javi didn't know if it had room for a true third.

Ále doesn't help much while Javi gets him dressed for bed, but he doesn't protest either. It's early for a Saturday night bedtime, but after a full day at the museum, he seems content to go directly to bed.

Gavin is waiting at the door when Javi finishes. When Javi turns to check on Ále one last time, he can feel Gavin follow his gaze. A moment later, he feels Gavin turn his eyes on Javi instead.

Javi's ears go hot and his heart starts to pound in his chest. He swallows and tries to focus on his breathing.

It's not that they haven't touched each other since their first time together. They have. It's just only been a couple of times.

Not to mention that they haven't moved beyond intentional hands and deep kisses. After the way Gavin chose today's museum outing especially for Ále and the ease and warmth of his support after his mother's phone call, Javi wants something more tonight. He wants to be as close to Gavin as he can be, wants to hold tight to the affection he has for his Provider and see where it can take them.

"Javier?" Gavin asks.

Javi looks at his Provider, feeling a little wild with what he's about to ask. Turning away from Ále, Javi shuts the door behind them. He kisses Gavin square on the mouth and then pulls away just far enough to whisper, "I want to blow you."

Gavin's pupils dilate, but Javi can see him holding onto his rationality. He rests his palm on Javi's chest, holding him back when Javi tries to lean in again "What changed?"

"Nothing changed."

"Javier. You know you don't owe me anything."

"I know that," Javi says with an eye roll. "But," he swallows, suddenly shy about what he's about to say, "you've already done so much for me. You were a perfect gentleman for my grandmother at the wedding and you didn't have to fake a minute of it. You've stepped in as a parent for Ále. And from the second we met, you've shown the kind of man you are in the way you treat Evelyn. I just..." There's nothing for it but to go all-in. "I'm grateful to you, Gavin, and I always will be."

Gavin tilts his head. "That still sounds like you're trying to repay me for something."

Javi worries his lip. Bows his head. Looks away.

That doesn't sound right. He wants this, because Gavin is so much more to him than he ever could have expected at the beginning of their relationship.

"I want this with you, Gavin," he says softly. "I want to have this with you."

Gavin puts a forefinger on the underside of Javi's chin, tilting it up. "What if I take care of you tonight?" His hand softly slides down Javi's chest, nearing his waist.

Javi shivers, not wanting him to stop there.

"And tomorrow you can take care of me?"

A few months ago, Javi would have rejected such an offer out of hand, deeming it too transactional. Their relationship was a transaction at that point, but sex was to play no part of it.

Now, after the beautiful day they've had together as a family, Javi can't feel more different. Gavin cares for him and his son. Ále loves Gavin in turn. And—Javi's ready for another step. What Gavin is proposing is a genuine offer from a place of support and affection. What he's offering is everything Javi hasn't let himself want.

"Okay." Javi kisses Gavin's cheek, then drags his lips to the hinge of his jaw and kisses him there, too. "I want this. I promise."

After a moment, Gavin pulls away and searches Javi's eyes. He must find what he's looking for, because his expression turns heated and he kisses Javi once more before taking Javi's hand in his and making his way to their bedroom. Javi doesn't feel dragged so much as gently encouraged to follow. He goes without a moment of doubt, following him all the way to their bedroom. To their bed.

Gavin sits Javi down on the edge of the bed. Then, wonder of wonders, he kneels in front of him. Javi's breath catches in his chest, that same sense of power that he'd had as he jerked Gavin off the first time flooding his veins. It's strange and discordant and not at all the way he'd expected things to go in this relationship, but Javi isn't about to complain. Gavin slips Javi's socks off his feet, followed by his pants and boxers. Then he pushes Javi's knees wide so he can settle his chest between them.

For a moment, he just contemplates Javi's cock, staring at it intently. Before Javi can say anything, though, Gavin leans in and traces his finger along the underside. Javi's breath catches, and Gavin's eyes flick up to his. A smirk crosses his lips and he leans in, his tongue following the same path as his finger. Javi groans and fists his hands in the bedspread beneath him. "Fuck, Gavin."

"That's me." Gavin mouths at the base of Javi's cock, his eyes trained on Javi's. "I'm gonna make this so good for you."

Javi grunts and has to hold back from punching his hips forward into Gavin's mouth. There's heat there, and pleasure, and Javi doesn't quite know what to do with it all.

Gavin doesn't hold back. He licks his way to the head of Javi's cock before wrapping his mouth around it, sucking sharply. Javi tightens his grip on the bedspread, feeling a flush on his neck from wanting to grip Gavin by the hair and just ride his face. Gavin hums around him, as though sensing his thoughts, but he doesn't do anything more than get up on his knees so he can suck Javi better. He bends his neck and twists slightly until he can take Javi's cock deeper, occasionally tightening his lips around his shaft and sucking hard. Once he's got Javi good and sloppy, he pulls off and takes him in hand, mouthing along the side of his shaft.

Javi shivers above Gavin as his fingers spasm in the bedspread. He can't take his eyes off of Gavin and the expression of sheer bliss on his face. It's different from the parental joy he's seen when Gavin plays with Ále or the boyish smile he tosses Evelyn sometimes. This is something all Javi's.

Most importantly, Gavin wants this.

As Gavin sucks even harder, Javi jerks in his hold. Gavin's incredible, and Javi can't help but want more of him. All of him.

Gavin starts moving in earnest, then, his head bobbing on Javi's cock as he sucks him off. His tongue is working magic around the head of his cock, his hand sliding lower and lower down his shaft as Gavin takes him deeper and deeper.

"You've done this before, I take it?" Javi's voice is breathless.

Gavin pulls off his cock with a pop, leaving a slim thread of saliva connecting his bottom lip to Javi's cock. He swipes his tongue across his lip and right through that thread, snapping it at the source. "That a problem?"

"No," Javi hurries to say. "No, it's hot."

There's a smile on Gavin's face as he looks up at Javi. He leans in close to mouth along the side of his shaft again. He drags his tongue along his shaft and, once his tongue circles the head of Javi's cock, he takes Javi's cock and slaps it against his cheek a few times. It isn't Gavin's actions that does Javi in, though.

It's the look in his eyes. Heated and wanting, lustful in a way that Javi isn't used to seeing.

It's that look that gets his fist in Gavin's hair.

Gavin's eyes flash with understanding. "You wanna fuck my face?"

"*Gavin*," Javi groans.

"You can, you know. You can fuck my face."

Javi tightens his grip in Gavin's hair. "God, you're a tease."

"Not a tease. I'm completely serious."

"Gavin," Javi says with a shake of his head, "I can't."

"If this is going to be some bullshit comment about the status of our marriage, I'm just gonna deepthroat you 'til you come."

The breathlessness immediately returns to Javi's voice, his body a live wire of attraction. "Is that supposed to be a deterrent?"

Gavin smirks up at him. "You tell me." Then he's diving in and taking Javi down his throat, swallowing around the head of his cock.

Javi grunts and tightens his grip in Gavin's hair. He doesn't pull, though, too caught up in the sensation of Gavin swallowing around him. He stays there for a long moment, then tightens his grip in Gavin's hair. Gavin groans around him, sending vibrations all through his cock. Javi jerks against him, unintentionally forcing his cock deeper into Gavin's throat, but Gavin doesn't choke. Instead he moves with the pressure, moves with the push, and still somehow takes Javi even deeper.

Although Javi has always prided himself on his control, this—Gavin on his knees in front of him making sounds of pure bliss—is enough to tip him over the edge. He tightens his grip on Gavin's hair and grinds deep into his throat as Gavin swallows around him. Javi *moans*, his whole body succumbing to orgasm before he falls back on the bed, limp and wrung out.

From somewhere between his knees, Gavin chuckles. He leans up over Javi with a smirk on his face and come on his lips. He licks the come away just as Javi realizes what he'd done.

"Oh my god, Gavin, I'm so sorry, I shouldn't have done that."

Gavin leans in and kisses the apology from his lips. Javi grips him by the bicep, holding him close so that he can taste himself on Gavin's tongue. "Nothin' to apologize for," Gavin says as he pulls away. There's a rasp in his voice that sends a shiver down Javi's spine. "Besides," he adds, taking Javi's hand in his own. "I liked it."

He places Javi's hand on the fabric covering his own cock, damp and covered in come between them, and Javi understands.

Javi's eyes go wide. "Just from sucking me off?"

"You're not *just* anything, Javier." Gavin says, laughing warm and bright. "You're my husband."

Javi doesn't slow down to think about what he's doing. Instead he reaches up and fists his hand in Gavin's hair again, taking note of the way he gasps, before tugging him down into a deep, fierce kiss.

Gavin responds in kind, sinking into Javi's touch and turning Javi's frantic kisses slow and languid. He grips Javi by the hips and rolls them onto the bed until Javi's sprawled across Gavin's chest with a thigh between both of Gavin's. Javi can feel his hip getting sticky where it rests against Gavin's spent cock, but he can't find it in himself to be even a little grossed out.

He did that. Well, Gavin going down on him did that, but on some level *he did that*. Gavin got his pleasure from Javi, and that is hotter than it has any right to be.

Javi pulls away from Gavin's kiss, but Gavin just goes on kissing his way down Javi's neck, leaving him moaning. "Fuck," he whispers. Then, a little louder, "So, what's the plan for the rest of the night?"

Gavin grins at him. "I mean, I'm perfectly content to just lay here and make out for as long as you'd like."

At first, Javi almost argues. There are dishes to put away and laundry to sort. But the chores will go faster with both of them and frankly they can wait until morning. "You gonna help with the dishes when we wake up?"

"If that's the price I pay for keeping you in our bed a little longer, then yeah, I'll help with the dishes."

Javi nods as though that solves everything, and grips Gavin's hair to pull him up to face him. "Then I guess we can go with your plan."

Gavin's grin is radiant, leaving Javi's heart skipping a few beats in his chest. He chalks it up to relief.

After all, he's never fallen in love with someone this fast, so it can't be that. Can it?

34

Aside from that first morning, even on the days Gavin needs to go into work, Javier is always the first one up in the morning. Gavin knows it started because Javier felt like he owed Gavin something. That he needed to do things "right" in order to keep Gavin. Even though they've been together for months, Javier hasn't broken that streak.

Until the morning after the night Gavin first goes down on him.

It takes everything in Gavin not to reach out and brush aside the loose curl on Javier's forehead. Javier looks plenty handsome with it, and, if Gavin is being honest, the reason he wants to move it aside is because he's jealous. Jealous of a lock of hair that gets to be closer to Javier than Gavin himself.

Ridiculous, but true.

Gavin's eyes trace over the arc of Javier's eyebrows, the slope of his nose, the curve of his jaw. The apple of his cheeks, which always go so red when Javier blushes. His lips are softly parted, and Gavin is tempted to lean in and kiss them until Javier wakes. But, no, better to let him sleep. He does so much, was on his own so long, that this, at least, Gavin can give him.

Alejandro's door creaks open down the hall.

Gavin slips out of bed as carefully as he can, throws on a pair of sweatpants, and slips out of the main bedroom.

Alejandro looks up at him in surprise. "Good morning," he says, seemingly out of habit rather than anything else.

"Good morning."

Silence lingers in the air as they both try to figure out where to go from here. "Is Dad still sleeping?" Alejandro asks.

"He is."

"Oh. Okay." Alejandro turns around, as though to go back into his bedroom.

Gavin moves toward him. "Are you hungry?" He doesn't know quite what time it is, but if Alejandro is venturing out of his room before Javier wakes up, that's probably the reason.

"A little," Alejandro hedges.

"Okay." The uncertainty is probably coming from the fact that it's rare for it to be the two of them alone, especially in the morning. Gavin tries not to take it personally. "Do you want to do your stretches with me?"

"I already did them."

"Oh." Gavin hesitates, then offers again. "You could help me put away the dishes so I can make breakfast."

"But Dad's sleeping."

"That's okay," Gavin says with all the lightness he can manage. He doesn't want to mess this up. "I bet we can keep *real* quiet while we do the dishes so we don't wake him up."

Alejandro considers this for a moment. Then a huge grin breaks out across his face. "'Kay."

Gavin heaves a sigh of relief. "Okay."

They make their way into the kitchen. Gavin pulls the step-stool over to the sink so that Alejandro can reach the draining rack more easily.

"Okay, big guy. Why don't you start handing me the dishes?"

Alejandro is relaxed in a way that doesn't always come on Sunday mornings, with homework breathing down his neck. He doesn't hesitate to reach for the dishes and help Gavin start putting them away.

"So, did you have fun at the museum yesterday?" Gavin asks after he's put away a cup, a fork, and two bowls. Rather than correcting him or telling Alejandro to hand him things in any specific order, Gavin moves around the kitchen in a zig-zag.

Alejandro giggles as Gavin turns the chore into a game. "Uh huh. I really liked it. I liked it more than the places my Abuela used to take me."

Gavin races to get back to Alejandro before he's ready to hand over the next item. By the third cup, Alejandro picks up on the game and is now grabbing and holding up dishes at a rate that leaves Gavin struggling to keep up, but the shared laughter is more than worth it. "Is that so?"

"Yeah. Dad says that they were doing their best, but I don't like the way they treated my CP."

"Why's that?" Gavin asks as he reaches for the mug in Alejandro's hand.

Alejandro shrugs his shoulders, suddenly making himself small. "Abuelo, he liked to pretend it away. Like if he ignored the ways I'm different, I'd stop having CP. And Abuela treated me like a baby all the time."

Gavin swallows down his frustration with Javier's parents. He taps Alejandro on the shoulder until Alejandro stands up straighter and hands him a plate. Gavin knows they weren't super supportive of Alejandro, but in that abstract way that he knows a lot of things about Javier. They haven't been together that long, and he still has a lot to learn. "What about Citlali, your great-grandmother? Did she do those things?"

Alejandro shakes his head, fiddling with two spoons even as a smile spreads over his face. "She lets me help in the kitchen like you and Dad do. She lets me cut up my own food when it's not too hard. And she doesn't hover when I'm playing in her yard. That might be because it hurts her to stand up," he allows, "but she doesn't make me stay close to her either."

Gavin weighs Alejandro's words against what he'd seen of Citlali at the wedding, and it sounds like the woman he'd met. Not to mention that Javier has always spoken more highly of his abuela than his parents.

"I liked spending time with her better than spending time with Abuelo and Abuela." Alejandro reaches towards a plate near the back of the drying rack. Gavin hovers, but doesn't reach out, letting Alejandro manage himself.

That settles it for Gavin. He's been glad that he got Javier and Alejandro out of Vegas, but hearing Alejandro's version of the way his grandparents treated his CP makes him even more grateful that they crossed paths. "Then I'm glad that she was able to come to the wedding," he says.

Alejandro gives him another wide smile. "Me too."

The warm weight of someone's attention settles over Gavin's shoulders. He glances over his shoulder, to see Javier standing in the doorway, watching Alejandro with a soft expression. His eyes are damp and all Gavin wants to do is cross the room and kiss his tears away.

Then Javier turns to him and mouths *Thank you,* with eyes just as damp and an expression just as soft and Gavin knows he's never been blessed with anything greater.

Javier must see the relief in his eyes, because his expression goes even softer. He crosses the kitchen to stand in front of Gavin and cups Gavin's jaw between his palms. "Thank you." He whispers it this time.

Gavin doesn't fight when Javier pulls him in for a lingering kiss. He just parts his lips when Javier's tongue begs entry, and wraps his arms loosely around Javier's waist.

Javier presses in closer at that, kisses more deeply, and

Gavin's mind starts spinning. He doesn't know what he did to have his husband in his arms like this finally, but he's damn grateful, and he wants nothing more than to keep doing it.

Because the alternative is losing them, and he knows that, after all this time, that would destroy him.

35

A glance at the clock in Javi's study shows less than half an hour until Evelyn's Zoom hearing is scheduled to start. With the time difference, they weren't sure if Gavin would be home in time, so Javi asked Haley's mom Melissa to pick Ále up and take him to school this morning so that he could be home for Evelyn. It's only been a few days since Javi unintentionally disrupted their morning routine by sleeping in, but he can already tell that things have changed in the house. He can feel Gavin's eyes on him a lot more frequently, and Ále is more open with Gavin than he'd been before.

Catching the two of them putting the dishes away last Sunday was an exercise in restraint. Not because he doesn't trust Gavin—he does—or because he's worried about Ále—he always is, but not about this—but because he'd wanted nothing more than to stay cocooned in the kitchen like that for the rest of their lives. Gavin was so soft and gentle, so easy and kind, and though Javi learned all these things months ago, knowing them and watching them in action with his son are two different things. It's not the first time he's realized he could fall in love with Gavin, but it's the first time he's been certain he will.

Javi is aware that Gavin was holding back some when it comes to decisions about Ále. He's been doing it more than Javi realized, though he knows it is born of those early days together. That he'd been following Javi's lead. Now, though, after watching Gavin move so smoothly around the kitchen while Ále handed him dish after dish, Javi knows he can trust Gavin. Knows it down to his bones and, if he's being honest, down to the blood under his skin, what with the way Gavin's touch lights him up.

"I know that look."

Javi startles and looks over at Evelyn, only for his cheeks to go red.

"It's okay," she says in an exaggerated tone, "I'm just here stressing about my first divorce hearing while you daydream about my brother." The explicit mention of her brother makes Javi check the time again. In this case, no news from Gavin is bad news, because it means he's probably still out on a call. It's not ideal, but they've prepared for it. "Everything's *fine*."

Javi cringes. "I'm sorry Evelyn. I didn't mean to get distracted. I'm just not good at waiting."

Evelyn's face sobers. "Neither am I." Her hands twitch, as though she wants to wrap them around herself. "I wish Gav could have been here," she mumbles.

"I know." Javi rests his hand palm up on the desk between them. Evelyn takes it. "I'm sorry I'm not him."

Immediately, Evelyn shakes her head. "I'm grateful to have you," she says quickly. "You're my brother, too, just not in the same way that Gavin is."

"I'll do my best to be here for you." Javi squeezes her hand.

"Javier," she starts, but the Zoom meeting they've been waiting for suddenly turns on. Evelyn turns her attention to the screen before her, her professional veneer immediately sliding into place.

Javier sits at her side through the half-hour hearing, alternately squeezing her hand and having his hand squeezed.

As they wait for the outcome, Javi squeezes her hand one more time. "You've got this," he murmurs, grateful that they're muted and not present for the hearing in person.

The other videos on screen include the judge, whose screen is currently blank as she deliberates, Evelyn's lawyer, Shane, and Shane's lawyer. Shane's eyes keep darting to one corner of his screen, and though Javi hopes that's where the judge's picture sits, he's worried he's watching Evelyn. Worried that, even if Evelyn's suit for a fault divorce goes through here, there will be more to deal with from Shane even beyond the custody hearings that are sure to follow. Shane keeps smirking at the screen and Javi thinks, if he were there in person, he might punch Shane in the nose for what he's done to Evelyn.

"Everything is going to be okay," Javi murmurs.

As the judge returns to lay down her decision, Javi almost loses feeling in his fingers with how tightly Evelyn is squeezing them. He keeps his face neutral, though, until the judge rules in their favor. Then Evelyn releases his hand and cups her hands to her face, trying desperately to hold back tears. She thanks the judge, waits for the screen to go dark, then waits a few seconds more before bursting into tears.

Javi immediately wraps her up in his arms and pulls her in close, rocking her gently from side to side. He doesn't tell her that it's okay. It is and it isn't, and that isn't the point of this moment anyway.

What is the point, is the way Elaine comes wandering over from where she'd been playing quietly with her sister, as though even she understands the solemnity of the moment. She tugs on Evelyn's pant leg until her mother looks down at her and scoops her up into her arms. Javi watches as Evelyn holds Elaine close, wishing that Gavin were here only because he deserves to have this moment with his sister. Javi is grateful to be here himself, but he knows Gavin would love to be here too.

Javi also knows what a relief it will be to Gavin to have this portion of the divorce finalized, as that's been weighing both him and Evelyn down for weeks. If Shane can't get to Evelyn because there's at least a temporary restraining order, then there's nothing left holding Evelyn back from really settling down in Denver. It will mean more of Gavin's time taken up by Evelyn, but Javi can't be upset; he's too busy being proud of all the work Gavin did to help Evelyn feel safe here.

Elaine lets herself be cuddled for a few minutes before she starts to squirm in her mother's arms. Evelyn lets her down, then, before getting up and going to sit with her daughters.

It's a sight that unsettles Javi. He watches them, trying to figure out why, until Evelyn looks up at him.

"You okay, Javier?"

Somehow it's that image—Evelyn looking up at him from the floor near two toddlers—that clicks the unsettling feeling into place. For a moment, he sees Casey on the floor with Ále, playing with him as a toddler the way she never had. Then the image vanishes, leaving behind the memory of the few times Gavin did Ále's stretches with him. "Oh," he says softly.

Evelyn gets up swiftly, crossing the room to stand over Javi in a few quick strides. "What is it?" she asks. "What's wrong?"

"Nothing. Well, it's something," he corrects at Evelyn's popped eyebrow. "It's just not anything we can fix right now."

"Tell me anyway?" Evelyn asks.

Fear almost holds Javi back. But her voice is soft enough and warm enough that he doesn't have it in him to hold back, at least his first thought. "It's Casey. You just reminded me of her for a second."

"Ále's mother?"

Javi nods.

"Oh." Evelyn's shoulders tense and she looks away from him.

There's no way of knowing what to make of Evelyn's tone, and Javi doesn't try. Now that the words are flowing, he can't stop. "She's always loved Ále, I have no doubt of that. She just doesn't want to be a family. Not with me and him, at least. Not the way I wanted."

"Is she with someone else?"

With a quick shake of his head, Javi continues. "It's not like that either. She just has bigger dreams than me. She always did." Some of the old resentment around Casey cutting him out of the decision-making bubbles to the surface, but there's no time or space for it when Evelyn is staring at him in disbelief.

"Bigger than this?" Evelyn asks, gesturing to the study. To the house. "Bigger than your son?"

The study they're in, with the wood paneling that's warm and deep enough to make the space homey, but not so dark as to be oppressive, is the first reminder of what this new family has done and been for Javi and Ále. Javi glances at his desk made from wood of a comparable shade, and the easy way it's set up for both him and Ále to use it simultaneously, another reminder. Then there are the tall windows that welcome in the midmorning light.

Javi is the one that put the finishing touches on the room—the lush green drapes, the slowly-growing collection of mystery novels, the half-dozen pieces of Ále's art that adorn the walls—but he can feel Gavin in every square inch of wood and wall, seeping into his bones. This isn't a home that Javi built on his own. This is a home that he built together with Gavin to make it safe and special for their family.

This is a home built on their mutual love for Ále and, he's realizing, their mutual love for each other.

When Javi looks back at Evelyn, she's smiling like she understands.

Casey made her request clear, but Javi needs to ensure that they're completely on the same page. She's always enjoyed spending time with Ále around the winter holidays, and with the cold breathing down their neck, that's sure to become an issue soon. Javi relaxes. "I need to talk to her, don't I?"

Evelyn's smile widens. "You know the answer to that better than I do."

He reaches out and wraps Evelyn up in a hug, holding her tight to him. Even though he was supposed to be here for her on this difficult day, she's returned the kindness in spades. "Thank you," he whispers.

She returns the hug. "I didn't do much. You and Gavin, you two did the hard work." She pulls away so she can look him in the eye. "Thank you. For trusting him," she says before Javi can ask. "For welcoming him into your family. For *building* a family with him. Thank you."

Javi almost argues that Gavin was the brave one, taking him in sight unseen. But Evelyn isn't discounting that. She's focusing on the work that Javi did in this relationship, but she isn't ignoring the work that Gavin did too. So he smiles at her and nods gently. "You're welcome."

Her smile widens and then she pulls him in close again. "Thank you, thank you, thank you."

"You're welcome." Javi tucks his face into her shoulder to fight down the tears that want to fall. "And don't worry. I'm not going anywhere."

Evelyn squeezes him even tighter "You'd better not. I like you too much."

Javi doesn't bother trying to hold back a laugh.

36

Javi shoves the thought of Casey aside when he grabs Gavin's hand and drags him to the bedroom.

Gavin presses him up against the bedroom door with his hands at Javi's hips and his nose tracing Javi's jawline when he asks, "What do you want?"

Javi blinks the haze from his eyes. He wets his lips and searches for an answer. When he finds one, it's perfectly obvious. "I want to blow you."

"Yeah?" Gavin groans and tightens his grip on Javi's hips. When he speaks, his breath is a whisper over Javi's lips. "You want to be my good little husband and go to your knees for me?"

Javi's knees go weak at the mere suggestion. "Yes."

Gavin gives a shaky exhale. He tugs on the loose, partially unbuttoned collar of Javi's shirt, and Javi stumbles a step closer. Gavin's breath fans over his lips as he speaks. "You gonna take me as deep as you can? Gonna let me take you apart?"

"Yes."

"Good." Gavin pulls him in for a kiss. As Gavin's tongue slips into his mouth, though, Javi thinks of something else of Gavin's taking its place. His gut goes hot, and he pulls away from the kiss.

Gavin tries to follow him, but Javi nips his lower lip once before pulling away the rest of the way.

"I wanna get your cock in my mouth," he whispers against Gavin's lips. "So do you want me naked for that or not?"

With a low, guttural groan, Gavin pulls away. "I want you naked, baby. Want you all laid out for me when you take my cock."

"Alright." Javi says with a shiver.

He pulls away from Gavin, his hands going to his waistband. There's a rush and a thrill under his skin that wasn't there before. He turns his back to Gavin again, his head turned over his shoulder to look at him. Gavin's already naked himself, hand on his cock but eyes drawn to Javi's ass as though magnetically. Javi lowers his pants inch by tantalizing inch until he can pull the waistband taut under his ass. Gavin makes an appreciative sound from behind him, and Javi takes that as a win. On a whim, he adjusts his stance slightly, his hips still moving to the rhythm of absent music, and slowly bends in half, sliding his palms along his legs and taking his pants and boxers along for the ride.

He knows what he must look like, his ass and thighs and calves on display for his Provider, but for once in his life he doesn't feel embarrassed or ashamed.

He feels powerful.

He steps out of the mess of his pants and boxers one foot at a time, widening his stance as he does so. He traces his fingertips along the backs of his legs and up to cup his ass, one cheek in each hand. He lets his fingers press against the plump skin there and revels in the way Gavin groans again as he does so.

"Careful," Gavin says without heat, "or I might start thinking you're ready for me to fuck that ass."

Javi's fingers tighten instinctively on his ass. It shouldn't be this easy, he shouldn't want this so much, but he does, he *does*.

But he's not ready for it yet.

So instead he moves his hands to his waist and gradually rises to standing, keeping his back arched and ass out and on display the whole time. By the time he's vertical and facing Gavin again, Gavin's hands are off his cock and fisted in the sheets. His cock is tall, proud, and leaking steadily from the tip, and all Javi wants is to get it in his mouth.

He doesn't even wait for the instruction. Instead he steps forward and goes fluidly to his knees. He traces his fingertips along the shaft of Gavin's cock and lets his eyes look their fill as saliva pools in his mouth. He leans forward, tracing the tip of his tongue around the head of Gavin's cock.

The taste sends a jolt of heat through him. It's just skin, yes, but there's a musky quality to it that makes Javi lightheaded. He mouths around the head of Gavin's cock for a few long moments before taking it in his mouth.

Gavin makes a choked-off noise, and when Javi tips his head back enough to meet his eyes, he can see the lust-blown quality in them. Javi smirks around the head of Gavin's cock, that powerful feeling zipping through his veins again. He takes Gavin's balls in his hands, massaging them idly as he sucks the head of Gavin's cock.

"Fuck," Gavin says, and Javi's spine lights up at what he knows is coming. "Such a gorgeous little thing, aren't you? Taking me so well. Fuck, Javier, if you could just *see* yourself..." Gavin shakes his head.

Javi's smirk widens as he dares to lower his head ever so slightly down on Gavin's cock.

"God, Javier," Gavin whines before he reels himself in, "you're just so... *Fuck*."

Javi pulls his mouth off the head of Gavin's cock with a pop before leaning down and licking along the shaft. Gavin's fingers tighten in the bedsheets, and for a fleeting second Javi considers letting him fist them in his hair. Letting Gavin take his mouth for a ride, letting him take and take and *take*. But he's not ready for that, and he knows Gavin won't do it, even if he asks. So instead he goes up on his knees and slowly bobs his head up and down, trying to take more and more of Gavin in his mouth.

But Gavin isn't small, and taking him like that is harder than Gavin made it look. Javi knows intellectually that trying to deepthroat Gavin the first time he blows him probably isn't the best idea, but he's tempted all the same. He goes lower and lower and every inch, every centimeter, is another reminder of how little he knows of this.

"Fuck." Gavin's voice is soft and reverent, and when Javi forces his eyes to flutter back open, Gavin is looking down at him with a face equally as soft and reverent.

That has to be a good sign.

He focuses on Gavin's cock and takes the head between his lips again before shifting his neck to take more of Gavin into his mouth.

Gavin slides his fingers into Javi's hair, and Javi already knows he's going to be holding him off instead of fucking his face. The last thing Gavin wants to do is hurt him

Javi pops one eye open and does his best to glare at Gavin. He has plans.

Gavin looks sheepish, but not sheepish enough to confess. "Go on, then," he says instead. "Suck me."

Javi doesn't need telling twice. He lets his eyes fall shut again and then leans in to take as much of him in his mouth as he can.

Despite never having given a blowjob before, Javi has a general idea of what feels good, what's hot, and what is mostly just ridiculous. Right now, though, he doesn't care about any of that. What he cares about is the look on Gavin's face and making it go hazy with lust and release. He adjusts his torso up a little higher to improve his leverage, and then just… goes to town. He licks and sucks and swallows and takes whatever Gavin will give him and gives it back in spades. He wants to sink into this, wants to take this moment and cradle it close to his heart like the precious thing it is.

Like the precious thing Gavin sometimes looks at him as.

He moves hand and mouth in tandem, working Gavin over. At some point, probably around the time Javi tongues at the slit in the head of Gavin's cock, Gavin grunts and falls back onto a free hand while the other stays fisted in Javi's hair, holding him at bay. Javi grins around him, and that must be enough for Gavin, because he starts making aborted little thrusts into Javi's mouth.

Through it all, Gavin keeps up a litany of praise and supportive desperation. "So good, Javier, fuck, baby, so good," and "All mine. You're all mine, baby, and that's never gonna change," and "Fuck, baby, you're so good at this. So good."

Javi moans at the praise, easy as anything. He wants to sink into it, wants to wrap himself up in it. So he does, he does, and there's nothing but joy and pleasure in the spaces under his skin. He wants it, needs it, leans into it, and there's so much heat and ease under his skin that that's all he can focus on. He relaxes his jaw, his throat, relaxes into Gavin's touch. It's perfection of the highest order and he wants nothing more than to lose himself in it completely.

But all good things must come to an end, and no matter how much Javi succumbs to this, Gavin's pleasure is what it's about. So when Gavin's thrusts grow erratic and rushed, Javi knows what's coming. He yields to Gavin's every touch and when Gavin holds him down, knees sprawling wide as he tightens his grip in Javi's hair, it's easy to relax even further and swallow around each and every drop of come Gavin spills into his mouth.

Javi is still swallowing around the last of it as Gavin's cock goes soft in his mouth. The sense of rightness seeps into Javi's pores, sinks into his skin, and he can feel the way that Gavin is giving himself over to this. To him. It's everything Javi wants and it's perfection of the highest order and he can tell that if he only ever gets to have this, he'll take every last bit of it. Every last drop.

Slow and steady, Gavin shifts to pull out of his mouth even as Javi moans and tightens his lips around him to keep him inside. He doesn't want to let go, doesn't want to release his Provider's length, and he has to do something to cling to the familiar taste and smell and touch of Gavin. He wants this for so much longer, but he can already feel the way that Gavin's thighs are trembling with overexertion and overstimulation.

Gavin collapses on his back before Javi, one arm draped across his chest and his thighs spread around Javi's shoulders as he catches his breath. "Damn," he says, "that was..."

"Yeah?" Javi moves to hover over him, a grin on his face.

Gavin sits up and kisses him gently, dragging the taste of himself from every corner of Javi's mouth. Javi runs his fingers through Gavin's hair, brushing it back from his face even as he tugs him in even closer.

"Mm," he says when Gavin pulls away. "You liked it that much?"

"I like you that much." Gavin nuzzles at the juncture of Javi's neck and shoulder. "The blowjob was just a bonus."

Javi flushes, but when he tries to look away, Gavin catches him under the chin and kisses him again.

"Yeah, baby," he murmurs. "It's all you."

Then he presses his shin against Javi's cock and Javi sucks in a breath. His body responds automatically, grinding into the offered friction, and Javi can feel the smile Gavin presses in a kiss against his neck.

"Yeah," Gavin says breathlessly, as though he's the one that's being stimulated. He grips Javi by the hips and lifts him onto the bed so that he's kneeling astride one of Gavin's thighs. "Yeah, go on. Ride my thigh."

"Gavin..."

Gavin must hear the uncertainty in Javi's voice, because he

grips him tight, one hand on his hip, one on his ass, and moves Javi's hips in a slow, steady grind against him.

Javi's head drops down until his forehead is resting against Gavin's shoulder. He whimpers, already feeling like it's too much. Gavin eases up just enough to give him space to lean into the pleasure. "Come on, baby," Gavin whispers, kissing Javi's temple. Javi turns to him without looking, finding his lips with his own, easy as anything. "I wanna feel you come for me."

A whine escapes Javi's bitten shut lips.

Gavin chuckles and reaches up to cup the base of his skull. "Come on," he murmurs against Javi's lips. "I wanna feel you. Wanna feel how much you want me. How bad you want my cock. Wanna feel you."

Javi can't really argue with that. Still, he tucks his face into the curve of Gavin's neck and shoulder and lets his body do the work. He rolls his hips against the hollow of Gavin's hip, chasing the feel of sweat and pre-cum on his skin.

"Look," Gavin whispers when Javi's been quiet too long. "Look at how pretty you are, riding me like that. Look."

Before Gavin, Javi wasn't one to obey without regard for who was ordering him around. Even though very little of that stubbornness came out again after Casey left for Colorado, he knows he's fought Gavin on more than one occasion when the order of command would have dictated that he fall in line.

But this? An easy instruction falling from Gavin's lips like a prayer? This he can do.

He looks down and his breath catches at the sight. His hips are jerking quick and easy, hard and fast against Gavin's thigh, riding him like there's no tomorrow. His cock is straining, long and proud, the head resting against Gavin's hip. It sends a shiver down Javi's spine. He turns away briefly, biting a bruise into the base of Gavin's neck, before turning helplessly back to watch his hips work against Gavin's.

It's hot. It's *hot,* and Javi may have known for ages that this thing between him and Gavin was exactly that—hot as fuck—but knowing and seeing are two different things. He leans into the want in his gut and pants against Gavin's shoulder as his Provider eggs him on.

"Yeah, that's it, baby. So needy. So fuckin' needy. All mine to take care of. To care for. Fuck baby, you're everything. Want you so bad. God, if I thought I could get it up again..."

The promise in Gavin's words sends a shudder down Javi's spine, and he leans into it with all the want in his chest. "Yeah?" he asks breathlessly. "What would you do? What would you do to me if you could get it up again?"

"Fuck, you're so pretty." Gavin bites his earlobe in mock retribution, but it just makes Javi moan and arch against him. "Covered in my marks. Wearing me like a second skin. You'd give it up to me in a heartbeat, and not complain at all, wouldn't you?"

"Not if you won't tell me what you'd do to me."

Gavin rakes his fingernails down Javi's back. Javi arches hard, his jaw falling open and his eyes rolling back in his head. The pain is just enough to tip him over into pleasure, and it's an easy thing to lean into the desire clinging to his ribs. Two more quick thrusts against Gavin's hips are enough to have him spilling between them, his jaw still slack on an unuttered cry. As he comes down, Gavin pulls him in close, biting at his lips in his haste to gain entry to Javi's mouth. Javi yields as soon as he gets his wits about him, though, and then Gavin's licking his way into Javi's mouth with no resistance.

Javi doesn't fight him. Not until he shifts his hips and winces at the cooling slick between them. He pulls away, making a face at the mess. Gavin laughs, and Javi swats at his chest. He almost snaps at Gavin before he remembers he still has leverage.

"You don't get to make a face like that at me when you haven't told me what you'd do to me if you could get it up again."

The laughter cuts short in Gavin's lungs. "What?"

Javi smirks, knowing he's got his man. "Why don't you join me in the shower and tell me all about it?"

He's across the room and halfway into the shower before Gavin gets *his* wits about him again, joining him with a pep in his step that makes Gavin join in the laughter with Javi once he starts. They still have plenty to do tomorrow, but for tonight, the time and space is theirs to enjoy.

37

Javi waits until he's alone in the house two days later to go for his phone. It took standing there, watching Evelyn sink into the relief of the safety of her new family configuration for him to understand what he needs from Casey. Why the radio silence he asked for was a blessing and a curse.

He taps her contact photo and calls her before he can think better of it.

"Javi." Casey sounds surprised to hear from him. "What is it? Is Ále okay?"

"He's fine. He's at school, actually."

"Oh. Well," she says, "are you okay?"

"I'm fine. But I'm not calling for small talk. We both know I'm no good at it anyway."

"Then why are you calling?"

"I need to know what place you want in Ále's life." Javi says.

Casey goes completely silent. "What?"

"I need to know what place you want in Ále's life," he repeats.

"Why are you asking me this?"

"You're his mother. You have a place in his life whether you want it or not."

"You have a spouse, Javi. A Provider. You need to lean on him, not me."

It's an expected deflection, but it still hurts to know that Casey doesn't even want to admit to how much she does—or, as he sometimes fears, doesn't—care for Ále. "And I have. Or, I've been trying to. But I need to know what you want from me and from Ále before I can do that. I need to know what expectations you have."

"I don't have any expectations." Casey sounds politely confused and Javi can't tell how much is genuine. "You've been his primary parent his whole life. I trust you."

"That's not what I'm talking about. You always used to want to see him when you were in Vegas for the holidays. Thanksgiving. Christmas. Even your spring breaks back before they were filled with grad school work. You used to come spend time with us when you were in town."

"Yeah, because you know what my parents were like."

Javi barks a laugh. "Mine were just different, not better."

"Fair enough," Casey allows. Then she sighs. "Javi, I don't know what you want me to say or what you want from me. I didn't think I got a choice in the matter this time around. Don't you want to spend time with Ále and your Provider over the holidays?"

"I do," Javi says, and he means it. "Of course I do. But you're his mother. You deserve to spend time with him, too."

"Do I?"

The words are spoken so quietly that Javi almost misses them. "What? Casey, of course you do, if you want to. You're his mother."

"I gave birth to him," she says, "but I've never acted much like a mother. I've been absent most of his life, only showing up on holidays like you said."

"You call him," Javi counters. "And you've never missed a birthday present."

"Sure, but I've missed plenty of birthdays."

Javi can't deny that. But it doesn't answer his underlying question. "That's not the point. The past isn't something we can change. What do you want to do from here? Do you still want holidays with him, now that we're out here in Colorado?"

Casey is quiet, at first, but when she speaks it's with a raw honesty that Javi appreciates. "I don't know."

Javi's throat is thick with her uncertainty. "Okay," he allows when he can speak again. "Then take some time. Think about it. And then call me when you know for sure."

Casey laughs wetly. "I can do that."

"Good. Thanks for letting me pull you away," he adds, softer. "I don't know if I could have been brave enough to ask you about this if I had to wait."

"Of course, Javi. After all, I may be the mother of your child, but you're the father of my son."

She hangs up before he can come up with an answer to that cryptic statement.

When Casey calls back a week later, Javi doesn't hesitate to pick up. "Hello?"

"Javi?"

"Hi Casey."

"Hi." She doesn't say anything for a moment. Then, "I am having such a hard time not making small talk," she confesses.

"Then ask how our son is doing. That's more than small talk."

"How is Ále?" she asks dutifully.

"He's doing well. He's just as popular as ever. I don't think he's been home for a full weekend since the beginning of October."

"And his friends, they're all kind to him?"

Javi has no trouble reading between the lines. She wants to know if they are truly his friends or if they're befriending him out of pity. "They are," he affirms. "Every one of them."

Casey sighs. "Good. That's good."

When silence lingers a little too long again, Javi asks, "Why did you call, Casey?"

Casey answers after a moment of hesitation. "I'd like to see Ále this Christmas."

The words knock the breath from Javi's lungs. "What?"

"It doesn't have to be the whole time," she says quickly. "I'd just like to see him at Christmastime. Both of you, if you want to come up."

"You're always welcome in Denver," Javi counters.

"Javi. Please."

"But you want us to come up to Boulder." Javi runs a hand through his hair.

"I do."

Javi weighs his options. On the one hand, he and Gavin are finally falling into a rhythm together. They're moving around one another in ways that make them both feel heard and understood. There's something about that rhythm that Javi doesn't dare interrupt.

Then again, Casey is still Ále's mother. She's been good to their son his whole life, even when she couldn't be a full-time mother. Ále deserves to know her, too.

But there may be a way around this.

"Are you flying home for the holiday?"

"Yes." Casey sounds surprised. "Why?"

"Why don't Ále and I come pick you up for your flight?" Javi offers. "Maybe we can grab breakfast or lunch or whatever on our way to the airport. That way you can see him, and we can come up to Boulder to see you and you won't need to leave your car at the airport."

Casey hesitates. "You really don't want to bring him up here?"

"We have a good thing going here, Casey. I don't particularly want to mess with that. Especially not with this short notice.

With Gavin's hours, we may not get a lot of opportunity to spend the holiday with him. I have to prioritize that. Okay?"

"Alright. But if I gave you more warning you could make it work?"

"It would certainly make it easier on me," Javi says.

"Okay. Okay, I can deal with that. I'll send you my flight information."

"Sounds like a plan." Then, softer, "He misses you."

"I miss him, too," Casey says. "If I can swing it. I'll try to get down to Denver a few times in spring semester, too. Just to make things a little more equitable for driving purposes."

A laugh bursts from Javi in spite of himself. "Yeah," he says, "that would be nice. I'm sure he'd love to show you the house, too."

Casey hums noncommittally.

There's something there that Javier doesn't know about, but he doesn't ask about it right now. There's still a couple weeks until Christmas and the last thing he wants to do is unintentionally turn away the olive branch that she's offering here. "Keep me posted, though, yeah?"

"Yeah. Sure thing." Casey lets the quiet linger between them as she gathers her words. "Thank you," she says softly.

"For what?"

"For giving me another chance."

Javi weighs his possible responses to that, before saying, "You're his mother. He deserves to know you."

"Right." Another moment of silence, and then, "I'll talk to you later Javi."

"Yeah. I'll talk to you later."

He doesn't put the conversation out of his mind completely as he heads over to Marion to pick up Ále. In fact, he brings it up to Ále once he's in the car.

He waits until Ále pauses in his reenactment of all the schoolyard drama at play right now. "What would you say to going up to Boulder to pick Mom for her flight to Vegas for Christmas?"

Ále tilts his head. "You and me?"

"You and me."

"Not Gavin?"

Javi pauses briefly at that question. "I'm not sure about Gavin, kiddo," he says. "We'll need to see what his plans are."

Ále processes this. Then he shrugs. "Okay."

"Yeah?" Javi checks.

"Yeah. But let's do presents in Denver."

Javi chuckles. "You got it, buddy."

Now all that's left is to tell Gavin.

38

"Casey asked us to spend part of Christmas with her."

Gavin stills with his knife and fork firmly embedded in the tri tip steak he'd made for dinner. Cold washes through his veins. He hasn't started planning anything for them for the holidays, but the thought that Ále's mother could swoop in and steal Ále from them doesn't sit right with him.

Javier talks about Casey occasionally, but never enough for Gavin to form a full picture or opinion of her. Any positive regard is shifting rapidly at the implication of shared holiday time when she's been an absent entity in their lives.

"Oh?"

Javier turns to him with wide eyes. "I turned her down. Offered to drive her to the airport instead. Is that okay? I mean, do you mind?"

Gavin is quick to shake his head. He won't get in the way of Ále's time with his mother. "No, not at all. If you let me know when you two are going to make that drive, I can arrange my schedule to be at work at the same time. So I can be here at the house with you two when you're here instead of at work," he adds at Javier's confused expression. This is probably something he wants to do just the two of them and Casey, so Gavin will need to keep himself busy.

"Oh." Javier's face does something complicated before settling on a light frown. "Right."

Rather than respond immediately, Javier leans over and cuts up some more of the tri tip on Ále's plate and nudges the Brussels sprouts toward him. It's a testament to Javier's attentiveness; Ále had PE today, and he tends to need extra help on such evenings as the fatigue sets in.

"You, uh. You don't want to make the drive with us? Meet her?" Javier asks lightly.

Ah. There it is. "I didn't think you'd want me to."

Javier goes still, glances at Gavin, then looks back down at Alejandro's plate. "Why not?"

"I just figured you'd want it to just be the three of you. At least this year." He's not sure why he adds the caveat. He doesn't particularly want to meet the woman that left Javier and Alejandro behind.

Javier takes a moment before he replies. "I guess we haven't ever had a Christmas together just the three of us. Might be nice. But, Gavin."

Gavin looks up.

"You're a part of our family too. I know our relationship didn't start the way either of us might have wanted, but I have felt you choose me over and over again since Ále and I moved out here."

Gavin turns away, his heart climbing up into his throat. It's true, but to hear Javier speak it so plainly is more than he'd expected when they sat down to dinner tonight.

Javier leans toward him from across the table until Gavin looks at him. "You have chosen him without hesitation every time that it mattered. Gavin, we're a family. And nothing you say will change my mind about that."

In the wake of those words, Gavin forces himself to hold

Javier's gaze. Family was always a challenging concept for him, something that consisted of Evelyn and Evelyn alone for years. He considers his team family, true, but, other than Tyler, they've always had their own kids and partners to go home to. He's still learning how to keep a partner of his own. "Gavin." Javier takes Gavin's hand in his and squeezes it gently. "If you want to come up to Boulder with us and meet Casey, I will do whatever it takes to make that happen."

"Thank you." Gavin swallows. He threads his fingers through Javier's and leans forward to kiss his knuckles. "I'm..." Gavin hesitates. The last thing he wants is to be placed beside Casey and be found wanting. He's not ready to put their relationship to that test yet. "I don't think it's the right time, but I'd like to meet her. Someday." Someday when he knows he's done enough to keep Javier.

Javier searches his features, then whispers, "As long as you know you're family."

The words settle in Gavin's stomach like hot cider. He squeezes Javier's fingers gently. "I know."

Javier doesn't look like he believes him, but it must be close enough, because he lets it slide. "Okay. As long as you know that." He squeezes Gavin's hand one more time before he pulls away. "You're not on shift this weekend, right?"

Gavin blinks at the change of subject. "No, I'm off. Why?"

"Don't make plans. I need your help with something."

"Help?" Javier hasn't asked for help with much, yet, and Gavin can't stop the leap of hope and relief at the request. Whatever it is that Javier's asking of him, it's something Casey can't help with. Something that perhaps only Gavin can do for him. "Help with what?"

Javier just grins at him, wide and unfettered. "Don't worry about it."

So, for the rest of the week, Gavin tries not to worry. That doesn't keep him from wondering.

. . .

Gavin wakes up on Friday afternoon from his post-shift nap to a pair of pants being thrown in his face.

"Get up," Javier says brightly. "We don't have a ton of time, so we need to get started."

"Started?"

"I told you we have a project this weekend." That part sounds familiar. The getting up so soon after his shift does not. "I want to get it done before Melissa drops Ále off tomorrow afternoon."

"Melissa?"

"Haley's mom."

"She has Ále?" Gavin blinks blearily at his husband.

"I asked her to take him." Javier stills in his flurry of movement to really take Gavin in. He softens, and crosses their bedroom to sit on the bed at Gavin's side. "The last of the back-ordered pieces for Ále's play structure came in this week."

The words take a moment to percolate through Gavin's brain. As soon as they do, he clambers out of bed and starts getting dressed. "It's ready?"

"Ready for us to put together, yeah."

"That's not the hardest part." Gavin waves a hand off at the distinction. "Javier, this is perfect timing." He's got the next few days off, which gives him enough time to help get everything assembled and still get to see Ále's reaction when he gets back tomorrow.

Javier laughs, warm and bright and radiant.

Gavin stumbles a little as he gets into his pants. He turns to look at Javier, who's grinning at him sunshine-bright and perfect. It takes Gavin's breath away.

"It really is," Javier says, not realizing that he's just turned Gavin's concept of their relationship on its head. "Come on, I want to at least get the footprint sorted tonight so we can get the bulk of the structure put together tomorrow morning and just worry about finishing touches in the afternoon."

"You got it."

Three weeks ago, Javier marked out three-quarters of the yard for Ále, but the weather was too cold to pour the rubber surfacing Javier chose. Since then, they've been waiting for the structures themselves. Now that they've arrived, the backyard is filled with carefully organized parts and pieces, lumber and plastic and several buckets of what looks like quick pour concrete. There's a bright blue slide and a pair of large yellow high-capacity adaptive swing seats.

Before Gavin can stare too long, Javier points him at a few piles of lumber. There are three sets of instructions, each attached to a specific pile. Gavin reads through each in turn, taking advantage of the QR code on each of them to access videos outlining assembly and installation. When he's done, he looks up to see Javier standing with his hands on his hips as he surveys the space. They'll need to set up the framing before they can do anything more, which means digging holes, pouring concrete, and setting up the associated lumber.

Javier has a clear vision of what needs to go where and what order everything needs to be done in, which means Gavin is mostly there to follow directions and carry heavy things. Not that Javier isn't strong enough otherwise do some heavy lifting. He's got a more wiry, deceptive strength when compared to the strength Gavin has from firefighting, but he leverages it well.

Between the two of them, they get the holes dug for the structures and identify the order in which to assemble everything. They measure twice, then measure a third time, just to be certain, before they start installing the framing. Gavin needs to look away more than he would like, lest he get altogether too distracted by his husband in ways that really have no place while they're assembling his son's dream backyard. He tries to put those feelings away, tries to set them aside, but he can't deny that there's something about watching Javier's strength that turns him on.

Once the posts are in, they move everything else into position so that they're ready to finalize the structure the next day. Javier is particular about all of it, and when Gavin half-jokingly mentions getting started on finishing everything tonight, Javier rolls his eyes.

"I'm not putting any stress or strain on those posts any earlier than we have to."

Dusk rolls in eventually, but they've made enough progress that Javier is satisfied. Gavin races Javier to the shower but lets him win.

Javier tosses a glance over his shoulder at Gavin as though he's guessed as much, but he still takes his win and hops in the shower first.

Gavin throws dinner sandwiches together for the pair of them and makes it more than halfway through his before Javier is out of the shower.

The beeline Javier makes for his sandwich happens to intersect with the one Gavin is making for the shower. Javier stills Gavin with a hand in his elbow and leans up to kiss the corner of his mouth. "Thank you."

Gavin smiles. "You're welcome."

They take a phone call from an excited but oblivious Ále before they head to bed early, both excited about getting up early the next morning to keep working through as much daylight as possible the next day.

Gavin lets himself be roused earlier than usual the next morning and dragged through an abbreviated morning routine. Then they're out in the chill mid-morning air, with Javier getting just as physically involved as Gavin. There's still a lot of Javier giving directions and Gavin following along, but the lifting this time around is such that Javier helps out a lot more than he had the afternoon before.

They don't talk much, other than when Javier is giving instructions and Gavin is asking clarifying questions. The silence is comforting, soothing, and a reminder that they can exist together in this way. That being said, it does go over well when Gavin insists on grabbing his little bluetooth speaker and running some degree of music through it while they work through the afternoon and into the early evening.

The air is a little warmer by the time Gavin convinces Javier to pack up for lunch. Gavin almost offers to share the shower, what with the chill in his fingertips that made it through even the gloves, but he knows they're still navigating that boundary.

Javier pauses just outside the bedroom door, as though he might be thinking the same thing, but Gavin just smiles and waves him off.

By the time Gavin is out of the shower, Javier is flopped down on the couch with his eyes closed.

"I'm never moving ever again," he says to Gavin when he makes his way out of the bedroom.

Gavin laughs. He reaches out to run his fingers through Javier's still-damp hair. Javier hums and tilts his head back toward him. "You hungry?"

"Ravenous," Javier admits.

"Okay. You want those soup dumplings from that place you like?"

Javier tilts his head back even further so that he can meet Gavin's eyes. "Yeah?"

"Mm hmm. I can go pick them up if you want to order."

"We can have them deliver it."

"It'll be faster if I pick it up and you know it."

Javier hums and tilts his head forward again. "You're not wrong."

"Place the order." Gavin kisses Javier's temple. "I'll go pick them up."

"Mmkay," Javier says softly. Gavin waits until he's reached for his phone to head for the garage. "You want that broccoli and beef thing you like?" Javier calls out.

Gavin swallows around the warmth that swells in his chest that comes from being known. "Sure." He hopes his voice doesn't come out sounding too strangled.

The drive is quick and the dumplings are ready when Gavin gets there, just as he'd predicted. He thanks the young lady at the desk and heads right back out to head home to his husband.

Their late lunch is easy and quiet and calm and Gavin doesn't quite know what to do with himself. It's not the first time Alejandro is away for a sleepover, but it's the first time he's stayed after this long the next day. Melissa must know that Javier is planning a surprise for Ále, because she'd called to confirm that she wasn't bringing him back until five.

Javier snags the leftovers from the center of the table, and Gavin follows helplessly with their plates and cutlery in hand. Javier puts the leftovers in the fridge and the dishes in the dishwasher, and pauses as the door snicks closed. Then he turns to Gavin.

Gavin has a split second to see the wild look in Javier's eyes before he's pressed back against the kitchen counter. As Javier pulls him into a heated kiss, Gavin rests his palms on Javier's hips. He tries to pull away from the kiss once, twice, and then, on the third try, Javier lets him. "Javier. What's this about?"

"It's not about anything. I just want to be with you."

"Why?"

Javier hesitates, then takes the plunge. "Because we made such a good team out there. Because we got so much done. Because you looked so damn good out there and I couldn't stop thinking about getting my hands all over you."

Gavin's breath hitches. "Yeah?"

"Yeah."

"Well, then. Lead the way."

39

Javi's all smiles and laughter as he tumbles Gavin into the bedroom. He kisses his Provider a dozen times before pulling up short outside the hall bathroom. "Let me get cleaned up."

Gavin's eyes widen. "You mean… what do you mean?"

Javi bites his lip. "I mean we can. You know. If you want?"

"Oh," Gavin says, "trust me. I want."

Javi offers Gavin one more kiss before heading into the bathroom with a spring in his step. He knows plenty of that is the lift in his own spirits from having the yard mostly done and the joy that Gavin brought him personally, but he also knows how much joy Gavin brings Alejandro, too. There's so much joy in this house that he thinks he could burst. It's too much and not enough and it means so damn much more than he ever could have thought six months ago.

Once he's clean to his exacting standards, he wraps a towel around his waist and makes his way to their bedroom and Gavin.

Gavin, who is standing in the middle of their bedroom, still fully dressed, with his back to the door. Javi approaches him with a wistfulness that he doesn't recognize, and an adoration that is all too familiar. He settles his hands on Gavin's hips and then buries his nose in the back of Gavin's neck.

Gavin stiffens beneath him briefly before relaxing into his touch.

"Touch me."

Gavin shivers at the words. "Javier…"

"You promised."

With a sharp breath, Gavin spins around and grips Javi by the biceps. He surges across the room to slam Javi's back against the door. With Javi in place, he leans in to devour his mouth.

Javi groans and presses into the kiss until it gets to be too much and he leans his head back. Gavin takes that as permission to start kissing his way down Javi's neck, biting at the sun-kissed skin that the collar of his shirts usually hide so well. He reaches up to follow the trail his mouth is setting with his fingers. He kisses and kisses and takes and takes and all Javi can do is stand there and shiver in his arms.

"Gavin."

Gavin grins and leans up to kiss Javi again, biting at his lips. Javi whimpers and lets Gavin devour him, lets him destroy him down to his atoms.

"Gavin, please."

Gavin bites at his lips, then the hinge of his jaw.

"Gavin…"

"Gonna take you apart, baby. Gonna fuck you til you can't breathe."

Javi shudders. There's nothing he wants more.

Gavin worships Javi's body, his mouth pressing to every square inch of Javi's skin. Once he's got Javi standing beside the bed, he goes to his knees. He sucks hickies into the insides of Javi's thighs, bites at the hollow of his hips, nuzzles at his stomach. Before he can get to Javi's cock, though, Javi reaches down and pulls him up into a proper kiss.

"You promised."

Something flickers in Gavin's eyes, but it's there and gone too fast for Javi to decipher it, and Gavin kisses him before he can ask. "Okay. If that's still what you want."

"It is," Javi says with a frown. "It's what I want."

"Then I'll give it to you." Gavin pulls him in close and nuzzles at his neck, almost as though he's hiding. "Whatever you want, Javier. I swear to you, I'll give you whatever you want."

There's a weight to the words and Javi can feel something niggling at the back of his mind, but then Gavin lifts him bodily to carry him to the bed and there's no space in his mind left to do anything but succumb. He tucks his face against Gavin's neck and moans, his hips already rocking involuntarily to press his cock against Gavin's abdomen.

Gavin lowers him to the bed carefully as though he's something special. Something precious. Tears start in the corners of Javi's eyes, but he doesn't let them fall. He knows Gavin will stop if he thinks there's something wrong, and he doesn't want to stop. Not now. Not ever. He wants Gavin inside of him, wants to feel Gavin so goddamn close, wants to *be* Gavin's in the last way that matters. The last way that he isn't. And as Gavin settles his body over Javi, Javi knows that this is going to be everything that he's been waiting six months for.

He tightens his fingers in Gavin's hair and pulls him closer to kiss his lips. Gavin goes, slithering up his body and letting the fabric of his shirt rub against Javi's overheated skin. Javi shudders and starts pulling at Gavin's shirt. "Off," he whispers. "Take this off."

Gavin kisses him once more before sitting back on his knees and stripping out of his shirt. Before he gets to his pants, Javi leans up on his elbows and parts his lips in request for a kiss. Gavin's lips part on a stuttered breath and he leans in to kiss Javi easily. Javi kisses him back deeply, nipping at his lips while Gavin retaliates. Javi leans back slowly, slowly, and Gavin follows him until he has Javi surrounded, arms on either side of Javi's head, body blanketing him. Gavin's expression shifts and Javi's breath catches at the possessive look in his eyes.

"Gavin, I..."

Gavin leans in before Javi can finish the sentence, which is good, because Javi doesn't quite know what he would say to that look. Gavin presses his face into the juncture of Javi's neck and shoulder and inhales deeply. "Gonna fuck you so good, baby," he whispers. "Gonna take you apart."

When Javi speaks, his voice is a whisper. "Please."

Gavin pulls away, stripping out of his slacks before manhandling Javi into a position that he likes. Javi shudders underneath him, fingers scrabbling at his shoulders, raking down the skin along his spine. Gavin groans above him and starts rolling his hips against Javi's, his cock sliding through the jut of Javi's hip. Javi smiles up at him, fingers of one hand finding purchase in his hair as the other pulls him into a deep embrace. Gavin moves with him, but Javi can feel his free hand reaching for the bedside table and the lube.

A tiny whimper slips from Javi's lips. Gavin stills and pulls back. "Javier."

"It's good," Javi whispers, trying to pull Gavin into another kiss. "It's so good."

"Yeah?" Gavin melts and leans in closer, kissing him again.

"Yeah."

Gavin nods and pushes one of Javi's legs wider with his knee. With a deftness that Javi knows comes from years of practice, Gavin slathers his fingers in lube and probes gently at his hole. Javi shivers once and then relaxes into the touch.

Gavin's first finger slides in easily, and Javi tenses, then relaxes and sighs at the stretch. Gavin circles his finger, tests, presses, and then, when he's certain that Javi's ready, he slides in a second finger. Javi whines and yields so easy. If he's putting on a little bit of a show for Gavin, well, that's between him and his body.

"God, you're beautiful."

Javi startles at Gavin's words, somehow whisper soft and siren loud in his ears. He shivers, something warm and molten sliding along his spine. "Gavin."

"So damn pretty for me."

"Fuck me, Gavin." Javi whimpers and arches against Gavin's touch. "Please, fuck me."

"You gotta let me stretch you, baby." Gavin kisses Javi's temple. "I'm not gonna hurt you."

"You won't," Javi says with conviction. "You could never hurt me."

Gavin freezes, but before Javi can turn to look at him he swears softly and slips his fingers out for an instant before slipping back in with three. "You're sure?"

"Never been more sure of anything."

Gavin's breath hitches, and he pulls away just far enough to be able to look at him. His pupils are lust-blown and Javi doesn't know if he's seen anything more beautiful.

Javi reaches up and cups Gavin's cheek, pulling him in for a kiss. "Gavin. Please. I promise you, I want this."

Gavin shudders above him once more. He kisses him again before leaning back and spreading Javi's legs with his knees. He meets Javi's eyes and parts his lips as though to ask one more time, but Javi raises a single, unimpressed eyebrow. Gavin laughs and settles on his haunches to line his cock up with Javi's hole. With his eyes fixed on Javi's face, he slides in, slow and steady.

Javi tries, desperately, to keep his eyes open and fixed on Gavin's face. But pleasure slides through his veins, desire overcomes him, and his eyes fall shut. His entire attention is settled on the feeling of Gavin inside of him, Gavin's heavy breath from holding himself back, Gavin's fingers landing on his cheek. And then Gavin bottoms out and Javi hears a high keening sound. Gavin's lips land on his and the sound goes silent. Was that him?

"So good for me, baby." Gavin pulls away and peppers kisses all over Javi's face. "So good, so good."

"Gavin." Javi pants against Gavin's lips. "Gavin, please."

Gavin goes on kissing him warmly, intentionally, carefully. "So good for me, baby. So damn good."

Javi throws his head back, baring his throat. "Move," he pants out. "Please, Gavin, *move*."

It's all the instruction Gavin needs. He pulls out slow and steady, every inch sliding out just as delicious as it was sliding in. Javi gasps and whimpers, cries out in desire while his fingers scrape down the line of Gavin's back. Gavin hisses in what might be pain, but when Javi tries to pull his fingers away, Gavin leans in to bite at his neck in retaliation.

"I want you to touch me too."

"Gavin..." Javi shivers at the growl in Gavin's voice.

"Yeah," Gavin whispers. "God, baby, I wanna hear you say my name. Wanna make you scream."

"Gavin..."

Gavin snaps his hips forward, shoving his cock into Javi in one sharp thrust. Javi cries out, with what might be Gavin's name on his lips. He's not sure anymore, too engrossed in the feel of Gavin inside of him. "Yeah," Gavin whispers against Javi's neck as he starts fucking him in earnest. "Yeah, come on, baby. Come on, come on."

Javi whines, his hips pushing back with the little leverage that Gavin is providing him. Gavin's teeth keep worrying at Javi's neck. Heat flares in Javi's gut at the knowledge that he's going to have one hell of a hickey in the morning. That there will be proof of what this night is to him. What Gavin is to him.

Gavin's hips snap forward into Javi's a few more times before he buries himself in deep, grinding against Javi's hips. "Javier," he whispers. "Fuck, Javier."

"Javi," Javi whispers. "Call me Javi."

Gavin stills, then pitches forward to press his forehead against Javi's shoulder.

"Fuck. Javi, do you..." He stops himself and bites his lip.

Javi turns toward him. "What is it?"

"Do you—" Gavin shudders, then seems to force himself to open his eyes and look at Javi. "Do you want to ride me?"

Javi pulls back with a gasp. He stares into Gavin's eyes, searching them for an answer to a question he can't articulate. "Yeah?"

Gavin's face splits into a smile wider than anything that Javi has ever seen on his face. "Yeah."

For a second, Javi can't think. Then *all* he can do is think. He wants that. He wants that for *Gavin,* and he wants that for himself. He wants this, wants everything with Gavin, wants to do whatever it takes to show Gavin that Javi is and always will be his.

"Okay." Javi smiles.

Gavin shivers and groans and grips Javi's hips, rolling them over in one smooth go. Javi cries out as the move shifts Gavin inside of him, sinking deeper into him.

"Javi."

Javi levels him with a glare before he shakes his head, leaning forward slightly and shifting his hips. "S'okay." Then, with another shift. "Feels good."

"Fuck," Gavin groans, his hands tightening on Javi's hips.

With an idle hum, Javi slips his eyes open and adjusts his hips experimentally, watching the way Gavin's face shifts beneath him. He grins. "You like that?"

"Javi," Gavin groans. "Babe."

Javi shifts his hips again. Then he plants his palms on Gavin's chest and finds the core strength to roll his body sinuously over Gavin. "You want that."

Gavin's eyes fly open. "You know I do."

"Then maybe you should tell me more about how pretty I am," Javi says lightly.

Gavin groans again and throws his head back against the pillow as Javi rolls his hips again. "God, you're gorgeous, Javi. So pretty, and so damn good for me. God, baby, I can feel you all around me, feel you taking me so good, god, your body is just so damn hungry for me."

"Yeah," Javi says breathlessly. "Yeah, it is. Want you so bad, Gavin."

"Taking me so good, baby, so fucking good. So pretty up there, riding me like…" Gavin's hips punch up and Javi whines at the way his cock shifts inside of him. "Get down here and kiss me."

Javi doesn't need to be told twice. He leans down and presses his lips to Gavin's, savoring the desperation he can feel in his Provider's mouth.

Gavin goes on muttering praise, desperate and aching while Javi rides him into oblivion. And as Javi rides him, clarity starts to spin down from the crown of his head to the tips of his toes. His lips part, his toes curl, and as orgasm starts to creep up from the base of his spine, the knowledge spills over his lips.

"I love you."

Gavin stills. The room goes quiet, the noise of their lovemaking suddenly silent with Gavin's reaction. Javi opens his mouth to say something, apologize, beg forgiveness, but before he can Gavin grips his hips and topples them over so that he's above Javi again.

"Gavin."

Gavin shakes his head and leans in to kiss Javi with a ferocity that makes Javi's gut clench. Javi moans against his lips, cries out into the crook of his neck, gasps as he arches against him. Javi scratches at Gavin's back and arches against his every thrust.

Gavin is silent save for the occasional grunt and groan from each thrust of his hips. Gavin fucks him and fucks him and Javi's pleasure spirals higher and higher. The knowledge of his love for Gavin—how deep it runs, how far it spans—is overwhelming, and taking him on like this feels like everything these last six months have led to.

"I love you," Javi whispers again. "I love you."

"I love you too."

Javi closes his eyes, grateful that Gavin isn't leaving him hanging. "Fuck, Gavin, I..."

"Come on, baby," Gavin kisses him deeply and then his fingers find their way to Javi's forgotten cock. Javi arches and cries out as Gavin starts to stroke him. "Wanna see you come on my cock."

Javi shakes his head, thrashes, arches, cries out, and when he comes in stripes across his belly, he falls down against the mattress, boneless and severely fucked out.

Gavin doesn't stop moving. He fucks deeply into him, hands leaving bruises on Javi's hips as he moves. Javi smiles up at him, his delirium making him want to speak into being one more whisper of love. But the intensity on Gavin's face stills those words in his throat. Instead, he reaches up and pulls Gavin into a kiss.

"Thank you," he whispers against Gavin's lips instead. "You're everything. Thank you."

Gavin squeezes his eyes shut and bites down on Javi's bruised and battered neck one more time for good measure as he spills inside of him. It feels like a revelation. It feels like perfection. It feels like coming home.

Javi closes his eyes and sighs.

He drifts for a while, only half paying attention as Gavin wipes them down. He protests lightly when Gavin eases him out of bed to stand by the door just long enough for him to change the sheets. The protests still in his throat as he curls up on the clean sheets.

Sleep pulls at him gently, but he clings to consciousness for as long as he can. Clings to consciousness until Gavin slips into bed behind him. From there, slowly, Javi lets himself sink into sleep.

And, as Javi finally falls asleep, he thinks he hears Gavin whisper one last time against the back of his neck. "I love you too."

40

Javi's nervous as they stand on the front porch waiting for Melissa to drop Ále off. He'd hoped being with Gavin would take the edge off, and it did, but apparently not enough. Even with the last few hours of hurried assembly, there's no other word for it; he's just plain nervous. No matter how many times Gavin tries to calm him down or remind him that Ále is going to be too busy playing in the backyard to be anything but ecstatic about it, Javi can't shake the nerves.

"He's gonna like it," Gavin says from where he's sitting on the living room couch watching Javi pace. "Seriously, come sit down, you're working yourself up over nothing."

"Nothing?" Javi snaps. "I've spent months on this, trying to get the whole space set up for him, making sure it will be safe and still fun. I have worked on this since we moved out here, Gavin. Maybe it was just a weekend project to you, but it's more than that to me."

When Javi settles, Gavin is watching him calmly, though there's a hint of hurt in his eyes. "Have you said your piece?" he asks.

Dumbfounded, Javi can only nod.

"Good. Then let me say mine. And listen this time, because I know you know it's true. Alejandro loves you. He thinks the sun rises and sets with you. You are the one constant in his life, and that matters. That *matters*, Javi," Gavin says, moving to keep Javi's eyes on him when he tries to look away. "Everything you give him is a gift of the highest order, and that is true no matter how big or small the gift is. So," he says, getting to his feet and approaching Javi, "yes. This was a big project. It's taken a lot of your time. This matters to you. That means it will matter to Alejandro."

Javi stares at Gavin, who has closed the distance into his personal space. It might be the closest Gavin has ever stood to him when they weren't kissing. He blinks hard and might have gotten away with ignoring the tear that slips over his cheek if Gavin wasn't standing so close.

Gavin smiles and brushes the tear away with his thumb. "You did a good thing, Javi. You're allowed to revel in it."

Before Javi can muster a reply, the doorbell rings. "That'll be Haley's mom with the kids."

"Are you ready to show him?"

Javi blinks a few more times before nodding. "I am."

"Good." Gavin presses a sweet kiss to the corner of Javi's mouth. "Then let's go get your son."

Melissa is all smiles when she greets them. Javi does his best to manage the requisite small talk while his mind is in the backyard doing an inventory of everything that could possibly go wrong.

Gavin more than holds up their end of the conversation, and Javi doesn't actually catch what he says to redirect the conversation toward the yard. As soon as Gavin closes the door behind the five of them, Javi's heart rate kicks up again.

Ále is already halfway to his room by the time Javi realizes that he needs to say something to his son about what he and Gavin did this weekend. Javi looks at Gavin just long enough to gather strength from him, and then he's walking down the hall after Ále while Gavin entertains Haley and her mother.

The door to Ále's room is open. Javi leans against it for a moment, watching his boy carefully sort the clothes he brought to Haley's into the hamper and put his toys back where they belong. Javi is loath to interrupt, so he waits until Ále puts everything away to get his attention. "Ále? There's something I want to show you."

"Is it the playground?" he asks, already hurrying forward. "Is it ready?"

Javi relaxes slightly. "Why don't you and Haley come with me and find out?"

Ále follows Javi out of the room toward the back of the house. His movements are confident and strong, and Javi knows that, in some ways, he owes that confidence in this space to Gavin.

Looking up to meet Gavin's eyes from where he's standing by the closed curtains that hide the yard from Ále, Javi realizes that Gavin isn't looking at him.

He's looking at Ále.

Javi turns his attention back to his son as well. There's a hint of knowing in Ále's eyes, and Javi can't shake a smile at that. "You ready?" he asks.

Ále looks up at him with those same shining eyes and nods.

Then Gavin pulls the shades open and Javi gets to watch as Ále takes in the yard that he and Gavin spent the weekend finishing up. His eyes go wide at the slide that's steep but not too steep, just enough that he can handle it. His hands start to tremble as he turns his head toward the swings, lower to the ground than usual with supports for his legs. When he turns to look at Javi, there's a light in his eyes that makes it clear that he is just as excited as Gavin predicted. He's distantly aware of the gasp that Melissa lets out, but his only concern right now is Ále.

Ále, whose face flickers briefly before he looks up at Javi. "Just for me?"

"And all your friends."

"Yeah?" Ále asks, timid, but hopeful.

"Yeah."

Ále indulges in a brief hug before squirming out of Javi's arms. "Can Haley and I go play?"

"That's why we invited her in," Javi answers. "Go on, you guys can have some time before Haley and her mom need to leave."

Ále grins and heads for the backyard, opening the back door carefully before leading Haley outside.

Javi is still useless at small talk, so he leans against the back of the house, watching his son and his son's best friend play. Ále is enamored with the slide, and he and Haley take turns making their way up the shallow stairs to the top before sliding back down. When they have their fill of that, they beg Javi to come push them on the swings. Not that it takes much begging. Gavin offers Melissa a coffee, and the two of them retreat to the kitchen, leaving Javi with the kids. The kids follow that up by begging Javi to climb up to the top of the structure and send them swinging down the slide.

After twenty minutes of this, Melissa comes to collect her daughter. There's all the requisite pleading and bargaining for "just a little longer, Mom." Melissa caves and allows Haley another fifteen minutes. It isn't until Melissa winks at him from over the rim of her steaming coffee mug that Javi realizes that was a ploy to get home when she actually needs to get home without Haley pitching too big of a fit.

Offering a smile in return, Javi wonders if maybe, next time, he can try to be good at small talk. Melissa and her daughter have been an absolute godsend since the move, and Javi thinks maybe it's time he got to know her better.

When the fifteen minutes are up, Melissa and Haley head out with only a little bit of fuss. Then it's just Javi and Gavin watching Ále exhaust himself on the new apparatuses. As dusk starts to gather, it's Gavin that calls Ále inside. "I thought you might want to call your mom before it got too dark," Gavin says to Javi's surprise. "I thought you might want to show her your new space."

Ále's eyes light up. "Yeah," he says, "I want to do that."

Javi pulls his phone from his back pocket. He pulls up Casey's contact info, hesitating for just a moment before he taps the icon for a video call. He waits for the call to connect, relief flooding his veins when Casey shows up on screen. She agreed to pick up any time he called, and this confirmation of her commitment to Ále calms him. He hands the phone off to Ále.

"Mom!"

"Hey baby." The warmth in Casey's tone is evident even though Javi can't see her face. "Are you outside? What's going on?"

"Dad and Gavin finished the yard. Do you want to see?"

"You bet I do."

Ále glances at Javi, then turns back to the phone. "Come on, I'll take you on a tour."

As Ále makes his careful way back over to the structure, Javi steps closer to Gavin.

Gavin takes the hint and wraps an arm around Javi's waist, pulling him in close.

Javi rests his head against Gavin's chest, his eyes never leaving his son. "He's so happy," he murmurs.

"He certainly seems that way."

Javi tilts his head so he can look Gavin in the eye, "Thank you."

"Javi, we've talked about this. You don't need to—"

"Thank you, I know. But, listen," he says, turning in Gavin's arms. "Gavin, I know that Ále and I did the hard work. I know that we put in the time to make this a life worth living. But you're the one that gave us that chance. I know this started out as just a business arrangement, the two of us helping each other. But, honey, we're a family, now, in ways that I didn't ever account for.

You and me, we've got this. Whatever life throws at us, we're gonna be okay. Okay?"

Gavin blinks hard a few times, as though fighting back tears. "Okay, baby," he says softly. He leans in and brushes his lips over Javi's. "I trust you."

The familiar words send a thrill down Javi's spine. He leans up and kisses Gavin even harder. "Promise?"

"Yeah. I promise."

MEET THE AUTHOR

H.L. Voss is an award-winning queer and nonbinary author. When they aren't writing short stories, doing blackout poetry, or trying to finish the manuscript that is currently plaguing their life, they spend their time training as a mermaid freediver and teaching computer science to high school students. Originally from Denver, they now live in Salt Lake City. You can find them online at hlvoss.com

OTHER TITLES FROM

5 PRINCE PUBLISHING

www.5princebooks.com

Come to the Cape *Emi Hilton*

Time To Byrne *S.E. Reichert*

Bookish *Bernadette Marie*

Dare You to Choose Truth *Lauren Lipp*

Enlightenment *Nicole Kelley*

All the Little Moments *Savannah Reed*

The Rocking of the Ocean *Barbara Matteson*

New to Newport *Emi Hilton*

Trusting the Alpha *Courtney Davis*

Sweet Summertide *Sarah Dressler*

No Words After I Love You *S.E. Reichert*

Demons and Tea Leaves *Courtney Davis*

Shadow of the Throne *Russell Archey*

Shadow Among the Stars *Courtney Davis*

The Pack *E.C. Saulness*

Keeping Kama *Emi Hilton*

A Winter's Wedding *Sarah Dressler*

Trimutant *April Marcom*

Soul Sacrifice *Courtney Davis*

www.ingramcontent.com/pod-product-compliance
Lightning Source LLC
LaVergne TN
LVHW041114080826
845145LV00007B/1818